GAP CREEK

ROBERT MORGAN

GAP CREEK

a novel

ALGONQUIN BOOKS OF CHAPEL HILL 1999

Published by
ALGONQUIN BOOKS OF CHAPEL HILL
Post Office Box 2225
Chapel Hill, North Carolina 27515-2225

a division of
Workman Publishing
708 Broadway
New York, New York 10003

Library of Congress Cataloging-in-Publication Data

Morgan, Robert, 1944–
    Gap Creek : a novel / Robert Morgan.
       p.   cm.
    ISBN 1-56512-242-9
    I. Title.
    PS3563.087147G36   1999
    813'.54—dc21   99-34995
                                                       CIP

New ISBN 1-56512-296-8

10 9 8 7 6 5 4 3 2

For my daughter Laurel

I would like to thank Shannon Ravenel and the staff at Algonquin Books of Chapel Hill for their crucial help in bringing this book to completion, and especially Duncan Murrell for his extraordinary persistence, tact, and insight.

GAP CREEK

One

I know about Masenier because I was there. I seen him die. We didn't tell anybody the truth because it seemed so shameful, the way he died. It was too awful to describe to other people. But I was there, even though I didn't want to be, and I seen it all.

Masenier was my little brother, my only brother, and us girls had spoiled him. If Masenier woke up in the middle of the night and wanted some hot cornbread one of us would get up and bake it. If Masenier wanted a pretty in the store in town we'd carry a chicken down to one of the big houses in Flat Rock and sell it to buy him the pretty. Masenier got an egg every morning while the rest of us just had grits. If he wanted biscuits and molasses, Mama or one of us girls would bake them for him.

I thought Masenier was the cutest boy in the world. He had these blond curls that stood out all around his head, and his eyes was blue as the mountains in the far distance. He loved to sing and sometimes Papa would pick the banjo by the fire at night and us girls would sing ballads like "In the Shadow of the Pines" or "The Two Sisters" and Masenier would clap and sing along. We didn't have music that often and it was a special treat when Papa got down the banjo.

Now the year I'm talking about was the year after Cold Friday, that day when the sun never did come out and it never warmed up. Cold Friday was the coldest day anybody had ever seen. It seemed like the end of the world, when the chickens never left the roost, and it put such a chill on everything we'll never forget that day. Papa took his coughing sickness then and it seemed like he never was well after that. But it was the year after Cold Friday when Masenier started acting poorly.

Masenier had always been such a healthy boy, even a little plump, from all the biscuits and molasses, and his cheeks was pink as wild roses. He had a pile of white sand out beside the house Papa had carried in the wagon from the creek. Masenier made roads and castles and all kinds of mountains and valleys in the sand. He even made him a church out of sticks and set it on a hill of sand, and he stuck little rocks around it to look like a graveyard. You might have knowed a boy that done that was marked in some way.

ALONG IN THE winter Masenier started to look peaked. He fell off a lot, and Mama thought it was because the cow was dry. So we borrowed milk from the Millers that lived further out the ridge. But the milk didn't seem to help Masenier. He got paler and he lost his baby fat.

"What that boy needs is a tonic," Cora Miller said. And she mixed up a tincture of herbs and roots that she kept in a cupboard in her kitchen with corn liquor. Mama give Masenier a tablespoon of the tonic before every meal. The tonic would bring the glow back to his cheeks for a while. We thought he was getting better. And for Christmas he got four oranges and a poke of peppermint candy.

But it was the day after Christmas when he woke up with the pains. My sister Rosie heard him holler out and she went to his bed in the attic. "My belly hurts," he said.

"Have you got the colic?" Rosie said.

"Hurts bad," Masenier said.

Everybody knows what you take for the colic is pennyroyal tea, and Mama boiled some as soon as the stove was hot, even before she cooked any breakfast. Masenier sipped the tea, and it seemed to make him feel better, maybe because Mama put a little paregoric in the tea, the way you do for babies with the colic. Papa said, "Too much store-bought candy will always give a body colic."

BUT AFTER THAT Masenier got the colic even when he didn't have any store-bought candy. After the Christmas candy was long gone he still had the terrible cramps and would wake up in the middle of the night crying. Mama would hold him in her lap and rock him by the fire. And Papa or one of us girls would hold him while Mama made pennyroyal tea. Then after he drunk the tea with some paregoric he would feel better and might even sleep a little.

That was a bad winter, not only because it was colder than usual, but because of the ice storms and the snows. It looked like the woods had been chopped down, there was so many trees broke by the ice. Sleet is hardest on pine trees, because so much ice gathers on their needles. I doubt if there was a pine tree standing whole on the mountain. And when it snowed it was a heavy wet snow that broke down more trees and made barns and sheds and even houses cave in. The church house at Poplar Springs fell down.

Because Papa had the cough, my sister Lou and me did the heavy work outside. We got in eggs and fed the stock and carried in wood and water from the spring. I hated how everybody expected me to do the outside work. If there was a heavy job it just fell naturally to me, and sometimes Lou, like it always had. The weather was bad so long we nearly run out of firewood. I took the axe into the woods and chopped up a blow-down tree. And then I hitched up the horse Sally to the sled and drug in a load. My hands liked to froze it was so wet and cold.

"Julie can work like a man," Mama said when I brought the load of wood into the front room.

"Somebody's got to work like a man," I said and dropped the logs on the edge of the hearth. My hands got rough from the cold and the hard work. I rubbed grease on them at night to soften the calluses and moisten the dry skin. I would have liked to keep my hands soft the way Rosie did hers.

DURING THE TERRIBLE winter when Papa took the chest consumption, we didn't hardly get off the mountain, and we almost run out of cornmeal. If Papa did the least little thing he would start coughing and get so weak he couldn't hardly set up. He had always been such a strong man before that it embarrassed him to be so helpless. Mama liked to say, "Now you can do without a lot of things, but a family can't do without cornmeal. If you run out of meal you don't have any bread and you don't have any mush. And you don't have anything to fry fish in, or squirrels. When the meat runs out, and the taters runs out, the only thing that will keep you going is the cornbread. You can live a long time on bread and collard greens, if you have collard greens. And you can live a long time on bread alone if you have to, in spite of what the Bible says."

We got down to the last peck of cornmeal in the bin, and then to the last gallon. Mama started skimping on the size of the corn pone she baked every morning.

"Masenier won't get better if he don't have plenty to eat," Mama said. "And your papa won't either."

"Maybe we'll freeze to death before we starve," I said.

"Don't talk that way," Mama said. "You take some corn down to the mill."

There was still ice on the trees and snow on the ground. But I seen what I was going to have to do. I resented it, but I seen what had to be done. The road was too slick and steep for either the wagon or the sled. I couldn't carry enough corn on my back down the mountain and back up. Even if my sister Lou went with me we couldn't carry enough between us. Lou was the toughest of my sisters. She was almost as strong as me. I saw that the only way to take a bushel of corn to mill was to sling it over the horse's back and lead her down the mountain. It would take both me and Lou to lead Sally.

"Lou, you're going to have to help me," I said.

"Why ain't I surprised?" Lou said.

Took us all day to get down the mountain, wait for the turn of corn to be ground, while the men eyed us and told jokes, and then lead Sally back up the trail. We got home a little after dark and the sacks was damp. But we had enough fresh meal to last a few weeks, until the weather opened up and Papa was well enough to drive the wagon down the mountain.

BUT EVEN WITH plenty of cornbread and milk to eat, Masenier didn't get any better. He kept falling off no matter how much he eat. And then he started to get a fever and the night sweats. He had terrible dreams that would make him holler out in the night. He yelled one time, "There is snakes dancing!" and when we woke him up he said there was a pit where snakes was swaying to music. He looked scared out of hisself. He was so scared by his dream he dreaded to go back to sleep. One of us had to set up with him after he drunk his tea with paregoric. There was some long nights that winter on into February and early March.

But it was after the weather broke, after it looked like things was opening up and Papa's cough was a little better, that Masenier took the terrible fever. One morning Mama felt him and he was hot as a coal and all day he just got hotter. By evening he was talking out of his head.

"Mama, why don't you have Gabriel come blow his horn?" he said. We knowed he was a little beside hisself. Mama had read him a story from the Bible the night before. After it got dark he just growed hotter. When a person has a bad fever they just seem to glow. Masenier was so lit up with the heat he looked swelled enough to bust.

"What can we do to bring his fever down?" Papa said.

"We can rub him in alcohol," Mama said. We stripped the clothes off Masenier and rubbed him all over with alcohol. The room was filled with fumes and you would have thought it would freeze him to death. But after all that sponging he was hot as ever.

"I've heard you're supposed to wrap up a body that has the fever," Lou said.

"He's been wrapped up all day," Rosie said.

"There's nothing else to do but bathe him in cold water," Papa said.

I went down to the spring and got a bucket of fresh water. It was a cool night with a full moon, and the water was near freezing. "This is liable to give him pneumony," I said.

"If we can't bring it down the fever'll cook his brain," Mama said.

Now I've heard that somebody in a high fever sees visions and speaks wisdom. I've heard you're supposed to gather round a fever patient to hear a message from heaven. But while we peeled Masenier's clothes off and bathed him in cold water, he didn't say a thing that made sense. When we put him in the tub of cold water he screamed, "It's the haints with no eyes!" That's all he talked about, haints with no eyes.

"There's no haints," Mama said to him. "There's nothing here but us." But it didn't do no good. He kept his eyes wide open and jab-bered on about what he could see.

It scares you when a fever keeps going up. It's like watching somebody slide toward a brink and you can't stop them. Masenier was so hot it burned your hand to touch him.

"We've got to make him sweat," Mama said.

"How do you make him sweat?" Papa said.

"By wrapping him in quilts and putting pans of hot water under his bed," Mama said.

"That'll just make him hotter," Papa said.

"Sweating's the only thing that'll cool him off," Mama said.

We got nigh every blanket in the house and piled them on Mase-nier. And we heated kettles of water on the stove and in the fire-place and poured boiling water in pans, which we slid under the bed. It got so hot in the house we was all sweating. I lifted the cov-ers and looked at Masenier. It was like his skin had closed tight and he couldn't sweat.

"He's going to die if we don't do something," Papa said.

"What else can we do?" Mama said.

"We can make him drink hot lemon tea," Papa said.

Rosie and me squeezed some lemon juice into hot water and they tried to make Masenier drink a cup of that. But he wouldn't wake up enough to drink anything. His eyes was closed and he wouldn't rouse.

"Drink some of this, darling," Mama said and patted his cheek.

"Maybe he should drink something cold," Papa said.

"I don't think he can drink anything," Mama said. She held the cup to Masenier's mouth, but his lips was closed.

"If we was to pour it down his throat he might strangle," Papa said.

It got to be midnight and Papa wound up the clock on the man-tel. As he turned the key he looked at Masenier, and you could tell how worried he was. Papa was still weak hisself from the lung sickness. "I'll carry him to the doctor," Papa said.

"You can't carry him to the doctor in the middle of the night," Mama said.

"I'll carry him down the mountain, and Julie can hold the lantern," Papa said. Papa always did depend on me when he needed something. If there was a hard job to be done, it just had to be me that done it. I didn't know but what Masenier had a catching sickness. I was near about afraid to touch him.

"Why does it have to be me?" I said.

"Because you're the strongest one in the family," Mama said. "And because everybody has to do what they can." Mama always did know how to make me ashamed when I tried to get out of a job.

"All right, I'll do it," I said, as I always did when they expected me to do something they didn't want to do.

It was a cold, clear night with the moon shining when we started out. We didn't even need the kerosene lantern in open places, but I lit the wick anyway and carried it like a pail of light down the path in front of Papa. He toted Masenier on his right shoulder wrapped in a blanket. Sometimes Masenier groaned, but he was so asleep he didn't know what was happening.

When we got to the woods we needed the lantern, and in the hollers where the moon didn't reach it was black as a Bible. The woods smelled different at night, and I kept thinking as we picked our way down the trail how I could smell rotten leaves and water in the branch. And I thought how it was almost time to find sprouted chestnuts, where they fell in the fall and got covered with leaves and was beginning to sprout now. Nothing is sweeter than a sprouted chestnut. It cheered me up a little to think of chestnuts.

I heard a dog bark somewhere off in the woods near the Jeter place. And then something up on the mountain squalled, like a person in terrible pain.

"What is that?" I said.

"Nothing but a wildcat," Papa said.

The scream come again, this time closer. "Must be following us," I said.

"Just a wildcat," Papa said, and I could tell from his voice he was nigh out of breath.

"Here, I'll carry Masenier," I said.

"You carry the lantern," Papa said. "I'm all right."

But Papa was winded. He was ashamed to admit it, but he was winded.

"Won't do Masenier no good if you get wore out," I said.

"I can carry him," Papa said. He kept walking a little further, too stubborn to admit he was tired, and then he had to stop to catch his breath.

"Here, let me take him," I said. I set the lantern down on the trail and turned and took Masenier from Papa. Papa was so weak his arms trembled when he handed the boy to me. Masenier didn't feel all that heavy, except he was limp as a sack of flour. I was afraid to touch him, but didn't have any choice. I slung him up against my shoulder and followed Papa down the trail. It took us over an hour to make it down the mountain.

DR. PRINCE LIVED in one of the big houses down in Flat Rock. He was the son of the old Judge Prince that had founded Flat Rock, and he lived part of the year in Charleston and part in the mountains. And when he was in Flat Rock he doctored the mountain folks same as the Flat Rock people. Sometimes he rode his horse with a doctor bag slung behind the saddle out on the ridges and to the far coves beyond Pinnacle.

I knowed the doctor had a big cur dog that he kept in a fence in front of his house. Everybody had seen the cur dog. I didn't know what we would do when we got close to the house, for the dog was supposed to be mean.

Though Masenier had not felt heavy when I took him on my shoulder, his little body got weightier and weightier as I stumbled down the trail. It was like somebody was adding pounds to him the further we went. I stiffened my back and locked my arm around him and followed Papa swinging the lantern. I was still mad that I had to carry him and that give me more strength.

When we come out of the woods into the open country around Flat Rock, the moonlight was so bright it seemed like day. I could almost see the green in the grass along the creek and the windows of houses made you think there was lights inside them. Dew on the fields sparkled like beads. I was so tired my arms ached and my legs trembled by the time we got to the gate of Dr. Prince's house.

Sure enough, the dog set up a growl and a bark. He come running from the porch and stood behind the gate snarling. He would have eat up anybody that come through that gate.

"You holler for the doctor," Papa said.

"Let me catch my breath," I said, and shifted Masenier to my left shoulder and called out, "Dr. Prince!"

The dog set up an even bigger fuss. And I heard a noise in the house.

"Hey, Dr. Prince!" I shouted.

A light was lit somewhere inside the house and a door opened. "Who is there?" a voice called.

"This is Julie Harmon and her papa. Masenier is bad sick."

"Is he with you?" the voice called.

"We carried him down the mountain," I said.

The doctor called the dog back and held him on the porch

while we climbed the steps and went inside. The cur growled as we passed him. It was a big fancy house with high ceilings and lots of mirrors and lamps. The doctor led us into his study, which was lined with books. Rich folks' houses always smell like toilet water and some kind of soap.

We laid Masenier on the table in the middle of the room and Dr. Prince brought a bright lamp over and looked at him. Dr. Prince had a big mustache like the German Bismarck. He pulled the blanket back and felt of Masenier's pulse. "How long has he had the fever?" he said.

"He got hot two nights ago," Papa said.

Dr. Prince bent down and sniffed Masenier's breath and listened to his heart. "Could he have milksick?" the doctor said.

"Too early for milksick," Papa said.

"Then it must be typhoid," the doctor said.

I was going to say hadn't nobody else on the mountain had typhoid, but I didn't. Who was I to argue with Dr. Prince?

Dr. Prince went to a shelf and got a bottle of something that looked like reddish syrup. "Let's give him a dram of this," he said.

I had to hold Masenier's head up and Papa pried his mouth open with his fingers. But I don't think Masenier knowed what was happening when the doctor poured the spoon of syrup in his mouth. Some dribbled out of the corners of his mouth, but I guess a little went down his throat. Masenier was too deep asleep to know the difference.

"You'll have to watch him closely," the doctor said and handed Papa the bottle of syrup. "Every fever is different."

"I'm afraid I don't have no money," Papa said.

"You can pay me later," Dr. Prince said. It was the way the doctor said it so quick that told us he was rich and didn't need our money.

"I'll bring you a dollar soon as I sell some chickens," Papa said.

"That will be fine," Dr. Prince said. He showed us to the door and held the big cur dog by the collar while we walked to the gate. I never did see any of the doctor's servants.

I know Papa was tired before we ever started back up the mountain. I was wore out myself in my legs and in my back, and my arms was sore. We had four miles to walk still, and they was up the mountain.

"Let me carry Masenier," I said.

"We'll take turns," Papa said.

"I should carry him now on the flat ground," I said. "And you can carry him when the trail gets steep."

"We'll both get wore out," Papa said.

"I can rest while you're carrying him," I said. I took Masenier from Papa. The boy was dead asleep. His head laid on my shoulder. I prayed, Lord, let us get Masenier home. Don't let him die out here on the trail in the damp night air. I had never prayed with such a will.

It was the prettiest night you ever saw, with the moonlight slanting on the creek and dew sparkling in the grass. The mountains rose like shadows ahead of us. It must have been three o'clock in the morning, and the mountains was so still and peaceful you would have thought the Millennium had come and all our trials was over. It was the first time I ever noticed how the way the world looks don't have a thing to do with what's going on with people.

I locked my arm around Masenier like I never meant to let go, and I stomped the ground hard to make my steps firm. If I had to carry him all the way up the mountain, I could. I was determined to get this over and done with. There was strength in me I had never called on, and this might be the time I had to use it.

Papa lit the lantern when we got to the woods and started climbing. It was so still I could hear our breath and the flutter of flame in the lantern. Sometimes a twig or an acorn dripped off the trees. I had never seen the woods that quiet. There wasn't even a dog barking anywhere, and the wildcat must have found its mate, for I didn't hear any more squalling.

When you make extra effort a numbness sets in, like your legs are walking on their own and you're not willing them to. But as I kept going a throbbing started in my back, and every step hurt, like I had cramps in my back and arms.

"Want me to take him?" Papa said after we had gone maybe a mile.

"I'll take him a little further," I said. I figured if I could get to the bench on the mountain where Riley's spring was we could rest and give Masenier a drink of cold water. Then Papa and me could take turns carrying him the rest of the way up the mountain.

"You are going the extra mile," Papa said.

The extra four miles, I thought, but didn't say it. When you are straining you have a short temper and a sharp tongue. Mama liked to say, "It weakens you to feel proud of yourself." Better use your breath to fight against the trail, to fight against the mountain, I told myself.

We had got a little further up the trail, up to where the beds of moss growed below the laurel thicket, when I felt Masenier stiffen in my arms. I thought he must be waking up and stretching, that the syrup the doctor had give him was having a good effect. But his back arched too stiff and fast. "Are you awake, little feller?" I said. I started to pat his back, but felt his whole body stirring.

"Is he awake?" Papa said.

"Must be," I said, for Masenier was twisting in my arms like a baby that will jump even while you're holding it. But there was something wrong, because the stirring continued, and his back kept jerking. "Hold the light here," I said to Papa.

Papa brought the lantern up close and the first thing I saw was Masenier's face. His eyes was open like he had seen something terrible and his mouth was drawed back in a scream, but no sound come out except the gnashing of his teeth. He looked like he had seen the awfullest thing and it had scared him to death.

"Is he dying?" I said.

"He's having a fit," Papa said.

Masenier's feet was kicking now and his whole body heaving. I didn't know what to do. Should I lay him down? Or hurry on up the trail toward home? Should we turn and go back down the trail to the doctor's house?

"Put him down here," Papa said, and held the lantern over a bank of moss beside the trail. I knelt down and laid Masenier on the ground, and it was the worst sight to see him twist and kick with both legs. I'd never seen anybody have fits before.

"What can we do?" I said and held his head off the cold moss. I felt helpless. It was like the night was crushing down on top of me.

"Put something between his teeth," Papa said. "So he won't swallow his tongue."

All I had to put between Masenier's teeth was a corner of the blanket we had wrapped him in. I folded it twice and stuck it in his mouth, which was foaming with spit. His head jerked as I pushed the fabric between his teeth.

And then he coughed and coughed again. I seen he was choking. I wondered if he had swallowed his tongue, or was he choking on his own spit? I stuck my finger in his throat to pull out the block and felt something rush up into his mouth.

"He's strangling!" I screamed.

Papa held the lantern closer and we seen that Masenier was throwing up. White stuff come out of his mouth and lines of white stuff. "My god," I said. For I thought he was throwing up milk or some white gravy. But what come out of his mouth was gobs of squirming things. They was worms, wads and wads of white worms. He kept coughing and throwing up, and more come out.

"He's choking," Papa said and reached his hand into Masenier's mouth and pulled out more gobs of the things. I shuddered, looking at what he was doing. Papa dug out more worms to clear Masenier's mouth and throat. And when he stopped, Masenier's mouth was open and his eyes was open, but he was still.

"Make him breathe," I cried and shook Masenier's chest.

Papa pushed on Masenier's heart and listened to his chest. "He's not breathing," he said. Masenier's mouth was open and his eyes was open in the lantern light.

"What can we do?" I said.

We just looked at his little body, and I couldn't think of anything else to do. Something twitched in a nostril. It was another worm that had found its way out through his nose.

I SET THERE on the cold ground feeling that human life didn't mean a thing in this world. People could be born and they could suffer, and they could die, and it didn't mean a thing. The moon was shining above the trees and the woods was peaceful. I could hear the creek down the ridge gentle as a dove, and the mountains was still as ever. The ground under me was solid, but little Masenier was dead. There was nothing we could do about it, and nothing cared except Papa and me. The world was exactly like it had been and would always be, going on about its business.

We must have set on the ground several minutes before we got the strength to pick up Masenier and carry him up the trail. Papa and me took turns toting the body, and we got to the house in the first light of day. Mama and Rosie was waiting up, with the lamp still burning on the mantel.

Two

After Masenier died there was just us four girls in the family, Lou and me and Rosie, and Carolyn the youngest. Rosie was the oldest, and Lou was next. After we lost Masenier Carolyn got spoiled almost as bad as he had and never did a bit of work around the place. It was like we had to spoil somebody, and with no brother it was just natural that Carolyn would be the one. Mama made Carolyn pretty pink dresses with lace and ribbons on them. And she fixed Carolyn's hair in ringlet curls and a pink bow. Carolyn looked more like a doll than a regular child.

Papa's lungs had started to get a little weaker. When he got overworked or soaked in a storm, or chilled by a draft in church, it would take him in the chest. He'd get his feet wet mowing along the branch and before midnight he'd be coughing and spitting into the fireplace. He had been a strong man, but the chest consumption weakened him all over. When his lungs hurt he couldn't sleep, and when he coughed none of us could sleep much either.

The rest of us, except Carolyn, sure worked plenty. As Mama got older she sometimes had back trouble and couldn't stand up straight and had to walk bent over. It might have been rheumatism, or something inside her way down. But it throwed more work on us girls when she was poorly.

Rosie didn't mind doing her share of the housework. She never did like to work outside in the yard and fields, but she would cook things. She liked to sew and to knit. She could do embroidery and knit socks and sweaters and shawls. And she liked crocheting counterpanes and fancy pieces. Rosie would help to dust and clean up, but she preferred to be in the kitchen, or setting by the fire with her yarn and hook with a cat in her lap. That needle pulled and pulled and pulled, looping the soft knots of the vest or throw she was crocheting. Her bag of thread and needles, scissors and extra hooks, set on the floor beside her chair.

But what Rosie liked most of all was cooking. She always kept a fire in the cookstove and a pot of coffee warm on top of the stove. Rosie would sip coffee while she was rolling out dough for a piecrust or cooking down strawberries for preserves. She had her own box of spices and seasonings on the shelf and she didn't want anybody else to touch them. She dried herbs from the little garden on the bank and put the leaves in bottles and jars like a druggist might. "I don't want anybody to touch my herbs," she said. "They might mix them up."

"How do you know they're not already mixed up?" Lou said once.

"I know by the look and the smell," Rosie said. She took the cap off a bottle and sniffed it.

LOU WAS THE only one of my sisters that was willing to work outside. I don't think she liked it, but she was willing to help out. Like I said, when Papa got sick it fell on me to take care of the stock and field crops. But Lou would pitch in and help. Biggest job the year round was to bring in wood, for we had to have fuel for the cookstove and the fireplace. We had to keep the house warm when Papa was coughing, and that meant load after load of wood.

Ever since I was a girl I had worked with Papa to cut firewood. I could pull a crosscut saw and chop with an axe. Since I was a barefoot girl I had been splitting kindling for Mama. But I was never good at splitting bigger chunks and logs. I had trouble lifting the sledgehammer, and I always did hate the harsh sound of steel on steel driving a wedge.

But helping is one thing, and having to do it all yourself is another. Once Papa started taking to bed for long spells, with his breath too short to get any air, Mama said somebody had to bring in the wagon loads and sled loads of wood, had to cut and saw and split and tote it to the porch where Mama or Rosie or even little Carolyn could reach it. Though Carolyn rarely touched anything as rough and heavy as wood. The job just fell to me, without anybody explaining why. And since it had to be done, I done it, and kept on doing it.

FOR FIVE WEDNESDAYS in a row that winter it snowed. And between the snows it would sleet. And after every sleet come a thaw where everything started melting. Then when it turned cold again the water froze, so there was layers of ice and snow like a fancy cake stacked in the woods.

The snow got so hard and slick the horse couldn't hardly walk on it. That was the month our cow slid off the pasture hill into the branch and lost her calf. The ground was slicker than a pane of glass.

"I don't think the horse can stand up, much less pull the sled," Lou said.

"Then we'll have to pull it ourselves," I said.

"I've heard of working like a dog, but never like a horse," Lou said.

There wasn't no other way to bring in the load of wood that I could see, except to pull the sled ourselves. We toted the axe and saw into the woods across the pasture where a bunch of trees had been knocked down by the ice. I broke a sheath of ice off a log before we begun sawing. It was like everything had been painted an inch thick with ice, and then coated again.

The first thing you have to learn about a crosscut saw is to just pull it. You don't ever push it. The other person pulls it toward them, and then you pull it back. If you try to push the saw it will buckle and wear you out before you get started. Pa had taught me that. But Lou had never done much sawing before. Every time she pulled the handle to her, she tried to push it back. The saw pinched and stuck in the log and made it twice as hard for me to pull.

"No, no, just let it go," I said.

"I'm trying to help you," Lou said.

The log was froze and hard to saw anyway. Fresh wood has a lot of water in it, and froze wood saws like a rock. And when Lou pushed on the saw it was almost impossible to pull it to me.

"Don't try to help me, just help yourself," I said.

For a few strokes everything went smooth. And then Lou started pushing the saw back without thinking. "Don't push," I hollered.

After you have held a crosscut saw for half an hour your hands get so stiff you can't open the fingers. Your fingers are curled around the handle and it hurts to let go. Your fingers ache when you straighten them.

We cut through the log three times in twenty-inch pieces. My back got stiff and my fingers hurt. "Let's rest a little," I said.

"We'll get cold if we stop," Lou said.

"I'm burning up," I said. Sweat was running down my back and around my temples, though it was below freezing in the woods. "I hope no man ever sees us working like this," I said.

Lou pulled the saw back to her and gasped, "Why not?"

"Because he would never think of us as ladies," I said.

"We're not ladies," Lou said.

"I don't want to be looked on like a field hand," I said.

"Maybe that's what some man would want," Lou said.

"Not any man I would want," I said.

"Now look who's being choosy," Lou said.

We stopped to rest when the log was sawed through. I stood up and put my hands on my hips. "Any man that just wanted a woman who could cook and bring in firewood would either be a cripple or too old to be any count," I said.

"When is a man too old to be any count?" Lou said.

"I don't know exactly," I said. "But when a man gets beyond a certain age he's no account for a woman."

"And how would you know before you married him?" Lou said.

"You'd just have to be smart," I said. As I rested I could feel the cold sinking in.

"Or you could try him out," Lou said.

"Lou!" I said. Lou always did like to say the worst things she could think of.

"That would be better than marrying somebody who was no account," Lou said.

When I let go of the saw handle my hands was numb at first. But as I straightened the fingers and stretched them they hurt like the bones had been bruised.

I knowed marrying was on Lou's mind. She was two years older than me and she had been thinking of getting married since she started walking home from church with Garland Hughes the year before. She was sweeter than a pound cake on Garland, and they went riding in his daddy's buggy several times, until she heard he had a girlfriend over at Pleasant Hill that he sometimes went to see, and who was going to have a baby. After that she wouldn't walk home with him no more. But the way she grumbled and took on, you could tell she was still studying about him. She was mad at Garland, but she hadn't got over him, not by a long rifle shot.

I might have been as crazy to think about boys and marriage as Lou was if I hadn't had to work so hard. There didn't seem to be any end to what I had to do to help Papa. Papa said he didn't know what he would do without me.

"Whatever man marries you will be the lucky one," Papa said to me. "For you're the best of my girls, the best one."

That give me a little chill of satisfaction, that Papa would say that to me. For he wasn't a flattering man, especially with his daughters. But I thought, he wouldn't talk so agreeable if a man actually asked for my hand. For what would he do without me to help him on the place? What would he do with nobody to bring in wood or hoe the corn? I could hitch up the horse as good as Papa and I could pull fodder and cut tops off corn. I even helped him butcher hogs, though he usually got another man to help him hoist the hog once it was scraped and slide the gambrel stick up a pole so it hung high enough to be gutted and dressed.

And because I was so busy, boys hadn't paid much attention to me. A girl knows how to invite attention. But I'd never had the time to prettify myself and primp, and to study how to be at the right place to get a man's notice. Oh, I had thought about it, as any healthy girl would, and I was pleased just to see a good-looking boy at church or in town. And sometimes it give me a thrill just to think of a good-looking boy.

When I thought of a boy I always thought of somebody I could give in to. Not one of these nervous boys that couldn't hardly look at you without blinking. I thought of a strong man that knowed what he wanted and could teach you. I wanted a body that meant to go somewhere. I guess I wanted a man instead of a boy.

But what was the good of thinking about boys when Papa needed me to help him, and my hands was so rough from holding an axe or shovel or hoe handle I didn't want any boy to see them, much less hold them and feel the calluses and swelled knuckles. Hard work will make the joints in your hands swell up so your fingers lose their pretty shape. I didn't know if my hands would ever get soft again. They hadn't been delicate since I was a little girl, since before I started working with Papa, sawing and digging ditches with a pick and shovel.

WHEN LOU AND me had sawed ten lengths of wood we loaded them on the sled. It was hard to roll the heavy pieces without slipping, but at least they rolled easier on the ice than they would have in leaves. You always load wood on a sled lengthwise, for the stakes on the sides keep it from rolling off. The ten sticks was heavy, and I had my doubts whether Lou and me could pull the sled.

But it was good to take a break from sawing. We picked up the ropes tied to the rings of the runners.

"I never thought I would have to be an ox," Lou said, "at least not this way."

I snickered, but I was already pulling too hard to laugh. The runners had stuck in the ice, and first we had to break them loose. The sourwood runners appeared to sink down in the ice a little. I pulled on one rope and Lou pulled on the other, but we couldn't budge the sled. Twice I slipped on the ice and hit my knees.

"It's too heavy," Lou said.

I saw that if we had to take off some wood and pull half a load it was hardly worth the trip. "Let's pull sideways," I said. We jerked the ropes to the left, but still the sled wouldn't loosen. I was confounded to know what to do. And then I seen a pole leaning on a downed oak tree. I took the pole and pried it under a runner of the sled. "Now pull," I hollered to Lou. She give a yank, and the sled runners broke free. I dropped the pole and grabbed one of the ropes, and we started dragging the load through the woods. We had to lean ahead almost until our knees touched the snow. But the sled moved forward and we kept going toward the house.

IN A HOUSE full of girls there is always disagreement about the work, about who is to do what. When Papa was too sick to do anything outside, it seemed natural they expected me to look after the stock and do the milking, as well as bring in firewood. But when Papa took bad sick and didn't get any better, somebody had to nurse him too, cause Mama couldn't do it all. And there was things my sisters didn't like to do, that had to be done, like lifting him onto the chamber pot, and bathing him once a week, and rolling him over when the bed clothes had to be changed. Of course they wanted me to do it, for who wants to watch their own Papa dookie in the pot, or who wants to wash him all over with a washrag?

But somebody had to, and somebody had to help Mama, and somebody had to stay up at night. And Mama had back trouble herself that winter and was too sore to do much lifting or bending over.

SO IT FELL on me a lot to stay up with Papa, when his lungs got so bad he couldn't breathe at night. After I'd worked all day in the fields I'd get a little sleep between maybe eight o'clock and midnight, either in bed or sometimes just dozing by the fire in a chair. Then I'd rouse myself to stay up with Papa after all the others had gone to sleep. A body can do with a lot less sleep than you might think. One of the others sometimes stayed up for a while, or got up at some point in the night. But it fell to me to be there for the longest time, on watch, so to speak.

So I kept a lamp burning in the tiny hours as Papa struggled. It was an awful thing to see and listen to, a grown man trying to get his breath like a child with the croup. I think that's one reason why the others wanted to get away from him. By late March Papa couldn't halfway take in any air. He rasped and panted in his throat and coughed like he didn't have the breath to cough and was going to break open. His face turned red and splotched like people with the hectic do.

THE NIGHT I'M talking about was windy and late in March. It had rained during the day and then turned off cold. The sarvises and the redbuds was already blooming, but I guess some of their blossoms got blowed away. It was so windy air pushed down the chimney and made the fire flutter and smoke a little. I don't think the wood smoke helped Papa breathe no better. You could hear wind roaring on the mountain like a thousand waterfalls. Everybody else had gone to bed, and every time a gust shook the house the windows rattled.

"Papa, would you like me to heat up some water, so you can breathe the steam?" I said.

"Won't . . . do . . . no . . . good," Papa gasped. He had spit up blood earlier and there was a bloodstain in the corner of his mouth.

"Want me to heat some rocks and put them under the bed?" I said.

He shook his head. It was like after the long struggle all winter to throw off the weakness in his chest, he had just give up.

Wind hit the house like the breath had been knocked out of somebody, and I heard something fall in the attic. It was dark except for the lamp on the table by the bed.

Papa coughed so hard it looked like his eyes was going to pop out. A cough raised his back up and run through his body in waves. As he tried to cough he stared straight up like he was looking a hundred miles away.

"Would you like some syrup?" I said. "Mama has made some

soothing syrup out of honey and liquor with a little paregoric in it."

Papa shook his head, but I got the bottle anyway and poured a tablespoon for him.

"No . . . use," he gasped.

"You got to quit coughing," I said. "You're going to choke." I held the spoon to his lip and tipped some into his mouth. But he coughed, and the syrup flew back out. I tried again, but he coughed that out too.

The thing about somebody with chest sickness is they don't have any lung left to breathe with. Their chest is so eat up there's nothing to take in and hold air. And the lungs think if they cough they can get rid of the congestion and take in more air. But the coughing don't do no good. And more coughing just makes it worse.

Now I was getting scared. The light of the lamp was glaring and everything looked sharp, just like itself, and more like itself than usual. I shuddered with the fear of what was happening.

What can I do? I thought to myself. I'm powerless to help Papa. I was scared as I bent down over Papa's bed and tried to make him drink some of the warm water with lemon juice in it. I knowed he was thirsty. He was dried out from coughing and from breathing so hard. He tried to drink, but he had to cough as soon as the liquid touched his throat. The warm water and lemon juice sprayed out on the bed. I had to wipe it off his face and the bed clothes. And then I tried again.

It hurt to see him so hungry for air, and so parched for liquid, and unable to take either. I held the glass to his lip and he coughed again, and lemonade dribbled on his chin. His lips was chapped, the way sick people's lips get. They cracked and bled when he coughed. It was hard to tell what was blood coughed up and blood from his lips. It reminded me of Masenier choking when he coughed. It made me sick to watch him.

Papa had been the strongest kind of man all his life. He had been able to lift two two-hundred-pound bags of fertilizer when he was young. He had once lifted a loaded wagon while his brother fixed the wheel. He could carry a deer out of the woods after shooting it. Now his chest was sunk in and pitiful. His arms was wasted, though his hands was still big and rough. It broke my heart to look at him.

There is a smell that lung sickness gives people. It's the smell of blood and congestion and fever. It's the smell of blood mixed with air that hangs over a bed and fills a sickroom. It's the smell of old blood, and blood that is fresh and already old. It's the smell of a festering wound.

Papa raised off the pillow trying to get his breath. He gasped like he was trying to swallow the whole world to get some air in his mouth, since there was no room in his lungs. He was sweating with effort to suck in more air.

"Lord," I said without even thinking, "please let Papa get his breath. I can't bear to watch him die."

Papa gulped two more times and his head fell back on the pillow, like he had got some air into his chest, like he was relaxing a little. His body settled down under the quilts like somebody getting ready to go to sleep. He had fell off so much he didn't look like a grown man in the bed. He resembled a bent old woman.

"Lord, let Papa get some rest," I prayed. I never had been one to pray a lot on my own, but I found myself saying the words without even thinking.

I tried to think if there was anything else I could do for Papa. Surely if I thought hard enough, I could find something helpful. All I wanted was for Papa to make it through till daylight. I knowed that most people die between midnight and dawn. I went to put another log on the fire, one of the logs Lou and me had cut and drug through the ice. The wood was too green to burn perfect, and that made the fire smoke a little. I had a few sticks of old pine, which I'd brought in for kindling, and I throwed them on the fire too.

When the new log caught it popped like a cap pistol and hissed as if there was a snake in the wood. Then it popped again. And I seen this green flame rising out of the log, and realized it must be fruit wood. It was a persimmon tree, not an oak, we had cut up. No wonder the wood was so hard, harder than oak. There was some blue in the flames too, but mostly it was bright green. Now I have never believed in ghosts and portents more than other people. I usually don't even listen when people are telling ghost stories. But Mama had told me a long time ago, and Grandma had told her, that a green fire in a fireplace means something is ending and something else is beginning. A green flame is a sign, like a green shoot in spring, or the green light that takes over the sky sometimes after a storm.

I watched the green flame prance and strut and spread its wings. The fire twisted and beckoned as if it meant for me to follow. The fire spread on the wood like fingers on a keyboard. The log popped and hissed and then started to whine. And the wood begun to moan, like somebody that was grieved. I listened for a little bit to the mournfulness and then I shuddered and turned away. I didn't have time for such stuff.

And that's when I knowed I couldn't stand to watch Papa die. I had been there when Masenier died, and I had seen it all because I had to, because I had to help Papa carry him down to the doctor's house. And now Papa was dying, and I was the one forced to watch him.

"I won't do it," I said out loud and stomped my foot on the floorboards. I guess I was as much scared as angry. I had had to clean up Papa and I had had to set up with him, and I had had to wait up with him instead of sleeping. And I had sawed down and hauled in and split the very logs that was keeping the house warm and burning the green portent. Everything that was hard fell to me, and everything nobody else wanted to do fell to me.

"I won't do it," I said again and stomped to the window. Wind shook the frame and trees roared on the mountain like giant animals.

"What won't you do?" somebody said. It was Mama standing in the doorway holding a lamp.

"I ain't going to do this no more," I said.

"What do you mean?" Mama said.

I didn't say nothing else. I couldn't think of what I wanted to say. There wasn't no words that fit how I felt.

"Somebody has got to stay up with Papa," Mama said.

I started to say I wouldn't watch Papa suffer no more, but I couldn't bring myself to say it. I had always done what Mama had told me to, and Papa had told me to. I had always done what was expected. I grabbed my coat from the peg by the door.

"Where you going?" Mama said.

"I'm going to split more wood," I said.

"In the middle of the night?" Mama said. "We've got plenty of wood."

"All the wood you have is what I brought in," I said. I couldn't say to her I would rather die myself than watch Papa die.

"It's too dark," Mama said, "and windy."

Rosie appeared in the door with a blanket wrapped around her shoulders like a shawl. "Where is Julie going?" she said.

In the kitchen I jerked the barn lantern from its nail and lit the wick. I made the flame high as it would go and closed the glass globe before stepping out into the wind on the back porch. I shivered as the blast hit my face and swirled up under my dress. The flame shuddered in the lantern but didn't go out. The gust felt like lips blowing cold air all over me.

The woodpile and woodshed was around the side of the house. I set the lantern down on the chips not too far from the chopping block. There was half a moon overhead and clouds churning and chasing theirselves around its light. The ridges looked like black waves raring up.

From the woodpile you could see the lighted window of the front room where Papa was. I turned away from the house so I could get my night eyes. Didn't want to see what was going on there. I had never refused what Mama had told me to do before, but I couldn't help myself this time.

The lantern throwed its yellow glare over the chips on the ground. The chips appeared to be floating like some kind of foam. I thought there was one chip there for every single lick of the axe on the chopping block. The chips was different colored, maple, oak, pine and hickory. The chips had stayed there like echoes from every chop.

Lou and me had piled the sections of logs in the woodshed, and I took one out to the chopping block and set it on its end. Wind pushed into my face except when I bent over. If a log is less than eight inches thick you can usually split it without a wedge. I raised the axe up into the wind and swung where I thought the wood was, but the blade glanced off. The light only showed the outline of the piece of persimmon. I raised the axe again and it sunk into the meat of the wood and wouldn't let go. Took me several yanks to pull the blade loose.

"Julie!" somebody was calling in the wind. I looked around but didn't see nobody on the porch. There was only the light in the window of the front room. I lifted the axe again and sunk it even deeper into the wood. This time the log split, the splinters tearing from each other right down the middle. It was a satisfying sound. I brought the axe down again, and with a crackle the wood separated into halves and fell apart.

"Julie!" somebody called as I turned around toward the house.

But there was nobody in sight. The voice seemed to come from out of the woods, or maybe up on the ridge. Maybe it was just the wind, but it sounded like somebody accusing me.

I laid the two halves of the split stick aside and got another piece from the woodshed. The torn wood smelled fresh and sour. I could smell the sap on the axe blade. I set up the new log and got the wedge from the woodshed. Much as I hated to split wood, here I was doing it. I didn't know what else to do.

Instead of going to the porch for the sledgehammer I just used the back of the axe head to pound the wedge in. When the wedge was set I brought the axe down hard, but my aim was off, and the wedge jumped out of the log to the ground. I hated the ring of steel on steel. It was a ring of pain, of bones breaking. There is a sourness of doom in the ping of steel driving steel.

I was so mad I kicked at the chips before picking up the wedge again. The iron was cold as a fish. But this time I set the wedge deeper before swinging down on it. The wood cracked and I knocked the wedge loose and set it again. When the log fell in two I split each half again.

"I won't do it," I said under my breath, and the wind sucked my words away. When the moon went behind a cloud I found I had got my night eyes a little. In the splash of lantern light I could see the ground and the log I had set up. As I got into the motion of splitting I found I could feel my way to the wedge with the back of the axe head. I hit the steel and hit the steel and hit it again. And the pieces of log fell apart like cracking shingles. As I worked I missed less and less.

"I won't do it," I said again. I was beginning to sweat, and my dress was sticking to my back under the coat. The wood fell apart like I knowed where to touch the nerve at its center with the blade. I aimed for the heart of a cut end and hit it. The wood cracked itself, and cracked again.

"Julie!" a voice called in the wind, but I ignored it. It was maybe three in the morning, and I had a lot of wood to split yet.

AFTER ALL THE logs was busted open and ready to be carried in, I got a piece of pine from the woodshed to hack for kindling. It was fat, knotty pine I'd gathered on the ridge above Papa's newground. Holding the axe close to the head I shaved off some splinters from the brittle piece and then split it into slivers. I needed little pieces to start fires in the cookstove and fireplace in the morning. The pine wood glittered in the lantern light like sugar or some yellow crystals. Some of the splinters was no bigger than matchsticks. And some was the size of knives and forks. I piled the kindling in a neat little heap beside the lantern.

My eyes was wet, but it was not from sweat. There was tears running down my cheeks as I started splitting another piece of seasoned pine.

"Julie," somebody said in the wind, but the voice was close by. I kept hacking at the wood with the axe, though I couldn't see too well.

"What are you doing?" the voice said. It was Rosie, who had come up behind me still wrapped in the blanket.

"I'm getting in wood, since nobody else will do it," I said.

"At four o'clock in the morning you're splitting more wood?" Rosie said.

"Somebody has got to keep the house warm for Papa," I said.

"Papa is dead," Rosie said. "You might as well come back in."

"I'll come in after a while," I said, and hit at the stick of pine again. In the lantern light I seen my tears drip on the axe.

Three

After Papa's death things hadn't changed as much as you might think. For Papa had been sick a long time, and I was already doing most of the outdoor work, me and Lou, and sometimes Mama helped. You didn't get Rosie much out in the fields or woods. She was a house worker. When things had to be done in the fields or woods, Mama would complain, and then she would tell Lou and me to go do it. But it was up to me to see that things got done. In any house somebody has to take the burden. Mama would say, "Julie, don't you think it's time to plant the taters," and I'd say, "Mama, I've done dropped the taters yesterday, and I'll plant corn today." She had never got over the death of Masenier, and then Papa died, and it seemed to leave her wore out, like she didn't feel up to trying no more. Wasn't anything for me to do but take over and get out and do the work, whether I liked it or not.

There was this Spanish oak that had fell in a storm the winter before, on the bank of the road. It fell in the wind on the night Papa died, but I had been too busy in the fields all summer to cut it up. So it laid there and dried out and seasoned a little, which made it easier to saw.

The first time I saw Hank I was too embarrassed to speak. But that was just because I was took by surprise. Because it was the last thing I was expecting, to fall in love. It was late summer after Papa died in early spring, and Mama and me was sawing the Spanish oak right on the bank of the road where it comes up from Crab Creek.

I reckon there's nothing awkwarder in the world than the sight of two women in long dresses at either end of a crosscut saw. It was still hot and my hair had come unpinned when I wiped the sweat off my forehead. My face was hot and there was big rings of sweat under my armpits. I was so busy working I didn't hear the horse until it snorted and kind of cleared its throat. And when I looked up and brushed a strand out of my eyes, I saw this wagon hitched to a chestnut mare. The wagon stopped and this man, really almost a boy, a big, strong boy, stood in the bed holding the reins.

"Howdy," he hollered to Mama, not paying much attention to me.

"How do," Mama said, standing up. She had took to saying "How do" the way Papa used to.

I can say without doubt the man in the wagon was the handsomest I had ever seen. His hair was black and he had this high rounded forehead. And already he had a soft mustache that hung around the ends of his mouth. He was tanned dark from working in the fields all summer. But the thing that caught my notice first was his shoulders. He had the straightest, widest shoulders, and you could tell how powerful he was, and how much he could lift. It was the way he was made, and not that he was such a terrible big man.

"I'm looking for the Willards that are selling sweet taters," he said.

"You ain't there yet," Mama said and pointed on up the road.

"Figured I had a ways to go," the man said.

"Where you coming from?" Mama said. It was not what she would have said when Papa was alive. She said it the way Papa would have.

"All the way from Painter Mountain," the man said. "I'm Hank Richards."

"I'm Delia Harmon," Mama said. "And this is my daughter Julie."

"Pleased to meet you," the man said and tipped his hat.

That was when I felt myself get red in the face. The sweat run down my temples, and I felt myself blushing all over. Because it wasn't till that second that I remembered I didn't have any shoes on. I was saving my shoes for winter and I didn't want to wear any heavy work shoes if I was just going to be standing in the leaves and sawing. And it was so much cooler to go barefoot. But at that instant I knowed I didn't want Hank Richards to see me barefoot, like a little girl or a pauper. It was bad enough that he had seen me pulling a crosscut saw.

I wiped the hair off my forehead and tried not to look at him. And trying not to show I was moving, I worked my feet into the leaves. My dress was long and I hoped the mayapples on the bank would help hide my dirty feet. It was like I was caught naked, though there wasn't anything bare except my face and hands and feet.

"I was sorry to hear about your man," Hank said.

"We have to believe the Lord knows what he's doing," Mama said.

"Hard as it is," Hank said and shook his head. I could see he was talking like a grown-up man, which he wasn't used to doing. And he was talking to Mama for my benefit, or at least partly for my benefit. I seen he had stopped for my benefit too, for he must have knowed perfectly well where the Willard place was. I was so pleased at the thought I must have blushed even more.

But I seen that Hank wasn't going to speak to me. He was just going to talk to Mama so I could get a good look at him, and he could steal glances at me, and I could hear his talk.

"Mr. Harmon was a mighty fine man," he said and shook his head to show he understood how hard it was to make sense of things that happen.

"He worked as long as he could," Mama said.

"He was a man you could count on," Hank said and spit tobacco juice over the side of the wagon. The horse stepped sideways and he hollered, "Whoa there."

"I'm pleased to meet you," Mama said.

"I don't get up this way too much," Hank said.

"You ought to come to church here sometime," Mama said. "We're having a singing a week from Sunday."

"Might do that," Hank said. "I might just do that."

"Come to church and then come on home with us for Sunday dinner," Mama said. She said it just like Papa would have.

"I'd admire to do that," Hank said and looked right at me.

"Do you like to sing?" Mama said.

"Better than I like to eat peaches," Hank said.

"Come by some evening and we'll raise a song around the fireplace," Mama said.

Hank lifted the reins and rippled them across the mare's back. It was time for him to go on. He had stopped in the road and talked as long as was polite. "You all come see us," he said.

"We don't never get as far as Painter Mountain," Mama said, "unless we're going to Greenville."

"You're welcome if you do," Hank said and tipped his hat, first to Mama and then to me. And as he did he looked right at me, right into my eyes, and I felt a jolt go through me like lightning from the back of my neck to my groin, and my knees trembled. I was so thrilled I looked right back at him. I couldn't look away.

Now a look can tell you more than hundreds of words, if it's the right look at the right time. A look can go through your face and eyes right inside you. The look Hank give me lifted me off my feet and burned into my heart. I was a girl that never had been around boys much, been too busy working and worrying about Papa. I guess Papa had been the man I had been in love with, in a way, more than any other person.

But I don't know why Hank's look stung me so deep at that instant. We don't ever know why we fall in love with one person as opposed to another. Let's say I was just a healthy girl that once Papa died was ready to fall in love. You can say it any way you want to, and it still comes out to mean the same thing.

I looked right back at Hank, and I couldn't take my eyes away from him. I'd never done anything so bold before, but I couldn't help it. The look may have lasted only a second, but it felt like we was fixed on each other and couldn't break loose. I'd never felt so scared or so inspired. Hank's look filled me with something that was sweeter than the sweetest sleep when you are tired. He flicked the reins again and the horse stepped up the road. I watched the wagon creak and rattle on the rocks, and Hank's straight back where he stood holding the reins.

"There's a young man that's proud of hisself," Mama said when he was out of hearing.

"I reckon so," I said. Mama looked at me and seen how I was blushing. I never could hide a thing from Mama. And she must have seen that look Hank and me had traded.

"Don't go getting ideas," Mama said. "You're not but seventeen, and you know we need you on the place."

"Wouldn't dream of it," I snapped. But I wasn't thinking about what I was saying. I was watching Hank's straight shoulders as he rode through the spotlights and dapples of sun that come through the oak trees, and I was wondering if he had seen my bare feet. I wiggled my toes in the leaves.

"Take hold of that saw," Mama said. "We've got to finish this log."

"Yes ma'am," I said.

. . .

THE VERY NEXT Sunday Hank come to church on the mountain. He wore a gray suit of clothes, like he was from town. He must have just bought the suit, for it looked brand-new. I saw him standing outside the church when we arrived. The other young men and boys was slouching on one side of the door and Hank was standing on the other by hisself. The Willards always said they wouldn't let boys from any other community come to court girls on the mountain.

Hank touched his hat as I walked past him up the steps. I didn't know if I should speak to him or not, since that would tell all the other boys he had come courting me. I glanced at Hank and walked by quick, but I had seen that look in his eye, like there wasn't nobody in the world except me and him. Something thrust up in my heart like water busting from a fountain.

All through preaching I could feel Hank's eyes on the back of my head and neck. He had come in and set down on the last bench with the backsliders and sinners and most of the boys in the community. I reckon they elbowed and shoved each other, and throwed lit matches in each other's laps during service like they always did. They didn't get a bit of good out of preaching, and the rest of us ignored them.

Soon as service was over I dreaded to go outside, for I didn't know what would happen. Would the Willard boys get in a fistfight with Hank? Would they let him get away? I knowed they was rough, mean boys and I was afraid for him.

But soon as I come out the church door following Mama and Rosie, there stood Hank with his hat in his hand like a peddler. "How do," he said to Mama. "How do, ma'am."

As I stepped by him he said, "Miss Harmon, may I have the honor of walking you home?" He said it just like he was a lawyer, an educated person from town. Everybody in the churchyard was listening. I couldn't think of what to say. "Why sure" wouldn't sound right, and "Yeah" wouldn't sound polite. All the other girls, and the Willard boys, and Mama and Rosie, and the preacher, was watching. Nothing I could think of to say sounded right. So I just nodded and Hank held out his arm for me to take.

As we walked out of the yard I could feel the pressure of all eyes on me. It was like a high wind coming at my back, pushing the cloth of my dress against my skin. I don't know if I was blushing or not. In the bright sunlight it didn't matter.

Don't ask me what we talked about walking down the road toward our place. I was just aware of holding on to Hank's strong arm. I think he talked about playing the banjo, and about how to make a banjo out of the skin of a cat. I think he asked if I sung alto or soprano, and I told him alto. He said he'd thought so. Mama and the other girls walked along behind us so we didn't have a chance to kiss, even if we had wanted to. People in those days didn't kiss anyway unless they was already serious.

We walked up that road and I thought about what those Willard boys might try to do. And I thought about how Lou and Rosie would tease me. And I thought about how even if Hank never did come back I would always remember how he had walked me home. A handsome boy from Painter Mountain had walked me home from church.

Back at the house Hank took his hat off and set on the porch talking to Carolyn while the rest of us helped Mama put dinner on the table. Mama had cooked her chicken before church and kept it warm in the oven. Mama asked Lou if she would take the bucket to the spring for some fresh water. It was a good thing I had killed and plucked the chicken that morning, because we didn't always have chicken on Sunday. I had hoped Hank might show up at church, and come home with us.

When we finally did set down to eat, Mama asked Hank to say

the blessing. He set at the head of the table where Papa had set, and bowed his head. "Lord," he said, "for what we are about to receive make us truly thankful, and for the struggles of this life make us strong and worthy, and for the beauties of the world make us humble and grateful."

It was an eloquent blessing, unlike any I had heard before. I looked at Hank just as he raised his head and caught his eye for a second. He didn't wink, but it felt like he had winked.

Everything went all right at the dinner until I had to go to the kitchen for the coffee. The chicken and rice and peas and peaches was good. And the cornbread was hot and just soft enough. Hank eat plenty of everything.

"Mr. Richards, you should have brought your mother," Mama said to Hank.

"Ma wouldn't go anywhere but Painter Mountain to church on a Sunday," Hank said.

"She would certainly be welcome," Mama said.

"Have you ever rode the train?" Carolyn said. Carolyn had not been able to take her eyes off of Hank since he got to the house.

"I took the train all the way to Chattanooga one time, looking for a job," Hank said.

"Did you sleep on the train?" Carolyn said.

"It's not polite to ask too many questions," Mama said.

"I didn't sleep in a berth," Hank said, "but I took a nap in my seat." We all laughed.

"Have you ever been to Greenville?" Rosie said.

"I go every year, me and my brothers, to sell hams and molasses," Hank said.

"I would love to ride the train to Mount Mitchell," Carolyn said. Carolyn was wearing one of the pink lacy dresses Mama made for her, the one that had smocking on the front.

Finally Mama said for me to go get the coffee off the stove, and she asked Rosie to bring in the coconut cake she had made. Rosie loved to make coconut cakes, even when she was a girl. And nothing goes better with coffee than coconut cake.

There was still a fire in the cookstove, and the coffee was boiling. I took the pot off the stove and carried it to the dining room. But as I got close to the table I wondered if I should pour the first cup for Mama, who was a woman and the oldest person at the table, or for Hank, who was our guest at Sunday dinner. I couldn't make up my mind, and that flustered me. I took a step toward Mama and then stopped.

"Julie, pour some coffee for Mr. Richards," Mama said. That settled it, but the damage was already done. My hand was shaking when I held the heavy coffeepot over Hank's cup. Coffee come out of the spout too fast and splashed out of his cup and on his knee. He jumped when the hot coffee touched him, and I must have screamed as I stepped back. I hit the buffet as I jerked around and the pot fell to the floor, throwing out a scarf of smoking coffee.

"Oh, Julie," Mama said.

Hank stood up and knocked the drops of coffee off his pants. "It's nothing," he said.

"Are you burned?" I said.

"Not a bit," he said.

Mama run to the kitchen for towels, and I helped her wipe up the spilled coffee.

"I'll wash your pants," I said to Hank.

"It's just a spot," he said.

I finished mopping up the coffee and carried the pot and wet towels to the back porch. Through my carelessness I had ruined everything. Everything! I figured Hank would just get his hat and go, as soon as it was polite. He would get away from all us girls gawking at him, and Carolyn flirting, and Mama calling him Mr. Richards. I knowed there was a lot of girls prettier than me closer to Painter Mountain, girls not so clumsy and nervous.

But I was wrong. Hank did get his hat, but he said, "Julie, show me where the spring is. I need a drink of cold water after that fine, hot dinner."

There was no way I could refuse to show him where the spring was. I wiped my hands on a dry towel and hung it on the nail by the stove.

"Somebody can bring a bucket of fresh water from the spring," Mama said.

"I want to drink it cold from the ground," Hank said.

It was the brightest day you ever seen outside, bright as only early fall can be. The grass and leaves on the trees and even the bare dirt appeared to sparkle. I don't know if it was the light, or the fact that I was falling in love, that made everything shine. The world was lit in a new way, and I was lit up in every finger and toe and part of me.

Our spring was down the hill behind the house, below the big walnut tree. The spring was hid by laurel bushes so it was always in shade. It was the boldest and the coldest spring on the mountain. Water pushed out from the sides of the spring, boiling up the white sand on the bottom and stirring the flecks of mica. There was little lizards around the edges of the pool, showing how pure the water was.

Hank took the coconut shell off the stick by the spring and dipped out a drink. He offered it to me and I shook my head. He drunk the water slow, like he was savoring the flavor and the coldness. "This here water tastes like it comes out of rock," Hank said, "like it's been running through rubies and emeralds."

It was pretty the way he put it.

"I wish I had a ruby; I would give it to you," Hank said.

"I don't need no ruby," I said.

Hank dipped up another drink, and then replaced the coconut shell on the stick. "Now my mouth is sweet," he said. He looked into my eyes and stepped closer. He took my hands and raised them, first one and then the other, to his lips and kissed them. Nobody had ever kissed my hands before. Then he put his hands on my elbows and pulled me closer to him.

"You are an unusual person," he said and looked right into my eyes. I couldn't think of any way I had been unusual except to splash coffee on his britches, but I didn't say that. He leaned closer and nudged my lips with his lips. It tickled, and made my lips tingle. He rubbed his lips sideways across mine, and I thought how gentle and careful he was, for such a big, strong man. I wondered if Mama or Rosie or one of my other sisters was watching us from the back porch. And then I remembered the laurel bushes was between us and the house. Hank pressed his lips to mine and the feeling was sweet, sweeter than the fresh water from the spring. Then he nibbled at the edge of my lip, at my upper lip and the corners of my mouth. He run the tip of his tongue along my upper lip. It was a feeling I'd never had before.

When Hank put his lips full against mine and placed his arms around my shoulders, I felt I was being gathered up in a spin and cut off from the air and light around me. It was like his arms made a separate world around me. His arms and lips and the feel of him against me made us apart from the woods and spring and bushes. We was our own world just by being together.

The feeling of the kiss went all over me. The kiss went through my arms and legs to the tips of my fingers and toes. That was the strangest part. Hank kissed my lips and run his tongue around my lips, and I felt the sweetness in the back of my head and down my back. So this is what kissing is, I thought. And I thought, This is not me. This is better than me. This is better than I deserve. And I thought, No, this is what I have been waiting for; this is what the future is going to be like.

Hank kissed me and we turned around like we was dancing real slow. We stepped around, but I wasn't hardly aware of stepping. I felt the trees and laurel bushes and the spots of sunlight was all circling. Everything was turning as Hank kissed me. My eyes was closed and I floated with the turning.

When Hank took his lips away and breathed, I caught a breath too. I took a breath and opened my eyes. And looking over his shoulder at the woods I seen somebody standing among the bushes above the spring. It was the oddest feeling, to open my eyes after my first kiss, after an otherworldly kiss, and see somebody staring at us from among the oak trees. It was like waking up from a sweet dream and finding somebody studying you.

I knowed it was one of the Willard boys. I think it was Clarence. He must have been watching us all that time. I couldn't know how long he had been watching. But if he was watching us, the rest of them must be watching us too. There might be half a dozen Willards spying on us.

"I want you to be careful," I said to Hank. I didn't mean to spoil everything by telling him we was being watched.

"Careful about what?" he said.

"You just be careful as you go down the mountain," I said.

And then I heard a squirrel bark. But it wasn't a regular squirrel. The bark was too steady, and a little too loud. It was one of the Willards making the noise, teasing us. And then I heard a bobwhite call, and though it sounded like a bobwhite, the call was too loud. It was another one of the Willards answering the first.

Hank must have seen the worry on my face, for he started to listen. Just then a turkey gobbled further up the ridge. "There's a lot of varmints about," he said and laughed.

"Don't you leave here by yourself," I said.

Hank pulled his coat back and showed me a pistol stuck in his belt.

"They may have guns too," I said. I knowed the Willard boys carried pistols with them, especially Webb. Sometimes on Sunday afternoons they would walk along the road with a .22 and shoot at rocks and cans.

"Don't you worry," Hank said. "Worry never made anybody live a second longer."

We walked around the edge of the yard and Hank held my hand. I think he wanted whoever was watching to see us together. I showed him the garden where the tomatoes was so ripe and many they had broke down the vines. And the summer squash had got so big they looked like yellow geese laying in the weeds. The tater vines was dead and the bean vines had turned yellow.

We walked to the edge of the cornfield where Lou and me had already cut the tops and pulled the fodder. "Who did all that work?" Hank said.

"I did some," I said. "And Lou helped, and Mama did some."

Hank looked at me and run his finger along my cheek. "You will make somebody a good wife," he said. I couldn't look into his eyes. I couldn't hardly bear for him to look at me. For I knowed that more than anything in the world I wanted to be married to Hank Richards. I wanted to live in a house with just him and me, and I wanted to help him work in the fields and raise chickens and pick apples to dry in the sun for winter. It seemed too much to hope for that I could be with him day after day, day and night. It was too perfect to think on. Nothing ever worked out that perfect in this world. And if I wanted it too bad it would never happen. The world was made so people never got what they wanted most. Or maybe they wanted most what they couldn't never get.

"You will make somebody a good husband," I said. I hoped he

didn't think I had cut all the tops in the cornfield by myself. I was a little ashamed of all the hard work I had had to do.

"Who is going to help you kill hogs?" Hank said. We had ambled close to the hogpen and the mud of the pen sent its stench over into the sweet smell of the garden.

"I guess Lou and me and Mama will do it," I said.

"I could come up and give you a hand," Hank said.

"You don't have to do that," I said.

"You'll need help lifting the hog," Hank said.

I didn't protest, because I wanted him to come whenever he would. And I didn't want him to think I was able to kill a hog and cut it up all by myself. We walked by the grape arbor where the bees was busy on the ripe Concords.

"Did you ever make wine?" Hank said.

"Papa used to make blackberry wine for his rheumatism," I said. "But nobody else ever did drink any."

"Pokeberry wine is better for rheumatism," Hank said. "It warms the joints and soothes them."

When we got to the front porch Mama come out and said she had made a fresh pot of coffee. She asked Hank did he want any.

"That would be perfect," he said. "I've got to leave soon, but a cup of coffee will set me up for the road."

Mama brought out two mugs on a tray and we set on the swing on the front porch. I never had coffee except in the morning, but I took the cup just to be sociable. Maybe it was because I was excited and in love, or maybe it was because I wasn't used to drinking coffee in the afternoon, but after a few sips it felt like lights was going through my veins to the ends of my fingers. And the yard and front porch got even brighter and clearer. Everything was so clear it hurt my eyes to look at it. And Hank was so handsome with his black hair and downy mustache and brown eyes and high forehead, it sent a pain through me just to glance at him.

I thought I heard Carolyn giggle inside. She must have been watching us through the window. She was nearly fourteen, and too big to giggle like that. But she was spoiled and I reckon she was jealous because Hank had come to see me and not her.

"What if I was to ask you—," Hank said. But just then there was a whippoorwill call on the hill above the road. Since whippoorwills never call till after dark, it didn't fool us. It was one of the Willard boys all right.

"That bird has got its clock wrong," Hank said.

"If you was to ask me what?" I said.

There was a dove call, slow and mournful, from the same place the whippoorwill had called from. "Those birds are singing up a regular chorus," Hank said.

"Those birds ought to be jailbirds," I said.

Next it was a mockingbird on the hill, sounding like the other birds, and a rain crow and a robin. And then a fox barked up there too. "The woods is full of noise," Hank said.

"If you was to ask me what?" I said again.

There was another bobwhite call, and a fox bark, and then a wildcat scream. "What if I was to ask you to be my wife?" Hank said. I couldn't believe what was happening. I had only walked home with Hank the first time that morning. Some girls had to wait months, even years to get engaged. I had first laid eyes on Hank less than a week before, and here he was asking me to get married. It felt like I was dreaming it all.

AFTER WE KISSED and held hands and looked into each other's eyes for what must have been an hour, ignoring the birdcalls from the hill, and Carolyn's giggles behind the window, Hank said he had to go, if he was to get off the mountain before dark. He didn't want to be caught on the mountain after nightfall. "Might step on a snake," he said.

"I'm afraid for you," I said.

He kissed me on the forehead. "Just do what I tell you to do," he said.

"What do you want me to do?" I said.

"I want you to hold my hat," he said. He took off his wide-brimmed black hat, and he went to the front door and thanked Mama for the dinner.

"I hope your pants ain't ruined," Mama said.

"A spot of coffee won't ruin good cloth," Hank said.

"You come back and see us soon," Mama said.

"I'll do that," Hank said.

Out in the yard Hank handed me his hat and told me to stand by the front gate and hold it for him.

"Where are you going?" I said.

"I'll be back," he said and winked. And taking off his coat and tucking it under his arm he headed down the trail to the outhouse. The outhouse was hid behind the arborvitae, and it was right at the edge of the pine woods. I heard the door of the outhouse slam. I smiled, thinking how delicate Hank had been about mentioning where he was going.

I held the hat and stood there beside the boxwood by the gate. Mama had swept the yard and sprinkled sand on it, but chickens had already tracked the sand and stained it. I would have to carry more sand from the branch for next Saturday. Shadows was getting longer across the yard, and I felt the coolness of evening in the air. A crow cawed in the pines on the hill. A dog barked down the mountain.

After a few minutes I started to wonder what Hank was doing in the outhouse. Was he sick? Had a spider bit him? It was embarrassing that he had gone there and was staying so long while I held his hat by the road. I looked at the soft felt hat. It must have been a seven and three-quarters size, for Hank had a large head. Mama come out on the porch and said, "Is he gone?"

I shook my head and pointed toward the outhouse. Rosie and Carolyn come out on the porch behind Mama and looked toward the arborvitae. I hoped Hank wouldn't step out and see them all looking at him.

I held the hat and looked down the road, but didn't see anybody. And then I looked up the road and saw the road that way was empty too. There was a dove call on the hill, and then another bobwhite call. I looked at the hat in my hand, and I looked toward the arborvitae. And then I smiled, because I knowed Hank had already slipped away into the trees and was far down the mountain. I was even more thrilled than I had been, to think he was safe, and that he had been so clever.

"Well, what happened to him?" Mama said.

"He's done gone," I said.

"He'll have to come back for his hat," Carolyn said. "A gentleman don't go anywhere without his hat."

Shadows was already reaching across the yard. There was crow calls from the trees on the hill. I tossed the hat up in the air and caught it. It was the happiest day of my life.

MARRIAGE WAS DIFFERENT from what I ever expected. Like all girls I imagined something wonderful, and it was wonderful, in most ways, but in different ways from what I had thought. Mama had always said that marriage is like everything else: it is work, hard work.

As I expected, Mama was angry when I told her I was engaged.

"You don't hardly know that boy," she said.

"How well am I supposed to know him?" I said.

"Well enough to know his mama's name," Mama said.

I didn't say nothing. I never was good with talk when somebody was upset. Besides, there was nothing I could say to convince Mama.

"When are you getting married?" Lou said.

"Next month," I said.

"Where are you going on your honeymoon?" Carolyn said. She was always reading stories in magazines about courtship and honeymoons.

"I don't know yet," I said. "He has only just asked me."

"I'll say," Mama said. "You only met him last week."

"I'll bake you a coconut cake," Rosie said.

"Who is going to do the work around here?" Mama said.

"The crops is already in this year," I said. "It's not like Rosie and Lou and Carolyn is helpless."

"This is a fine come off," Mama said, "after your Papa died in the spring. And you not much more than a youngun." But I don't think Mama was as mad as she acted. Or if she was she got over it. Maybe she seen the advantage of getting one of her girls married off. Or maybe she seen there was nothing she could do to stop it. "I just hope he's a good man," Mama said, "though he's really just a boy."

"He's eighteen years old," I said.

"That's what I mean," Mama said. "You're both just younguns."

Four

Now the week before we was married Hank rented a house over the line in South Carolina. It was way down a little valley called Gap Creek, and it was the farthest I had ever been from home. Hank said he wanted to live there because it was a pretty place, and because it was cheap, and he had work where they was building a cotton mill at Lyman. He had worked before as a carpenter and mason's helper and he already had a job lined up at the site in Lyman, helping to make brick. I thought later he moved to South Carolina to get away from his ma, because when I got to know her I could see why he would want to.

We got married on a Saturday, nearly a month after we first met, and we stayed that night at Mama's house. I felt embarrassed to be spending my first night as a married woman in my own house, but Mama knowed what to do. Since there wasn't no extra bedroom she told Hank to sleep on the couch in the living room, and I stayed in the bedroom with Lou and Rosie and Carolyn like I always had. I didn't get hardly any sleep that night, and Lou giggled and teased me.

"Do you reckon Hank is lonesome out on the couch?" she said.

"Shhhhh," I said and pretended to be sleepy.

The next day we walked down to Gap Creek.

Like any bride, I thought my husband was wise and on his way to riches. And when I seen the valley of Gap Creek I thought it was one of the prettiest places in the world. The house wasn't so fancy, but the narrow valley with steep mountains on either side looked like a picture out of a magazine. The valley floor was flat, winding peaceful back into the steep mountains. It was still green in the slender cove, though it was already fall on the higher slopes.

The worst thing about the house was that Mr. Pendergast, who rented it to us, lived there hisself. He lived in the bedroom at the front of the house, and our rent was the meals I fixed for him and the washing I did for him. He was a crusty old widower and I seen I was going to have to humor him. I was just a young bride and Hank took me down there to start housekeeping in that little place, and to cook for old man Pendergast.

Mr. Pendergast was a short man with a huge head of gray hair and hair growing out of his ears. He always looked at you with a squint when he talked. "Don't you worry about me," he said the night we arrived, when I come in with all my clothes tied up in a pasteboard box and a pillowcase, after walking all the way from Mount Olivet, "I don't eat hardly nothing, and I'm so quiet you'll never know I'm around."

He showed me where the kitchen was and where all the pots and pans was. His wife had died three or four years before, and he had let the house go the way most men would. Every inch of the floor needed to be scoured and scrubbed. You never seen such filth as was built up around and behind the cookstove. I seen it would take me a week to get the place cleaned up so it didn't turn your stomach.

"What do you like for breakfast?" I said.

"Just fix me some biscuits and gravy," Mr. Pendergast said, "and maybe a poached egg."

I had heard of poached eggs, but I had never made a poached egg. I'd have to ask Hank what a poached egg was.

"We won't have no bacon until we kill the hog," Mr. Pendergast said. "But it's almost time for hog killing."

LATER WHEN WE went to bed that first night I was almost afraid to move in the attic bedroom, for the floorboards creaked and the bedsprings creaked. And I was afraid Mr. Pendergast was right below us listening to every sound we made. The floorboards groaned and the bedsprings moaned when we got in. "Shhhh," I said to Hank.

"Pendergast is deaf as a fencepost," Hank said, not even lowering his voice.

"Even a fencepost can hear this bed creak," I said.

After Hank blowed out the lamp we laid in the bumpy bed in the room smelling of old wood and smoke. Hank turned over to face me and the springs banged on the slats of the bed. I giggled cause I was a little nervous. But I wasn't scared or worried like so many brides are supposed to be. I had thought all my life about this first night in our own house, and now that it was here I was more worried about waking up Mr. Pendergast than anything else.

"Shhhh," I said again.

When Hank put his lips to my ear it felt so odd and good it made me shiver. And when he put his finger on my nipple it felt like funny bones all over my body had been touched. When he run his hand over my shoulder and under my armpit and down to my belly, I thought little sparks must be jumping off my skin in the dark.

I felt something pulling my nightgown up over my knees and over my thighs and over my belly. I giggled and the bed creaked as Hank moved over me. And then I felt something hot and wet in my belly button, and I knowed it was Hank's tongue going in and out and round and round the navel. He licked the little hairs around my navel and stuck his tongue in the hole. I hoped there wasn't any lint in there.

It was all so strange and different from what I had imagined. I didn't hardly know what was happening. It was like the world had been tilted and turned in some way. And time had stopped, or slowed down. Time had been turned on its side and moved in a curve. When Hank got on top of me and rocked the bed, I felt numb with his weight, and I heard the headboard of the bed knock on the wall. I thought of Mr. Pendergast below listening. I wondered if this was it. Was this what everybody talked about and thought about so much?

Stop, I wanted to say. You stop that. But I couldn't. You quit that, I thought of saying, but I didn't. As Hank rocked faster the bedposts scooted on the floor a little. What he was doing hurt a little, but it felt good too. A sweet hurt, a hot sweetness.

"Oh," I said. And I thought, You'll have to stop this. We can't go on like this, for I was getting short of breath. And Hank was getting short of breath. Stop that, I thought. Or maybe it was: Don't stop. Don't stop now. Don't stop.

All the colors started running through my head in the dark. Purples and greens and yellows and blacks. They blended into each other and poured over each other. And the colors was like milk, so soft and warm and pouring over and into each other. And the colors was swelled, bigger than I had ever thought they could be. The colors was melodies, like shaped note singing.

Now quit this, I thought. We've got to stop or we'll wake up old man Pendergast. We'll wake up the chickens in the henhouse and we'll wake up the horse and the hog in the pen. We'll even wake up the stars over the mountains, and the birds roosting under the eaves of the barn. But the colors poured on behind my eyes, the purples and blues, the salty colors like orange and yellow. Yellow is salty as butter and popcorn. Yellow was swelled up and buttery. And there was a golden brown that was saltiest of all.

And I felt a sneeze coming down there. It was the best feeling, of a sneeze coming right out of my middle and swelling through me to get rid of what I was holding back. And I sneezed quick, and again. It was the sweetest cachoo, and cachoo, so deep and full it hurt too.

Hank was shoving too and pushing with his feet against the foot of the bed like he was running while laying down or dancing while laying down. And there was a wrench of boards and a squeal of nails pulling out. We fell and slammed onto the floor. It sounded like the house had fell down, but I knowed what had happened, even though it was dark and I couldn't see. That old bed had pulled apart and the footboard had fell away. The springs and mattress had slid onto the floor.

I was laying on the floor, and I knowed Mr. Pendergast must have woke up beneath us. But I giggled a little and Hank put his head on my neck and giggled too. We was both tired out, and it felt good just to lay still. I listened to see if Mr. Pendergast was moving around below. But all I could hear was my own breathing, and Hank's breathing. And then something crashed, and I could tell it was the headboard of the bed falling over on the floor.

"Lord a mercy," I said in the dark. I thought I heard somebody laughing below, but I couldn't be sure. It might have been a screech owl off in the woods, or wind in the eaves.

MY FIRST TROUBLE with Mr. Pendergast come the next morning when I fixed his breakfast. Hank got up early to go to the mill at Lyman where he was helping to tend the brick kilns. I fixed him some biscuits and butter and jelly to take in his lunch pail. After he was gone I went ahead and boiled a saucepan of water to fix Mr. Pendergast's poached egg. Hank had said a poached egg was just a slightly boiled egg. Rosie would know how to do it.

When the water was bubbling and rolling I put an egg in for what I figured was a minute. But I didn't have an egg timer or clock with a sweep hand. So I just had to guess. And then when I took the egg out of the water and put it on the table beside Mr. Pendergast's plate, he had still not come out of the bedroom. I kept waiting and finally eat my own breakfast of grits and gravy and drunk a cup of coffee. I finished and still Mr. Pendergast had not appeared. I got up and heated more water to wash the dishes, and after I had finished washing and drying the plates there was still no sign of him. I put the biscuits back in the oven and soon the grits was cold and getting a skin. Could Mr. Pendergast have died in the night? A chill went through me down to my tailbone. Had he heard the bed fall down in the night and was too embarrassed to come out? Had he got up early and left? Or could he be expecting me to serve him breakfast in bed?

I put the dry dishes on the shelf and got the broom and swept the kitchen floor. The fire was dying in the cookstove and I put a couple more sticks in. By then it was daylight and I could see the early sun turning the tops of the mountains copper. I heard a noise behind me and turned. There was Mr. Pendergast with his hair uncombed and his overalls with only one gallus buckled. He drug his feet as he walked to the table.

"I'll pour you some coffee," I said. I got the pot off the stove and hoped the coffee was still hot. The fire was blazing up again, but it might not have heated the pot yet.

Mr. Pendergast took a sip of the coffee and put it down. "This coffee is cold," he said.

"I'll heat it up again," I said. I took the cup and poured the coffee back into the pot.

"A man can't drink cold coffee," Mr. Pendergast said.

I took the pot of grits off the stove and put it on the table beside his plate. He took the serving spoon and dug into the grits and seen a skin had dried on them. "When did you make these, last night?" he said.

"I'm sorry," I said. "I made them for Hank at six."

"I wouldn't feed them to a hog," Mr. Pendergast said.

"I can make you some more," I said. I got more sticks of wood out of the box and put them in the stove.

"Don't bother," Mr. Pendergast said. "I'll just have biscuits and an egg."

I took the biscuits out of the oven and put them on the table. The jam and molasses and butter was already on the table. Mr. Pendergast looked at the egg and said, "I thought I said a poached egg."

"I can make you another one," I said.

Mr. Pendergast cracked the egg on the edge of his plate and started peeling it, then stopped. "It's not half boiled," he said.

"I tried to boil it for a minute," I said.

"I can't eat this," he said. He looked at me like he blamed me for everything wrong in the world. He dropped the egg on his plate like he had touched a rotten tater.

When the coffee was hot I poured Mr. Pendergast another cup, but I couldn't hardly stand to look at him. He hadn't told me when he was going to get up, and he hadn't told me how to poach an egg. But I didn't want to argue with him, because it was his house and I was going to have to live there.

I put more water on to boil, but Mr. Pendergast said, "Forget about the egg. I'll just eat biscuits and molasses." He set at the table like he had been offended and he didn't even want to look at me. I stood by the stove wondering where I could go. It was his house, but I had to take care of it. I didn't have anywhere to go except up to the bedroom to make up the bed. But the bed had fell apart and would have to be put back together. And after that I could sweep the front room and the porch.

I left Mr. Pendergast at the table eating hot biscuits and drinking coffee and climbed the stairs to the bedroom. The bed was in pieces, and the quilts and sheets all tangled up. To let in the light I pushed back the curtains. Everything was going wrong. Except for the memory of the night, I wished I was back home on the mountain. I almost wished I could go out and work in the fields or woods, like I was used to doing. At least Mama and Rosie wasn't as hard to please as Mr. Pendergast.

I thought of packing up my things in the cardboard box and lighting out for home. It would take all day to climb the mountain to North Carolina and then on up to the ridge. It was a pleasing thought, except when I got there I would have the same old work, and the shame of a failed marriage. Rosie and Lou would laugh if they seen me trudging up the road with my things in the box. And Mama would shake her head at the sadness of it all. And I would have to go back to cutting firewood and planning to butcher the hogs.

It was the thought of the work that cleared my head a little. If I was going to have to work so hard anyway, I might as well be working for Hank and myself. I might as well work where I was, now that I was down on Gap Creek.

I set the headboard up against the wall and got the sides out from under the mattress. I seen the bed could be fitted together again, but where the post had cracked it was going to have to be nailed. If it wasn't nailed, the bed would just fall down again. I looked at the crack in the light from the window and seen it had been made a long time ago. Whoever had set the bed up had knowed it would come crashing down as soon as the frame was shook. And I was certain it was Mr. Pendergast who had set it up without nailing the crack. He must have been waiting in the night to hear the bed crash. And it was him laughing I had heard after we fell on the floor and everything was quiet.

I marched down the steps and turned toward the kitchen table to ask where there was a hammer. But Mr. Pendergast was gone. His coffee cup and greasy plate and knife and fork was there, but he had disappeared.

"Where is a hammer?" I called, but nobody answered. I looked on the shelf at the back of the kitchen, and then on the back porch where all kinds of tools hung on nails. I didn't find a hammer, but discovered a hatchet that had a hammer back. And after a little more looking I found a half-rusty nail under a ball of binder's twine.

AFTER NAILING THE bedpost so it would hold the side, I put the bed together. It was an old bed and would creak no matter what you done to it. But I made it as firm and tight as I could. Since Hank and me would be sleeping there every night, I wanted to make it as quiet as possible. Mr. Pendergast might be downstairs listening every night, but at least the bed wouldn't fall again.

When I got back to the kitchen Mr. Pendergast was setting beside the cookstove whittling on a stick of kindling. He shaved curls off the piece of pine into the kindling box. He scratched with the knife on the white wood and hollowed out with the tip of the blade. It was a little figure of a person he was cutting. I didn't want to speak to him again, because I thought he would say something short. He would take advantage of anything nice I said and give me an order to do something else. He seen I was just a young girl that had never been away from home. He seen I was at the disadvantage of being married and in a new place for the first time in my life. I figured it was better not to say anything.

"I got some clothes that needs to be washed," Mr. Pendergast said. He opened the door of the stove and throwed shavings into the fire.

I hadn't thought of doing a wash on my first day on Gap Creek. At home we had just washed on Mondays. And then I remembered that this was a Monday. We had got married on a Saturday and walked down to Gap Creek on Sunday.

"Where is your clothes?" I said.

"In the bedroom, behind the door," Mr. Pendergast said.

It was already nine according to the mantel clock. When I washed clothes I liked to heat water early in the morning. I'd have to build a fire and carry water from the spring. I looked in the front bedroom where Mr. Pendergast slept and you never seen such a mess. His clothes was scattered everywhere. The room looked like a rag pile. The bed probably hadn't been made up in months. Clothes was piled on the bureau and on the nightstand. The room smelled of pneumony salve and camphor. I reckon Mr. Pendergast had rheumatism and rubbed the liniment on his joints. But there was a smell of dust also, and clothes that hadn't been washed in a long time.

I looked behind the door and there was a pile of clothes up to my waist, overalls and shirts, underwear and socks, heaped up and spilling over when I pulled the door back. Mr. Pendergast must not have washed clothes in months. It would take three armloads just to carry the clothes out to the backyard.

I marched out of there and right back to the kitchen. "Where is the washpot?" I said.

"I like a little starch in my shirts," he said.

I stepped out to the back porch and looked in the yard. Like in any backyard, there was a woodshed and a smokehouse, a clothesline, a path to the toilet on the right, and a path to the spring on the left. And further out there was a barn and hogpen. The washpot was on the trail to the spring. And there was a table and a wooden tub on the trail next to the pot. I looked around the porch and found a washboard and a bucket. And by the water bucket was a cake of Octagon soap.

I grabbed that bucket and carried several gallons of water from the spring and poured them in the pot. And then I got some kindling and wood from the shed and started a fire under the pot. There was a little wind, and the fire whipped around from side to side. But I put on more pine to make it blaze up.

It took me four trips just to carry Mr. Pendergast's clothes out to the wash table. With my arms loaded I tried not to smell all that sour cloth and soiled long handles. But when you have a filthy job the only thing to do is jump in and get it done. Won't hurt your hands to get dirty; you can always wash them. The quicker I got the clothes in the boiling water the quicker I would be done. I tried not to even look at the dirty clothes, but dumped them on the table and went back for more.

"Don't boil my linen with the overalls," Mr. Pendergast said as I passed through the kitchen. I could see now he was whittling the figure of a naked woman from the piece of pine. He was picking with the point of his knife at the rounded shape of the buttocks. "Don't want the linen to fade," he said. I didn't even answer him. He lived in such filth and never washed or cleaned up, and here he was worried about his clothes fading. Anything I said would just show him how angry I was, and I didn't want to quarrel on my second day on Gap Creek. It was not what I had thought the beginning of married life would be.

As soon as the water was boiling, I dumped in underwear and light-colored shirts. I heated the water extra hot to scald away the filth and grease in the clothes. Nothing will purify and sterilize like boiling water. The water bubbled and churned up into foam and flattened into spreading scars. I dumped the dirty long handles in and stirred them with the troubling stick, then let them boil for a minute and lifted them out with the stick and dumped them smoking on the wash table. I dipped two buckets of boiling water and mixed it with cold water in the tub. And then I took the washboard and the cake of Octagon soap and started to scrub every piece of underwear and every shirt. I rubbed them up and down, up and down, on the washboard, and the soapy water steamed up into my face. My hands got red from the soapy, hot water.

There is something chemical about the heat of washing, like the fire burns away filth and the soap turns the dirt into something clean. The bitter soap melts grease and soil. The slick soap eats away filth and oily stains. Much as you hate it, doing washing makes you feel you're starting out new. You have put your face in the smoke and steam, and your hands in the dirty slick water. And then you lift the pieces out and rinse them in fresh water and wring them out in the wind.

I took each piece of Mr. Pendergast's clothes out of the rinsing tub and twisted it hard as I could. The water squirted out and the cloth was merely damp as I hung it on the line, in the cool breeze. The line run along the trail to the spring, and I hung the clean underwear and shirts and socks along the big thread. And after that I hung the overalls so they looked like people walking as they flapped in the breeze.

"Have you washed my socks?" Mr. Pendergast called from the back porch.

"Done washed them," I said.

"Don't you lose none," Mr. Pendergast said.

"Wouldn't think of it," I said.

When the washing was done I felt a little better. For even Mr. Pendergast and his grumpy manners couldn't keep me from getting things done. I didn't know what to say to him, but if washing his stale clothes was part of my job, then I had done it. If waiting on him was part of my married life, then I had got it started that morning.

I LET THE FIRE die down and emptied the two tubs in the grass by the trail. The washing hung on the line like a whole army marching in the sunlight. Where the underwear hung and the shirts hung it looked like angels and not soldiers. But they didn't make any noise. The sun behind the cloth made them blinding.

I carried the bucket and soap back to the porch and Mr. Pendergast was standing on the back steps watching me. With the tip of his knife blade he was putting the finishing touches on the sharp little breasts of his naked woman. I glanced at the figure and looked away. I didn't want him to see me studying the carving. He held the pine woman up to the sunlight, and I could see how rounded her behind was and how big her breasts was. The face was still rough, but the shape of the body had been smoothed by the knife to look like real sculpture. When I glanced at the figure I seen Mr. Pendergast was looking at me and grinning. His face had flushed a little. I hurried past him. It was time to fix dinner.

MY HANDS WAS soft and water-sobbed from the washing. I wished I had some lanolin to rub on them, but I didn't. The skin on my fingers felt tender as a baby's as I loaded wood into the cookstove. I wanted to bake some cornbread and sweet taters for dinner. But first I would have to ask Mr. Pendergast where the sweet taters was kept. I hated to ask him anything, since my best idea was to avoid him. I was pretty sure the taters was in a hole or cellar somewhere, but I didn't have time to go searching. Not if I got everything done by dinnertime. Once I got the fire snapping in the stove, I looked out on the back porch and seen Mr. Pendergast still holding his doll and scratching at the face with his knife.

"Where is the tater pit?" I said.

He looked around slow at me and grinned. "You're standing right over it," he said.

I didn't want to ask him where the steps to the cellar was. I would just find them for myself. He watched me as I walked out into the backyard and looked to the right of the house. I didn't see any door or steps there. I looked on the left side of the house, and at first didn't see anything but weeds and the chimney. And then I saw a door like a lid on a trunk. The door was covered with tin and when I lifted it back, sure enough, there was steps going down to the cellar.

The steps was made of logs and covered with dirt, and they went right down into the dark under the house. I wished I had a lamp or a lantern. "Go ahead, ain't nothing to be afraid of," Mr. Pendergast said. He had come up behind me.

Cobwebs hung from the door frame. I went down the steps and stooped to avoid the dirty webs. It was so dark inside I couldn't see a thing at first. But the smell was sharp. It was the smell of old wood and damp ground that hadn't seen the sun in a long time. It was a smell of dead things, of dead beetles and dead mice, and the pee mice leave on nests of straw and string. Something buzzed by my ear, and I tried to slap it away. A moth fluttered to the door behind me.

I seen the gleam of eyes in the dark, but knowed it must be lids on mason jars. And something moved at about the level of my eyes, on a shelf, like a mouse or a snake sliding over dry ground.

"Don't you see the taters?" Mr. Pendergast called from outside.

"I can't see a thing," I called back.

"On your right," he yelled.

I stepped aside on something slick and soft. And then I seen the taters. They looked like twisted swollen bodies with tails. I grabbed up half a dozen and put them in my apron. Before leaving I looked around the cellar again. As my eyes adjusted to the dark a little I seen shelves loaded with jars of canned stuff, quart jars and pint jars, jelly and green beans. Some of the stuff looked like it had bleached or faded from being in the dark too long. Something that looked like a snake head was poking out of one of the jars. A tongue flicked in the dim light. I turned toward the door and banged my head on the lintel. A cobweb caught in my hair.

"Did you see my pet snake?" Mr. Pendergast said as I climbed the steps.

The sunlight burned my eyes and I wanted to brush the cobwebs away. But I didn't want Mr.Pendergast to think I was scared. "Didn't see no snake," I said.

"He's a cute little feller," Mr. Pendergast said, "about three feet long."

I hurried past him with the taters in my apron. I didn't want him to think he could get my goat.

To MAKE CORNBREAD, to make good cornbread, I had to have some buttermilk, and I knowed the buttermilk would be in the springhouse. I took the water bucket to fill and rushed out to the springhouse. It was a low log building over the branch. The floor was water, except for a row of stepping stones from the door. And in the water set jars of milk and pitchers of cream, butter inside tin pails. As I was bending down to get a jar of buttermilk I seen something watching me from the corner of the building. It looked long as a furry snake. But I knowed it must be some kind of animal like a weasel. It was long and its eyes sparkled. It was looking at me from a little face that was pointed. I stamped my foot and it slipped away under one of the logs of the sill. It must have been a mink, for it was too black and long to be a weasel.

When Hank come home that evening I could see he was tired. He had walked all the way to Lyman and he had worked all day at the brick kiln and then he had walked back. His face looked burned a little from the heat of the kiln where he had kept the fire blazing.

I had been ignoring Mr. Pendergast all day, ever since breakfast, and I went on ignoring him after Hank come home. Hank went out to milk the cow and when he brought the warm milk in I strained it into one of the earthenware pitchers. I figured the milk would keep colder in a pitcher than in a mason jar. I tied a cloth over the top of the pitcher and was going to carry it out to the springhouse when Mr. Pendergast come into the kitchen. Maybe he forgot Hank was there. I don't know. He said, "No no no, don't put all the milk in the springhouse like a fool. You've got to save some to clabber, if you want any butter."

Hank had just washed his hands and set down at the table. "You hadn't ought to call her a fool," he said to Mr. Pendergast in a low voice I hadn't heard before.

Mr. Pendergast wheeled around. "Somebody has to give orders around here," he said.

"You don't give Julie orders," Hank said. He stood up and shook his finger at Mr. Pendergast.

"This is my house," Mr. Pendergast said.

"And she is my wife," Hank said. "Don't nobody give her orders but me."

I started to say don't nobody give me orders, but I figured I better keep my mouth shut.

Mr. Pendergast looked like he had been caught by surprise, like he wasn't used to arguing with another man. "I ain't used to a girl that don't know nothing," he said.

"If you don't like the way she does things you can find somebody else to live in your dang-blasted dirty house," Hank said.

Mr. Pendergast turned like he was going to walk away, and then he looked at me by the stove. He started to say something, but didn't.

"We can pack up and get out of here tonight," Hank said. "You can find somebody else to clean up your nastiness."

"Now hold on," Mr. Pendergast said.

"We can take our things and head back up the mountain," Hank said. He thought he had the advantage over Mr. Pendergast, and it was advantage he was going to use. It was the first time I ever seen Hank do that.

"Now hold on," Mr. Pendergast said again.

"We can do a lot better than live in this place on Gap Creek," Hank said. His voice trembled, but I didn't know if he was really that mad. Mr. Pendergast heard the tremble in his voice.

"You can go if you want to," Mr. Pendergast said.

"I won't have you giving Julie orders," Hank said. "And I won't have you interfering with us."

"I'll do what I damn well please in my own house," Mr. Pendergast said, his mood changing.

I seen Hank was caught, because we couldn't leave after living on Gap Creek only one day. We didn't have a place to go. He had thought he had the advantage of Mr. Pendergast, but it turned out he didn't. I waited to see what he would say.

"If Julie has to look after this place we shouldn't have to pay for any groceries," Hank said.

"You don't have to pay for no groceries," Mr. Pendergast said. "But I'll damn well say what I please in my house."

"You just be careful who you say it to," Hank said.

"And you watch out who you're talking to," Mr. Pendergast said. But Mr. Pendergast and Hank had to stop, because even though they was mad, neither could afford to quarrel anymore. Mr. Pendergast probably couldn't find nobody else to look after his house and cook for him, and Hank and me didn't have anyplace else to go. Hank went back outside without saying another word and Mr. Pendergast set there looking at the table in front of him, and he set that way till supper was ready.

IT WAS THE next week while I was doing the washing again that I heard a voice around the front of the house. I ignored it at first,

thinking maybe it was a crow calling across the creek or a fox barking in the woods. Sometimes a sound will carry a long way when
the wind is right.

"Piieendergaaassss!" somebody called. Something was wrong
with the voice. It sounded all stretched and twisted. "Piieendergaasss!" it said again, as if the person hollering couldn't talk plain.

As far as I knowed Mr. Pendergast was in the house, setting at
the kitchen table where he had eat breakfast. Surely he could hear
the voice if I could.

"Piieendergaaassss!" the man yelled, as if he was strangling on
the name as he said it.

I started to run around the house to see who it was, but something about the voice made me not want to go. We didn't get many
visitors there on Gap Creek. I hurried to the back door and looked
in the kitchen, but Mr. Pendergast wasn't setting at the table. I tried
to adjust my eyes to the dim light but didn't see him anywhere.

"Mr. Pendergast," I said, a little louder than a whisper. I didn't
want whoever it was calling to hear me.

"Piieendergaasss!" the man yelled from the front yard.

I started toward the living room to look through the window
and see who it was, but almost run into Mr. Pendergast in the doorway. He was standing stooped over with his finger to his lips.

"They're calling for you," I said.

"Shhhhhh," Mr. Pendergast said. He looked like he was trying to
shrink into hisself.

"Piieendergaasss, I know where you arrrrrre," the voice hollered.

"Who is that?" I said. It didn't make sense for Mr. Pendergast to be
hiding in his own house. I stepped toward the window to look out.

"Don't let him see you," Mr. Pendergast hissed.

"What does he want?" I said.

"Piieendergaasss, you ooooowe me," the man shouted.

"It's just Timmy Gosnell," Mr. Pendergast said, "on one of his drunks."

There was a bang on the porch, like a rock or piece of iron had hit the planks and rolled till it slammed the wall. I had a cold, sour feeling deep in my belly.

"Can't you ask him to leave?" I said.

"He's drunk," Mr. Pendergast said. "And when Timmy's drunk he's crazy."

"Piieendergaasss!" the man screamed. "You got to make it riiiighghghttt."

I leaned over to where I could look between the curtains. The man in the yard wore a long black coat with no buttons. His overalls looked like they was hanging on him by only one gallus. His hat resembled a ragged bird perched on his head, and there was a cut on his forehead. He leaned as though he was bracing hisself against a hard wind and shaded his eyes and stared at the window.

"Piieendergaasss!" he yelled.

"Ain't you going to talk to him?" I said to Mr. Pendergast.

"Won't do no good," Mr. Pendergast said. "You can't talk sense to Timmy Gosnell when he's drunk."

The man in the yard picked up a rock and flung it at the door. The bang made my heart stop for a second. I had not been around drunk men very much. Papa only took a little blackberry wine for his rheumatism. And when one of the Willard boys got drunk and come around the house Papa always persuaded him to go on home.

"Piieendergaasss," the man hollered, "when you die smoke will come out of your graaaaaavvveee!"

"What does he mean?" I said.

"He thinks I never paid him for some ginseng," Mr. Pendergast said. "I paid him, but he was too drunk to remember."

Another rock hit the front door. The bang made something in

the marrow of my bones ache. It was awful to stand in your own living room and be hollered at.

"I'm going out there," I said.

"Don't you go," Mr. Pendergast said. "Timmy can be ugly when
he's drunk."

Lurching from one foot to the other Timmy Gosnell climbed the
steps to the porch. There was a stick Mr. Pendergast used as a walking stick leaning against the door jamb, and the drunk man picked
it up and banged on the door. It made a terrible racket, and the
licks seemed to shake the foundations of the house.

"Go way!" Mr. Pendergast hollered.

"Ssssssmoke will come out of your graaaavvveee!" the drunk
man yelled. He beat on the wall like he was punishing the house.

"Ain't you going to do nothing?" I said. My breath was short and
my ears humming.

"You ooooowe me," Timmy Gosnell screamed. He rapped on
the wood like he wanted to wake the dead on the faraway hill. I
couldn't take any more of the rapping. The noise tore something inside of me. I marched to the door and flung it open. The drunk man
staggered back in surprise and dropped the stick. He shaded his
eyes to see who I was.

"You ain't Pieendergaasss," he said.

"You ought to be ashamed of yourself," I hollered. I was so mad,
and scared, I was trembling. I could smell the drunk man in the
breeze. He stunk like soured fruit and foul rags and pee. He shaded
his eyes and looked at me sideways, squinting.

"Are you Piendergaasss's whore?" he said.

"You get away from here," I said. I picked up the walking stick
like I was going to hit him with it. I felt like swinging the stick right
at his grizzled face.

"Piieendergaasss is a coward," he said, "letting a wo-wo-woman
take up for him."

"You get away from here!" I hollered.

The drunk man looked at the door and he looked at me, and he looked up the road. He acted like he couldn't remember where he was, or what he was doing. He looked at the ground like there might be a clue there. Then he reached into the coat pocket and pulled out a bottle. He jerked out the stopper and took a drink, then put the bottle back in the pocket. "Piieendergaasss!" he hollered.

"Go on now, get," I said. But I was shaking as I held the stick and watched him stagger back to the road. I didn't know what I would do if he lunged at me, or swung at me. He stopped once and started to say something, then swept his hand like it wasn't any use and went on. I watched him lurch and reel all the way to the bend in the road.

WHEN HANK GOT home I told him what happened, and he was so mad his face turned white before it got red. He wheeled around at Mr. Pendergast. "You mean you let him throw rocks at the house?" Hank said.

"He didn't break nothing," I said.

"And you let Julie go out to deal with a drunk man?" Hank said.

"I begged her not to go," Mr. Pendergast said. "I told her it wouldn't do no good."

"I told him to go away, and he went," I said.

Hank was so mad he walked up and down in the kitchen, slamming his fist in his palm. "I wish I'd been here," he said.

"You can't talk sense to a drunk man," Mr. Pendergast said, "not to Timmy Gosnell."

"Not if you hide in the house you can't," Hank said.

"It didn't amount to much," I said. I was sorry I had told Hank about it.

"Next time I hope I'm here," Hank said.

"I hope you are," Mr. Pendergast said.

But I hoped Timmy Gosnell never did come back to Mr. Pendergast's house. And I hoped that Hank would not be there if he did.

"That man needs somebody to knock him sober," Hank said.

"And you're just the man to do it," Mr. Pendergast said.

Five

H ank had told me at the time we got married that his mama, Ma Richards, would be coming down for a visit. She was going to get a ride down from Painter Mountain, and she was going to stay for several weeks. I had never met Ma Richards, and I was looking forward to her visit, for I had not seen many women since we moved to Gap Creek. It was getting up toward late fall by then, toward hog-killing time.

One day Hank got a letter from his ma, scribbled with a pencil on tablet paper. "Hank, you come up here and get me on a Saturday," it said. "I'll be ready by ten o'clock." That was the whole letter.

"How're you going to get her?" I said. For Hank didn't even have a horse, much less a buggy or wagon. He walked to work every day to the mill at Lyman. Mr. Pendergast had an old mare with a bad foot, but Hank doubted if she could make it up the mountain and back. There was an old buggy in the barn, but it was buried under dust and harness and other junk.

"You're going to have to write your ma and tell her you can't come," I said. "She'll understand."

"She's expecting me," Hank said, like there wasn't a choice.

We dug the buggy out from under the hay and trash and dusted it off. I got a bucket of warm water and a rag and washed the whole thing. There was a shaft broke, and Hank whittled a new one out of a hickory pole and smoothed it with a piece of glass. He took the wheels off and put grease on the ends of the axles, then replaced a spoke in one of the wheels.

"Now all you need is a horse," I said.

"I have a horse," Hank said. He caught Mr. Pendergast's mare out of the pasture and showed me the sore on her right front foot. It was a place with pus coming out, right on the frog of her hoof. "She'll just have to go slow," he said. "And besides, I'm going to put a sock on her foot."

"What do you mean a sock?"

Hank took a piece of leather and put cotton inside it. Then he tied the leather around the mare's foot. It looked like she had a swelled hoof.

I DIDN'T EXPECT to be nervous because Ma Richards was coming for a visit, but I was. After Hank left before daylight to go to Painter Mountain, I started thinking of all the stories I'd heard about mothers-in-law. I had heard a hundred tales about how mean they was to girls that marry their sons. And I never had made a lot of friends with women anyway.

All day while I waited for Hank to come back with his ma, I thought about what I was going to say to her, and what she would think of my cooking and housekeeping. I had fixed up the bedroom upstairs next to ours, cleared out all the dust and rags and cardboard boxes, and went up to the attic to look for a single bed. Mr. Pendergast said the bed was there, but when I climbed up to the loft there was such a mess I couldn't see the bed at first. There was fruit jars and old chairs, and cobwebs hanging from everything. There was some roots hanging from rafters that I thought was ginseng. But everything was covered with dust.

When I finally found the little bed I had to scour it with soap and water. And I washed the floor in the little bedroom and the one window and hung curtains there. Mr. Pendergast watched me and didn't say much. Since the quarrel with Hank the second night, he had been a little quieter, though he still liked to snap at me from time to time. Some days he didn't get out of bed until after noon. When he set at the table in the kitchen while I was working, he complained that he didn't have no relations but his stepchildren, and they never come to see him.

"How long has it been since Mrs. Pendergast died?" I said.

"Four years," Mr. Pendergast said. "And I ain't seen my step-younguns since the funeral."

I was not good at waiting for somebody. When I'm waiting I get flustered and hot and think about all the things that could go wrong. And the more nervous I am, the more I worry and get aggravated. When I'm waiting time slows down till it mocks me. When I keep waiting for somebody to come I feel like I'm going to fall to pieces. The only thing to do is not wait at all, but to get on with whatever you're doing.

After I fixed up the bedroom for Ma Richards, I killed a chicken and plucked and dressed it for supper. And while the chicken was frying, I baked some biscuits and made an apple pie out of Northern apples from a tree beside the pasture. I was worried about my cooking because Rosie had always done the cooking at home. I never really had learned to cook except what I taught myself.

I set the table and Mr. Pendergast come into the kitchen and set down by the stove when it got dark. I left the chicken on the stove with a lid on to keep it from drying out, and took the biscuits out of the pan and put a cloth over them to keep them warm. The clock said it was past six.

"Maybe they been killed," Mr. Pendergast said.

"Bad luck to say such things," I said.

I heard a noise outside and run to the window. But it was somebody else going by in a wagon.

"Won't do no good to watch for them," Mr. Pendergast said.

"What will do some good?" I said.

"They may have run off the mountain," Mr. Pendergast said.

Instead of waiting for his supper, Mr. Pendergast got the jar of molasses and had hisself some hot biscuits with butter and molasses. It was one of his favorite things to eat. I just hoped he didn't eat up all the biscuits before Hank and Ma Richards arrived.

"We always look forward to people coming," Mr. Pendergast said, "then look forward to their leaving."

Finally it was near seven o'clock when somebody opened the door, and there was Hank in the lamplight and this little dried-up looking woman beside him. Because Hank was a big man I expected Ma Richards to be big too. But she was built like a banty hen, with black eyes and a sharp chin. Her head was tied up in a scarf and she stalked into the room like she was claiming it for her own.

"I'm cold and I'm so hungry my backbone has rubbed a blister on my ribs," she said. She walked around the kitchen looking at shelves and at the stove and bread safe.

"We're mighty proud to have you come," I said. I didn't know whether to hold out my hand or not. She looked at me and said, "You're not as tall as I expected." I had just thought how short she was, but I didn't say nothing.

"This is Mr. Pendergast," Hank said. Mr. Pendergast stopped eating and wiped his hand on his pants. But when he held it out Ma Richards didn't take it.

"Are you the Pendergast that was run over by a horse?" Ma Richards said.

"That was my brother," Mr. Pendergast said. "He's been dead twenty years."

Ma run her finger along a shelf and then looked to see if there was dust on it. She lifted the lid of the pan of chicken and steam come out of the pan. "Why don't we have something to eat?" I said.

"I'm so cold I need a cup of coffee," Ma said.

"It won't take but a minute to boil coffee," I said.

"Is the beans already ground?" Ma said.

"No, but won't take a second to grind them," I said. "If you can wait that long."

"Good, for I don't like stale coffee," Ma said. Ma acted so demanding and uppity I couldn't hardly believe it. I wanted to tell her she should have brought her own coffee, but I held my tongue.

Hank and Ma set down at the table with Mr. Pendergast. I took a lantern out on the back porch and ground some coffee beans. After I come back in and started the coffee to boiling I set down at the table.

"A woman should always be ready for her guests," Ma Richards said. She put butter and then molasses on a biscuit. "She should know what they will need," she said.

"I'm sorry," I said. I don't know why I said I was sorry. It just come out. I guess I was too mad to say how I really felt. I'd had everything ready for over an hour.

"We was late because an axle broke," Hank said.

"We're lucky we wasn't killed," Ma Richards said. She held a spoon up and looked at it in the lamplight. I was glad I had polished all the silver.

"I had to patch it up with a hickory stick," Hank said.

"Never been so scared in my life," Ma Richards said. "We was on the edge of a cliff when the buggy wheel broke. Where did you get that buggy?"

"It belonged to my pa," Mr. Pendergast said.

"Are you sure it wasn't your grandpa?" Ma Richards said and laughed. Mr. Pendergast laughed with her.

After I set down at the table, with Ma Richards at the end where I usually set, Hank said a longer blessing than usual. And it was more politely said too. "Lord make us truly thankful and worthy . . . ," he begun. I thought how careful he was around his ma. She was such a tiny woman, and yet Hank acted like a little boy trying to please her.

"I'm so upset I don't think I have any appetite," Ma Richards said when the blessing was over. I passed her the platter of chicken and she took a drumstick. She held it up in the lamplight and looked at the crust, which had got damp from waiting so long in the pan.

"A crust won't stay crisp if there's too much flour on the skin," she said.

I was going to say it was waiting so long in the pan that made the crust soggy, but I stopped myself. I didn't want to sound like I was arguing with Ma Richards. She was not only my mother-in-law, she was my guest. And I was just learning to cook.

Ma took a biscuit and sliced it. The biscuit had got a little soft from waiting under the cloth also. Ma held the biscuit half up in the lamplight. "A biscuit that ain't cooked long enough will never be crisp," she said. I felt my face get hot. Ma Richards was testing me in front of Hank and Mr. Pendergast. I wasn't going to let her get my goat. I passed her the rice and the green beans. I passed her the butter and molasses. I seen the coffee was boiling and got up and poured her a cup. I asked Mr. Pendergast if he wanted any coffee.

"Couldn't sleep for a week if I had coffee for supper," he said.

"Anybody with a clear conscience can sleep," Ma Richards said.

Mr. Pendergast started to answer but then couldn't seem to think of what to say. He couldn't admit his conscience wasn't clear, and he couldn't argue that it was. Ma had made a statement that was unanswerable. I set down at the table again and helped myself to the rice.

Ma Richards took a sip of her coffee like she was testing it. "Is this the house where a woman died of TB?" she said.

"That was my wife," Mr. Pendergast said.

"I heard she was sick a long time," Ma said.

"Nigh on to three years."

Ma looked around the kitchen like she expected to see Mrs. Pendergast still there, in one of the dark corners. "I hear germs from TB will stay in a house for years," she said.

"No germs has bothered me," Mr. Pendergast said.

"What room did she die in?" Ma said. She sipped the coffee and took a bite of biscuit and molasses.

"The front bedroom," Mr. Pendergast said, "where I still sleep."

"You've been a lucky man," Ma said. She took a bite of her chicken then put the drumstick back on the plate and spread more molasses on a biscuit.

"How did your husband die?" Mr. Pendergast said, his mouth full of chicken.

Ma Richards looked at Mr. Pendergast like he was accusing her of something. She spread the molasses careful and then took a bite of the biscuit. "Died setting on the porch," she said. "He was helping me to churn and just pitched forward into the yard. The churn spilled all over the place and chickens run to peck the clabber."

"Died of a stroke?" Mr. Pendergast said.

"Died of a stroke or a heart attack," Ma Richards said.

"Must have eat wrong," Mr. Pendergast said.

"He eat what I fixed him," Ma said, "which was plain, wholesome fare."

"I had a warning that Pa was going to die," Hank said.

"What kind of warning?" Mr. Pendergast said.

"My brother Russ and me was setting on the milkgap waiting for Pa to come back from mill," Hank said. "It was getting late, where the air has got gold in it, and it was time for Pa to be home. We was looking down across the pasture and I seen Pa coming up the slope. Except he wasn't wearing overalls, but a new suit of clothes. And I thought, He must have been to town and bought a new suit."

"Was you dreaming?" Mr. Pendergast said.

"Russ seen him too," Hank said. "If it was a dream we was both dreaming it. We watched Pa walk across the pasture, and when he got close enough to speak I was going to say how come you have got a new suit. But just when I opened my mouth he was gone."

"Where did he go?" I said.

"He just disappeared," Hank said. "Both Russ and me had seen him, and then he just vanished in the evening air."

"And you never seen him again?" Mr. Pendergast said.

"We looked around all over the place," Hank said. "And after a few minutes we seen Pa coming across the pasture again. Except this time he was wearing his overalls and his old black hat and carrying the sack of corn on his shoulder."

"And he didn't know nothing about the suit of clothes?" I said.

"We asked him about the suit, and he thought we was just fooling him," Hank said.

"And you never did explain it?" Mr. Pendergast said.

"We never could figure it out," Hank said. "But a few weeks later Pa died all of a sudden. It was a portent, but we didn't know how to cipher it."

"The Lord sends us a warning," Ma said, "but we ain't listening."

"There was a portent before Pa died," Hank said, "and one after."

"What do you mean after?" Mr. Pendergast said.

"Uncle Calvin seen Pa after he died," Hank said.

"How could he see him?" Mr. Pendergast said.

"After Pa was dead and buried, Uncle Calvin seen him in church at Sunday service, setting in his usual seat," Hank said. "He was setting in the Amen Corner and he was singing like he always did."

"Did he speak to him?" Mr. Pendergast said.

"After the service he was gone," Hank said. "Except Uncle Calvin seen him there the next Sunday, and the next. But after three Sundays he didn't see him again."

"It was a sign," Ma Richards said.

"A sign of what?" Mr. Pendergast said.

"A sign of how much he hated to leave us, even to be with the Lord," Ma said. "It was a sign he will always be watching over us." Ma took her handkerchief out of her sleeve and dabbed at her eye. Then she replaced the handkerchief and begun to butter another biscuit.

"I think the dead are watching us all the time," Mr. Pendergast said.

"Of course they are," Ma Richards said. "That's why we should be careful what we do and what we say. They are with the Lord and watching over us. At least some are with the Lord."

"We don't know a tenth of what there is to know," Mr. Pendergast said. "Why we don't even know a sixth."

The kitchen was so hot I had to go outside. I went out to the back porch to get the pie I'd put there to cool. Soon as I opened the door I felt the cold wind. It was good to get out of the kitchen, but I hurried back in with the apple pie and took off the lid.

"That wind has ice in it," Ma Richards said.

"If it comes a freeze we should kill the hog," Mr. Pendergast said.

"It would have to be a Saturday for me to help," Hank said.

"You help me butcher the hog, I'll split the meat with you," Mr. Pendergast said.

"I'll help you out," Hank said. "And Julie can too." He sounded just like Papa or Mama back at home. If there was heavy work it just naturally fell to me. But we sure needed the meat.

"I can help," I heard myself say.

IT WAS ON a Monday that I helped Mr. Pendergast kill and butcher his hog. Hank had to work at the brick kiln in Lyman, or he would have stayed and done the heavy work. The killing had to be done when there was a freeze. Then after the meat was salted down in the smokehouse it didn't matter if the weather turned warm again.

"You shouldn't ask a girl to help butcher hogs," Ma Richards said that morning.

"I always helped Papa," I said. "Wasn't nobody else to help." I didn't like to butcher hogs, but if it had to be done I might as well go ahead and do it. And I didn't want to take any advice from Ma Richards.

"Hog killing's no work for a girl," Ma said, like she expected that to be the end of it. She was used to giving orders and having her sons obey them. Hank didn't argue with her so I didn't either.

"Maybe you could wait till Saturday," Hank said to Mr. Pendergast.

"The weather may have warmed up by then," Mr. Pendergast said.

"I can help today," I said, and didn't even look at Ma Richards.

Hank had to leave at daylight, and I got up to fix grits and gravy and eggs. I packed a dinner bucket full of biscuits and boiled eggs, and before Hank left Ma Richards opened the bucket to see what was in it. "A man working all day has got to have some belly timber," Ma said, and she looked at me when she said it.

Soon as we eat our grits and gravy and Mr. Pendergast eat his poached egg, he took his rifle out to the hogpen. He had laid down scalding boards by the washpot the day before.

"Be easier to shoot the hog by the scalding boards," Ma Richards said.

"If you know how to lead a filthy hog you're welcome to do it," Mr. Pendergast said.

There was a frost that made the grass white as shavings of coconut. I had put on a coat and gloves. My breath smoked in the first light of dawn. Puddles had a paper of ice on them. In the cold, still air you didn't smell the stink of the hogpen till you got close beside it. Ma Richards stayed back in the kitchen.

I didn't look while Mr. Pendergast shot the hog in the head. Instead, I started a fire under the washpot and piled on wood to make it hot. I carried several buckets from the spring and filled the pot. And I sharpened two butcher knives, and two paring knives for the scraping. A small thin blade is always better for scraping the hair of a hog.

A shot cracked in the first light and when I got to the pen Mr. Pendergast was tying a string to one leg of the hog laying on its side. He had slit the throat and dark blood was pooling on the mud. There was nothing for me to do but wade into the filth and tie another rope to the other hind leg.

It took both me and Mr. Pendergast pulling on the ropes to drag the hog over the froze ground to the scalding boards. The way a hog is soft and quivery it spreads on the ground and is hard to drag. The water in the pot was beginning to boil and send a column of steam up into the sky. There was no wind, and the steam and smoke rose straight up into the air. I dipped a bucket into the water and splashed it over the hog. The carcass spread out its fat on the boards, and the water smoked wherever it splashed and spilled onto the ground.

After I had scalded one side and scraped it clean we rolled the hog over. The body shook like jelly, and the eye stared blue in the first sunlight. I dumped several more buckets of water on the hide and bent over to shave away the hair that was left. I always hated the stink of hog bristles and scalded skin. It's a stench of half-boiled flesh and wet hairs. I scraped and cleaned the knife on the corner of a board, and scraped some more. Mr. Pendergast stood by the fire and watched. I seen that by "helping" he had meant for me to do the work. He seemed so short of breath, maybe there wasn't much else he could do.

Now after a hog is scraped comes the real work. What goes before is just the start. With the hog scalded down and shaved, I took a butcher knife and slit the shanks of the back feet so there was room between the bones and the tendons. Then we drug the hog over to a pole leaning in the forks of an apple tree. I fitted a gambrel stick over the pole and stuck the sharpened ends through the slits in the hog's hind legs. It took both me and Mr. Pendergast to push the gambrel stick up the pole, sliding wood on wood until the hog was hanging off the ground. Then I tied the gambrel stick to the fork of the tree, and it was time to get to work.

Taking a sharpened butcher knife, I drove it into the fat of the hog's belly, but not too deep. I didn't want to cut any of the guts inside. I'd always hated butchering hogs, and here I was married and doing it again. Slicing through the skin and fat I brought the blade right down the hog from one end of the belly to the other. And then with the axe I chopped through the breastbone. Hot guts started falling out, and I had to push them back until we got the tub underneath. Then with my sleeves rolled up I raked the smoking guts into the tub, the slick coils of entrails, intestines like blisters and bubbles of manure with big worms inside, as well as liver, heart, lungs, stomach. I took the axe and finished splitting the chest bone and then raked out the rest of the innards.

It took both me and Mr. Pendergast to lug the tub into the garden to bury the guts. They had a sickening smell of blood and manure. I had blood up to my elbows.

"Never seen a woman work like you," Mr. Pendergast said.

"Work ain't nothing but work," I said.

Now THE NEXT job was to cut off the head. I knowed Hank liked fried hog brains, so I meant to save the brains. I took the butcher knife and carved off the head down to the spine, and then I chopped through the bones with the axe. The head was so heavy I could just barely carry it over to the wash table. The skull would have to be cracked later.

The sun was high over the ridge and making everything gold by the time I started carving up the carcass. First I had to cut off the shoulders, which you can leave whole, like hams, and put in the smokehouse. Next you have to section the belly and back into middlings and loins. With the axe I hacked through ribs and backbone. Bits of fat and blood and bones splattered on my clothes.

"Look at you," somebody said behind me. It was Ma Richards, who had brought a dishpan out to the wash table. I thought how easy it would be to swing the axe at her. But I was quick ashamed of such a thought. I had to watch myself, cause I got riled while working hard.

"We'll need every pan and bucket in the house," I said.

For the fine work of cutting ribs and tenderloin along the back I got a saw from the barn and sawed up the ribs in sections about four inches long. But instead of sawing up pork chops I sliced out the tenderloin so it could be fried in thin pieces without the bone.

The last job, except for salting the hams and shoulders and bacon, was to separate the fat from the meat underneath. With a paring knife I carved off the streaked bacon we would need for cooking. And I sliced the fat into sections between six inches wide and a foot long. My hands got so greasy they wouldn't hardly hold a knife. I heaped up three tubs with chunks of fat.

"I'll start dicing up the fat as soon as somebody brings it in the kitchen," Ma Richards said.

"I can't carry no bucket of fat," Mr. Pendergast said.

It took both me and Mr. Pendergast to wrestle the tubs and dishpans of fat to the kitchen table. It appeared dark as a cave in the house after the blinding sunlight.

Mr. Pendergast got a box of salt from the smokehouse and we sprinkled down the hams and shoulders and slabs of bacon before we carried them to the shelves of the smokehouse. We crusted the meat on every side with salt. When we was finished I looked at the mess around the scalding boards. The fire was smoldering in the sun and swatches of scraped hair was scattered on the grass. There was blood and bits of fat and skin on the table. Bloody buckets and tubs and knives laid in the grass. I could still smell the guts and scalded skin.

My hands was greasy and bloody. I walked down to the branch and washed up as best I could. It was time to carry the tenderloin and ribs into the house. It was time to render the lard and make sausage. I had been working since before daylight, and it was way past dinnertime.

Ma Richards had put three canners on the kitchen table, and she had started dicing up the tubs and dishpans of pork fat. "I'd about as soon die as render any more lard," she said. Her hands was already shiny with grease.

"I can do it myself," I said.

"Don't be so proud." Ma said. "It'll take us both to finish by dark."

I was going to tell Ma it wasn't exactly pride that made me work so hard, but I didn't. "I'll fry up some tenderloin and make grits for dinner," I said. One of the pleasures of hog killing was to have fresh meat. I was hungry. I throwed more wood in the stove and sliced some of the tenderloin into a pan. Then I put on water to boil for grits. Mr. Pendergast wandered into the kitchen. "Ain't we going to have dinner?" he said.

"Won't be but a minute," I said. There was just a little cold coffee in the pot and I throwed it out in the backyard. While the meat was frying and the grits boiling, I ground some more beans on the back porch. I was so tired my arms felt a little numb. I just wanted to set down and rest. It would be only two or three hours before Hank got home and was ready for his supper. But I would be working long past that, rendering the hog fat down into lard.

When you're tired it's like all the force in the world works against you. Takes extra effort just to do little things. You feel it takes willpower just to breathe. If Ma Richards said something snide, I didn't know but what I'd bust into tears.

"They's streaks in this fat," Ma Richards said.

"A streak won't hurt the lard," Mr. Pendergast said.

"It's a waste of bacon," Ma said.

"We've got plenty of bacon," I said.

"It's a waste; that's all I'm saying," Ma said.

"I'll try to do better next time," I said, as dry as I could. The tiredness made me slow and calmer than I expected. I turned over the slices of tenderloin and stirred the grits. The coffee started to boil.

"Nothing smells better than fresh tenderloin," Mr. Pendergast said. The fresh meat, as it crackled and turned brown, smelled sweeter than any pastry. Fresh meat has a perfume of its own. The steam that went up from the pan of tenderloin filled the kitchen with a golden flavor, mixed with fumes of the boiling coffee. The smells made me a little light-headed, and out of myself.

When I cleared a space at the table and put the grits and tenderloin there, Mr. Pendergast brought a chair from the corner and set down. I poured three cups of coffee and put down three plates with knives and forks. Mr. Pendergast helped hisself to a slice of tenderloin. I put butter on the table and set down myself.

"Only heathens eat without asking a blessing," Ma Richards said.

"You say the blessing," I said to her. As far as I knowed Mr. Pendergast wasn't a praying man. At least I had never heard him pray. Some men will pray out loud and some won't.

Ma bowed her head and closed her eyes. "Lord, make us thankful," she said. "Forgive our forgetfulness and unworthiness. Punish our faults, but forgive our sinfulness, for we are all black sinners inside. And forgive the folly of youth, and the foolishness of old age."

There was no doubt Ma was referring to my youth and folly in her prayer, but you can't argue with what a body says in a prayer. What they say in prayer is between them and the Lord. I passed the tenderloin to Ma and then took a slice for myself. I had browned the meat till it was gold and crisp on the outside, but white and tender on the inside. The meat was so tender it almost melted when you bit down on it. I put butter on the hot grits and stirred it in. I had warmed some biscuits left over from breakfast in the oven and sliced one of them and put butter on it.

"Nothing's better than grits and tenderloin," Mr. Pendergast said. And it was true. The fresh meat went perfect with the taste of grits and butter. I poured a little milk into the coffee and took a sip. The coffee taste was different from the sweetness of the meat and grits and went just right with them.

"This coffee is too strong," Ma Richards said.

"You can put some milk in it," Mr. Pendergast said.

Ma stirred butter into her grits and took a bite, but she didn't say nothing. I thought she kind of grunted with the pleasure of the taste. She cut off a piece of tenderloin and put it in her mouth, but still she didn't say nothing.

I took a sip of coffee and felt the brightness of the coffee in my belly and in my veins. The grits and butter and meat and biscuits was making me warm inside. But the coffee made the air in the kitchen seem shiny and cool, and even the buckets of fat looked clean.

"I never got enough tenderloin," Mr. Pendergast said.

"Tenderloin is better with gravy," Ma Richards said. But she kept eating the grits with butter.

"Tenderloin is good with anything," Mr. Pendergast said.

I got another helping of grits and a second slice of meat. It was hard to believe this golden flavor had been the smelly hog just a few hours before. I tried to forget the smell of scalded hair and skin.

"Best hog meat is fattened on acorns," Mr. Pendergast said. "When hogs run loose they tasted better."

"I don't remember tenderloin tasting better than this," Ma Richards said.

"We could gather acorns and bring them to the hog," I said.

"It would take a week to pick up a bushel of acorns," Mr. Pendergast said.

"They used to kill pigeons and feed them to hogs," Ma Richards said. "Back when there was millions of pigeons come through every year. Of course that was before my time."

"Before my time too," Mr. Pendergast said. He had grease on his chin, but he didn't stop to wipe it off.

I felt like eating was the best thing there was. People eating together felt bound to each other, like it says in the Bible about the breaking of bread.

"I went all the way through the war without any pork to speak of," Ma Richards said.

"I did too, except that we would steal a hog from a farm we was passing," Mr. Pendergast said.

"That's why we didn't have meat," Ma said. "The bushwhackers stole our hogs."

"We wasn't bushwhackers," Mr. Pendergast said. "The army had nothing but a little cornmeal to give us."

Since I was a little girl I'd heard stories about the Confederate War. I wanted to think about something more pleasant. "Times is better now," I said.

"Times was worse after the war was over," Ma said. She helped herself to more grits. "When Fate come back from the army and we got married, we didn't have a dollar between us. We took up house-keeping in the cabin on Painter Mountain without a horse or cow. For a long time I cooked soup in the washpan. We had to borrow Fate's daddy's horse just to break a garden. I had to make coffee in the water bucket. And everybody else was near about as poor."

I had not heard Ma talk so much. It was the sweet tenderloin and grits and coffee making her feel better than herself. Her tongue was loosened and softened.

"For ten years after the war you couldn't find a nickel," Ma said. "People traded work and paid each other in kind. I finally got me half a dozen hens and it was their eggs I traded for coffee and sugar. We didn't have nothing else but what we raised. When Dave come along we still didn't have a cow. By the time Hank was born the worst was over."

"Hank said he was born little," I said.

"Didn't weigh much more than two pounds," Ma said. "He come almost two months early. It's a miracle he ever lived." She took another slice of tenderloin and a sip of coffee. And she buttered a biscuit. "Nobody expected him to live. I don't reckon he ever would have except for the sugartit."

"What kind of sugartit?" I said.

"It was just a rag dipped in milk or dipped in honey we'd let him suck on. I'd soak it in a little chicken broth and let him suck it.

That's what kept him alive. He was the littlest of my younguns, and he growed up to be the biggest man."

"I've knowed it to happen with dogs," Mr. Pendergast said. "The runtiest of the litter will grow into the biggest of the pack."

"The Lord has his own way of doing things," Ma said.

"Hank sure don't look like a runt," I said.

"I spoiled Hank because he was so little," Ma said. "I fed him better and never made him work hard as the other boys. That's why he growed up so big."

"Hank works hard," I said.

"He works hard, but he don't finish what he starts," Ma said. "He loses his temper too easy. The hard work is staying with a job till it's done."

I wanted to stand up for Hank, but I didn't know what to say. Ma Richards had knowed him longer than I had. And I didn't want to argue while we was eating. "Hank is working mighty hard at the brick kiln," I said.

"And we're working mighty hard at hog killing," Ma Richards said.

I don't know what brought us together in such a fine fellowship unless it was just the tenderloin and grits and coffee, and maybe the work of hog killing. But it was like we formed a special kinship in the kitchen, at the table piled with tubs and dishpans full of pork fat. Maybe it was the tiredness that made me a little light-headed, and the prospect of all the work ahead.

"If there's anything better than fresh tenderloin the good Lord kept it for hisself," Mr. Pendergast said, like it was something he had said before. But like all familiar sayings, it had truth in it.

"The good Lord made the world so we could earn our joy," Ma said. "But it's no guarantee we'll ever be happy."

"There's no guarantee of anything except we're going to die," Mr. Pendergast said.

"Let's start rendering lard," I said.

. . .

IT WAS TIME to get to work. The sun was halfway down the sky and Ma had only started dicing up the fat. I carried our plates out to the back porch where I'd wash them later. And then I got a paring knife and sharpened it on the stone Hank kept beside his razor strop.

You cut up fat by slicing it in slabs. And the slabs you put on a board and slice ten times one way and then ten times the other. That way you end up with little boxes of fat that will cook down quicker than big chunks. With the knife as sharp as I could make it, I started cutting. I drawed the blade through the white jelly flesh again and again. And soon as I had the little pieces cut I scooped them up and dumped them in the canner.

After the canner was mostly full I set it on the cookstove, which was already hot. Then I threw more wood in the stove and started cutting up more fat. I figured there would be three full canners to render down. That would give us maybe ten buckets of lard and enough cracklings for crackling bread all winter.

Now when hog fat begins to heat up the little cubes start to sweat. They get bright with oil drops and glisten as they melt. The oil just melts out of them and the pot steams and bubbles as it comes to a boil. Ain't nothing dangerous as rendering lard because of all that hot grease on a stove. A pot gets tipped over it will burn you up. If the grease falls in the fire it will explode. You know the saying: The fat is in the fire. Fat'll flare up like kerosene.

But the main thing I worried about was getting burned by the grease. For sometimes a canner of rendering lard would spit out a gob and burn you. Or if you knocked the pot it would splash out faster than boiling water and burn you alive. I had been rendering lard every year with Mama and I knowed how uneasy boiling grease was.

"SET THE CANNER further back on the stove," Ma Richards said. All the good feeling from the dinner table was gone from her voice.

"I've got to leave room to set the other one on," I said.

"You won't need room if that tips over on you," Ma snapped. She had changed back to her old self.

Instead of answering I started carving up more fat at the table. I sliced twenty times this way and twenty times crossways. The fat sliced easy as clotted cream or thick jelly. My left hand was so slick with grease I couldn't pick up anything but the blocks of fat. I raked the knife across the board harder than I needed to, to show how determined I was to get the job done and ignore Ma.

There was a little blood on the fat and on the board also, and I hardly noticed when I felt a nip at the end of my middle finger as I held a slab down to slice it. But when I saw the bright blood on the white fat I knowed I'd cut myself. A drop fell from the end of my finger, and then another. "Oh no," I said.

"What have you done?" Ma said.

"Just a nick," I said.

"Don't get blood on the lard fat," Ma said.

I grabbed a dishcloth and wiped the grease off my finger. I'd cut a place on the tip about the size of a pinhead. But it kept bleeding bright red drops. I cleaned off the left hand with the cloth and tore a strip from a fresh linen rag. I bound up the finger as best I could to stop the bleeding.

"That's what comes of being in a hurry," Ma said.

"I'll have to be more careful," I said. I wasn't going to take the time to get mad at Ma, and I wasn't going to stoop to the level of her snideness. With the bandage on my finger I finished slicing up the second pan of fat and then lugged the heavy canner to the top of the stove. But as I slid the container onto the stovetop I pushed it too far to the right and hit the canner already there. The boiling fat rocked like a wave had been sent through it. I backed away and seen a tongue of boiling lard spit up and over the rim as the wave sloshed on the side of the canner. The flung grease hissed on the stovetop and turned to crackling bubbles and smoke. But there must have been enough grease so that some of it busted into flame, for I seen fire on top of the stove. That might not have amounted to nothing, except the rocking and sloshing continued in the canner and the hot oil spit out again and leapt right into the flames. With a whoosh the fire flared on the stovetop. I think it would still have been all right and just burned there sizzling on the metal except a little more grease sloshed out of the pot and the fire caught onto that and followed the splash back into the pot. That was when the fire blazed up in the canner itself. All the hot oil caught at once and the flames jumped to the ceiling, lighting the kitchen.

"Oh my god," Ma said.

I looked around for something to throw on the flames. There wasn't a blanket or quilt anywhere. There wasn't anything bigger than a dish towel.

Now a grease fire is a worse kind of fire than usual. A grease fire hisses and jumps from one spot to another. There was grease all over the stove and all over the kitchen. The flames darted from one spot to another.

Ma run out to the back porch and got the water bucket. I'd heard that throwing water on boiling grease is the worst thing you can do, and I hollered for her to stop. But she flung the bucket of water right onto the flaming pot. You would think cold water would put a fire out, but the dousing exploded in a hiss and made the boiling lard splash in all directions. The flames followed the leap of the splash. The water just spread the fire. Flames landed on the second canner of fat and on the dishpans full of fat on the table. The whole kitchen seemed to turn to flames before my eyes. The curtains on the wall caught fire, and heat blistered my face.

"We'll have to get out," I yelled to Ma. I pulled her toward the back door. Smoke was already so thick you couldn't see much but the flames in the kitchen.

Mr. Pendergast come running in with another bucket of water. I guess he must have been to the spring. "Don't throw no water," I hollered. But he flung the water right on the fire, making even more smoke and steam.

"I've got to get my money," he shouted.

"What money?" I said. It was so hot I could barely stand in the doorway.

"My pension money," he yelled.

"You come back," I said, and grabbed at his arm. But he had already jerked away. He dropped to the floor and crawled under the smoke. I knelt down where I could see, out of the worst smoke, and watched him work his way to the right of the stove.

"Get back here," I hollered.

"You better stop him!" Ma screamed.

I knowed Mr. Pendergast kept a can of kerosene sometimes used to start fires behind the stove, but I had forgot about it. He reached into the corner behind the wood box and brought out a pint jar. And I think he would have made it out except for this explosion that flared up behind the stove. It must have been the kerosene catching fire. I screamed as the flames covered Mr. Pendergast up.

"Let him go," Ma shouted. But I couldn't just leave Mr. Pendergast laying there in the fire. I had to try to help him. He was screaming and the fire seemed to be right on top of his head.

"Take his foot," I hollered to Ma, but she was already out the door and on the back steps coughing and trying to get her breath. "Grab hold of his foot," I said.

I took hold of Mr. Pendergast's feet and yanked as hard as I could, and he moved a little. I was coughing too and felt smothered from the smoke. I jerked harder and got Mr. Pendergast halfway out the door. And then Ma took one of his feet and helped me pull him onto the porch.

Mr. Pendergast's hair was burning, and part of his shirt was burning. I didn't have nothing but my apron, and I put my apron over his hair and snuffed out the flames. I burned my hands a little, but got the fire out. And just then Ma brought a bucket of water still warm from the washpot and throwed it on his shirt. We rolled Mr. Pendergast over on the wet porch and seen how bad his face and forehead was burned. The skin looked black on his forehead and scalp where his hair had been. His eyebrows was burned off and the skin on his cheeks looked red and peeling, and bloody in places under the soot.

I was thinking we had to put something on his face and on his back where his shirt had burned. What you put on burns is butter or lard or some other kind of grease or oil. There was butter in the spring house, but the lard was burning up in the kitchen. And then I thought, No, I'd better try to put the fire out first. If I can I've got to save the house. I stood up and looked in the door.

"You stay out of there," Ma Richards hollered. "Nothing you can do."

Smoke poured out the door and out the windows. You couldn't see nothing in the kitchen. I couldn't even see any flames. That made me think nothing was burning but the lard, and maybe that could be put out. I looked around the porch and seen a pile of tow sacks by the hoes and shovel and mattock. They had been used I guess for taking corn to mill or carrying leaves to put in cow stalls. I grabbed up eight or ten sacks and run to the washpot.

"What are you doing?" Ma Richards called.

"Putting out the fire," I hollered back. I plunged the sacks into the pot and pulled them out streaming warm water. With my arms around the dripping sacks I run toward the back door.

"You stay out of there," Ma yelled.

I leaped up the steps and run past Mr. Pendergast into the smoking kitchen. The smoke was so thick I couldn't see much. Bending close to the floor I walked to the stove and throwed wet sacks on the burning canners, and then the smoke boiled up worse and I couldn't hardly see what I was doing.

I run back out to the pile of sacks and got eight or nine more and carried them to the washpot.

"You stay out of there!" Ma screamed. But I didn't pay no attention to her. I carried the hot dripping sacks against my chest and hurried through the back door. I figured if the house could be saved I had to try. I'd started the fire, and I had to stop it. I stepped across Mr. Pendergast laying on the porch. He was starting to wake up from the smoke swoon, and hollering.

Fighting my way into the smoke, holding my breath and bending down low as I could, I put sacks on the burning grease on the table. I flung sacks on the burning can of kerosene and used the rest of the sacks like a shield to walk up to the burning curtains and jerk them down and smother them.

I started coughing, and every time I coughed I breathed in more smoke. Smoke burned my eyes so I couldn't see nothing. I put a hand over my eyes and started toward the door. To keep from breathing smoke I held my breath, and it felt like my chest was going to bust. The longer I held my breath the more it felt like my chest was ready to explode. And then I couldn't find the door. Smoke was everywhere and my eyes stung so I couldn't see. And I couldn't breathe for coughing and smothering myself. The smoke was so thick I couldn't tell up from down, or remember where the door was or where the table was. I was so weak I couldn't hardly stand up. My knee knocked against something hard, and my head banged on a sharp corner. There was nothing to breathe but smoke, dirty, greasy smoke.

Somebody pushed me and lifted me, and the next thing I knowed I was hobbling and tripping down the steps out into the yard where the air was cool. It was Hank helping me outside. The air was fresh, but every time I took a breath I coughed, and smoke burned in my lungs and in my throat. I bent over and felt something wet leap in my throat, and found I was throwing up on the ground. I was trying to throw up all the smoke I had swallowed, but puked out tenderloin and grits and butter, now sour and bitter. I had to throw up everything. I heaved until tears come to my eyes and I was so weak I was trembling.

"What in the world happened?" Hank said.

"Julie bumped a canner and the lard caught fire," Ma Richards said.

When I was empty I stood up straight and wiped my mouth and brow. "You could have been killed," Ma Richards said.

"The fire is out," Hank said. He looked through the doorway into the smoke. "You put it out just in time, before the floor or walls caught." He stepped out on the porch fanning the smoke with his hand. I looked through the back door and seen the smoke was settling in the kitchen. The top half of the room was already clear. And I seen Mr. Pendergast laying on the porch floor groaning. His face looked awful with its burns, but he was still holding the pint jar, and in the jar was dollar bills and coins like sliced pickles. A silver dollar had rolled out of the jar onto the porch.

IT TOOK ALL of us to carry Mr. Pendergast to his bedroom. While the smoke was still settling in the kitchen, we lugged him around to the front door. Hank held him by one shoulder and I gripped him by the other, and Ma Richards carried his feet. Mr. Pendergast was half awake and moaning.

"I want to rub butter on your face and hands," I said to him.

"You near about burned down his house," Ma said. Ma was the kind of person who was always blaming somebody. If something went wrong she was more interested in pointing a finger than in fixing the problem. I have met a lot of people that way, but nobody as bad as Ma Richards.

"How did the fire start?" Hank said as we toted Mr. Pendergast up the front steps.

"Grease splashed out on the stove," I said, "when I bumped one canner against another."

"Everybody knows you throw baking soda on a grease fire," Ma said.

Before I could stop myself I answered Ma. I hadn't meant to stoop to her level, but I was tired. "You spread the fire by dumping a whole bucket of water on the lard," I said.

"At least I tried to do something," Ma said.

"You didn't think about baking soda no more than I did," I said.

Hank opened the door and we squeezed through into the dark living room. The bitter smoke smell hit me soon as we was inside. The house smelled like ashes.

"Somebody will have to get a doctor," Ma Richards said as we carried Mr. Pendergast into the bedroom.

"I don't even know where a doctor is," Hank said.

Mr. Pendergast's bed looked like a pit of rumpled quilts and blankets. After we laid him down I tried to fix the bed so he was at least under the covers. His hands was burned, but he was still holding on to the jar of money. I tried to take the jar out of his hands.

"No!" Mr. Pendergast hollered, and jerked the jar away from me. "That's my war pension money."

Hank lit a lamp on the nightstand and I bent down close to Mr. Pendergast. "Nobody is going to take your money," I said. "We'll put it right here on the stand where you can see it."

I don't think Mr. Pendergast believed me. He wouldn't have trusted anybody with his money. But he was in so much pain he couldn't think what to do. I took the jar from his hands and put it on the table. Skin hung in shreds off his hands where he had reached into the fire to get the money. "I'm going to put some butter on your burns," I said.

"No!" he hollered.

"He's beside hisself," Ma Richards said.

"He's hurting," I said.

I hurried out to the springhouse to get a fresh cake of butter. It was starting to grow dark. Hank had gone to milk the cow, and Ma Richards set in the living room by the fireplace. "I can't stand to look in that kitchen," she said.

I didn't see any way to rub the butter on Mr. Pendergast's burns except with my bare fingers. And I knowed the burns was going to be tender. But when I rubbed my fingers in the butter and made it melt, and put my hand to Mr. Pendergast's forehead, I was startled by his scream. I'd never heard a man holler that way. When Papa was sick and in pain he was always calm and well behaved, until near the very end.

"This will make you feel better," I said. I tried to touch him with the butter again, but he howled and jerked away.

I knelt beside the bed with butter on my left hand and tried to think what to do. It was the hardest and longest day of my life. I was wore out from killing the hog, and cutting up the meat, and from cutting up the fat and fighting the fire. I was weak from throwing up. And I was to blame for the fire, as Ma Richards had pointed out. And I was to blame for Mr. Pendergast getting burned, except I had tried to keep him from going into the flames for his money jar. It was my job to do what I could to help, to make up for the bad I'd done.

The grit on the floor cut into my knees. "I'm trying to help you," I said. But talking to somebody in great pain is like talking to a youngun or a dog. They just want to feel better and can't think clear about it. And they don't want to listen to what you have to say. Somebody suffering is as selfish as a baby.

Mr. Pendergast's lips was cracked and bleeding. "I'm perishing of thirst," he hollered.

I was going to call Ma Richards to bring me a dipper of water, but I thought better of it. I wiped my hands on my apron and hurried out to the spring to get a bucket of cold water. It was dark now, and the dirt of the path was already froze.

"What are you doing?" Hank called from the cowshed.

"I'm getting a drink for Mr. Pendergast," I said.

"He needs a drink of liquor," Hank said.

When I brought the bucket into the bedroom and held the dipper to Mr. Pendergast's lips, he drunk like a man dying on the desert. The fire had burned him and parched him, and he was burning up inside. He gulped the water like a mad dog trying to quench its thirst. He gulped so fast he threwed some of the water up. His lips was so cracked and tender it hurt him to touch the dipper. His eyes stretched wide as he tried to drink faster. His eyebrows and lashes was burned away and his skin peeling like old paint with soot and blood on it.

"You'll get sick if you drink too fast," I said.

"I'm already sick," he gasped and swallowed.

He drunk three dippers of water, and then he belched and throwed up. Mr. Pendergast was so weak he couldn't raise his head, and when he throwed up the water just come out of the side of his mouth and run down his burned cheek. I took a towel and tried to wipe off his cheek and neck, but he screamed and pushed me away. He pushed me away and twisted on the bed and screamed again.

I had to do something to ease his pain. That's when I remembered the shelf in the kitchen where there was all kinds of bottles and jars and little boxes. I had sorted through them looking for herbs and seasonings. But there was a number of jars and bottles and cans I hadn't opened. I took the lamp and started out of the bedroom.

"Don't leave me," Mr. Pendergast hollered.

"I'm just going to get something," I said.

"Don't leave me," he said again. I seen that he was afraid of the dark. I left the lamp on the nightstand and went to get another lamp in the living room.

Ma was setting by the fireplace. "He will die," she said.

"We need to ease his pain," I said.

"He'll die in any case," Ma said.

The kitchen was a mess of wet sacks and spilled lard, half-burned fat, soot, and charred boards. The fire in the stove was out, and the room was already cold. I climbed on a chair to look at the shelf. You never seen such a collection of old cans and bottles as Mr. Pendergast had there. Snuff cans was filled with sage and thyme, pepper and allspice. There was camphor and rubbing alcohol. There was oil of cloves for toothache, and Epsom salts, castor oil, and tincture of lobelia for snakebites. I opened several bottles and sniffed them. I didn't know what some of them was.

But there was a dark blue bottle with a stopper in it. I pulled out the cork and smelled. It had the scent of alcohol, but smelled like something else too, an inky, earthy, musky smell. I had sniffed the scent before. It smelled of black wetness in the dirt, and yet was metallic too. If I remembered right that was the smell of laudanum. I took the bottle back to the front bedroom.

"God help me!" Mr. Pendergast called.

"If you pray to the Lord, he will help you," Ma Richards said. She had come into the bedroom with me. Mr. Pendergast's face now had blisters on it, with dried blood and strips of burned skin.

"The Lord help me, please," Mr. Pendergast said.

"You take a tablespoon of this," I said and poured a spoonful from the bottle. The liquid was brown and cold. It give off chemical fumes. I held the spoon to his lips, but he jerked away, like the cold spoon hurt his lips.

"Don't spill it," I said. "There's only this little bottle."

"He's contrary as an old mule," Ma Richards said.

"Help me," Mr. Pendergast said and rolled his eyes.

"I'm trying to help you," I said. "You drink this quick; it'll make you feel better." I put the spoon to his lips but he jerked away again.

"He's got a devil in him," Ma Richards said.

"I'm freezing in hell," Mr. Pendergast said. He shivered so hard his teeth chattered. I had heard that people who had been burned felt like they was freezing to death, but I'd never seen it before. Mr. Pendergast jerked like he was naked in the snow.

"This will warm you up," I said. I held the spoon just above his lips, and the instant he opened his mouth I tipped the liquid in. A little dribbled out of the corner of his mouth, but most of it went down.

"Water," Mr. Pendergast called. I got the dipper and give him a drink. As he swallowed the water you could see a change come over him. His eyes got darker and wetter in the lamplight. Some of the in-flamed look started going out of his neck and throat.

"He needs to sleep," Ma Richards said.

Hank come to the door and looked in at Mr. Pendergast. "This is a pretty come off," he said. He looked more disgusted than I had ever seen him.

"You've got to get a doctor," Ma Richards said.

"Where?" Hank said. "I don't even know where there's an herb granny."

Hank had worked all day and walked to Lyman and back and then had saved me from the smoke. He was as tired as I was. "Maybe we can get a doctor in the morning," I said.

"This old man won't live till morning, unless he's doctored," Ma Richards said.

Everything had turned out so bad, I couldn't think what to do next. The kitchen was half burned up, and the lard was burned up. The sausage wasn't made and I was so tired I was not at myself. Ma

Richards was quarreling at everything I did. And Mr. Pendergast was so bad burned he was in pain and in danger of dying, and I was partly the cause of it all. But it was no good to think about blame. Ma Richards had showed me that. The first thing was to take care of Mr. Pendergast, and all the rest could wait. Everything else could be sorted out the next day, or even the next week.

"Surely there's a doctor in Tigerville," I said. "Or somebody that can tell you where to find one."

Hank come closer to Mr. Pendergast. "Where is your family?" he said, loud, like Mr. Pendergast was hard of hearing.

Mr. Pendergast mumbled something, but I couldn't understand what he said.

"Where is your children?" I said. He mumbled again, but it didn't make sense.

"We can find out tomorrow," I said.

After Hank got his coat and left, I told Ma she might as well go on to bed. "I'll stay up till Hank comes back," I said.

"It's in the fine hours that people suffer and die," Ma Richards said.

"Hank will be back with a doctor soon," I said.

I took a lamp back to the burned-out kitchen and looked for a fruit jar of liquor I'd seen on the shelf. I figured the liquor would go well with the laudanum. Together they might make Mr. Pendergast comfortable. The lamp throwed its yellow light and shadows on the table where the cold biscuits and tenderloin from our dinner remained. Only a few hours before we had set there eating and feeling so good. The biscuits and grits had soot on them. I found the jar and took it to the front bedroom.

Mr. Pendergast had not gone to sleep as I had hoped. His eyes was open and he watched me come through the door. "No!" he hollered. "You're not coming after me."

"I'm going to make you feel better," I said.

"No," he said and wrenched around in the bed like he was trying to get away from me.

"Everything is all right," I said. "You're going to feel better tomorrow. You're going to feel better after a drink of this."

But Mr. Pendergast looked at me like I was trying to poison him. He pulled away, and his eyes stretched wide in fear. "I'm just Julie," I said. I poured some of the liquor into the dipper and held it out to him.

"No!" he screamed and pulled further away.

"Who do you think I am?" I said.

"I know who you are," Mr. Pendergast said. "You're the angel of death."

"I ain't no kind of angel," I said, and held the dipper close to his lips.

"There was an angel of death in the prison camp," Mr. Pendergast said. "Now you have come back for me."

"Drink this and I'll put some butter on your burns," I said. I held the dipper in front of him but he didn't drink. He was quiet for a few moments.

"I have committed the unpardonable sin," he said.

"Ain't no such thing," I said.

"You're taking me to hell," Mr. Pendergast said.

"I'm just giving you a drink until the doctor comes," I said.

"I have committed the unpardonable sin without even knowing it," he said.

"What have you done?" I said. I wanted to keep him humored until the doctor arrived.

"I've sinned against the Holy Ghost," he said.

"You're talking out of your head," I said. "All you did was get burned looking for your money."

"Where is my money?" he said, his face in a panic.

"Your money is right here, see," I said and pointed to the jar on the nightstand, beside the lamp and bottle of laudanum.

"You can have the money," he said, "if you'll leave me alone."

"I don't want your money," I said. I held the dipper to his mouth and he gulped some of the white liquor and coughed. He took another big swallow and coughed again. I hoped with both the liquor and laudanum in him he could rest a little, and I could rub butter on his burns. I wanted to soothe him and keep him soothed until the doctor come. He laid back on the pillow and I reached for the butter. But before I rubbed any on my fingers he jerked up in bed again.

"Can you smell it?" he said.

"Smell what?" I said. "All I smell is this corn liquor."

"It's the pit of hell," he said, "the stink of brimstone like rotten eggs burning."

"Just the smoke from the fire in the kitchen," I said. "Let me put some butter on your burns."

Tears was streaming out of Mr. Pendergast's bloodshot eyes. "It's the fire that never dies," he sobbed.

"You just smell the grease fire," I said.

He cried like his heart and will was broke. I had never seen a man cry like that. "I will burn for all time," he said.

It was as if the liquor and the laudanum had soothed the burning on his face and head and hands but made his conscience burn worser. He was truly afraid. "You should get some sleep," I said.

The house was quiet except for pops and creaks here and there in the attic. Ma Richards must have gone on to bed for I didn't hear her stirring. A wind had rose in the dark and gusted against the windows, rattling panes.

"Don't you smell the stench?" Mr. Pendergast said.

"I don't smell nothing but burned lard and soot from the kitchen," I said.

"It's the stink of hell," he said and sobbed. The salt of his tears stung the burns on his cheeks. He rubbed a cheek with a swelled and blistered hand. Skin hung in little rags off his fingers.

"Let me rub butter on your hands," I said. I figured if I could get grease on his hands he would let me spread some on his face.

"No," he said, and jerked his hand away from me.

"Nothing else will help you heal," I said. I was so tired it sounded like somebody else talking. I was kind of floating and knowed if I stopped I would collapse. I felt so bad for what I had done that I couldn't think about it. I had to keep going. I had to. The awfulness of the world and the evilness of the world was in the air with the stink of the fire. The scariness was in the air like ghosts that wanted to press on my mind and haunt every second and every thought. They wanted to get in behind my eyes where the worst pain was. The devils gathered around my head and mocked me.

"Hell is scorching every inch of me!" Mr. Pendergast hollered.

"You're in your own bed, in your own house," I said. "And I'm here to help. I'll rub butter on your burns and you'll feel better." What he needed more than anything else was soothing in his mind.

"I didn't mean to tell a lie on my brother Jonathan," Mr. Pendergast said, out of breath, like he was talking to a judge. "And I didn't go to break Papa's watch."

"That was a long time ago," I said.

"I didn't mean to play with myself," he said.

"Mr. Pendergast, there's no need," I said. I didn't want to hear no more. The pain in his mind was unbearable.

"It was laughing at the preacher," he said. "That's how I sinned against the Holy Ghost."

"Now, Mr. Pendergast," I said.

"It was old Preacher Liner up there hollering, 'And the half shall never be told.' One of his suspenders broke and I busted out laughing. The preacher pointed his finger at me and said, 'Them that mock the Spirit sin against the Holy Ghost.'"

"You was just a boy," I said.

"Them that mock the Spirit are in danger of hellfire," Mr. Pendergast quoted.

"But surely you have been forgive," I said. "It was just a little thing."

"I will burn forever," Mr. Pendergast said. It was like he had give up. He even took pride in his damnation. He acted like he took some comfort in his own terror. I heard the mantel clock strike two. It was the darkest and loneliest time of night. Wind shoved against the wall of the house and a mouse or rat scratched in the wall behind Mr. Pendergast's bed. It sounded like the rat was gnawing a nut or chewing on a piece of wood. Something swished inside the wall and then overhead, in the ceiling. I didn't know if it was a rat running. It sounded like a big snake sliding over paneling. It sounded like something ten feet long sliding dry scales over wood.

"Please help me," Mr. Pendergast cried.

"I'm here to help you," I said. I put my hand on his shoulder.

"I can feel the fire on my feet," he said.

"Your feet are right here in this cool bed," I said.

"I'm freezing," he screamed.

"I'll get you another blanket," I said.

"Hell is ice," he said. His teeth was chattering. He looked like he seen something in the air in front of him. "Get back," he cried.

"There's nobody here but me," I said.

"Leave me alone," he shouted.

I put both my hands on his shoulders and tried to push him down on the pillow. He swung at me and hit me in the face with his burned hand. The pain made him groan. "I won't go," he whispered.

"You don't have to go nowhere," I said. I seen that the laudanum had wore off. The pain was coming back worse than before. I got the blue bottle from the nightstand and poured a spoonful of the cold liquid. "You need to drink this," I said.

"Won't do no good," he said.

"It helped before," I said.

"You'll poison me," he screamed.

I had to think of some way to make him drink the laudanum. Otherwise the pain would kill him. Even if I had to trick him, I had to make him take it. "If you don't drink this I'll have to leave," I said.

"No," he cried.

"I'll have to leave you to holler by yourself," I said. It hurt me to say a lie, but I couldn't think of any other way to make him take the laudanum. He closed his eyes and opened his mouth and I poured the liquid between his lips. Some of it dribbled out of the corner of his mouth, but most of it went down. It was a bigger dose than the first one. I used all the rest of the laudanum.

"The devil has long, dirty claws," Mr. Pendergast said, "and his claws are poison."

"He won't get his claws on you," I said. I felt like I was talking to a little child.

"The devil is trying to get in bed with me," Mr. Pendergast said.

"You lay back down and rest," I said. I pushed him gently back on the pillow.

"The devil is going to choke me," he said.

"Ain't nobody here but you and me," I said.

As the laudanum took effect I seen his eyes get wet and glassy, and blacker than ever. He was still troubled in his mind, but numbed by the tincture. His eyes roved around the room like he was trying to see where the evil spirit was hiding.

"You get some sleep," I said.

He laid on the pillow and took this deep breath. It was the kind of breath you hear somebody take when they're asleep. You expect them to take it in and then let it out. I waited without hardly knowing I was waiting. But Mr. Pendergast did not breathe out. I looked at him, and his eyes was open but not moving.

"Mr. Pendergast," I said. I put my hand over his nose but didn't feel any breath. I put my ear to his chest but didn't hear any heartbeat. Mr. Pendergast was dead. One moment he had been alive and afraid, and the next he was dead. He went just like that. It was amazing how easy it was for a human life to end. A person could die and you wouldn't hardly know it. I put my fingers on his eyes and closed them. Just then I heard Hank at the door.

THE DAY AFTER Mr. Pendergast died I felt ten years older. The doctor Hank had found on the other side of Tigerville said he thought Mr. Pendergast had a stepson in California and a stepdaughter in Columbia, but he didn't know their addresses and didn't even know their names. I was wore out and the kitchen was a ruin. Ma Richards blamed me for all of it. And that seemed mighty unfair to me. I *had* knocked the grease out on the stove, but it was me that drug Mr. Pendergast out of the burning kitchen, and it was me that put out the fire with wet sacks. Hank was irritated because he didn't know what to do about the house, and about reaching Mr. Pendergast's relatives.

"We may not have a roof over our heads," he said the morning after Mr. Pendergast died.

"We don't even know where to bury him," Ma Richards said.

There we was, in somebody else's house down in South Carolina, and him laying a corpse in the front bedroom. We might be throwed out, and I might be accused of burning the kitchen, or maybe even of killing Mr. Pendergast. Everything looked so bad the weight crushed down on me.

"Carry him into the kitchen," I said to Hank. I cleaned off the big kitchen table so it was bare. That was the only clean place in the kitchen. Everything else was black with soot.

"You can't lay out a corpse," Ma Richards said. "That's a job for an older woman."

"I helped lay out Papa," I said.

"We don't even know what his kin wants to do with him," Hank said.

"He's got to be laid out in any case," I said.

"You ain't even got a cooling board," Ma Richards said.

"We'll have to use the table," I said.

I cleared the stove and washed the burned grease off with soap. When I started a fire in the box the stovetop smelled like burned lard and soap as it heated up, but that was soon singed away. I brought a kettle of water to a boil. There was so much to be done, and I had to work my way through it. But the more I done the calmer I got. I scrubbed the soot and grease off the floor. And then we carried in Mr. Pendergast's body and I stripped off his clothes. Since he was already getting stiff, he needed to be laying on something flat and hard.

I washed every inch of him with soap and water, and put a handkerchief soaked in camphor on his face to keep it from turning brown, the way I had seen it done with Papa and Masenier. And then I rubbed oil all over his skin. Mr. Pendergast's bowels had moved after he died and I had to clean that up too.

"You oughten to have to do that," Hank said. I'd never done anything Hank told me not to. I didn't even know if I could, or if a wife should do something her husband said not to do. But if Hank just fussed, as he usually did, I felt justified in going ahead with what I was doing.

"Somebody's got to make a casket," I said.

"I need to go down to the crossroads and tell the preacher," Hank said. "There'll have to be a service."

"There'll have to be a casket," I said.

"You think you could do that too?" Hank said.

"I was thinking you could," I said, but wished I hadn't.

"I'll decide what I do, and when I do it," Hank said, and looked at me hard. A chill went through my bones, a sick iciness sunk in my belly. Hank and me hadn't quarreled before. It was the surprise of Mr. Pendergast's death, and Ma Richards being there, that made him lose his temper.

"Hank," Ma Richards said. I hadn't noticed she was standing in the doorway. "Hank," she said, "you've got to show who's wearing the britches in this house."

"Don't it look like I'm wearing the britches?" Hank said.

"You're used to things being easy," Ma Richards said.

Instead of answering her Hank walked out of the room, slamming the back door.

I looked at Ma, and I looked away. I was so mad I couldn't think of anything to say. I kept washing Mr. Pendergast's legs. I scrubbed his feet, between the toes and under the arches. His toenails was black, but I decided I wouldn't trim them or clean them. Soon as I finished washing his body I wet his hair and combed it with a comb I found in his room.

Dressing the body was harder than washing it. I found some drawers in the bedroom, and a shirt I'd washed myself. And I found a suit of clothes hanging on a nail, but they was wrinkled. I sprinkled the wool and heated the iron on the stove and pressed the suit. It took a lot of lifting and rolling of the body to get it dressed. The arms and legs was setting stiff as wood. The eyes come open when I moved the head, and I had to brush them closed again.

Hank had gone out in the backyard, and I heard him sawing and hammering. There was a stack of old boards in the barn, and I seen he was hammering together a box from chestnut boards. With the corpse dressed and laying on the kitchen table, I started thinking about fixing some breakfast. None of us had eat since the day before. I hated to fix something to eat with the corpse laying there, but there was nothing else to do. We had to eat, and we had to get on with things. And I meant to show Ma Richards I could go on in spite of whatever she said.

I wiped the soot off the top of the meal bin and scooped out some cornmeal.

"You're not going to cook with that thing laying here?" Ma Richards said.

"I won't touch the body," I said.

"I'm not eating around a corpse," Ma Richards said.

I didn't answer her. I wasn't used to talking back to older people. And it wouldn't do no good to snipe at her. I wiped off the coffeepot and poured some fresh water in it. "Would you grind some coffee?" I said to Ma. Without answering me, she took the can of coffee beans out to the back porch.

I got some fresh ribs out of the dishpan where they had been setting overnight. They had been partly cooked in the fire and soot made them black. I rubbed the smut off and put eight or nine in the frying pan. Soon the kitchen smelled like frying meat. And boiling coffee and baking cornbread. Hank was still hammering when I called him in.

"Where are we going to eat?" Hank said. Mr. Pendergast laid on the kitchen table like he was in state in a public place.

"There's nowhere to put the body till you get a casket made," I said.

"I'm not half done," Hank said.

"I'm not eating with that thing in here," Ma Richards said.

I give everybody a plate and served the cornbread and molasses and fresh ribs. We set as far away from the table as we could, eating on our laps. I was near starved, and Hank and Ma Richards was near starved too. We eat everything I'd fixed, and drunk all the coffee. It didn't matter that Mr. Pendergast was laying there a corpse after we took the first bite.

"This is like a wake," Ma Richards said, her mouth full of cornbread and molasses.

"We are like sin eaters," Hank said.

"I never believed in such dreadful stuff," Ma Richards said.

"What is a sin eater?" I said.

"Somebody the family pays to eat supper off a corpse, like they are taking on all the sins of the dead person," Hank said.

"What an awful idea," I said.

"It's just a story," Hank said.

AFTER HANK FINISHED the chestnut box and we put Mr. Pendergast in it with his hands folded, we set the coffin on two chairs in the living room. And there he laid until the funeral on Wednesday. I kept handkerchiefs soaked in camphor on his brow. And I tried not to look at him as I went about my work. But it was hard not to glance at the face under the handkerchief, like I was expecting it to come awake and say something.

One of the neighbors, George Poole, who run the store at the crossroads, come by and I asked him about Mr. Pendergast's children. George Poole was a big man whose belly punched out below the bib of his overalls. "Last I heard Butch was somewhere in Californy," he said.

"You don't know what town?" I said.

"All I heard was he went to Californy," Mr. Poole said.

"And how about his stepdaughter?" I said.

"Now Caroline is down in Columbia somewheres," Mr. Poole said. He looked closer at Mr. Pendergast. "Everybody looks younger in death," he said. "I wonder why."

"Because they have stopped worrying," Ma Richards said. "All the grief goes out of them, if they went to heaven."

"Does anybody know Caroline's address?" I said. "Is there any cousins, or aunts or uncles, here on Gap Creek?"

"Now Caroline and Butch was stepchildren," Mr. Poole said. "I don't think they kept in close touch."

"His wife was married before?" Ma Richards said.

"She must have been," Mr. Poole said. "She already had the younguns when she come here."

George Poole set with us for several hours, looking at the chestnut box and making conversation. It was his way of being neighborly, of keeping vigil. But it all felt a little strange, because we wasn't even Mr. Pendergast's kin, and George Poole and Mr. Pendergast had not been close friends either.

"Pendergast kept to hisself," George Poole said. "He hunted ginseng and trapped for muskrats. He done anything he could do on his own. He never liked to go off on public works. In the last year or two he was too feeble to go out in the woods much. But he would buy ginseng from other diggers."

"I never seen him go beyond the cowshed," Hank said.

"He hid his money somewhere," Mr. Poole said. "Everybody thinks he hid a lavish of pension money somewhere."

I didn't say nothing about Mr. Pendergast's jar of money, and Hank didn't bring it up either. It didn't seem like any of George Poole's business.

"Where did he keep his money?" I said to George Poole.

"People say he hid it in a fruit jar somewhere in the backyard," Mr. Poole said.

"Maybe that was just a rumor," Hank said.

"People is liable to say anything," Ma Richards said.

"I'm just saying what other people has said," Mr. Poole said.

THE FUNERAL FOR Mr. Pendergast was the pitifullest thing you ever seen. There must not have been more than a dozen people there. Mr. Pendergast didn't have relations on the Creek, and it was a cold rainy day. Gap Creek Church was open to the rafters, and the preacher's voice seemed to echo up into that empty space. I expected bats and rats to be scratching around up there over the congregation.

Preacher Gibbs and his wife sung a song, and it was the mournfullest thing you could ever hear. They sung "On Jordan's Stormy Banks" and it was slow and sad. A song like that can sometimes make you feel sweet with the sadness. Music can make time, and a lifetime, seem precious. But the way they sung "On Jordan's Stormy Banks" was like all the life and all the joy was draining out of the world. There wasn't a thing to hope for. It was the bad kind of sadness. It was the sadness of sin, not the sadness of love and piety.

"When we come to the end of the way," Preacher Gibbs said, "what will we have to say for ourselves?" And the way he said it you felt nobody would have anything good to say for theirselves, that it was hopeless from the beginning, and there wasn't nothing anybody could say for theirselves. I always hated that kind of preaching, especially at a funeral. For if somebody is dead there ain't nothing you can do for them. And it's too late for them to change their ways. All that kind of sermon can do is make other people feel bad. They leave a funeral feeling worser than when they come. A funeral should make people feel glad they're still alive.

"The wages of sin is death," Preacher Gibbs said, and his words rumbled and rattled in the loft. Every word he said was swallowed up by the stillness and darkness up there in the rafters. "This generation of vipers," Preacher Gibbs said.

I had the awfullest feeling, watching Mr. Pendergast laying there in his box with no kinfolks around to mourn and bury him, and the preacher talking sad and harsh to the empty church. It was like we had come to the end of things, almost before my life and marriage had got started. Ma Richards was setting on my right, and Hank on my left. There was no place I could go except forward in time toward death. The bottom was falling out of the world. The bench I set on was still there and the floorboards was solid under my feet.

But everything important was falling away, and when I closed my eyes I felt like I was falling into a pit and being hit over the head with the preacher's words.

When the funeral was finally over, it took all the men there to carry the box out to the graveyard on the hill behind the church. After the preacher's words, even the cold rain felt soothing. I had a headache, and my belly hurt like I had eat a green apple. Yellow leaves still hung on the hickories and a crow called its heckle from the pines further up the mountain. The mountains was so steep on both sides of Gap Creek it felt like we was at the bottom of a big grave.

Hank had dug the grave hisself that morning and the heaped dirt by the hole was so red it seemed to blister and sparkle in the gray light. Something about the raw dirt around a grave always shocks you, like it was a hungry mouth that human flesh is fed to.

"First comes death," Preacher Gibbs said, "and after that the Judgment."

The crows cawed in the pines.

"As for man his days are as grass. As a flower of the field so he flourisheth. But the wind passes over and it is gone, and the place thereof shall know it no more."

As Hank and three other men lowered the casket into the hole with ropes, the preacher and his wife sung "Shall We Gather at the River." And I must say, it was the perfect song to be sung over a grave. It was a song I had always loved. And even in the rain and wet dirt, I begun to feel better about the funeral, and about the preacher. Preacher Gibbs was just doing what all preachers do at funerals. It was the cold, empty church that had made his words so sad and made me feel so sad. Preacher Gibbs and his wife kept singing by the grave in the rain, and they sung every verse of the song. They had fine, clear voices.

. . .

As we walked back to the house after the funeral Ma seemed more cheerful than I had ever seen her. I guess the fact that she was older than Mr. Pendergast, and she was still alive, had cheered her up. You would have thought his funeral had reflected glory on her. She was smiling to herself, and she walked tall and fast. She grinned like she had a special secret. I'd never seen her so sweet. I was tired out and wrung out, and she walked up the Gap Creek Road like she was fifteen years old.

Six

W hen we got back to the house I was so dragged out I
dropped on the sofa. Two chairs was still facing each
other in the middle of the living room where the casket
had laid. The house needed a cleaning and the kitchen needed to
be fixed up, scrubbed down from ceiling to floor. Mr. Pendergast's
room had to be cleaned up and his stuff sorted and washed. But the
house didn't even belong to us, and I didn't know who should do all
that work.

"You rest," Ma Richards said. "I'll fix some supper."

"I'll get up in a minute," I said. "Just need to rest my feet."

"Hank, you got to look after Julie," Ma Richards said. Hank was
warming his hands by the fire. We was all cold and wet.

"I'm fine," I said.

"You're expecting," Ma Richards said, "unless I miss my guess."

"Is that a fact?" Hank said to me. But he acted embarrassed, or
maybe took by surprise.

"I don't know," I said.

"How long has it been?" Ma Richards said.

"Nearly two months," I said.

"That settles it," Ma Richards said, like she had took charge of the house. Her face was bright and her eyes sparkled. Suddenly I seen why she had been so cheerful. Just the thought of becoming a grandma had cheered her up.

"Settles what?" Hank said.

"Settles the fact that I'm going to stay here and help Julie out," Ma Richards said.

"Don't need help," I said. A chill passed through me. I had thought Ma would be leaving in a few days. It was the one thing that cheered me up, the thought that she would be gone and Hank and me could get back to living our lives.

"You're going to need a lot of help," Ma said.

I looked at Hank. He stood by the fire and didn't say nothing. Though I had never said so, I was sure he knowed how much I resented Ma Richards being there. I couldn't say nothing against his mama, but she irritated me. And she irritated him too, but he was a man and she treated him different. And besides, she was the only mama he had ever knowed.

"I don't even know for sure I'm expecting," I said. It seemed to me that if Ma Richards stayed with us any longer I would have to leave myself. I would walk back up the mountain and stay with Mama and my sisters.

"You are," Ma Richards said, like it was somehow a credit to her.

I got short of breath. I felt if I didn't get Ma out of the house, I was going to have to run away.

"We probably won't even be staying here," I said. "We don't know whose house this is now."

"You don't want to move, in her condition," Ma said to Hank, like I was a little girl and they had to decide for me. It was what she wanted to do, take charge of the house and of Hank. She wanted to treat me like a little child, her child. And she wanted to be in charge of the baby even before it was born.

"I don't know what we'll do," Hank said.

"We may have to leave here any day," I said.

"You can stay till one of Mr. Pendergast's heirs shows up," Ma said. "I don't see what's to stop you."

"The county will sell this place for taxes if somebody don't show up," Hank said.

"Then you pay the taxes, and you can buy it," Ma said.

"Don't have enough money," Hank said and spit his tobacco juice in the fire. His jaw always tightened when he talked about money. He didn't like to talk about money.

"We don't know where we'll be living," I said, "and we don't know if I am expecting for sure."

"Well, if I'm not wanted here, I sure don't mean to impose myself," Ma said.

I didn't answer her, for I didn't want to ask her to stay.

"We want you to stay as long as you can," Hank said. He looked at me. "But we may be moving back to Painter Mountain with you."

"With me?"

"Where else would we go?" Hank said.

"I'd have to fix up the loft for you," Ma said. "There'd be no other place for you to sleep."

"Exactly," Hank said. "I'll take you back to Painter Mountain and you can fix up the attic for us."

"You'll need a lot of help here," Ma said. "Julie can't clean up this place by herself."

"They may throw us out any day," Hank said. "And besides, I'll help her do what has to be done." Hank knowed how to talk to Ma Richards. He had growed up with her ways and knowed what to say.

"When do you want to go?" Ma Richards said. All the cheer had gone out of her.

"I was thinking Sunday, because I don't have to work," Hank said.

"I hate to travel on the Lord's day," Ma said.

"The Lord will understand," Hank said.

But Ma Richards had to get in the last word. "Somebody will have to take care of this house," she said.

"I think I can manage," I said.

I felt like I was falling in love with Hank all over again, because he had understood how much I wanted Ma Richards to leave, and because he had helped me. I wanted to run to him and kiss him on the neck and on the cheek. He was dearer than he ever had been. He had saved me from his mama. While everything else was going wrong or up in the air, at least I was going to have the house to myself again. That seemed to mean everything. If I could just be alone in the house to do my work and to clear my mind, I might be happy again.

THE NEXT SUNDAY morning Hank hitched up the horse and buggy and helped Ma Richards into the seat. I stood in the yard and waved to her as they drove away.

"Don't strain yourself now," Ma called.

"I think I can manage," I said.

"Whenever you feel tired just go and set down," Ma said.

"I am seventeen years old," I said.

"That's why I worry about you," Ma said.

"Don't worry about me," I said.

"And remember, almost all women get sick in the morning," Ma said.

I stood on the steps and watched the buggy get smaller and smaller up the creek road. The farther away it got the better I felt. When the horse's head, and then Ma's and Hank's heads, disappeared around the bend, I felt a peacefulness settle through me, like all kinds of dust and soot had settled to the ground, leaving the air fresh and bright.

. . .

THE WEEK AFTER Mr. Pendergast's death it turned cold again. Hank went back to work at the cotton mill at Lyman, and I was sick nearly every day. Each morning I throwed up in the chamber or off the back porch, and then set in the kitchen sipping some hot tea. After having Ma Richards there all those days, and after worrying about Mr. Pendergast ever since we moved in, I enjoyed the peacefulness each day, soon as my belly settled down.

You wouldn't believe how good I felt those days after my stomach calmed. I washed the dishes and dried them and put them on the shelf. Then I took a bucket and rag and washed the floor. It made me feel strong to get down on my knees on those rough boards. It was like a morning prayer, kneeling on the cold boards and crawling backwards to rub away any dirt with the rag. That's when I felt how much it meant to have a home, a place to live in day after day and night after night.

As I scrubbed the floor I was scrubbing part of the world. And I was scrubbing my mind to make it clear. It was work that made me think clear, and it was work that made me humble. I could never talk fast, and I could never say what I meant to people, or tell them what they meant to me. My tongue was never loosened by my feelings. It was with my hands and with my back and shoulders that I could say how I felt. I had to talk with my arms and my strong hands.

When I finished scouring the floor I took the bucket of dirty water out to the back porch and emptied it. I was rinsing out the bucket with fresh water when I seen a buggy pull off the road. I didn't think nothing about it at first, for peddlers and buyers of ginseng and herbs come around from time to time. This buggy looked new and its black top and sides sparkled. The horse that pulled it was black and its sides sparkled like they had been shined with shoe polish. My breath tightened in my throat the way it always did when I seen a stranger.

I rinsed out the bucket and throwed the water in a flashing

streak across the yard. A hen got hit and run away cackling. Another hen rushed to peck where the water had splashed. The buggy stopped in the yard and I put the bucket down and hurried out to meet it.

"How do," the driver in a black suit said and tipped his hat.

"Howdy do," I said.

He stuck the whip in its socket and tied the reins to a ring on the side of the buggy. "My name is Jerrold James," he said. "I'm an attorney from Greenville."

"Pleased to meet you," I said. "My name is Julie Richards." But a chill rung through me. I knowed a lawyer couldn't be bringing good news.

"Is this the property owned by Vincent Pendergast?" he said.

"It is," I said. "But Mr. Pendergast died last week and was buried on Wednesday."

"Precisely," the lawyer said. "Precisely."

"I took care of Mr. Pendergast, and of the house," I said. There was a cold wind coming down the valley, and I was starting to get chilled without my shawl.

"I saw the notice of Mr. Pendergast's death in the Greenville paper," the lawyer said. He took a sheet of paper out of his case.

"Do you represent Mr. Pendergast's heirs?" I said.

"Not exactly," Mr. James said. "Since Mr. Pendergast has no will, or at least not one anybody has found, it's not clear who his heirs are. His stepchildren, wherever they are, may or may not have a legal claim to the property."

"I see," I said.

"For all I know your claim may be as good as theirs," Mr. James said.

"My claim?" I said.

"By right of occupancy," he said. "That would be for a court to decide."

"We would have to go to court?" I said.

"Precisely," Mr. James said. It was his favorite word, and he made it sound like a sharp knife cutting through fat.

"My husband and me don't want trouble," I said. I wished Hank was there to talk with him.

"But I'm here on another matter," Mr. James said. "I represent the Bank of Greenville, which holds a lien against the property." He took two more sheets from his case and held them out for me to see. I didn't really look at them. I figured he would tell me what they said.

"Do we have to move out?" I said.

"Not necessarily," the lawyer said. "That's what I'm here to talk about."

I invited Mr. Jerrold James inside. I was shivering in the wind. When we got into the living room I asked him to set down on the sofa and I throwed another log on the fire.

"Would you like some coffee?" I said.

"That would be splendid," he said. "I did get a little chilled driving up the valley."

There was still some warm coffee in the pot and I poured him a cup and brought it to the living room. Mr. James pulled his chair closer to the fireplace and took a sip of coffee. "I understand there was a fire," he said.

"I was rendering lard and some grease caught fire," I said.

"Was there much damage?" he said.

"The curtains burned, and some boards on the floor got charred," I said. "I put it out with wet sacks."

"And Mr. Pendergast got burned?"

"He got burned on his head and face, and on his hands," I said.

"How did Mr. Pendergast get burned so badly?" Mr. James said.

"He was trying to put out the fire, and save his property," I said. "A can of kerosene flared up and caught his hair." And that was the truth. I wasn't telling Mr. James a lie.

"Did Mr. Pendergast tell you where he kept his money?" the lawyer said. Wind made the house shudder and the windows rattle. A puff of smoke come out of the fireplace, as it always did when there was a gust from the north. The smoke reminded me all too much of the fire in the kitchen.

"He never did," I said. And that was true. Mr. Pendergast had never let on he had money until he crawled into the fire to save the jar behind the stove.

Mr. James smiled at me. "What are you folks planning to do now?" he said.

"We will stay here and look after the place, until the heirs come," I said.

"I can see that you're honest folks," he said.

"We try to be," I said.

"That's why I would hate for the bank to foreclose," he said, and took another sip of coffee.

"What do you mean?" I said.

"We want to do the Christian thing," he said. "But if the bank can't collect the interest due on the loan, it will have to seize the property."

"I wish my husband was here to talk to you," I said.

"The case is very simple," Mr. James said. "If the bank can't collect the interest due on the loan it will have to foreclose."

"But Mr. Pendergast's heirs don't even know he's dead yet, as far as I know," I said.

"I understand that," he said. "But the bank will have to act in any case."

"When Hank comes back you can talk to him," I said, feeling flustered.

"I'm sorry to bring you bad news," Mr. James said.

"We don't have a place to move to," I said.

"There's no reason you would have to leave, if the bank can collect its interest," the lawyer said.

"You mean we could stay here?" I said.

"As long as the payment was made, I don't see why not," Mr. James said.

It seemed to me I owed it to the heirs not to let the bank take the house before they even knowed Mr. Pendergast was dead. It was my job to look after the place until they showed up. I just wished Hank was there to help me decide what to do.

"I can see you've taken very good care of the house," Mr. James said.

"I've tried my best," I said.

"I'm sorry to surprise you this way," he said.

"You have to do your job," I said.

Mr. James finished his coffee and put the cup down on the floor. "I would like to help you if I could," he said.

"Would you like another cup?" I said.

"No thank you, I'll have to be going."

I knowed there was something I ought to do; I had to do something. "When will the bank seize the house?" I said.

"They will have to act before the end of the year," Mr. James said. "I'm sorry it has to be that soon."

"What if you was to get the money," I said, "for the interest?"

"If the interest was paid the bank wouldn't act," Mr. James said. "Could you pay the interest?"

"We don't have much money," I said.

"The heirs could reimburse you later," Mr. James said, "when they're found."

"What if they ain't found?" I said.

"Then you could keep living here, as far as the bank is concerned."

I seen it was the thing to do, to pay the interest. It was the only thing to do, to not let the bank take the house before the heirs even knowed Mr. Pendergast was gone. And if the interest was paid, Hank and me could keep living there.

"How much is the interest?" I said.

"That depends on the period you're paying it for," the lawyer said, "a month, a quarter, or a year."

"How much for a year?" I said.

"I'll have to check my papers," Mr. James said.

"I think I might know where to get it," I said.

"That would save us all a lot of trouble," Mr. James said.

I got my shawl and hurried back through the kitchen. Mr. James followed me and stood on the porch as I run to the outhouse. Behind the two seats and the Sears and Roebuck catalog we kept to use as toilet paper, was the jar full of Mr. Pendergast's pension money. Hank had put it there after Mr. Pendergast died. He said it was one place nobody would look for money.

The jar was cold as if it was full of ice. I carried it in both hands to the porch.

"That belonged to Mr. Pendergast?" Mr. James said.

"It was his pension money," I said.

"Let's count it and I'll give you a receipt," Mr. James said.

I lit the lamp in the kitchen and the lawyer poured the money out of the jar on the table. You never seen so many silver dollars and half-dollars and quarters, mixed in with dimes and dollar bills. There was even a five-dollar gold piece that sparkled in the lamplight. There was so much money I felt scared.

Me and Mr. James made separate stacks of all the different kind of coins. Some was so old and had stayed in the jar so long they felt sticky.

"Let's make sure this is not Confederate money," Mr. James said and laughed. When it was all counted there was forty-seven dollars and eighty-six cents.

"Is that enough for interest?" I said.

"That's almost enough for a whole year," Mr. James said.

I felt so relieved I almost cried, for I had found a way to save Mr. Pendergast's house for his heirs. And Hank and me still had a place to live.

"The Bank of Greenville will remember that you helped us," Mr. James said. "And we may just be able to help you in the future."

Mr. James opened his case and took out a sheet of paper. With his fountain pen he wrote on the page several lines and handed it to me. "Received from Mrs. Julie Richards, $47.86, interest for the loan on Mr. Vincent Pendergast's house on Gap Creek. Jerold James, Attorney."

"Thank you for helping us," I said.

"The Bank of Greenville knows it can help itself only by serving its customers," Mr. James said. I walked out into the front yard with him and watched him climb into the buggy. He untied the reins from the post and said giddyup. I watched him turn the buggy around and start back down the road. I stood there and watched till he was almost out of sight before it got so cold in the wind I had to run back into the house.

ALL DAY AS I worked I thought about Mr. James and how he had come out of the blue and collected Mr. Pendergast's interest for the bank. I was proud of what I had been able to do. Even though Hank wasn't there, I had paid the interest and saved the house from the bank. But the whole thing appeared stranger the more I thought about it. I had expected Mr. Pendergast's heirs to show up and demand the property and the money, not some lawyer from a bank in Greenville. There was something odd about the whole business, but I couldn't put my finger on what it was. What the lawyer said made sense, but I dreaded to tell Hank what had happened. The more I thought about it, the more I saw he wouldn't be pleased that the money was gone.

I HAD RIBS and cornbread and fresh collards ready when Hank got home from the mill. I poured him a glass of sweet milk and set down myself before I told him about the lawyer and about the bank having a lien on the property.

"He said we have to leave?" Hank said.

"No, he didn't say that," I said. I listened to the wind outside. There was a steady roar on the ridge above the creek.

"What did he want?" Hank said.

"He said Mr. Pendergast owed interest to the bank," I said.

Hank stopped eating and looked at me. He had grease on his chin. "You didn't tell him Mr. Pendergast had any money?" he said.

"I paid the interest," I said. "He said the bank would take the house if the interest wasn't paid. But he was very nice about it."

"I bet he was," Hank said.

"He said we could stay if the interest was paid," I said.

"You didn't tell him about the jar of money?" Hank said.

"I give him the jar of money, for the interest," I said.

Hank stood up. His mouth was full of cornbread, and he didn't say anything for a long time. "You stupid heifer," he finally said.

I felt ice around my heart when he said that. I felt a cold vise crush my heart in its jaws. "I had to," I said. "He said they would seize the house. I had to pay the interest."

Before I knowed it Hank swung back and hit me across the face. My cheek stung and my head rung, but I didn't hardly feel it. It was Hank's words that burned right into my heart.

"He snockered you," Hank said. "You didn't even know who that man was. He tricked you. He didn't even know Pendergast had any money until you told him. You dumb heifer."

And I seen it might be true. The "lawyer" had fished around until I went after the jar of money. And he had talked me into giving it to him. He had talked so convincing I had give it all to him. Tears squirted into my eyes and I run into the living room. I was ashamed of what I had done. And I was ashamed of what Hank had done. It was a shame I'd never felt before. It was a shame that cut through my stomach like a razor. I was so ashamed for Hank. Papa had never hit me, and Mama had never hit me since I was a little girl. When I was little Mama used to switch me with a hickory when I sassed her. But that was when I was maybe five or six.

I set on the sofa and put my head down on the arm. But I didn't sob like a little girl that's heart was broke. There was tears in my eyes, but I couldn't empty my grief out in sobs. I guess I was too shocked, and too angry. I buried my eyes in my arm and expected Hank to come in and say he was sorry. I thought he would take me by the shoulders and stand me up and kiss me. He would comfort me, and then maybe we could go back to like it was before, before Ma Richards come, and before Mr. Pendergast died.

But Hank never come into the living room. I was ready for him to come put his hands on my shoulders and tell me how sorry he was. I was going to resist him at first. I was going to show how disappointed in him I was. I was going to make him work to win my forgiveness; I wouldn't be so easy to woo back.

Instead of feeling his hands on my shoulders, I heard the back door slam. I raised up and listened. There was only the sound of the fire in the fireplace and wind brushing the eaves and the roof. Hank had gone out into the dark. Instead of comforting me, he had left me to my shame. I felt weak in my knees I was so disappointed. Worse than the shame of being slapped was the shame of being left alone.

I stood up and walked to the fire and held out my hands to the flames because I was cold inside. People are supposed to feel hot with shame, but I felt my bones had turned to chalk. I felt I had shrunk to joints and knobs of chalk and ice. I stood by the fire and waited for Hank to come back in. I studied what I would say to him. For I was awful sorry for what I had done with Mr. Pendergast's money. I had give away money that was not mine, money that would belong to the heirs by rights. I had done a foolish thing. The man that pretended to be Mr. James was a true shyster. And Hank had done a worser thing, when he raised his hand against me.

The longer I stood by the fire the less I warmed up. The sound of the wind made me shudder, and the cold was deep inside me, in my bowels and in my bones. If I stood any longer and waited for Hank to come back in I was going to freeze to death. I dreaded to go back into the kitchen, where Hank had slapped me, but there was nowhere else to go, in the whirl of feelings and the twisting around of everything.

Most of the supper was still on the table, the cornbread and ribs, the collard greens and the glasses of sweet milk. Everything had got cold, except the milk, which had got warm. The plates had half-eat stuff on them, and the lamp on the table throwed a yellow light on the clutter.

I got a handful of kindling and tossed it into the stove, and took the kettle out to the back porch. In the dark of the backyard I couldn't see Hank anywhere. I wondered if he was out in the barn or maybe beyond the woodshed. Was he standing out there watching me? I poured the kettle full of water and carried it back into the kitchen. Was my marriage over before it had hardly started?

While the water was heating up, I scraped the plates into the slop bucket for the chickens. And I put the cornbread and collards and ribs into the bread safe. I wiped the table off and throwed the crumbs out the back door. With a wet cloth I washed the table and put the dirty dishes and spoons and forks into the dishpan. When the kettle was hot I poured the pan about half full of water.

The hot soapy water felt good on my hands and wrists. I buried my arms up to the elbows in the steaming pan and put my face close to the dishpan to feel the warmth on my chin and neck. I wished I could sink my whole body into a tub of hot, soapy water. I needed to soak myself and cleanse myself. I needed to melt away the stain of shame. I scrubbed each knife and fork, each glass and dish and bowl. I rinsed them in a pan of fresh water and dried them with a clean towel. I was finished and ready to throw the dirty water out the back door when Hank appeared in the door.

"What did that lawyer look like?" he said.

I had thought of a thousand things to say to Hank. I had thought of everything from apologizing to trying to shame him for smacking me. I had thought of telling him I would get a gun and shoot him if he ever hit me again. And I had thought of getting on my knees and begging forgiveness for the stupid thing I had done. But now that Hank had finally come back into the house I couldn't think of a thing to say. I wrung out the dishrag in the pan of dirty water.

"Can't you remember what he looked like?" Hank said.

"He was just a man," I said. None of the things I had thought of to say would come to my tongue.

"Is that all you can say?" Hank said.

"He was a man wearing a suit, and driving a buggy," I said. I tried to recall what Mr. James's face had looked like, but I couldn't remember a single detail. What was the color of his hair? The color of his eyes? Did he have whiskers or not? It had all slipped out of my mind.

"Was he tall or short?" Hank said.

"He wasn't as tall as you," I said. "And he was a little stoop shouldered."

"That don't tell us much," Hank said.

"He said his name was Jerrold James," I said.

"He could be anybody," Hank said.

"I wasn't studying him to remember him," I said. "I was worrying about saving Mr. Pendergast's house."

"You didn't worry enough," Hank said.

This was the first bad quarrel Hank and me had, and I didn't know how it was going to turn out. I didn't know if it was the end of us, or not. Mama and Papa had had tiffs, but Papa had never struck Mama as far as I knowed. Papa had never struck anybody as far as I was aware.

I didn't say anything to Hank that I didn't have to say. For I was still ashamed of what he had done, and what I had done. I was ashamed that I couldn't think of what I wanted to say. So I just kept quiet while he fussed and fumed about the money.

"Can't you remember nothing?" he said.

I shook my head.

"Could you recognize him again?" Hank said.

"I might."

"And you might not," he said. Hank was worried and he was nervous. It confused him and consternated him that I didn't say much. He was used to a woman carrying on like Ma Richards. He was used to tongue-lashing and insults. By keeping quiet I was throwing him off balance. It was the first time I seen what power I had over his blustering bad temper. If I just waited, he would get worked up and keep butting his head against my quietness. I seen I didn't have to say much at all, could just let him fret and worry. He would use his rage against hisself.

"Would you recognize his horse?" Hank said.

"I might," I said.

He talked that way in the kitchen, and then followed me into the living room, thinking up one question after another. But I didn't tell him much. I couldn't tell him nothing that would help. I let him fuss and fret and wear hisself out. When it was time to go to bed I didn't say nothing. I took the combs out of my hair and put them on the mantel, and then I got a lamp from the bureau to carry up the stairs.

I DON'T KNOW what it is about a quarrel that stirs a body so. But when I got under the covers in the cold bedroom it felt like my flesh was going wild and glowing. The work had burned the chill away, and as I listened to Hank rage I had got warmer and warmer. The fuss and the shame had spirited something inside me. As I got in bed by myself I could feel the heat give off by my skin warming up the covers and mattress under my back. I listened to the wind in the eaves and in the chimney and waited for Hank to climb the stairs and come into the room.

I guess waiting stirs the flesh also. There is nothing like waiting to whip up the pulse and make the blood sing in your ears. I could feel the blood in my neck and chest, and even in my arms, so warm it was purring. I laid in the dark feeling the covers touch the tips of my breasts and my belly and my knees. You was a fool, I said to myself. You are nothing but an idiot. But the thought was not entirely painful. For if I knowed I was a fool and admitted it, at least I was standing on firm ground and could see clear where I was going. If I knowed I was a fool I might learn to be better and to do better.

Wind brushed against the roof and I shivered, not because I was cold but because I was so warm sparks flashed off my body. There was electric currents in the covers and in the air, and every bit of my body had a charge and sting, like soda water on a tongue. You are a pure fool, I said to myself.

BUT HANK DIDN'T come on up to bed. I laid in the dark waiting minute after minute. After maybe an hour I heard the front door slam, like he had gone out. And after that I must have dropped off to sleep, for I never did hear him come in. But in the wee hours I was woke by the sound of steps on the stairs.

Hank climbed up the stairs and opened the door. He was carrying another lamp and he set the light on the little bureau. He had to stoop a little under the slope of the ceiling. He'd left his shoes downstairs by the fireplace like he usually did, and he padded around in his socks. First he unbuckled one gallus of his overalls, and then he unbuckled the other. To take off overalls you have to unbutton the sides at the waist, but before he done that he blowed out the lamp. I listened to him slide off his overalls and hang them on the bedpost. I heard something rattle in the corner and couldn't think what it was. And then I remembered the tin can where Hank sometimes spit out his tobacco. Next I heard something creak and felt a draft of cold air. He had cracked the window just a hair, as he always did before going to bed.

When Hank set down on the bed to take off his socks, it shook the mattress and springs like they was jelly. I quivered with the bed and tilted as he laid down and pulled the covers over him. He was so much heavier than me that the bed shifted and I felt I was laying on a hillside. I had to prop myself with one hand and elbow to keep from sliding over.

Would Hank touch me? Would he get over his anger enough to forgive me? Had the quarrel stirred him up and spirited him up the way it had me? Would he roll over and put his hand on my breast the way he did when he felt loving? Would he whisper something in the dark that would send sparks through me down to my groin? He shifted his shoulders and pushed up against the pillow. His weight made the bed sway. Every inch of my skin stung with the itch to be touched and the need to be touched. Every place on my body itched.

I wanted to reach out to him, but I knowed that wouldn't do. I had never reached out to him before. I was sure he didn't want me to do that. He wanted to be the one to reach out. If he was ready to love me he would reach out. There was nothing for me to do but wait for him to make up his mind. I had seen him do it so many times, just make up his mind all of a sudden that he wanted to be loving.

I listened to the little clock ticking in the dark on the nightstand. It was the alarm clock we used to wake up at five-thirty or six. Its tick was fast as my heartbeat. Its tick made my ears itch. The tick tickled and prickled my skin.

Hank turned over and put his hand on my hip. But what he said was not love words. He didn't whisper that I was his honey or his sugar pudding. He didn't whisper that he was sorry and that I was his sweetheart love. At first I didn't even hear what he said, it was so different from what I expected, what I wanted to hear. You know how words can seem strange if they're not what you're waiting for.

"I got fired today," he said.

He said it like he was almost too tired to say it. And he said it like he was explaining why he had got so mad about the jar of money too. I knowed that instantly. He was saying in his own way he was sorry he had hit me.

"How come?" I said.

"Cause all the bricks is made," he said. "They've got bricks enough to build the cotton mill and they don't need me for anything else."

I reached out and put a hand on his leg. I put my hand on his hip and raised my leg and put it on his. I could feel his sadness, in his words and in the loose way his body laid. He was heavy with sadness. He was slow and hot with sadness.

I run my hand down his hip and his leg. I smoothed the hairs around his crotch and felt him get bigger. My excitement and his sadness made me bolder than I had ever been before. I stroked him until he was long and hard as iron. I heard his breath getting deeper. "You will get another job," I said. But it seemed to me that didn't matter. In the dark what mattered was we was together and naked. Wind shoved the side of the house, way down on Gap Creek in South Carolina. We would always find a way to live, a way to get back, as long as we could love. I was going to have a baby, and that was what mattered.

I run my hand through the hair on Hank's chest and pinched one of his nipples. I had not done that before. It was like everything I did was the right thing. When Hank pressed against me I felt the sparkle in my skin where he touched. The glow had centered in my belly where the baby was. It was a coal of fire. Mama had told me you shouldn't love in the later months of a pregnancy, but it was too early to need to worry. I was free to do whatever I wanted, and what I wanted was to love Hank in our own bed in our own way. Our quarrel and the uncertainty of things made it even more important to love.

As Hank rolled on top of me, it was like time slowed down and every second stretched out and strained to its limit. The dark got bigger, and everything in the dark got bigger. Hank's shoulders and elbows and hands got bigger. The seconds groaned with bigness. Every inch of flesh was large and hurt, it felt so tender. Hank worked like he was climbing a hill against me. He crawled like he was climbing up a tree. He crawled faster, and then he slowed down. He slowed down again, and then he climbed farther. He pushed like he was galloping. He climbed like he was going to the top of the tallest mountain, and he was bringing everything he had to me.

Now the strangest thing was I seen all kinds of things to eat in my mind. I must have been still hungry after not finishing supper. I seen bright strawberries, and carrots and tomatoes. I seen Red Delicious apples and shelled peas and boiled taters. I seen new potatoes in butter and sweet milk. I seen ripe pears so big you couldn't hardly take a bite out of them. I seen grapes so ripe and tight they would bust on your tongue.

"It's going to be," Hank said. But I didn't know if he was talking about the baby or our love, or the wealth of love, which was more important than money.

Hank hollered out and climbed faster. And then it was like he busted out inside me. It felt time turned inside out on the hot tongue that flicked inside me. And I felt my bones melting and my legs melting in the color that roared through me. But it was not a red flame or an orange flame. It was a blue flame that started at the back of my head and burned down my spine to my belly and out to the tips of my toes, as the blue turned to purple.

When Hank rolled off me I was covered with sweat, and I was plumb wore out.

Seven

The day after I give away the jar of Mr. Pendergast's money and the day after Hank lost his job at the cotton mill, it was like we had to start out all over again. The only reason we had come to Gap Creek, as far as I could tell, was the job building the mill at Lyman. Gap Creek wasn't the kind of place you'd think of moving to unless you had a purpose or kinfolks there. And the fact that I had give away money that was not mine made me see how hard the world was, and how much I had to learn. And the fact that Hank had slapped me made me see how troubled our marriage and our lives was going to be.

I was stiff the next morning from the strain of our quarrel and from worry. But I felt cleaned out by the force of our loving, like I had been stretched, both in my body and in my mind, and that left me stiff and a little sore, the way you feel from working too hard and using new muscles.

Hank rose early but didn't make a fire in the kitchen stove. By the time I got up the kitchen was still cold, and I had to start a fire and put on a pot to make coffee. The grass in the backyard was thick with frost. Hank brought in a bucket of milk steaming in the cold air. "Set that on the porch," I said. "I'll strain it later."

I guess he was embarrassed about our quarrel, for he didn't even answer. He strained the milk through a piece of floursack and carried the pitcher out to the springhouse. I'd never seen him so quiet. I cooked grits and fried some eggs and pieces of shoulder meat. When we set down to eat I said, "Can't you get a job at another cotton mill?"

"Ain't another mill in walking distance," he said, "except Tigerville."

"Then get a job at Tigerville," I said.

"I've already tried," Hank said.

"We could move," I said.

"Move where?" Hank said.

"Move closer to another cotton mill," I said.

"That's for me to worry about, not you," he snapped. He put his coffee cup down and looked angry at me. I froze inside. I was just trying to be helpful and cheerful. I didn't say nothing else. I looked at my plate and eat my grits. I remembered what Ma Richards had said about Hank being spoiled, and about him quitting when things got hard. I saw that he got mean when he thought he wasn't in charge. He would get scared and mean if he thought he wasn't the boss. When he was angry it was better for me not to say nothing, even if I was mad too.

The wind had died down during the night and I listened to the fire pop and mutter in the stove as I put some jelly on a biscuit.

"They're building a store in Pumpkintown," Hank said. "But that's nearly ten miles away."

I didn't say a thing. I would just let him do the talking, if that made him feel better. I'd let him talk all he wanted to. It was having the last word that was so important to him. Since he was raised by

Ma Richards it made sense he would feel that way. He paused like he expected me to say something. I didn't.

"There are houses going up here and there," he said. "I could ask for work on one of those jobs."

I listened to wood settle in the stove, and a crow cawed somewhere on the ridge above the creek. A hen cackled in the chicken house.

"We could go back to North Carolina," I said.

"Where would we live?" Hank said. "There's no room on Painter Mountain, even if we wanted to live there. I don't think we can live with your mama and all your sisters."

"We could find another house up there," I said.

"And what would we use to pay the rent?" Hank said.

"Gap Creek is fine with me," I said. Because he was worried, Hank wanted to pick another fuss. It was something he was used to. When you're unhappy you find a way to get angry and make somebody else angry. But I wasn't going to fall into that habit.

"We might just stay here for a while," he said.

I got up and started gathering the dishes into the dishpan. I scraped the plates into the slop bucket and put the leftover biscuits and meat in the bread safe. "I'm not worried about staying here," I said.

"Nobody has asked us to leave," Hank said.

I THOUGHT HANK would probably go off looking for another job that day, but he didn't. Instead he took Mr. Pendergast's shotgun and a box of shells from Mr. Pendergast's bedroom and put on his mackinaw coat and cap. "I'm going to get us a wild turkey," he said. But he didn't look happy about going hunting. His jaw was set in a grim way and he looked like he just wanted an excuse to get out of the house.

"I ain't seen any wild turkeys," I said.

"The wild turkeys is up the holler," Hank said, "up the branch, way back toward Caesar's Head."

AFTER HE WAS gone I cleaned up the kitchen. And then I decided to have a look around the place. With no money coming in from wages, I had to know what we had to last the winter. I would be eating for both me and the baby, and I had to see what there was to get us through till the spring, assuming we was allowed to stay in the house till spring. I didn't have but thirty-six cents in my purse, and I didn't know how much Hank had in his pockets. But whatever it was, we would soon run out of cash. I was not going to ask Mama to help us, unless there was no other way, and I was not going to ask Ma Richards for anything. But if there was enough stuff on Mr. Pendergast's place, we might make it through the winter anyway, until the baby was born.

I lit a lamp and took it down to the cellar. I doubted that Mr. Pendergast had done much canning on his own. But his wife must have at one time. I had seen those jars down there before.

I held the lamp high over the jars and looked around the musty basement. There was old boards piled above the bank, and a dough board with mold on it. Mold growed white as baking soda on the beams. And then I seen the bin of taters. I had forgot the bin of taters. There was two bins actually, Irish taters and sweet taters. The spuds must have been dug in mud for they had dirt crusted on them. They was little taters, but there might have been two or three bushels of them. Only problem was some had already begun to get soft and wrinkled. The skin of the taters was puckered in places, like they had been dug a long time ago. I squeezed several and some was soft, but most wasn't rotten. I'd have to pick through the pile and get rid of the rotten ones.

The sweet taters looked cleaner, like they had been dug in dry dirt that crumbled off them. Sweet taters look more like roots than Irish taters; they look swelled up, like big blood vessels. Some was perfect as a football, but most was crooked and wrenched around. I picked through the sweet taters and found them hard and cold, like they had been dug that fall just before we moved to Gap Creek.

There was a few old buckets and rusty hoes in the cellar, but I couldn't find nothing else that could be eat. The basement looked like it had long been forgot, a place that was about to be buried under cobwebs and low sills and joists. I climbed back up the plank steps to daylight and blowed the lamp out. The fresh air tasted so good I breathed deep to get the cellar taste out of my mouth and nose.

Next I inspected the corncrib. It was a regular old-time crib made of two-inch slats with wire mesh nailed to the inside. It was the kind of crib with slanted sides, bigger at the top than at the bottom. There was moss and lichens growing on the slats, showing how old it was. The door was a crawl-through door, more than waist high. I pulled out the peg that held the door and looked inside.

A basket on the floor held some ears of shucked corn, and a bucket of shelled corn set beside it. It was the corn I used to feed the chickens. But most of the crib was filled up with a great heap of unshucked ears. I guess there was a wagon load of corn there, the shucks gray and weathered. Grains scattered on the floor had the hearts eat out by weevils, like beads that had been drilled through. I climbed in and took an ear and pulled the shuck back. Some of the grains had been hollowed out and some not. The corn must have been two or three years old, and some of it was not fit to use. But there was enough good corn to make some meal, five or six bushels anyway.

There was strings of dried peppers hung on the back porch. But I wondered if there was anything else on the place to eat. Wasn't anything in the woodshed but wood. I knowed what was in the spring-house. That left the old smokehouse where we had put the ham and shoulders and middles on the day of the hog killing. There was some jugs on the bottom shelves of the smokehouse I wanted to look at. I opened the door of the little building and let the sunlight fall on the floor where the ashes from hickory fires was heaped. The salted meat laid on the shelves, and the place smelled like salt and uncooked lard. The smell of salt made you think of cooked meat.

The jugs on the lower shelves was heavy earthenware. I lifted one up and took it out into the sunlight. It was the kind of jug you think of as holding moonshine. I pulled the wooden stopper out and sniffed. It was the smell of sorghum, rich, maybe overcooked sorghum. I tilted the jug and a tongue of molasses licked out slow through the mouth. I dipped a finger in the dark syrup and brought it to my mouth. It was sorghum all right, with a golden redness inside. No blackstrap syrup, or cane syrup, but sorghum with its special smell. It was a little overcooked and thick, almost rubbery in the cold air. But the molasses could be warmed up, and they had the right flavor. There was four jugs of them. That would last through the winter, with syrup for biscuits and cornbread, as well as sweetening for cakes and gingerbread. There was molasses to be put on cornmeal mush in the morning, and on oatmeal.

The only place I hadn't been to was the barn loft. I knowed what was in the feed room on the ground floor, the barrels of crushing and dairy feed and cottonseed meal, the bag of shorts for the hog, the laying mash and oyster shells for the chickens, sweetfeed for the horse. The steps to the loft was outside the feed room, and as I climbed the steps I seen two dusty china eggs on the shelf by the harness. Old horse collars and plowlines, hames and trace chains, singletrees and doubletrees hung on nails. Mice scurried around the sacks and coils of rope as I climbed.

The barn loft was a great room open to the rafters. The roof was held up by poles, and there was heaps of sweet, moldy hay in the center, near the hatch where forkfuls could be throwed down to the ground. Mice trickled along the eaves, as daylight sparkled through cracks. There was a pile of shucks in the corner, and grains of corn was scattered on the floor where ears must have been piled at one time.

I looked to the side of the hay pile and seen something with a wick, like the tip of a giant candle. Stepping closer I seen it was the stem of a winter squash. There was maybe ten squashes there, acorn squash and winter squash. They was hard and cold. And then I seen the pumpkins. They wasn't big pumpkins like you make jack-o'-lanterns from. They was sugar pie pumpkins, not much bigger than the squash. I counted seven of them.

Standing beside the hay pile I smelled something sweeter than the hay. It was just a whiff, a trace. I looked around but couldn't name the scent, except I was sure it wasn't just the smell of old seasoned hay. I searched in the gloom and found the perfume come out of the straw. It was the scent of apples. I poked around in the edge of the hay pile until I touched something hard. There was round, hard things under the straw. I pulled the hay aside and seen the apples. They was spotted gold and orange apples. They was what Mama called "horse apples" except a little bigger than horse apples. They had been gathered from the tree at the side of the barn. Mr. Pendergast must have gathered them and hid them in the hay. The apples was sticky with natural wax on their skin, and they had hay dust stuck to them. But they was firm, fresh fruit. Must have been a peck or two of them, buried in the hay waiting to be made into pies in January or February, as long as they stayed cold. I picked up an apple and wiped it on my sleeve and bit it. The flesh was yellow, sweet and coppery, an old-timey taste. The firm flesh turned to juice as it was crushed.

While I was eating the apple, I looked around the loft and seen a string of what looked like tinsel hung from the post on the left.

Looking closer, I found they was beans, dried beans still in the pod and threaded together to stay dry. There was yards and yards of beans. They looked like bunch beans and cornfield beans that had been dried. They had dust on them, but they could be washed and boiled to make soup, to make soup beans.

But the strangest thing I seen in the barn loft was this old basket, a split hickory basket, made like a saddle, with high ends and bulges on either side. It was the kind of basket you don't hardly see anymore. Inside was all these little paper bags closed with clothespins. There must have been twenty of them. The bags looked wrinkled and reused many times. I was going to open a bag when I saw there was writing on the side of it. Somebody had wrote in pencil "Blue Lakes" on the brown paper. I opened the bag and found it was white bean seeds. Other bags said "Half-Runners" and "Barnes Mountain Beans," "Big John Beans," "Seay Beans," "Brown Speckled Beans," "Long White Greasy Beans," "Edwards Beans," "Goose Beans," "Greasy Cut-Short Beans," "Johnson County Beans," "Lazy Wife Beans," "Logan Giant," "Nickel Beans," and "Ora's Speckled Beans."

It was a basket of old bean seed, sorted and labeled. Mr. Pendergast's wife must have left them there. They was all ready to be planted. If I stayed till spring I would put them in the ground.

WHEN I CLIMBED down from the barn loft I tried to think what else I might look for that could be eat. There was the cow and the horse and the dozen chickens. But there was no guineas and no sheep on the place. Maybe Mr. Pendergast had buried some cabbages. It would mean a lot to have fresh cabbages to eat in the winter. And if I had enough heads I could make sauerkraut.

After the wind of the night before, the sky looked like it had been scrubbed and polished. The air was clean and everything sparkled. The creek shimmered where you could see it between willows, and the yellow leaves still on the hickories flashed across the pasture.

I always loved the late fall. The cool air was thrilling and the purple leaves on the oaks and gum trees was a feast for the eyes. Here and there on the other side of the pasture a sumac bush or sassafras was bright red, like a touch of lipstick. But the woods was yellow and gold more than anything else. The woods looked painted, like a rainbow had crashed onto the mountain and spilled its colors down the valley. Since we had moved to Gap Creek, and since Mr. Pendergast was burned in the fire, I had been too busy to get out and look over the place. I had been to the hogpen, and to the springhouse, and to the toilet, but I had not walked out to the end of the pasture. I had been too much in the daze of being married, and moving to a strange place, to look around Mr. Pendergast's property. And I hadn't felt much like poking around for the fun of it.

Where somebody has buried cabbage, all you see is the roots sticking out of the ground like pigtails. Cabbages are buried upside down. I looked in the stubble along the edge of the garden, and in the edge of the orchard beyond the hogpen. There was loose dirt and weedstalks where the taters had been dug up, but I didn't see cabbage roots. I searched along the pasture fence beyond the smokehouse and didn't see no buried heads there either.

At the milkgap I climbed up on the bars and jumped down on the other side. The grass in the pasture had been cropped short by the cow and horse, but indigo bushes growed here and there. For some reason stock won't eat indigo, as long as there's anything else to graze on. There was cowpiles scattered over the pasture like big brown buttons. The barbed wire fence looked old and needed patching. In places rails had been nailed between poles where the wire had rusted and broke. The fence leaned this way and that way and staggered along the edge of the woods.

The pasture was bounded by the branch on one side, and in places the stream had washed out posts so they hung on the wires above the water. It was a wonder the cow hadn't got out by going under the wire. Leaves had washed down the branch and piled up in the pools in wads and wedges.

"*Eeeeeerrrrrr,*" something whistled in the sky above. I looked up and seen a hawk floating up there. I didn't know what it was watching, maybe a field mouse, or a squirrel. There was no baby chicks for it to catch that I was aware of. I walked along the fence to where the pasture started up the side of the mountain. I guess bottom land along the creek was too valuable to use for pasture on Gap Creek, for only a few acres of pasture was near the creek flats. Where the pasture was steep, some of the ground was cleared and some under trees. I had not been out in the woods since I got married and come down to South Carolina. It felt good to be in the open, and to smell the old leaves in ditches and in the branch.

I turned to look at the valley. Gap Creek was just a narrow, twisty cove that wound for a few miles between the ridges. There was a rock cliff high on the opposite ridge that looked like a wrinkled face frowning at the fields below. "Fussy Face," I named it, speaking out loud. Old Fussy Face, that like a statue kept watch on the seasons passing and the people on the road below. The rock looked down like a silent idol on the passing seasons. It made me feel something I couldn't name. Gap Creek valley was so narrow, so pinched between the flanks of the ridges, it looked like a toy valley, a model of a cove in the mountains. The tops of the ridges had been stripped bare by the wind, but the lower slopes and the holler itself still had color.

I turned around and climbed a little more, and seen this white thing through the trees. It looked like a face, or a piece of snow. I stopped and tried to think what it might be. Was it somebody watching me? Was it a piece of white cloth? The thing was about waist high, best I could figure. I started walking, for I guessed whatever it was couldn't hurt me.

As I got closer something run away from the white spot. I seen a flash of white disappear and knowed it was a deer that went bounding off to jump the fence and disappear into the woods. Still closer I saw what appeared to be a white skull on a stob, except it was too square to be a skull and the eye holes was wrong. I thought it was a piece of ice. And then I saw it was a salt lick. Mr. Pendergast had put a block of salt on a stick for his cow to lick, and the deer had come out of the woods to lick it too.

"Mr. Pendergast is gone but his salt is still shining up here," I said, not sure what I meant. I turned and looked toward the trees and seen a deer watching me from the shadows. It was waiting to come back and lick the salt, waiting for me to get out of its way. I thought how everything craved salt.

Mama had told me that during the Confederate War when you couldn't buy nothing at the store, and there wasn't any money, salt was the scarcest thing of all. Salt was ten dollars a pound, then fifty dollars a pound. It got to where you couldn't buy it for any price. Where there was a salt spring back in the mountains, people went there to boil the water down to catch the salt. They fought over water there and at least one got shot. People got so hungry for salt they dug up the dirt of their smokehouse floors and boiled it to get the salt drippings out.

I LEFT THE salt block so the deer could come back to lick and savor it. I wanted to climb higher so I could see more of the valley. I wanted to get out in the woods by myself the way I used to on the mountain. I wanted to stretch my lungs and my legs, and to get up high on the ridge. I wanted to get away from the house and not think about Hank for a while. I wanted to forget how unhappy he was, and how I had give the money to Jerrold James.

Just as I got to the edge of the woods a gust of wind hit the hickory trees and gold leaves floated out across the valley like flocks of birds. Leaves swirled and fluttered. The air was filled and the sky was filled as trees all over the side of the mountain give up their leaves to the gust. Red leaves and yellow leaves and orange leaves shivered in the air. Wind raked across the mountain and combed through the trees, and it looked like the whole mountain was breathing out leaves.

I run through the leaves like they was butterflies whirling around me. I slapped at the flying leaves like they was colorful snowflakes. I would be too heavy to run and climb in the woods before long. So I might as well run while I was thrilled by the wind and had a chance. I climbed over the fence and run through the hickories and under the maples and poplars. The air was alive with leaves bright as goldfish. I slapped at a floating leaf and turned and run up the ridge.

The ground was deep in fresh-fell leaves, and leaves sparkled like they was waxed and oiled. I kicked up a cloud of leaves. I kicked up a fog of new-fell leaves. I kicked away the leaves in front of me like deep fresh snow. Leaves swarmed around my head, clicking as they touched. I waved my arms and swatted them away. I danced with the leaves and made them swirl faster. I laughed out loud and laughed at the top of my voice. I caught leaves in my apron and pitched them away.

When I got out of breath I was almost at the top of the mountain. The wind was colder there. I skipped and stumbled through poplars to the very top. Just under the summit, where a kind of bed was protected from the wind, I laid down on my back in the clean, fresh leaves. I wanted to rest in a spot out of the breeze. I laid back with my arms spread out in the leaves the way you do to make angels in snow. I'd never heard of "leaf angels" but I guess you could make them.

The trees was thinner at the ridge top and their limbs had already been stripped of leaves. I looked right up through the lightning shapes of limbs to the blue sky. There was a few leaves flying by up there, and I saw a bird, and then I seen a flock of geese going by in a point, like the head of an arrow. But after the geese went by I saw nothing but blue sky. Through the gray lightning of the limbs I looked right into the deep sky.

Now it was the strangest thing to look deeper and deeper into the blue. Most times you look into the sky and just see haze and blue. Unless there is clouds and you look past the clouds. But this time I looked into the clear sky and saw the *depth* in the sky. I looked past the clear air into the further miles of air, and still deeper where the air was thinning out to nothing. I looked until I could see nothing but emptiness, out toward the stars, though I couldn't see the stars in daylight.

I looked so deep and long I felt I was falling. I was following my sight right out and through the limbs and into the empty air. Instead of looking up, I felt I was hanging from the ground and looking down, further and further down, miles and years down, mile after empty mile. I was falling far down into the nothing. I was whooshing down deeper and deeper into the emptiness. And the thought of falling forever and forever froze me. I stiffened myself like I was flying faster and faster. I felt like I was going to explode.

I closed my eyes and the feel of falling stopped. I felt the fresh leaves on my back and opened my eyes and seen the trees around me. A daddy longlegs prickled on the leaves nearby. It had already throwed its perfume, as they do when they're scared, and I smelled the musky odor.

Standing up I looked at things close by: a fallen sourwood, a little holly tree. It felt so good to have my feet on the ground again, I stomped into the leaves going down the ridge. I stepped firm to grip the ground. I stomped hard to make dints in the soft ground under the leaves, digging my heels into the steep side of the mountain, making steps. I didn't want to go back down the way I had come up and tended to the left, to come out of the woods further down the valley. I had never been in the woods below the Pendergast place. I wanted to see a little more of Gap Creek before I returned to the house.

As my balance come back I took bigger steps down the mountain. I swung around trees and fairly jumped between trees. I skipped, and one time slid in the leaves right on my behind. But it felt good, almost like skidding on a board or a sled. I scooted down in the leaves and then stood up and run, pretending I couldn't stop myself, and slapped at sourwoods and young hickories. I run until the ground leveled out and I was standing almost on the valley floor.

THAT EVENING I was thinking about fixing supper, about making some cornbread and baking taters, and opening a can of beans from the basement, when I seen Hank coming into the back yard carrying a big old bird. I thought at first it must be a goose, but it was too big even to be a goose.

"Fix this turkey," he said and throwed it down on the back porch. "I'm tired. I had to walk all the way to Caesar's Head."

"I walked to the top of the ridge," I said.

"What for?" Hank said, taking off his mackinaw coat.

"I was looking for chestnuts," I said. I didn't want to say I went walking just to see the woods, to be outdoors in the fall weather. That wouldn't have sounded right.

"Did you find any?" Hank said.

"A few," I said. I didn't want Hank to think I went gallivanting around the woods just to be footloose. After all, I was carrying a baby. I didn't want to tell him I had gone dancing around in the woods with the flying leaves, and that I laid on the mountaintop looking into the sky till it felt like I was falling out toward the stars. The best way I could show him how helpful I was was to keep my mouth shut and fix the turkey.

I BOILED A pot of water on the stove and carried it out on the back porch. A turkey is harder to dip than a hen, because it's bigger and longer, and the feathers are so long and stiff they don't even want to fit in the pot. I held the turkey by the neck and by the feet and doused it into the smoking water. The water was so hot the steam near about burned me. I plunged the bird in and let it soak. Then when I pulled it out, the water streaming from the feathers smoked in the cold evening air. The drops almost scalded me as I pulled out the big tail feathers and wing feathers. Even the back feathers of a turkey are stiff and long.

I pulled out handfuls of feathers and throwed them in the yard, thinking I'd clean them up later. But the wind swept them across the yard and into the weeds. I plucked until my hands was covered with little feathers and pin feathers and down stuck to my wrists. I plucked the carcass until the skin looked bumpy and hairy. And then I lit a piece of newspaper and singed away the rest of the pin feathers and down. Nothing looks as naked as a plucked and singed bird.

After that I had to wash my hands and dry them on my apron. Taking the sharpest knife in the kitchen, I rubbed it some more on the whetrock on the back porch and then took the bird out to the chopping block and cut off the head and feet. The blood had darkened and thickened, but a good bit still poured out the neck. Now the messy part of dressing a bird is when you have to slice open the belly and take the guts out. There's a stink when you scald the feathers and pluck them, but it's not as sickening as the smell of guts. The smell that come out of the belly was worse than the stink of chicken piles and the chicken house. The bird was cold but the smell was hot as something burning.

This is what I have to do for Hank, and for myself, I thought. It made me mad to have to pull out the squishy cold guts and rake them into the weeds beyond the chopping block. Dogs would come in the night and eat them up. But I had to make Hank feel good about hisself, to make him feel strong and in charge of things. If he wanted to go off into the mountains to kill a turkey and bring it back for me to fix, then that was the least I could do.

I cleaned out the turkey inside and washed it with dippers of water. I thought about cutting it up the way you do a chicken, but the body was too big to fry. I didn't have a pan that would hold it. I would have to bake it in the oven. That would take about four hours, and we would have to eat late. But the turkey would be a feast. Maybe it would cheer up Hank and make him forget he had lost his job. Maybe it would make him happy he had moved to Gap Creek. Maybe he would forget I had give away the jar of money to the man in the buggy. I tried to think about what I had to stuff into the turkey. My supply of herbs and spices was meager. But I did have some biscuits left over from breakfast, and some sage and pepper. I crumbled the biscuits and sliced some taters into them, and sprinkled four or five herbs into the mixture. I stirred it up and added a little vinegar before stuffing it inside the turkey. Then I slid it all into the oven.

"It'll take at least four hours," I said to Hank as he lifted the milk bucket off its nail.

"There's a thousand turkeys up there," he said.

"Up where?"

"In the holler below Caesar's Head," he said.

"In the gap where Gap Creek comes from?" I said.

"No no no, in the gap to the west," Hank said. "There is turkeys in the trees and in the bushes. They was eating chestnuts on top of the ridge. There is enough turkeys to last all winter."

"Then we won't starve," I said. But the second it come out I was sorry I'd said it.

"Do you think I'm gonna let you starve?" Hank said.

I was about to answer that I hadn't meant it that way, but he had already slammed the door and was gone.

WITH HANK NOT making any wages, and with winter on its way and Christmas on its way, I begun to think of some means of getting a little cash. I never cared a thing about money, except when I needed something, or to buy presents. I wanted to send something to Mama, and to my sisters up on the mountain. And I figured Hank would want to buy something for Ma Richards, if not for his brothers. We wouldn't likely have a chance to go up to Painter Mountain or to Mount Olivet, but we could mail some presents if we had them. And I wanted to buy a present for Hank too. I could always make him something, but I wanted to order something from the Sears and Roebuck catalog.

I didn't have any money of my own. I looked in my purse and found I still had only thirty-six cents. That wouldn't even buy a present for Mama, much less Lou and Rosie and Carolyn. I counted the money and put it back in my purse. There must be something on the place I could sell. The chickens belonged to Mr. Pendergast, but I had fed and watered them and gathered the eggs. Maybe I could sell a few eggs down at the store at the crossroads for twenty cents a dozen. And if I made some extra butter I might sell it for fifteen cents a pound. But the cow wasn't giving much milk now, and the milk she did give didn't have a lot of butter in it. I wouldn't be able to make more than a few pennies out of butter before Christmas.

Could I make any money out of gathering chestnuts? There was plenty of chestnuts on the ridges above Gap Creek. But I'd have to take them to Greenville to sell. It wouldn't be right to sell Mr. Pendergast's taters, or anything else of his on the place. I wished I was better at sewing. I wished I had practiced with my needle the way Rosie and even Lou had, while I was out sawing wood or hoeing corn. I wished I could do fancy embroidery or quilting. I wished I had a sewing machine. I didn't even have any cloth to make new clothes for Hank and me.

TWO DAYS LATER there was a banging at the front door. Who could be knocking so loud on the front porch? Hank had gone off I didn't know where, and I didn't know when he would be back. The curtains was closed in the front room so I couldn't even see out the window. Before I could get to the front door it opened, and somebody said, "Anybody home?"

"I'm home," I said. I said it stiff, for I didn't know who was coming in.

It was a woman that entered the front room, followed by a man wearing a black hat.

"Howdy do," I said.

"I can't bear it," the woman said and buried her face in a handkerchief. I couldn't see too well with the light behind her, but I didn't think I knew her, or the man either.

"You all come on in," I said. It was the only thing to say.

"Just give me a minute to get hold of myself," the woman said.

"I'm Julie Richards," I said and held out my hand.

"I'm Caroline Glascock," the woman said, "and this is my husband Baylus." She sobbed and put the handkerchief to her nose.

"Is anything wrong?" I said.

"I'll be all right in a minute," the woman said.

"You all pull up a chair by the fire," I said. I throwed another log on the fire. It had got chilly in the room as the fire died down.

"Thank you, darling," she said and wiped her eyes.

I set down with them before the fire and the man held out his hands to the flames. I knowed I had to be neighborly, the way Mama would be. "It's cold out there today," I said.

"Cold weather makes this place even sadder," she said.

"Cold weather is good for hog killing," I said.

"Honey, you don't know who I am," the woman said. "I'm Mr. Pendergast's daughter, stepdaughter."

"I was awful sorry when he died," I said.

"I didn't even know until this week," she said, and cried again. Her husband didn't say anything.

"Hank and me have took care of the house," I said.

"Tell me how it happened," Caroline Glascock said. She looked at the pictures on the mantel and shook her head and dabbed at her eyes.

"We was rendering lard when the kitchen caught fire," I said.

"And he died in the fire?" she said. "How awful."

"He died later that night," I said. I didn't want to tell her no more than I had to.

"After he got burned?" the woman said.

"He did get burned," I said, "on his face and head and hands. It was terrible."

"Pappy and me didn't always gee-haw," Caroline said. "But it broke my heart to hear how he died."

"I stayed up with him the night he died," I said. "We did what we could for him."

"How long have you lived here?" she said, wiping her eyes.

"We just moved here this fall," I said, "from up in North Carolina."

"How long did Pappy suffer before he died?" she said.

"Like I said, he died the night after he got burned," I said. "We went after a doctor, but it didn't do no good." I felt bad to have to tell her about that night, but there was nothing else to do. I looked at the man. He set in front of the fire turning his black hat in his hands. He was listening, but didn't say nothing.

Caroline stood up and lifted a picture from the mantel. "Wasn't Mama a pretty woman when she was young?" she said.

"She was beautiful," I said. Caroline was a big woman. I guess she weighed about two hundred pounds and was forty, maybe forty-five.

"Did he tell you who this place belongs to?" Caroline said.

"No, he never did," I said.

"It belongs to me," she said.

"What about your brother?" I said. "The one that lives out in California?"

"Mr. Pendergast, Pappy, meant to leave the place to me. I bet there's a will somewhere in this house that proves it."

"I ain't found a will," I said.

"Don't matter," she said. "Nobody's thinking of property at a time like this."

"Could I get you all some coffee?" I said.

"It upsets me so much to come back here," Caroline said, "I don't think I could drink anything."

"I'm awful sorry about what happened," I said.

"What started the fire?" Caroline said. I looked at her and then I looked away. I felt a wave of sickness inside like I was going to throw up.

"I had helped Mr. Pendergast kill his hog," I said. "And we was rendering the lard."

"You helped butcher the hog?" Caroline said.

"Wasn't nobody else to do it," I said. "Mr. Pendergast couldn't lift much."

"Word is he burned hisself trying to save the house," Caroline said. "Pappy ever was a fool when he got scared."

"He got burned in the kitchen when the kerosene exploded," I said.

"But the house didn't burn down," she said.

"I got some wet sacks and put the fire out," I said.

"Bless you, honey," Caroline said. "We owe you."

There was a pause and the fire popped and whined, like it was coming a rain or even snow. I didn't want to talk any more about the fire. I knowed it would just make her sadder. I wondered if she was going to tell us we had to move out of the house.

"I think Pappy Pendergast had a lot of money hid away," she said.

"Where did he hide it?" I said. I couldn't bring myself to admit I had give the jar of money away. I wasn't going to tell her that.

"I reckon he hid it in different places," Caroline said. "Sometimes he had it in a shoebox in the closet, and some money he had buried in a tobacco can in the backyard. I've knowed him to keep his money in a old leather shot pouch that hung in the attic."

"I never seen any of those," I said.

"And sometimes he kept it in a fruit jar," she said.

"What kind of jar?" I said.

"Why a mason jar, honey, a half-gallon mason jar, like you buy corn liquor in," she said.

"There is mason jars in the basement," I said. "Would you all like to search the house?"

"Honey, it don't matter," Caroline Glascock said.

"I ain't searched the attic," I said. "But I've cleaned the rest of the rooms and washed all of Mr. Pendergast's clothes."

"Bless your heart," Caroline said.

"We have tried to take care of all Mr. Pendergast's things," I said.

"Pappy was a squirreler," Caroline said. "He would squirrel away just about anything. He could have left his money out in the smokehouse or the woodshed. He could have put it in the springhouse, or under the crushing in the barn."

I felt a flash of pain in my belly, like a cramp was coming on. I wished they wasn't there so I could make some herb tea and rest. I felt like there was some big change in my life about to happen. I wished Hank would come and talk to them about paying the rent on the house. "Mr. Pendergast was here by hisself for a long time," I said.

"I know he was and I feel bad about it," Caroline said. "Baylus works in Columbia and that's where we have to live. It's too far to come up here more than about once or twice a year. We come when we could."

"How long does it take?" I said.

"It's not just the train ride to Greenville. It's finding a way to get from Greenville to Gap Creek that is the trouble. You have to hire a carriage or a buggy or some such. It's an all-day operation."

"So you growed up here on Gap Creek?" I said.

"Only for a while," Caroline said. "But I have such happy memories of this house." Her voice broke and she cried again.

I hoped I didn't have to throw up while they was there. I didn't want to have to turn my back on them and run away and puke. I was embarrassed enough as it was. I felt sorry for her, and I was scared she would find out I had give away the money.

"How much rent are you all paying?" Caroline said and blowed her nose.

"I don't know," I said.

"You don't know?" she said.

"Because I kept the house and cooked for Mr. Pendergast," I said.

"You mean you was the housekeeper?"

"Hank, my husband, made an arrangement with Mr. Pendergast for us to live here," I said. I had never knowed exactly what the arrangement was.

There was a wrenching in my belly and I felt something push like a fist right up in my throat. The sour taste reached the back of my mouth before I could stop it. I stood up and put my hand over my mouth and started running toward the kitchen.

"Are you all right, honey?" Caroline Glascock called after me.

As I run into the dark kitchen I tried to think what I could throw up in. There was the slop bucket behind the stove, but it would take too long to find it and get it out in the open. There was the dishpan, but if I used that I'd have to wash it out. The kitchen still smelled like the baked turkey, and that made me even sicker. I run out the back door and down the porch steps. At the corner of the porch I bent over and retched so hard it felt like my tailbone was coming up through my belly. I heaved like I was trying to get rid of everything I had ever eat. I heaved like I was trying to turn myself inside out.

When I quit heaving I was so weak I had to hold on to the post of the porch. I was wet with sweat and felt like I had just been born.

"Are you all right?" Caroline Glascock said. She had come out on the back porch and her husband Baylus stood in the doorway behind her.

"I must have eat something," I said.

"You must have been poisoned," Caroline said.

I was so stiff and weak I had to walk slow to the steps and up the steps. I was sore inside, like every muscle in my belly had been strained. I hobbled up the steps one at a time.

"You be careful, girl," Caroline said.

They followed me back to the living room where I stood by the fireplace trying to catch my breath. I felt clean and steady, but weak.

"How much do you want to charge for rent?" I said.

"We'd rather sell the place than rent it," Caroline said. "We already have a house in Columbia."

"I don't reckon we can afford to buy a house yet," I said.

"Leasing is better than renting," Caroline said.

"I don't think we've got much money," I said.

"We need to find somebody to buy the house," Caroline said. "Much as I hate to sell Pappy's place, I know it has to be done."

Hank come in the front door. He looked cold, like he had walked a long way, cold and tired. I was so relieved he had come back I could have cried. "This is Caroline Glascock," I said to him, "and her husband Baylus. She's Mr. Pendergast's stepdaughter."

"Pleased to meet you," Caroline said.

"How do," Hank said and took off his mackinaw coat. He stretched out his hands to the fire.

"Mr. and Mrs. Glascock say we might be able to rent the house," I said. It seemed polite to mention both of them, though Caroline had done all the talking.

"We'd like to sell the place," Caroline said. "Baylus and me don't have any use for it."

"What are you asking?" Hank said.

"We want to be reasonable," Caroline said. "We just want to get a decent price for the place, don't we, Baylus?"

Her husband nodded and didn't say anything.

"I ain't got a lot of money," Hank said.

"This place will pay for itself in a short time," Caroline said. "Pappy raised a ton of hogs and sold the hams down in Greenville. He raised everything here, corn and sorghum and cotton."

"Ain't seen no sign of cotton," Hank said.

"It's been a while since he raised cotton," Caroline said. "He got too old and feeble to raise cotton after Mama died."

"I thought this was above the cotton line," Hank said. "I thought they never did grow cotton north of Traveler's Rest."

Caroline looked at Hank and wiped her eyes. "Pappy knowed how to do it," she said. "It would grow here on the valley floor, protected by the mountains." The fire popped and I heard a wagon rattle by outside. My sides was sore from all the throwing up, and there was a sour taste at the back of my mouth. I needed a drink of cold water to freshen my mouth and clean my throat. But my belly felt cool inside, almost cold. I was glad it was settling.

"Mr. Pendergast let us stay here cause Julie kept house for him and cooked his meals," Hank said.

"We need to sell the place," Caroline said, "much as we'd like for you all to stay on."

"But you might rent the house to us?" I said.

"We'd prefer to sell," Caroline said. "And we could use the money. Just last summer I had an operation we're still paying for."

"How do I know you all are who you say you are?" Hank said.

"Who else could we be?" Caroline said. She opened her purse and took out a card. Hank looked at the card and then handed it to me. "Mr. & Mrs. Baylus Glascock" it said on the card, and give an address in Columbia.

"I just wanted to be sure," Hank said.

"I don't blame you, the way people are these days," Caroline said.

"How much would you rent it for?" Hank said.

"We could only rent it till we found a buyer," Caroline said.

"If we could afford to we'd like to stay here," Hank said, "at least till the baby's born."

"I thought you might be going to have a baby," Caroline said and smiled at me. "When is it due?"

"Around May or June," I said.

"We need to sell," Caroline said, "but you all look like decent people." She looked around at her husband and back at me. "Maybe you could stay here till after the baby is born."

"How much rent would you charge?" Hank said. "I ain't got a lot of money."

"Did you say you are a carpenter?" Caroline said.

"I do carpentry and masonry," Hank said.

"Maybe in the spring we could hire you to fix up the place," Caroline said, "to get it ready to sell."

"I can do any kind of work," Hank said.

"How much could you pay now?" Caroline said. "We want to be reasonable."

"I ain't got but five dollars to my name," Hank said. He reached into his pocket and took out five silver dollars. I reckon that's all he had left from working at the mill in Lyman. The coins sparkled in the firelight as he held them in his outstretched palm.

"Ain't you got something you could pawn?" Caroline said.

"All I've got is my tools," Hank said. "And I have to keep them if I go back to work this winter."

"I've got a necklace and a brooch Mama give me," I said.

"I couldn't take your brooch," Caroline said.

"It's got gold around the edges," I said, "like a little picture frame."

I got the brooch and necklace from the bedroom and showed them to her. "They're worth about five dollars," she said. She held on to the jewelry. I tried to think of something else that could be sold. Mama had give me an alarm clock, but it was only worth a dollar or two, even when it was new.

"Tell you what we'll do," Caroline said. "Give us the five dollars and the necklace and brooch as a kind of down payment, and we'll give you a receipt. Then the rest you can work out by fixing up this house. That should be good enough, don't you think, Baylus?"

"That is mighty understanding of you," Hank said.

"It's hard to sell a house in the wintertime anyway," Caroline said.

"We're obliged to you," I said.

"You all helped take care of Pappy," Caroline said. "I'd like to know a young couple was getting some good out of this place. Besides, it needs some fixing up."

"We'll take good care of it," Hank said.

"We'll come back in March to talk about the repairs," Caroline said, "and to buy what materials you need."

I couldn't believe what was happening, that we was renting the place and would have somewhere to live until after the baby was born.

"Don't you all want to stay the night?" I said. "It's getting late and there's plenty of room."

"Honey, we've got to get back on the road," Caroline said. "We've got to go back to Greenville to catch the train to Columbia. Baylus has to work tomorrow."

"You can at least stay for supper," I said. "We have plenty of turkey left."

"That's sweet of you," Caroline said. "But we really do have to be on our way. And this place makes me sad. I have too many memories here." She opened her bag and looked inside, and then closed it. "I will mail you a receipt for the five dollars and the jewelry," she said.

"You don't have to do that," I said.

"Business is business," Caroline said. "I believe in doing things right and proper."

I was so thrilled my head was buzzing.

"You all should stay the night," Hank said.

"We're much obliged for your invitation," Caroline said. "But there are a few things in the house we should take. They belonged to Mama and they have sentimental value."

"You take whatever you want," Hank said. It had been a while since I had seen him so cheerful.

"I'll just get a few of Mama's things," Caroline said. She took the clock off the mantel and handed it to her husband. Then she went into the kitchen and gathered a lot of silver from the drawer into her big handbag. There was a little silver cream pitcher on the table and she took that too.

"Is there anything you can't find?" I said. I could understand why she would want her Mama's things.

Caroline took a lamp into the front bedroom and looked through all the drawers of the bureau. She got some jewelry and a comb and brush set. Baylus come back in and carried another load out to the carriage. There was a mirror on the bedroom wall and Caroline took it down. She got Mr. Pendergast's rifle out of the closet, and a revolver she found in a drawer. She looked in the attic but didn't find anything she wanted to take.

"You all come back and see us," Hank said as they climbed into the carriage.

"We'd love to come back to the mountains in the summertime," Caroline said. "We'll come back and have a picnic by the creek."

"You all come back any time," I said.

"We'll see you along about March," she said as Baylus drove them away. "And I'll send you a receipt for the rent."

Eight

But there wasn't ever any receipt come from Columbia for the rent on the house. We waited every day and Hank walked to the little post office down at the crossroads. I got a letter from Mama, and Hank got a letter from Ma Richards. But nothing ever come from Caroline Glascock or her husband Baylus. As the days passed and Christmas got closer, I wondered if they had been who they said they was. After two weeks I figured they wasn't.

It was hard enough to lose the five dollars and my brooch and necklace, and all the things they had took from Mr. Pendergast's house. Christmas was coming and we didn't have no money at all, and no way of getting any. But that wasn't as bad as what it done to Hank. He could blame me for giving away the jar of Mr. Pendergast's money, and I had to take the blame. It made Hank feel better that he could blame me and call me a stupid heifer. But now it was him that had been outfoxed. There was no way he could deny that he had give the money and the jewelry and all the things from the house away. And he had been just as pleased as I was at the thought of renting the place with such a little payment, and fixing up the house in the spring. His feelings was hurt because he took such pride in his judgment of people. Hank never liked to admit he had made a mistake. Men are like that. They care more about their pride than anything else. It made him mad that I knowed he had been suckered just as bad as me. It made him angry at me more than at the Glascocks or whoever they was.

I seen how he felt and tried to soothe him. "It was me that was fooled by them first," I said. I wanted to make it sound like I was taking part of the blame.

"You should have seen them for what they was," Hank said.

"I know I should have," I said.

"Any fool could have seen through them," Hank said.

"I should have knowed better when Caroline didn't remember what Mr. Pendergast kept his money in," I said. If I let Hank criticize me it would make him feel better and then he wouldn't be so mad at hisself. Nobody likes to be criticized, and I hated to be criticized, but I seen it was easier to let him blame me than to live with a man who was enraged at hisself. And once he got over his anger I hoped he would be fair to me again. When Hank pouted like a little boy the best thing was to treat him like a little boy.

"You should have threatened to call the law," Hank said.

"Except I didn't know any law to call," I said.

"They'll never be caught," Hank said. He was feeling so bad he talked in a low voice, almost a mutter.

"If we tell the sheriff what they took, they might be caught selling the clock or silverware, the cream pitcher. That would prove we didn't take them."

"I ain't going to the sheriff," Hank said.

"What if we get accused of selling off Mr. Pendergast's things?" I said.

"Nobody knows what was in this house," Hank said.

"It would be better if we made a list of what they took," I said.

"That way if the real heirs turn up, we'll have something to show them."

"Are you telling me what to do?" Hank shouted. He looked at me hard, like I had insulted him.

"I'm just saying it might pay us to make a record of what happened, and let the sheriff know," I said.

"I'll decide when it's time to tell the sheriff," Hank said.

"I know you will," I said.

"What does that mean?" Hank said.

"That you will tell the sheriff when you want to," I said.

Hank was ready to answer like I was arguing with him. But there was nothing to argue with in what I had said. He opened his mouth and then turned away. He picked up the sugar bowl and throwed it at the stove, and sugar scattered all over the stove and floor like snow.

"It don't matter," I said. But he didn't answer. He was already out the back door, and I didn't see him again till after dark.

MOST TIMES WE stayed away from the store, because we didn't have any money to trade there. A store is a sociable place in a valley like Gap Creek. But after losing our money to Caroline Glascock we didn't feel like seeing anybody. And women don't hang around a store that much anyway, not the way men do. Some men seem to slouch around the store every day, setting by the stove in winter spitting tobacco juice in a bucket and playing checkers, or setting on the bench out front in the summer. They keep up on the gossip, I reckon, though most of the time you don't hear them say much. It's one thing for a woman to go to the store when she has money to spend. But I didn't have money, and I stayed away from the store at the crossroads.

But along in December we run completely out of coffee, and

then we got so low on sugar I done without it in everything but the rare cake for Sunday dinner. Now you can live without coffee, though it don't hardly feel like living when you get up in the morning and have nothing to go with your grits but water. And you can use honey or molasses if you have them, instead of sugar. But nobody would do without either if they had any choice.

I tried to think of something to trade at the store for coffee and sugar. We didn't gather enough eggs to have one a day for ourselves, so it would take weeks to save up two or three dozen, even if we didn't use none. I didn't have enough butter to sell.

But sometimes the Lord puts a thought in your mind at the right time. I recalled that people had said Mr. Pendergast had been a digger of ginseng roots. Several had mentioned that to me, and I had seen a little sang hoe on the back porch. But I hadn't seen any roots around the place. He must have been too feeble lately to climb up on the ridge looking for ginseng, which was usually found far back on the ridges. Then it occurred to me I had seen some roots hanging from a rafter in the attic when I climbed up to the loft to get the single bed for Ma Richards. I had noticed the roots up there and then forgot all about them.

I dropped what I was doing and run right up the stairs and climbed the ladder to the attic. I'd not been up there since we first come to Gap Creek. There was light from the two windows in the loft, and I was struck by the powerful smell of smoke and old wood. I hadn't stopped to bring a lamp, so I had to let my eyes get used to the dim light. There was chairs and old trunks, dirty fruit jars, coils of rope and rusty steel traps. Some leaves of bleached-out tobacco hung from nails in a rafter, with hammocks of spiderwebs between them. It was warm by the chimney.

And then I seen the roots, hanging on a piece of twine not far from the chimney. Mr. Pendergast must have hung them there and then forgot them. There must have been thirty roots, all covered with cobwebs. Some looked like dried sweet taters and some like shriveled figures of people, and some like the private parts of a man. I felt one and found it dry and scaly. Was it too dried up to sell? I untied the roots from the string and gathered them in my apron. If there was a pound of them they could be worth two or three dollars, maybe more. But I didn't think they amounted to a pound, they was so dry and brittle. Holding the closed apron in my left hand I climbed back down the ladder.

Hank had gone out in the woods looking for another turkey, I reckon. He had been feeling so bad lately I didn't want to ask him too many questions. And I didn't want to wait for him to come back to take the ginseng to Poole's store. I got a paper bag to carry the roots in and put on my coat. It was a sunny day, and the road was a little muddy from thaw.

The crossroads was only a mile and a half away. When I reached the store I seen George Poole setting by the stove playing checkers with a man named Slim Rankin. And Pug Little was watching them play. I had met them before at Mr. Pendergast's funeral. George looked surprised to see me, because I almost never come to the store. "Hey, Miss Julie," he said. He always called me Miss Julie, never just Julie.

"Howdy," I said and nodded to him and Slim and Pug.

"To what do we owe the honor of your visit?" George said. He turned his eyes back to the checkerboard.

"I have brought some roots," I said, and placed the bag on the counter.

"What kind of roots?" George said.

"Sang roots," I said.

George made a move on the checkerboard. "It's mighty late in the season to be digging sang roots," he said.

"These was dug last year," I said, "and have been drying ever since."

All the men looked at me, for they must have guessed the roots was Mr. Pendergast's. George stood up and walked around to the other side of the counter. He emptied the poke I had brought on the counter. The roots looked littler than they had in the attic.

"You ain't been digging sang roots, have you?" Slim Rankin said.

"I didn't know Hank was a sang digger," Pug Little said and grinned at Slim.

"Mr. Pendergast left them in the attic," I said.

"Pendergast wasn't able to go digging for the past year," Slim said.

"I don't know when they was dug," I said. All the cans on the shelves behind George looked like roosting birds staring at me. The store smelled of harness leather and coffee and wood smoke.

"These is awful dry," George said. He took a pan off his balance scale and heaped the roots in the pan. Then he placed the pan on one side of the scale and added little weights to the other side.

"Preacher Gibbs used to dig ginseng," Slim said.

"Everybody used to dig sang," Pug said, "back when there was still some to dig."

"There ain't but three quarters of a pound here," George said.

"Is that all?" I said.

"And these is so dry and old I don't know if the man in Greenville will take them," George said.

"He just sells it to the Chinese, and the Chinese will buy any kind of ginseng," Slim said.

"Being dry don't hurt sang," Pug said.

"The price is down for roots anyway," George said. I figured George was going to tell me he couldn't buy the roots, that I had wasted my time taking them down there. I wondered if he thought the roots wasn't mine to sell.

"Whatever you give me I'll later give to Mr. Pendergast's heirs," I said. "When they can be found." I was glad nobody knowed about us giving the things to Caroline Glascock.

George worked with a pencil on a sheet of brown wrapping paper on the counter. "At two dollars and seventy-five cents a pound I can pay you two dollars and six cents," he said.

"You mean you'll pay me two dollars?" I said.

"And six cents," George said.

"Make sure he gives you the six cents," Slim said.

"You have to watch old George," Pug said.

I had not seen that much money since Hank give his five dollars to Caroline Glascock or whoever the woman was.

"Honey, I wish it could be more," George said. I guess he seen the astonishment on my face.

"George is a terrible skinflint," Slim said.

"I would hate to see George try to go through the eye of a needle into heaven," Pug said.

I decided not to ask any more questions. I wanted to take my coffee and sugar and get out of there. I wanted to tell Hank about our good fortune. Maybe it would cheer him up. "Can I get five pounds of sugar and five pounds of coffee beans?" I said.

"If you can carry that much," George said. He scooped out the beans and sugar into paper bags and tied them with string. I took a bag on either arm like twin babies.

"You have twenty-seven cents left over," George said. I put the bags back on the counter and took the coins.

"Thank you, George," I said.

"I almost forgot: you have a letter," George said. He stepped over to the pigeonholes that was the post office at the far end of the counter and brought back an envelope with pencil writing on the front. I put the letter in my pocket because I didn't want to read it in front of George and Slim and Pug.

As I walked up the road with the bags in the crooks of my arms and the envelope in my pocket, I kept thinking of the letter. From the handwriting I could tell it was from Mama. Was she writing to say that somebody was sick, or a relative had died? Was she asking how I felt? Was she coming down for a visit?

There was a big white pine by the road about halfway back to Mr. Pendergast's house. When I got to the big tree I told myself I needed a rest. I was breathing for two and didn't want to hurry. And I couldn't wait no longer to see what was in the letter. I climbed the bank and set down in the needles under the tall tree.

The letter was wrote on two sheets of lined tablet paper in Mama's neat hand. "I hope you are well, we are well. I hope everything is allrite with the baby," Mama wrote. "There is no news here accept that Lou and Garland is getting married and they are coming down to Gap Creek for a visit afterward."

I turned over the page and read the back, as the breeze fluttered the papers in my hand. "And Carolyn is coming with them," Mama said. "Carolyn is going to stay a few days with you and Hank while Lou and Garland goes on to Greenville."

My hands was shaking with the news. It would be so wonderful to see Lou. Except I hated for her and Garland to see how poor we was. I turned to the last page to see when they was supposed to arrive.

"They will come down to Gap Creek next Wednesday," Mama said. I tried to recall what day of the week it was. It was already Wednesday, because it had been four days since Hank went hunting for turkeys on Saturday. They was coming today. They might already be there. I stuffed the letter in my coat pocket and gathered up the two paper bags. I hoped they hadn't arrived at the house while I was away and seen my dirty dishes, and the bedroom where nothing had been picked up.

   . . .

YOU KNOW HOW it is when you're trying to hurry. You stretch your legs but your feet stick to the ground. The road ahead grows longer and longer. I hurried toward the house, and finally when I come around the bend I seen Daddy's old wagon parked in the yard with Sally still hitched between the shafts. Lou and Garland and Carolyn was already there. They had seen my dirty house. I slowed down and caught my breath. My belly felt uneasy, and I stopped to rest a little before climbing the steps. There was voices in the living room. Hank's gun was leaning by the front door, but I didn't see no sign of a turkey.

"Well look what the cat drug in," Lou said as I come through the door.

"And look what washed down off the mountain," I said. Lou shrieked and run to me for a hug. I hadn't seen her in nearly three months.

"Don't want to press you too hard," she said and patted my belly. It felt so good to see Lou.

"You're looking mighty pert," I said, and set the paper bags on the sofa.

"I said to Garland when he asked me to get hitched," Lou said, "I said, I'll marry you if you'll take me down to Greenville so we can stop and see Julie and Hank on the way."

Garland stood by the fireplace and tipped his hat to me. "Take off your coats and stay awhile," I said. I wondered why Lou had decided to take Garland back. I figured she would tell me when we was alone.

"And welcome, Carolyn," I said.

Carolyn was talking to Hank in the doorway to the kitchen and I patted her on the shoulder.

"Mama sent you some things," Carolyn said and pointed to a box on a chair. There was a ham wrapped up in brown paper and several jars of jelly and jam.

"Why don't we all set down," I said. "And I'll take these things to the kitchen."

"We'll help you out," Lou said, and picked up the bags from the couch.

"I can do it," I said.

"You ought to be careful," Lou said. "Grab that box," she said to Carolyn.

"Expecting a baby is not a sickness," I said.

"Didn't say it was," Lou said.

"I was going to clean this house up," I said, "but I had to go to the store."

"We can help you," Lou said. "Can't we, Carolyn."

"Hank said he would show me the barn and the springhouse," Carolyn said.

"You can do that later," Lou said, sounding just like Mama. I had forgot how much Lou's voice was like Mama's.

"I wish Mama could have come," I said.

"Mama won't never leave the place anymore, except to go to church," Lou said. "I think she's got arthritis in her back, because she walks stooped over."

"I wish I could see her," I said.

Carolyn walked around the kitchen looking into pots and boxes and inspecting cans and bottles on the shelves. She opened the sugar canister and seen it was empty. "Where is your sugar?" she said.

"I got some today at the store," I said. "And some fresh coffee beans."

"You don't need to fix anything special for us," Lou said.

"It's your honeymoon," I said.

"Yeah," Lou said and hugged me again. I'd never seen her so happy.

"I want to go to Florida when I have a honeymoon," Carolyn said.

"You will, darling, you will," I said. Carolyn had never had to work like the rest of us, and she was the most romantic of all us sisters.

"I sure don't want to go to Greenville on my honeymoon, or Gap Creek," Carolyn said.

Lou and me looked at each other and grinned.

"Honey, whoever you marry will have some say about where you go," Lou said.

"I want to marry somebody that likes to travel," Carolyn said.

"Well, I hope you do," I said.

Carolyn drifted back into the living room, and Hank took her and Garland out to the barn to unhitch Sally and look around at the outbuildings. Lou and me lit in to clean up the kitchen and get some supper started. I poured the coffee and sugar into their cans and ground some fresh coffee beans.

"Fresh coffee always reminds me of Rosie," I said.

"Don't nobody love coffee like Rosie," Lou said.

"She likes her coffee and baking better than she'll ever like any man," I said.

"She may be right about that," Lou said and laughed. I looked at her and broke out laughing myself. It was like old times, when we talked about boys and made light of boys, and girls that was in love with boys. Now we was both married, but it was fun to be like our old selves.

"If boys is so bad why did we both get married?" I said.

"'Cause it's the bad in boys we like," Lou said, and we laughed again.

I swept the kitchen and Lou got a bucket and the mop and mopped the kitchen and living room floor. Then we attacked the bedroom and picked up everything and made the bed in Mr. Pendergast's room. Hank and me would sleep there while Lou and Garland was visiting.

When we finished downstairs we climbed up to the bedroom Hank and me had been using. "Only problem with this bed is it falls apart when it gets shook," I said.

"Well, thanks," Lou said.

"That's what happened to us our first night here," I said. "But the next day I fixed it."

Lou looked at the bed and patted the post. I expected her to make some smart remark. But of course she didn't. She was a woman on her honeymoon. I told her the story of the bed crashing down on our first night while we dusted the room and put on fresh sheets and pillow cases.

"You think old man Pendergast left it that way on purpose?" Lou said.

"The bed was ready to collapse," I said.

"What a dirty old man," Lou said.

"You should have seen the figures he liked to carve with his pocketknife," I said.

I was waiting for Lou to tell me why she had decided to marry Garland after all. I knowed she wanted to tell me. Out the window I could see Hank pointing out to Garland and Carolyn the boundaries of the pasture where it run up the mountainside. At a distance Carolyn looked like a full-grown woman. Her figure had filled out since I had left home in early fall. She took Hank's arm as they walked around the barn. Carolyn was laughing at something Hank or Garland had said.

"Was you surprised to hear I was marrying?" Lou said.

"I was, a little," I said.

"You know I always loved Garland," Lou said.

"I know you did," I said. I was going to let her tell me in her own good time. I was not going to hurry her with questions.

"I finally decided that it didn't matter about that girl over at Pleasant Hill," Lou said.

"Really?" I said, and plumped a pillow with a fresh case on it.

"He said he had give her up," Lou said. "He said she never meant anything to him."

"Didn't she have a baby?" I said.

"She had a baby, but Garland said it didn't belong to him," Lou said. I thought there must be a grin on her face, but there wasn't. When Lou talked about Garland she always got serious.

"I just want you to be happy," I said.

"I don't think Mama was too happy I got married," Lou said.

"Mama always worries," I said.

"Older women don't believe in romance," Lou said.

"Mama is just afraid for you," I said.

IT WAS THE first time Lou and me had ever cooked together. We had sawed wood together and we had hoed corn together and pulled fodder. But it was always Mama or Rosie that was busy in the kitchen at home. It felt good to have Lou in my kitchen.

"Now you just set down while I fix supper," Lou said.

"I will not," I said.

"You've been on your feet long enough," Lou said.

"How would you know?" I said and we both busted out laughing.

I was so glad I had bought the sugar and coffee, for my cupboard was bare, and there was only what was left of the canned stuff in the basement. But there was the ham Mama had sent, and that would give us a feast for two or three days. I put the ham in a pan and basted it with brown sugar and molasses. It was just like Mama to send a ham. I bet she had sent the best piece of meat left in the smokehouse.

"You could put a little mustard or vinegar in that sauce," Lou said.

"I want this ham to be all sweet," I said. After sliding the ham in the oven I got more wood from the back porch for the stove. Garland and Hank and Carolyn was standing out by the bee-gums, watching something above the trees. I shaded my eyes and seen a wedge of geese going over. They sounded like a pack of beagles running after a rabbit. The geese was high enough to go right over the ridge. They was flying south, and by dark they would be far out of the mountains.

"Who has done the work at home since I left?" I said.

"Most of the outside work has fell to me," Lou said.

"I figured that would happen," I said.

"We sure have missed you, Julie," Lou said.

"Missed my wood chopping and hog killing," I said.

"Missed your complaining," Lou said, and we both laughed.

"Who is going to do the work now we're both gone?" I said.

"Mama and Rosie will have to take turns," Lou said. "And Carolyn is going to have to learn to do her share."

"Why did Mama want Carolyn to come with you?" I said as I mixed batter for cornbread.

"It was not so much Mama wanting her to come as Carolyn begging to come," Lou said.

"She wants to see new places," I said.

"That girl is so spoiled I could smack her sometimes," Lou said.

"We have all spoiled her," I said, "after Masenier died."

"I wouldn't have minded some spoiling myself," Lou said.

"Maybe it won't hurt her," I said. "She just turned fourteen."

"What does a fourteen-year-old girl know?" Lou said.

"About as much as a seventeen-year-old girl," I said. We both laughed. I opened a can of green beans into a pan and placed them on the stove. I wished I had got some sweet taters to bake, but I hadn't.

"Was you scared when you got married?" Lou said. "I mean on your wedding night."

"I guess everybody's a little scared at first," I said. But I couldn't look at her as I said it. Lou and me had talked about marriage before I was married, but in a general way. I was embarrassed to talk, now that I was married and going to have a baby. I would not have thought I would feel that way, like I would be violating a confidence.

"I'm a little scared of being hurt," Lou said.

"No need to be afraid of being hurt," I said. I still couldn't look at her. Lou was older than me, and here she was asking me questions. "At least in that way," I added.

"What way?" she said. I looked at her and we both laughed.

"If you get hurt it will be your feelings that are hurt," I said. I started setting the table and Lou got the silverware from the drawer and begun to lay it in place. I was glad I had polished what was left of Mr. Pendergast's silver a few days before.

"I just hope I can make Garland happy," Lou said.

"You will," I said.

"I would hate to think he will be disappointed," Lou said.

"You have married him," I said. "That should make him happy."

"You know what I mean," Lou said.

"I know he's mighty lucky to have you," I said. "After the way he's acted."

"That has all been forgive," Lou said. "I told him I would forget."

"He's a lucky man," I said.

The coffee was boiling and I set it off to the side of the stove. The smell of coffee and the baking ham filled the kitchen. It reminded me of Mama's kitchen.

"I wish Rosie was here to bake one of her coconut cakes," I said. I had only two eggs, and I certainly didn't have a coconut.

"Rosie sent you a cake," Lou said. "I forgot all about it."

"Where is it?" I said. I looked in the box where the ham had been. There was only jars of jam and jelly.

"It must still be in the wagon," Lou said. She run out the back door and around the house and come back in with a box tied up with string. I untied the string and looked inside. It was a beautiful coconut cake, the kind that Rosie always made. But the bouncing of the wagon had made the top layer shift and slide over.

"Dear lord!" Lou said when she saw it. "Rosie would be mortified."

"Rosie will never know," I said. With a pie server I lifted the edge of the top layer and scooted it back on the cake. The icing was broke and flakes of coconut had fell off in the box. I took a knife and smoothed the icing around the sides like a mason would a joint of mortar and then sprinkled the spilled coconut over the repaired seam.

"That'll be as good as new," I said.

Carolyn come to the back door and looked in the kitchen. "Where is the milk bucket?" she said.

"Right here on the counter," I said.

"Hank is going to teach me to milk," Carolyn said.

"Don't you ruin your Sunday frock," Lou said. Carolyn was wearing one of her pink dresses with lace and ribbons on it. And her shoes looked new.

"Don't treat me like a baby," Carolyn said.

"Don't you act like a baby," Lou said.

"We just don't want you to get your dress dirty," I said.

Carolyn did not slam the door as she went out, but she banged the bucket on the door post loud enough so you knowed it wasn't no accident. It was her way of showing her resentment.

"That girl has some growing up to do," Lou said.

"She'll grow up," I said. "She better."

"But grow up to what?" Lou said. And we both laughed again. I felt a little light-headed with all the smell of coffee and ham and bread baking, and all the talk with Lou. I wasn't used to much conversation with another woman, and I hadn't seen any of my family since I got married.

"YOU KNOW, I never could see Mama and Papa together," Lou said.

"What do you mean?" I said.

"You know what I mean," Lou said, "as man and woman."

"What else could they be?" I said. But I was just pretending not to understand her. I knowed what she was saying. It was something I had thought about before. I could not imagine Mama and Papa together in bed. It just seemed impossible. It was silly to think that, since they had all us girls. But I just couldn't think about them in bed naked and loving.

"If they wasn't together as man and woman, how do you explain us?" I said with a giggle. That got us to laughing again.

Before we set down at the table for supper, I got some candles I'd found in the bedroom closet and put them right at the center of the table. The candles give the kitchen a glow warm as a ripe peach.

"How romantic," Carolyn said when we was all seated.

"It's a romantic occasion," I said, and looked at Lou and Garland. Their eyes was bright in the candlelight and Garland took Lou's hand. "Nothing is more romantic than the day you're married," I said.

We all held hands around the table while Hank said the blessing. "Lord, give Lou and Garland a long and happy life together," Hank prayed. "And bless their union with children. And give them work worthy of their talents, and give them the bounty of your love."

"Amen," we all said.

"When I get married I want to ride on the train somewhere far away," Carolyn said. Carolyn read novels and magazines when she could get them, and the way she talked showed the things she had been reading. "Maybe to the Rocky Mountains, or even to California," she said.

"I'm sure you will, honey," Lou said, "if you're lucky." Lou looked at Garland and they smiled at each other.

Hank sliced the ham with our sharpest butcher knife and passed the plate of slices around. Everything looked gold and mellow in the candlelight.

"We're celebrating Julie and Hank's baby also," Lou said.

"I don't want no baby," Carolyn said, "till I'm at least forty years old."

"Forty is too old to have a baby," Lou said.

"It is *not*," Carolyn said. "Is it, Hank?"

"There are women that have babies at forty, and even forty-five," Hank said.

"But it's more risky," I said, "the older you are." I felt so warm and at ease to have some of my folks around me, to have Lou with me. Hank had been feeling too low to be good company for the past few weeks.

"It's not romantic to have babies when you're young," Carolyn said.

"How would you know?" Lou said.

"Ain't that right?" Carolyn said to Garland. All eyes turned to Garland, and in the candlelight his face went red. I felt my own face get hot. I don't know if Carolyn intended to speak to Garland because his girlfriend at Pleasant Hill had had a baby or not. Maybe what she said just slipped out. Everybody looked away from Garland to pretend there was no special meaning to Carolyn's words. I got up to pour the coffee and cut everybody a slice of Rosie's cake.

"Where are you all planning to live?" I said to Garland when I set down again.

"We're going to rent Cyrus Willard's old house," Lou said. Garland wasn't much of a talker and I could see that Lou was going to answer for him most of the time.

"That's a mighty pretty place out on the ridge," Hank said.

"You can see Mount Pisgah from Cyrus's place," I said.

"I've heard there's snakes in that old house," Carolyn said. She helped herself to a second piece of cake.

"Where did you hear such talk?" Lou said.

"I heard it from Wilma Willard," Carolyn said. "I heard that when her grandpa was old and sick and living there by hisself a snake fell through a crack in the ceiling onto his bed and he had to lay still all night till it crawled away."

"You never heard such a tale from Wilma," I said. "Papa used to tell that tale about one of the Edneys a long time ago."

"Wilma swore it was the truth," Carolyn said.

"A snake could get into any house," Hank said. "Snakes like to crawl up into attics where it's warm. I've heard of people finding fifty rattlesnakes in an attic in October or November."

"I'm glad we got off on a romantic subject," Lou said. "You all are as bad as Papa to tell snake stories at bedtime."

"Speaking of bedtime," I said. "I know you all has had a long trip today. And you'll have an even longer trip tomorrow. Whenever you want to go to bed, the room is ready upstairs." I didn't want Lou and Garland to feel embarrassed when they went off to bed.

"It's too early to go to bed," Carolyn said.

"When does Mama make you go to bed?" I said to Carolyn.

"She has to go to bed by nine," Lou said.

"That was last year, when I was little," Carolyn said.

"That was last week, when you was little," Lou said.

"You can sleep in the room with the single bed upstairs," I said to Carolyn. I got up and started clearing the table.

"I'm going to help you wash the dishes," Lou said.

"No you're not," I said. "You're going on to bed, and Carolyn is going to help me clean up."

"I can help with the dishes," Hank said.

"If them is my orders I might as well go on to bed," Lou said.

"Them is your orders," I said.

"Come on, Garland," Lou said. "Julie wants to get us out of her way."

"I reckon we might as well," Garland said.

"Let's have a short prayer," Hank said. We stood there in the kitchen and held hands in a circle while Hank prayed. "We are thankful for the fellowship of our family, and our family in Christ," he said. "We are thankful for the promise of salvation and for the watchful eye over our lives. We are thankful for your love and for human love. Guide us as we go ahead in our lives, and help us to accept the gift of life and your blessings." It was good to see Hank in a better mood.

"Good night," I said and hugged Lou, and then hugged Garland.

"Good night," Lou said as they started toward the stairs, holding hands.

"Let's you and me start cleaning up," I said to Carolyn as soon as they was gone.

"Can't we wait till morning?" Carolyn said.

"You should always clean up a kitchen before going to bed," I said.

"I can help," Hank said.

"We will all help," I said. I gathered up the knives and forks and spoons and plates and cups and made as much noise as I could scraping the plates into the slop bucket and putting leftovers in the bread safe. I made even more noise going out for water to boil in the kettle.

When the water was boiling, we formed a line. I plunged the dirty bowls and dishes into the pan of hot soapy water and scrubbed them with a rag. Then I passed a suds-covered plate to Hank, who rinsed it by pouring water from the dipper over it into the second dishpan. Hank handed the dripping plate to Carolyn, who rubbed it with a towel and set it on the counter. As she waited for a plate to be handed to her, Carolyn stood with one hand on her hip, like she was bored. I ground the spoons and knives and forks on the bottom of the dishpan, making them rumble and rattle.

"I don't see why we have to do everything right now," Carolyn said.

"Everything will be clean and fresh in the morning," Hank said and glanced up at the ceiling. Then he looked at me and grinned. It had been weeks since I had seen him grin.

"It's hard to sleep knowing you have a kitchen full of dirty dishes," I said.

"That wouldn't keep me from sleeping," Carolyn said.

"It's hard to rest if you ain't done your work," I said.

"When I get married I'm going to have a servant to wash dishes," Carolyn said.

"In that case you won't need to worry," I said and giggled.

We washed every single cup and saucer, bowl and fork and spoon. I took a wet rag and wiped the table and counter. "Would you sweep the floor?" I said to Carolyn.

"You can sweep the floor and I will mop," Hank said.

"I never heard of mopping the floor in the middle of the night," Carolyn said.

"You will sleep better, knowing the floor's clean," I said. I took a damp cloth and wiped off the shelves in the kitchen.

"You never used to work in the kitchen at home," Carolyn said.

"Didn't need to," I said. "Rosie and Mama done it all."

When we was done and the kitchen was sparkling, there was nothing to do but go into the living room. There was still a fire in the fireplace and Hank throwed on some more sticks.

"What we need now is popcorn," I said.

"Too bad there's no popcorn in the house," Hank said. The wind had rose and rattled in the eaves and at the windows.

"Mama sent a bunch of popcorn," Carolyn said.

"She did?" I said. "Where is it?"

"In a jar, in the box," Carolyn said.

I run to look in the box in the kitchen and sure enough, one of the jars I figured was jam or preserves was filled with popcorn. "Mama thinks of everything," I said.

I got a pan and salt shaker from the kitchen, and a lid for the pan. After I poured corn in the pan, Hank held it over the fire. For a long time the pan was quiet. As he shook the pan you could hear the seeds rattle around inside.

"Maybe the popcorn is too old," Carolyn said.

"Takes a while to heat up," Hank said. Suddenly there was a plunk in the pan.

"We'll get at least one kernel to eat," Hank said. There was a ping on the lid, and then another. Then two more little explosions, and a pause. And suddenly it sounded like a string of firecrackers going off in the pan, chattering on and on.

"Glory be," I said.

"I'm too full to eat popcorn," Carolyn said.

AFTER LOU AND Garland left the next morning in the wagon for Greenville, I asked Carolyn what she wanted to do while she stayed with us. I was determined to treat her not only as my little sister but as a guest. She was growing up, and it was time to treat her like she was growing up. Because I had usually worked outside at home, and because I had always thought she was spoiled, I'd never made friends with Carolyn the way I was friends with Lou and Rosie. It was time to become friends with her, if I was ever going to, while she was visiting us, and while she was still young.

"What would you like to do for the next week?" I said.

"I don't know," she said. "What is there to do on Gap Creek?"

"We could start a quilt," I said. "There's an old frame upstairs."

"I don't like to sew," Carolyn said. "Every time I use a needle I prick my finger."

"You could wear a thimble," I said.

"Too boring," Carolyn said. She was at the age to belittle everything somebody else suggested or praised. I could remember being that way myself, though not as bad as Carolyn. It's a way of showing people that you have your own mind, that you will not be pushed around, or too easy to please. I was going to act like a mother and not be put off by Carolyn's contrariness. It would be good practice.

"We can go down to the store," I said.

"Would we have to walk?" Carolyn said.

"It's not even two miles," I said.

"I need to rest up from the awful trip down here," Carolyn said. "I'm sore all over from being banged around in that old wagon."

"The Pooles have a mighty handsome grandson," I said.

"Who are the Pooles?" Carolyn said.

"They run the store at the crossroads," I said. "Their grandson is named Charles, I think. And there is other boys in the community too."

"I bet they all have pimples on their faces," Carolyn said.

"I've only seen them once or twice," I said.

"I'll bet they're just mountain hoojers," Carolyn said.

"All boys act like mountain hoojers when they're young," I said and laughed. Carolyn laughed a little. It was good to see her laugh. It was the talk about boys that had cheered her up.

"We can walk down to the store one day and buy a candy bar or some soda pop," I said, remembering the twenty-seven cents I still had from selling the ginseng.

"Do they sell magazines at the store?" Carolyn said.

"They sell a few," I said, "but they cost ten or fifteen cents."

"Mama give me fifty cents," Carolyn said. "I want some magazines that has pictures of new dresses in them."

"I have a Sears and Roebuck catalog," I said. "That has lots of pictures of new dresses."

"The catalog just has old, ugly stuff," Carolyn said. "I want to see some really new things."

"Fifty cents won't buy you a dress," I said. But I wished I hadn't said it, just when Carolyn was showing interest in something.

"I know what we can do today," I said, with all the cheer I could muster.

"What?" Carolyn said, like she knowed already it would be something boring.

"We can go up on the mountain and look for chestnuts."

"It's too late for chestnuts," Carolyn said.

"These are chestnuts that got lost in the leaves," I said. "We can bring them back and roast them by the fire."

"I don't like chestnuts," Carolyn said.

Just then Hank come in from the barn. I guess he had been out to feed the horse and turn it loose in the pasture. He stepped to the fire to warm his hands. I think Hank felt a little awkward with two women in the house. I was afraid his moods would return. "It's a pretty day," he said.

"Too bad it's cold," I said.

"Going to warm up by this evening," Hank said.

"Maybe it's a good day to look for buried chestnuts," I said.

"I found some on the ridge above the pasture yesterday," Hank said.

"We could find all that the squirrels have missed," I said.

"Let's go up there and gather some chestnuts," Hank said and clapped his hands. He patted Carolyn on the shoulders with both hands. "We'll have a good old time," he said.

"Let's go," Carolyn said with a big smile, like it was what she had been waiting to be asked to do.

"I'll have to get my boots on," I said.

"I'll have to get my scarf," Carolyn said.

It was a bright sunny day, but the wind coming across the ridge had a razor in it, like it had crossed ice and snow not too long before. There is something exciting about winter wind. Clouds flew by overhead with their bottoms flattened, a sign of strong winds. And cloud shadows raced over the valley. The bare trees on the mountain sparkled.

As we crossed the pasture Hank took my left hand in his right, and Carolyn's right hand in his left, and we walked along swinging our arms like we was playing the game Red Rover. I had not seen Hank feeling so carefree in a long time. It was seeing people from home that had cheered him up. I reckon talking to Lou and Garland had took his mind off his own worries.

As we got to the upper edge of the pasture we almost run, past the salt block on its post, past the sweet gum trees, to the fence. When we stopped to crawl over the fence I was almost out of breath.

"You shouldn't be running," Hank said to me.

"I can run as well as I ever could," I said.

"I'm afraid you're not in any condition to climb either," Hank said.

"Who says?" I said and laughed.

"You've got to be careful," Hank said and patted my stomach.

"I'm just fine," I said.

But as we started climbing on the dry crackly leaves I found myself out of breath more than I expected. My chest felt tight and sore. It was like I couldn't take in as much air as I needed. I stopped and put my hands on my knees. I should not have run across the pasture.

"You don't have to climb up here," Hank said.

"You don't have to hurry so," I said.

Hank and Carolyn stood about ten feet ahead of me up the mountain. I didn't feel like I wanted to climb another step. I felt like setting down in the leaves.

"Maybe you should go back to the house," Hank said. "We can bring you some chestnuts."

"I want to help you find them," I said.

"Where is the chestnuts?" Carolyn said.

"Up where the chestnut tress are, and all down the ridge below," Hank said.

"We'll bring you some," Carolyn said.

"We'll bring you a poke full to roast by the fireplace," Hank said.

"If you want to go on without me, fine," I said.

"I just don't want you to overdo yourself," Hank said.

"We'll bring you a bag full," Carolyn said.

Without another word I turned and started down the mountain. I kicked the dry leaves and didn't look back. But by the time I reached the pasture fence I told myself it was silly to get mad. Hank was just worried about me because I was out of breath. And Carolyn was just a silly girl trying to get the attention of any man around. She was my little sister, and my guest. I was supposed to look after her, not get mad at her.

WHEN HANK AND Carolyn come back from the mountain it was late afternoon. They was laughing and their faces was flushed from being out in the wind. They had a bag full of chestnuts, which Hank put down on the kitchen table. "Carolyn didn't find a one of these," he said and laughed.

"How could I find them?" Carolyn said. "You always run ahead and grabbed them first." She shoved his shoulder.

"I think Carolyn needs glasses," Hank said.

"I didn't know what to look for," Carolyn said.

"I think you need some granny glasses," Hank said. He was teasing Carolyn, like he was fourteen hisself. I'd never seen him so lighthearted.

"I'm glad you all had such a good time," I said.

"It was terrible," Carolyn said. "Hank walked too fast and found all the chestnuts before I could get to them."

"They're mighty sweet chestnuts," Hank said. "Ain't you going to try one?"

"My stomach don't feel too good," I said.

"I was afraid you overdone yourself climbing the ridge," Hank said.

"It has nothing to do with climbing the ridge," I said. "I've been working ever since getting back to the house."

"You ought to set down," Carolyn said.

"I'll set down when I feel like it," I said.

"We picked the chestnuts for you," Carolyn said, "to bake by the fireplace."

"Maybe I'll feel like eating them later," I said.

I knowed I shouldn't let Carolyn irritate me so much. She was only fourteen, and Hank and me was supposed to make her feel at home. She was at the age to be crazy about every man she seen, specially one as handsome as Hank. But she was spoiled, and already a flirt in her ribbons and pink dresses. That's what got to me, I told myself. She never had done no work. She thought her purpose in life was to have a good time. She was so young she thought other people was there to serve her.

I was used to being alone with Hank. I wasn't used to other women paying attention to him. Maybe I was a little spoiled myself. A man will pay attention to any woman that flirts with him. A man won't understand how a woman knows how to play up to him. Any girl can get a man's attention just by looking him in the eye.

I told myself that Hank had had a hard time that fall and deserved to be cheered up. Carolyn's visit seemed to make him feel good again. He seemed to have got over his terrible blues. I should be grateful to Carolyn instead of resentful, I told myself. And I should give her a good example of how to behave.

"Go down to the cellar and see if you can find any taters that are still good," I said to Carolyn.

"It's dark down there," Carolyn said.

"You can take a lamp," I said.

"I'm afraid of the dark," Carolyn said and giggled. "What if there is a booger down there?"

"You'll scare it away," I said.

"In the dark I can feel wet fingers touching me," Carolyn said.

"Don't be silly," I said.

"I'll go look for some taters," Hank said. He took the pan from the counter and headed toward the door.

"I'll go with you," Carolyn called.

"Takes a lot of hands to get a few taters," I said.

"LET'S BURN OFF the creek bank," Hank said two days later.

"Oh goody," Carolyn said.

"Why do you want to burn off the bank now?" I said.

"To get rid of the stubble and brush," Hank said. "Everybody down here burns off their creek banks."

"Why can't you wait till spring?" I said.

"If we do it now the ashes will soak into the ground," Hank said. "Ashes make the best fertilizer if they mix with the dirt."

"Can I set fire to the brush?" Carolyn said. "I love to set fires."

"You don't want to get dirty in the smoke and dust," I said. Carolyn had on another one of her pink dresses with lace around the neck and sleeves.

"I won't get dirty," Carolyn said. "All I want to do is watch."

Hank took the box of matches from the shelf beside the stove, and got his hat from the nail by the door. "What we need is a hoe and a rake," he said.

I followed him out to the back porch. There was a light breeze coming down the valley, but it was a perfectly clear winter day. The sun was bright on my face.

"I hope the wind don't get any stronger," I said.

"Wait for me," Carolyn called, and run out wearing her pink shawl.

"There's just enough wind to take the smoke away," Hank said.

"Can I light the fire?" Carolyn said again.

"Don't get that dress dirty," I said.

"You sound like Mama," Carolyn said.

"Here, carry this hoe," I said to her.

I seen I was going to have to go along to see she didn't ruin the dress. I was responsible for Carolyn for two more days, and Mama and my other sisters would never forgive me if I let anything go wrong. I got my jacket and grabbed another hoe off the back porch.

"You better be careful," Hank said to me.

"Don't worry about me," I said.

"What if you was to fall?" he said.

"Then I'd pick myself up again," I said.

"You don't need to come," Carolyn said. "I can help Hank."

"Somebody has to look after you both," I said.

MR. PENDERGAST'S FIELD run right along the bank of the creek. The field was full of stubble of cornstalks and bean vines and big briars and weeds. And the bank of the creek was even worse. There was stalks big as saplings of ragweeds and hogweeds, goldenrods and Joe Pye weeds, ironweed and pokeweed. It must have been a jungle the summer before, full of snakes and spiders, hornet nests and sting worms. Mr. Pendergast had not touched it with a mowing blade. The stalks was higher than my head. They must have been higher still when they was green.

"You want to set the fire upwind," I said, "and dig a fire break downwind."

"There's hardly any wind," Hank said.

"But one could spring up," I said.

I had helped Papa burn off the field by the branch and seen how the wind can change before you know it, once a brush fire is going.

Hank give the box of matches to Carolyn and she struck one and held it to the leaves of a dry rabbit tobacco stalk. I didn't see any flame at first, but smoke lifted from the gray curled leaves. That's the way it is with a grass fire. You see smoke, but hardly any flames. The weed stalk smoked more and more and a little rag of flame jumped to the next stalk. There was a pop and crackle, and another stalk caught fire.

"Just look at that," Carolyn said, proud of herself. She stood holding her shawl in each arm, watching the tiny fire she had set fling from stalk to stalk, spreading itself from weed to dry weed. The fire spread out like a wave flung slowly through the stubble, tossing smoke on the breeze down valley. It was quite a sight, the sparkling water in the creek, the glitter of the silver weeds, and the fire chewing the brush and stalks into smoke that jumped away.

As I watched the fire turn the stubble into ash and clear the ground to soot, I seen why people liked to burn off their fields so much. It was a purifying thing, a sweeping away of the old clutter so things could start again and sprout again, down where the old weeds had been a mess and tangle. The fire turned the banks to bare ground. The fire made the ground naked and fertile.

"Whee!" Carolyn sung and clapped her hands as the flames

leapt to the tops of the stalks and danced and spun in the breeze. Hank grabbed up stubble from the corn patch and tossed it on the flames. The weeds popped like there was firecrackers and cap pistols inside them. Sticks and stalks snapped in the fire and spit out sparks as the canes and damp roots got hot. White smoke billowed and turned around and leaned far out over the creek. Giants of smoke loomed above the stream and marched down the valley in ranks and choo-choo puffs.

"You better dig a firebreak at the lower end," I hollered to Hank.

"The branch is the firebreak," he yelled back.

The flames and the smoke give me a soaring feeling. The flames appeared to clap their hands and the river cane by the water barked and spit puffs of smoke.

Now the thing about fire in dry grass and weeds is it spreads in any direction. It will seem to be headed left and then jump to the right. It will leap ahead and then back into the left corner of its track. I seen that Carolyn was standing too close to the fire as it edged into the thatch at the side of the cornfield.

"You'll get smoke in your hair and clothes," I called to her. But she didn't hear, or she didn't pay no attention. She tried to fan the flames with the ends of her shawl, like she was shooing chickens or flies away. I was going to tell her again to be careful, but stopped myself. I was sounding more like a mama than an older sister.

But the breeze must have made an eddy where she was standing, or there was a sudden change in direction of the wind. For I seen a flame jump right back on the hem of her dress, like it reached up to grab the cloth. I don't think she even seen it in the smoke and crackly noise. It was a full pink skirt, flapping where she swung it around. It was like the flame leaped back to attach itself to the lacy, silky material.

"Watch out, Carolyn!" I yelled.

"What?" she said and looked toward me. I pointed at the skirt and she seen the smoke coming from the fabric. She screamed and run back from the flames.

"Don't run," I hollered.

She shook her skirt like she was trying to shake the flames out of the cloth, but that only made the fire take hold. Carolyn started screaming.

"Hold still," I said. But she kept backing away into the muddy cornfield. I picked up wet dirt in both hands and throwed it on her skirt, but it didn't smother the flames enough. Carolyn kept backing away and shaking her skirt like it had bees in it. I wondered if I could tear the dress off at the waist.

"Watch your shawl," I said. But Carolyn was too scared to listen. She was screaming and backing into the muddy stubble. The flames was climbing up toward her waist.

"Lay down and roll in the dirt," I yelled. That was her only hope. But she didn't listen. She fought the flames with her hands and the ends of her shawl.

Just then Hank come running across the field. He had been at the lower end where the branch runs into the creek. "Lay down!" he hollered to Carolyn.

But Carolyn was too panicked to hear anything. She turned to run across the field, with the smoke and fire crawling right up her dress. "Please, Lord," I prayed. "Don't let anything happen to Carolyn."

Hank run right up to Carolyn and pushed her down on the ground. Then he grabbed her arm and rolled her over. He took her shoulder and rolled her over again. I run up and started throwing wet dirt on the skirt. Hank grabbed up handfuls of dirt too and we covered the flames until there was nothing but muddy cloth and smoldering. I pressed mud into the smoke with my fingers.

"Are you burned?" Hank said to Carolyn. But Carolyn was crying so hard she couldn't answer. She had mud on her face and pieces of stubble stuck to her tears and in her hair.

I lifted the muddy hem and seen her legs was not burned. There was not even any holes in her stockings. Her dress was ruined and her shawl was covered with mud. But it didn't look like she got burned at all.

"You're all right," I said. Carolyn kept on crying and I helped her up. Hank got on one side and me on the other and we started walking toward the house.

"Oh leave me alone," Carolyn said and flung our hands away. She walked out ahead of us so we couldn't see her face.

THAT NIGHT I woke in the dark and thought there had been a noise. I remembered there had been a loud noise. But since I had been asleep I couldn't recall what it was. I listened to the house creak and to the roar of the waterfall up the valley. It was impossible to tell what time it was. The dark was so thick it felt like two or three in the morning.

I rolled over on my side trying not to disturb Hank. When I got up to pee I tried not to bother him. Once he was woke up it was hard for him to get back to sleep. My belly felt a little uneasy and I reached out to turn myself again. But I reached out further than I had meant to, into Hank's side of the bed. And that side was cold, and empty.

Maybe the noise I heard was Hank getting up. But the sheet beside me was so cold he must have been up a long time. I listened to the dark house and thought I heard a noise. Setting up in bed I listened, and it sounded like there was a groan or moan somewhere in the house. There was a knock, like wood had hit wood.

Should I get up and see what was happening? Had Hank took sick in the night? Had he gone out to relieve hisself? He did not like to use the chamber pot in the bedroom except in the worst weather. But he had been gone too long to just be relieving hisself. Should I get up and see what had happened to him? Maybe I didn't want to see what was happening. Sometimes it's better to let well enough alone.

Then I heard somebody talking. I thought it was Hank's voice, but it was still so low I couldn't be sure. It was like somebody whispering almost. And then I heard the moan again, like an "Oh" drawed out. And somebody said, "Shhhhh."

I told myself I should not go look. And then I told myself I had to see what was going on. Whatever was happening was happening in my house. Had somebody arrived in the night? Had Lou and Garland come back from Greenville early? Had Hank took sick?

The bed groaned when I got out of it, and I stumbled on the cold floor. It was so dark I had to feel my way to the wall where my robe hung on a peg. I tied the robe around my waist and stepped quietly as I could to the door. From the living room I could see there was a light in the kitchen. And I could hear low voices. It was definitely Hank and Carolyn muttering about something.

I stood and listened and then thought it was bad to spy on them. If I stood and eavesdropped I would show how suspicious I was. I stepped forward still trying to be quiet. When I got to the door of the kitchen I saw a lighted lamp on the table. Carolyn was setting in a chair and Hank was bent over her with his arm around her. "Take this," he whispered to her. "It'll make you feel better."

I must have bumped into a shelf when I stepped into the room, for a pot rattled on the wall. Hank and Carolyn jerked around to see who was there.

"What are you all doing?" I said.

"We didn't want to wake you up," Hank said.

"Wake me up for what?" I said.

"Carolyn has a terrible colic," Hank said.

"I think it was the smoke I breathed that made me sick. I have a pain down here," Carolyn said and rubbed her lower belly.

"I have fixed some soda water for her," Hank said.

"You should have waked me," I said.

"Carolyn didn't want to wake you," Hank said. "She was trying to be considerate."

"I just feel bad," Carolyn said. There was tears in her eyes.

"Soda water won't do her no good," I said.

"Oh!" Carolyn cried out.

"You go on back to bed," I said to Hank. "This is a problem for women." There was a look of embarrassment on Hank's face. He took a step back.

"Let me know if there's anything I can do," he said.

"You don't need to do nothing," I said.

I got kindling from the box and tossed it in the stove. And I poured some water in the kettle. "I'll make a hot water bottle for you," I said to Carolyn.

"Won't do any good," Carolyn said.

"Sure it will," I said.

I set up with Carolyn for about an hour while she sipped hot tea and held the hot water bottle to her belly.

"You have been good to me," she said.

"You are my little sister," I said and put my arm around her shoulder.

Nine

A package come to us from Mama later that month, just a week before Christmas. One of the Hensleys that was driving a wagon load of hams to Greenville stopped by the house to leave it. It was Mama's Christmas presents for me and Hank: a cardboard box with jars of jam and preserves and honey. And there was things Mama and Rosie and Lou had sewed for the baby. Mama had crocheted a blanket and made several little gowns with embroidery on them. Rosie had knitted booties and a little cap. Lou had made a baby quilt. It was the prettiest little quilt I had ever seen, with orange and brown and yellow squares with a green underside.

I got all the pieces out and laid them on the sofa to look at. Tears come to my eyes when I thought of all the work Mama and my sisters had gone to to make those things.

There was one other present in the box. It was wrapped up in tissue paper and had Hank's name wrote on the paper with a pencil. But I could tell what it was. It was a pocketknife. Mama had gone down to the store at Flat Rock and got Hank a new knife.

"Hank, look what Mama has sent you," I said.

"I didn't ask for no Christmas present," Hank said.

"She wanted to give you something," I said. "It's Christmas." It was a fine knife with a bone handle. Hank tested the sharpness of the blade with his finger, then folded the knife and put it in his pocket.

After Lou and Garland had come back and picked up Carolyn, Hank had got moody again. He would go for days without hardly saying anything. I didn't say much either when he acted like that, for I had learned that when I tried to cheer him up he just snapped at me, like a dog that has been hurt and don't want to be bothered. It grieved me to see him so unhappy, and to know there wasn't a thing I could do about it.

WHEN IT WAS three days before Christmas I made up my mind to decorate the house, even though we didn't have any money to buy presents and had not felt like celebrating. It was a cold morning without any frost, and I told Hank we ought to get a Christmas tree. And put some holly and mistletoe in the living room.

"Nobody will see it," Hank said.

"We'll see it," I said.

I wanted to make Mr. Pendergast's house feel like a home that Christmas. I imagined the baby, even though it was unborned, would somehow know there was a Christmas being celebrated, and that it was in a home where people loved each other and give each other gifts and celebrated the birth of Jesus. And I thought trimming the parlor and fixing up a tree might make Hank feel more like his old self too. He had lost faith in hisself. And because he had lost his job, and was ashamed of hisself, it kept him angry. And because he was always angry, I was beginning to get angry. I had to try something. I guess my own patience was starting to run out.

"I'll go out looking for a tree," I said, "but you'll have to help me carry it in."

It was one of those mornings when my belly felt gray inside and off balance. When I was grinding coffee on the back porch I could hear my stomach muttering. While I was frying eggs and boiling grits, my belly was starting to churn, but I swallowed hard and moved real slow. And by the time I had got breakfast on the table I felt a little better. I had found that if I went slow enough the sickness would pass.

I set down at the table with Hank and sipped some coffee. I wouldn't feel like eating breakfast until later in the morning.

"You're not in no shape to go looking for a Christmas tree," Hank said.

"I'll be all right directly," I said.

"We don't have to have a Christmas tree," Hank said.

I felt you couldn't have Christmas without a tree, and you couldn't end one year and start another without a tree with candles on it. It was hard to say why I felt a tree was so important. But I didn't want to live through Christmas in a house without a tree. I wanted to do what needed to be done. "I want me a Christmas tree," I said.

"I'm going down the creek to look for muskrat sign," Hank said. "I may do some trapping later."

It took just about an hour for my stomach to settle down. I sipped the coffee and nibbled on a biscuit. Then I washed the dishes and set the rest of the breakfast in the bread safe, to eat later. I put on my coat and tied a scarf over my head and got out my old gloves that I used for chopping wood. It was cold outside and there was plenty of sun, winter sun. But you could see clouds gathering in the north, over the ridge. I got an old saw from the shed by the barn and started across the pasture, going slow so as not to make myself sick again. The best place to find a Christmas tree was in a growed-over field, where the pines and cedars had come up full and thick. I'd seen such a field beyond the pasture, beyond where the salt block was at the foot of the mountain.

In the field beyond the pasture there was mostly blackberry briars and dried weed stalks. The goldenrod stalks give off thistledown when I touched them, a glittering smoke that drifted in the breeze. There was pines scattered here and there among the brush, but they was mostly yellow pines, bastard pines Papa used to call them. Yellow pines and black pines don't have any shape for a Christmas tree. And their color is not so pretty either as a white pine. I was looking for a white pine, or a cedar. A cedar is fuller and stronger for holding ornaments, but a white pine has that icy blue color and is usually rounded and pointed at the top.

It was on the other side of the field that I found the white pines. They had been planted there by two big pines that loomed on the ridge above. There must have been a dozen little white pines scattered among the scrub. And in the weeds there was dozens more seedlings, growing in the stubble like blue sparks of needles. I looked for the right one. Each seemed to have something wrong with it. One was too lean and too long between its levels of limbs. A white pine grows its limbs in a circle around the stem, one set of limbs for each year it's lived. Another had been crowded by briars so it was lopsided. And another had lost its top. Some trees was too little, and one was too tall. Some didn't look round enough.

I searched across the field to see if there was any cedars in sight. Didn't seem to be any cedars in the field or along the edge. Cedars will often grow in ditches or along fences. They will plant theirselves in thickets and in a gully. I was going to have to choose the white pine that was least wrong and make the best of it. I walked around the trees, parting the brush to get a better look. There was one that was almost perfect in its shape, prouder and fuller than the rest. Its flaw was a hollow place near the bottom, where the limbs had been broke or died. I figured I could turn that side to the corner of the living room and the tree would look almost perfect.

It was getting cloudy by the time I sawed the tree down and carried it to the edge of the pasture. I left the Christmas tree by the fence while I climbed higher to find some holly and other greens. It would be good to have mistletoe, but the only way to get it would be to shoot out a bunch with a shotgun, or climb one of the oak trees on the mountain. I didn't feel like climbing no oak tree.

Just while I was looking for the Christmas tree, the clouds had moved in and blotted out the sun. The pasture and the valley looked different in the shade, like they had shrunk or got closer. The clouds filled every space in the blue sky. It felt colder all of a sudden. I pulled my coat tighter around me and started climbing.

What I was looking for was turkey's paw, what some people call ground pine. It's a kind of club moss and grows in thickets, and on the north sides in damp shady places. It grows along a vine that runs under leaves and litter and lifts up yellow green leaves that look like turkey's feet. It's the perfect decoration for hanging along mantels and over doorways. It can be wound around porch posts and along the railings of stairways.

It was too far to walk to the north side of the ridge, but I found some turkey's paw in a dark place above the maple swamp. There was a small bed of it just below a laurel thicket and I pulled five or six strings out of the leaves like I was unlacing or pulling out thread. Holly was easier to find, for there was a tree with berries on it in the maple swamp just below the laurel thicket. I broke off several limbs and headed back to the house. When I come to the cut tree I took the white pine by one of its lower limbs and drug it across the pasture. The clouds was thick and dark by the time I got everything to the house. It looked like it was going to snow, but I didn't think it was cold enough.

WHEN HANK SEEN the tree the first thing he said was, "That thing is lopsided as a goose." I thought about saying You could have got one yourself, but I didn't. I didn't want to make him even more moody. It wouldn't be Christmas without a tree, and I had got the prettiest one in the field.

Hank sawed out four sections of a plank and nailed them to the bottom of the pine to make a stand. We put the tree in the corner of the living room so the hollow place didn't show. I strung the strands of turkey's paw over the doors and along the mantel. And I put holly in vases on the mantel and on the table.

"Don't see any reason to make such a fuss," Hank said. "This house ain't even ours."

"It's ours for the time being," I said.

"I don't feel much like celebrating," Hank said.

"I know you don't," I said. Hank was like Ma Richards. He looked at things in the hardest way and said things in the harshest way. I was glad I had decided to celebrate Christmas. If you waited till everything was perfect to celebrate, you might never celebrate anything. I would try to act like things was going to turn out all right, and it just might happen. I had to make a house for me and Hank, and the baby.

I had looked in the closets and in the attic for Christmas decorations that Mrs. Pendergast might have had. The only thing I found was one glass ball that must have hung on a Christmas tree years ago. I brought it downstairs and tied it to a limb of the pine tree.

It was up to me to think of decorations. There had to be a candle on the tree. I fixed up a holder out of wire and put a candle on the very top.

There was some sheets of tinfoil in the kitchen, and I sliced them with the scissors and hung the strips on the tree to look like icicles. The strips glittered in the firelight and in the candlelight. Next I popped a bunch of Mama's popcorn and strung it on threads, which I wrapped around the tree. Last I cut some angels out of the pages of a magazine and hung them on the limbs.

With the candle lit on the top, the tree really did make the room look like Christmas. I set down by the fire and just looked at the tree, I was so proud I had got it done.

When Hank come in with an armload of wood I hoped he would say something about the tree. But instead he announced it was starting to sleet. I run to the door and looked out. Sure enough, there was white on top of the fence posts and on the fence wire, on the boxwoods and on the trees across the creek. The limbs of the arborvitae was beginning to droop like they was weighted with lead. Icicles stretched along the eaves and hung from the clothesline.

I had been hoping for snow on Christmas, and instead it was coming an ice storm. It was getting dark, but everything outside appeared to glow with the ice on it.

"The road up the mountain will be slick as glass," Hank said.

"Do you think it'll turn to snow?" I said. I wanted to see a white Christmas.

"Sleet always turns to rain," Hank said.

"Why is that?" I said.

"It always warms up after a sleet," he said. "I don't know why."

I FIXED SUPPER and we eat quiet. In the house you couldn't tell it was sleeting. It's almost never windy during a sleet. Sleet is like the most gentle rain that don't run off and don't drip and patter on the roof or windows. A sleet is silent because the fine droplets turn to ice as soon as they touch. Sleet attaches itself to everything and thickens like coats of paint, and you don't hear it. We eat warmed-over turkey and cornbread and gravy, and you wouldn't have thought anything was going on outside.

It was later, as we was setting by the fireplace, that we heard the first pop and crash. I couldn't tell exactly what direction it come from.

"Was that an apple tree?" I said.

"Most likely an arborvitae," Hank said. "Sleet is heaviest on evergreens."

"Hope it don't fall on the house," I said. Pretty soon we heard another pop and crash, but this time from farther away.

After we went to bed I heard a crack in the woods across the creek, like a rifle had been fired. Limbs was breaking all over the woods, and the tops of trees was snapping with the weight of ice. The house groaned and creaked with the load of ice on the roof. Everything was heavy as if it was wearing armor. I hoped the barn didn't crash down on top of the horse and cow.

After we went to sleep I was awakened by a crack and a whoosh, as a tree on the mountain broke and fell. I hated to think of all the hemlocks and pines that was falling. The woods would have gaps and roads would be blocked by knocked-down trees. The sleet was doing its work in the dark. There was so many pops on the ridges above it sounded like somebody was hunting or starting a war. Even after I went back to sleep I heard in my dream a boom, and then another boom. I dreamed the trees was skeletons of ice breaking up into little bones as they walked in the glare of lightning.

But by the time we woke in the morning the popping and creaking had stopped. It was still dark when I got up to start a fire in the kitchen stove. As I laid in the kindling and cobs, I heard the dripping from the eaves, like all the ice was melting. And it did feel a little warmer, though the air was so damp the chill soaked into your bones.

When I opened the door to get more wood off the back porch I heard the rain. It was a quiet steady rain. The yard was a sheet of ice, but grooved where runoff had started melting it. "Didn't I say it would warm up?" Hank said as he took the bucket out to milk.

"You sure did," I said.

"Too late to do the trees any good," he said.

After daylight we could see the trees down along the edge of the pasture and across the road. The ridge above the creek looked like it had been hacked with a mowing blade in places. There was still ice on the trees on top of the mountain. But in the valley most of the sleet was gone. There was only the broke trees, and the limbs laying everywhere, to show what a sleet had passed in the dark.

It was the day before Christmas and I had hoped to get outside and look for some ivy to string along the mantel and doorways with the turkey's paw. And if I couldn't find ivy I would gather galax, for I had seen a whole bed of galax on the ridge below the laurel thicket.

But all day the rain kept on. I expected it to slack off and the sun to come out. But instead it rained harder. It was a steady straight-down rain. Water stood in pools in the yard and the pasture looked more like a lake, or a bunch of little lakes. It was so wet the horse didn't want to go outside, and the cow stayed close to the overhang of the stall. Hank got soaked just carrying in wood from the shed.

"Creek's getting up," he said.

I walked to the living room and looked out the window. The creek was an ugly red and frothed high between its banks. Where it rushed against a log, the creek water seemed to clap its hands and reach out for the weeds along the bank.

"We could have a flash flood," I said.

"We're already having a flash tide," Hank said.

IT RAINED ALL day, never a lashing, harsh rain, but steady rain that filled every bucket and tub and sinkhole. The yard looked like a garden growing necks and blossoms of splash. The road looked like a creek, and the creek was running wild and red and wide as a river.

Floodwater appears angry because it's dirty and goes where you don't expect to see water. All the ice on the mountain had melted far up as I could see. "The barn is leaking," Hank said when he come in from milking.

"No wonder," I said.

And when I started to make supper, lighting a fire in the stove and grinding up some of the chestnuts gathered by Hank and Carolyn to make chestnut bread, I heard a plop in the corner of the kitchen. I took the lamp and looked and seen a puddle on the floor. I raised the lamp and seen a nipple of water stretching from a wet spot on the ceiling. Wasn't nothing to do but put a dishpan under the drip and mop up the mess on the floor. Before I got the chestnut bread mixed and in the oven, I heard another drip and got a bucket and put under that. And while I was getting the bread and grits and applesauce and sidemeat on the table, I seen the wet streaks coming down the wall behind the stove. It was leaking around the flue. It looked like the whole house was going to melt.

"Not supposed to come a flood on Christmas," Hank said when we set down to eat. "Nobody ever heard of a flood on Christmas."

"That's because we've always lived on mountaintops before," I said. And even as I said it I thought how narrow the Gap Creek valley was and how steep the ridges on both sides. We was below all the water that was falling on the mountains. All the rain on the mountains had to gather down into the slender valley.

"What does that mean?" Hank said.

"It just means we never had to worry about floods because we lived on the ridge," I said.

I don't reckon Hank had thought about floods in Gap Creek until then. We had moved there in early fall when it was dry. The little creek had behaved itself, staying in the bed of rocks that run like rough cobblestones between the fields and woods, twisty as a playful kitten. I could see by the look on his face how he thought for the first time of the narrowness of the valley and how close the house was to the creek.

"We are a good ways back from the creek," I said.

"Not far enough," Hank said.

I had hoped we would be feeling some Christmas cheer, but instead a wet, gray gloom had descended over us.

"If the creek rises we could climb up the mountain tomorrow and visit Mama and my sisters," I said.

"If the creek rises we won't be able to get out of the house without a boat," Hank said. He said it like he was talking about the end of the world. He said it like Ma Richards would have said it, like there was no hope anywhere.

"This house has been here a long time," I said. "It must have seen a lot of floods and not washed away yet."

But Hank didn't answer. He buried his face between his hands.

"Do you think we might ought to go on up the mountain tonight?" I said.

"We can't leave the horse and cow here," Hank said.

"We can take the horse," I said. "And we can leave the cow if we have to."

"I don't think anything but a fish could travel in this rain," Hank said.

When I went out to the back porch to get water to wash the dishes, it was raining hard as ever. In the dark you couldn't see nothing but lamplight shining on falling drops. It was like the air was sheets and curtains of falling water. Rain was coming down in ropes and clots and tattered rags of water. It felt like the sky was falling and the weight of the rain was pushing everything down to the ground, down the hill, down the valley.

After I finished the dishes and went to set in the living room, we listened to the rain drumming on the roof. The rain was harder and faster now. It sounded like an army marching over our heads, and it sounded like millstones rubbing each other. I heard a drip and seen water splash right on the hearth. It was leaking around the chimney. Hank got the ash bucket to put under the drip. "This house is going to fall apart like cardboard," he said.

"It is not," I said, trying to sound like the rain was a little thing. But looking out from the back porch into the steady rain had unnerved me too. In the dark it was like some force was coming out of the sky to drown us in the mud and flood. Whoever thought of an evil force coming from the sky? But it was like the air was threatening to smother us and crush us.

To work against the gloom I got up and lit the candle on top of the Christmas tree. The tree stood in the corner pointing up toward where all the rain was coming from. I thought of a description I had heard of the host of fallen angels being throwed out of heaven. The air was full of black angels falling in the dark, thick as snowflakes. Crowflakes, I thought. But the lighted candle pointed upward.

"We ought to sing some Christmas carols," I said. I thought if we sung it would make us feel better. Hank always loved to sing. It would make me feel better to hear his fine baritone voice.

"I can't remember any Christmas carols," Hank said.

"I don't believe that," I said. "You know all the Christmas carols." I started humming "Silent Night" and then begun singing it. But Hank didn't join in. I sung the first verse and stopped.

"We should have an organ," I said.

"We couldn't even afford a mouth harp," Hank said.

"I wish you had kept your banjo," I said.

"Ma made me give it up when I got saved," Hank said.

"You'll have to get another one," I said.

Hank looked toward the front door and fear come on his face.

"What is it?" I said.

He pointed to the door and I seen a tongue of black water

reaching over the threshold. It was in the shape of a bib spreading on the floor.

"It's just water from the porch," I said.

"That is the creek coming into the house," Hank said.

"Put something under the door," I said. I run to get an old blanket from the bedroom and stuffed it along the bottom of the door, the way you would to stop a draft. Water soaked through the blanket quick.

"Won't do no good," Hank said.

"What will?" I said. We couldn't open the door, for that would only let in more rain. Rain must be blowing right across the porch, I thought. But all I heard was steady rain on the roof.

"Nothing," Hank said. I looked at him, and listened. And then I heard the lips sound, the kissing sound and sucking that rising water makes when it touches a building or rock wall.

"You mean that's creek water?" I said. Gap Creek had rose out of its banks and crossed the road. In the dark it had reached into the yard and licked against the porch, then swirled up onto the boards of the porch and was now pouring under the door. Hank looked so worried I felt sorry for him. I tried to think of something to stop the water from coming into the house. I grabbed a lamp and run to look at the back door, for I thought it was lower than the front. But I had only took one step into the kitchen when my foot hit something thick. There was a splash and I seen water already standing on the kitchen floor.

I lowered the lamp to look at the water and seen pieces of kindling floating around under the table. And there was cans and bottles floating, and a cardboard box with some pinecones. Even as I looked I could see the water rising, washing in little tides across my feet. I turned to run back to the living room where Hank stood by the fireplace, leaning against the mantel.

"There's water already in the kitchen," I said.

"It'll put out the fire in a minute," he hollered.

Sure enough, water seeping under the front door had spread across the living room to the hearth. When it rose another inch it would be in the fireplace and the fire would go out in smoke and steam. I tried to think of some way to protect the fire, to build a wall around the hearth. There wasn't no way.

"We've got to get out of here," Hank said.

"We can't go out in a flood in the dark," I said. "We'd get drowneded."

"We can't just stay here," Hank hollered. I didn't like the look in his eye and the shrillness that had come into his voice.

"Only a fish could get through a flood in this dark," I said. "You said so yourself."

"We've got to make a run for it," Hank said. The tone of his voice scared me as much as what he said.

"We can't go up the valley to the mountain," I said. I wished more than anything that we had gone home for Christmas. I wished I was on top of the mountains with Mama and my sisters.

"Do you want to drown here?" Hank shouted, like I was responsible for the flood. He sloshed through the water in the kitchen and grabbed his mackinaw coat off the peg, and he lit the barn lantern. "Get your coat," he said.

"Where are you going?" I said.

"We've got to get out of this house," Hank shouted. I seen there was no use to argue with him.

"What can we take?" I said.

"We can't take nothing if we have to swim," Hank yelled. I'd never seen him so scared. The water was getting deeper by the second in the kitchen, and his words echoed off the walls in an odd way.

I tried to think what was most valuable in the house. We didn't have any money left but a few cents in my purse. There was a few pots and pans I had brung with me, and the comb and brush set Rosie had give me when we got married.

Hank swung the lantern like he was going to bash it on the wall, but stopped hisself. "You don't want to burn down the house," I said.

"What difference would it make?" he said. He started stomping in the water so the splashes flung out like wings. I grabbed my coat off the peg. I hated to get the bottom of the coat wet, but there was no way not to.

Hank acted like he was beside hisself. He stomped into the bedroom and got Mr. Pendergast's shotgun, which was about the only thing Caroline Glascock had left. He broke down the barrel and put a shell inside, and he put another shell in his coat pocket.

"What are you doing?" I said, shivering in the icy water up to my knees.

"Let's get out of here," Hank said. Holding the lantern and shotgun in one hand, he grabbed my arm with the other and pulled me through the kitchen to the back door. When he opened the door more water swirled into the room. In the lantern light the flood looked an evil brown, dark and smelly. It was water that had poured through outhouses and barns, graveyards and trash gullies.

The wind hit my face like somebody had slapped me with a cold wet hand. The air was whipping sheets of rain. Suddenly the air turned to shining blue powder, and I seen it was lightning. And I could see clear across the yard to the barn and pasture. There was nothing but water curving and swerving in a rush as far as you could see. Then it was dark again.

"Where are we going?" I yelled.

"To higher ground," Hank shouted. "Or hell." He pulled me into the current and it felt like a sow or horse had rolled against my legs. The water hit so hard it bruised me and wrapped around my knees and thighs and pulled at my coat.

"I can't stand up," I hollered.

"Got to hurry!" Hank yelled into the rain. He held the gun and lantern high and jerked me along with his left hand. Every time I lifted a foot it nearly got swept away from under me. We lurched and wrestled our way across the river toward the barn. The closest high ground I could think of was in the pasture, up where the salt lick was. But that was beyond the barn and across the pasture. I didn't see how we could get that far in the awful waves. In the dark I couldn't even tell if we was past the woodpile or chicken coop. It was black and the rain and current made you feel crazy. The glow from the lantern was weak as a lightning bug.

"Lord help us," I hollered. Something hit my side like a floating board or body. The rain smothered me.

But we kept going, from one foothold to another, and I think we might have made it to the barn, or even to the pasture fence, except that Hank stumbled. I don't know what happened exactly, but it was like he stepped into a ditch or sinkhole, or the flood jerked his feet out from under him. I don't think he meant to let go my hand. But down he went, and his hand was wrenched away from mine, and I was on my own in the middle of the raging water.

"Hank!" I screamed, and seen the lantern go bobbing away until it went out. And then everything was black as tar around me, with wind and rain in my face and water slurping and pawing at my legs and between my legs. I didn't know what direction to go in. I couldn't remember where the barn was, and where the house was.

"Hank!" I yelled again. But the wind hit me in the face and covered up my voice. I tried to listen, but heard nothing but wind. I took a step and the water got deeper. Was Hank under the water? Had he been swept down the valley? At the speed the water was moving he could already be a long way off. Should I try to look for him? I couldn't hardly stand up myself. I couldn't think what to do because I couldn't swim, and I didn't even know in what direction to move.

I don't know what I would have done, standing deep in that wild, stinking water, twisting myself against the current, except just then it come another flash of lightning that blinded me, and through my squinted eyes I seen the barn ahead. For a second the barn wall glared like it was lit, and then it was gone. Quick, before I lost the direction, I pushed myself toward the barn. Took all my strength to reach one foot, and then the other, through the tide, bracing myself and leaning against the current. If I fell down in that flood I was a goner.

As I worked my way step by short steps toward the barn I wondered if I should go back to look for Hank. Was he out there somewhere clinging to a fence post or tree? Was he deep in the mud of the creek? But I would be lucky to save myself and the baby inside me. It wouldn't do nobody any good if I got carried off in the flood.

When I finally reached the barn I put my hands flat against the wall and felt my way along to the door. The cow bawled inside and something banged like the horse lunging in panic. The barn felt like it was trembling in the grip of the flood. I eased my way along to the hallway door, and soon as I got into the passageway the current wasn't so fierce. The water was swirling through the stalls and it smelled like manure and rotten leaves.

"Hank!" I hollered, and held on to the slats of the cow stall. I could try to find the ladder to the hay loft and climb up there out of the water. But I couldn't just climb up to the dry hay and leave Hank out in the flood. If only I could see. If only I had some rope or a long pole I could help him.

"Hank!" I yelled again. The cow bawled inside her stall and something banged against the barn like a log or floating outhouse. I didn't want to go back out in the flood, for I had to think of the baby. It was my job to save the baby. But I felt bad about leaving Hank in the raging water.

I worked my way along the wall hung with harness, plowlines, and hames and horse collars until I reached the ladder. As I put my hand on the step of the ladder to pull myself up out of the water I felt a wet shoe. At first I didn't know what it was, and then I thought, has somebody left a boot out here? And then I wondered if a stranger was hiding in the dark barn. Was it somebody like Timmy Gosnell?

"Who's there?" I said. There was no answer. I pulled my hand away from the wet boot. "Is that you, Hank?" I said.

Suddenly there was a flash of lightning from outside, and in the glow from the doorway reflected from the water I looked up and seen it was Hank above me. He was holding the shotgun, and he was trembling and had a terrible look on his face.

"I thought you was drowneded," I said.

"You almost pulled me under," he said.

"You let go of me," I said.

"I couldn't help you," Hank said. He sounded like a little boy that was scared.

"I thought you was drowneded," I said.

"I'm going to shoot myself," he said. It was dark and I couldn't see his face, but it was like I could see his face in his voice.

"Don't talk crazy," I said.

"I didn't go to leave you," Hank shouted.

"I know you didn't," I said. I was glad I couldn't see his face.

There was a flash of light, and at first I thought the shotgun had gone off. But it was just another lightning.

"I ain't no good for nobody!" Hank hollered.

"It's not your fault," I said. I was afraid of what he might do with the gun in the dark. I didn't know what else to say. I had never seen Hank in such a state, or anybody else for that matter. There wasn't anything I could think of to say.

"You go on back home," Hank hollered. "I have ruint your life."

"You ain't ruined nothing, yet," I said. "This is all the flood."

Tears was mixed with rain in the corners of my eyes and down my cheeks. Lightning flashed again and I seen the water outside the door like wrinkled satin pulled away. Hank had had his moods, but he'd never done anything this crazy before.

"I ought to kill us both," Hank shouted.

"No!" I screamed. "You'll feel better tomorrow. The Lord will help us, if we pray," I said, my teeth chattering. I was jerking I was so scared and cold. The horse whinnied and rammed against the side of its stall.

I expected Hank to answer, but he didn't.

"The Lord loves everybody," I said. I was saying whatever come into my head. I couldn't think of what to say.

"The Lord has kicked my ass," Hank said.

"Don't talk like that," I said. I expected the lightning to hit the barn and burn us up. Instead thunder boomed on the roof like it was a drum. The pressure hurt my ears. I put my hand on Hank's dripping pants leg. "Come on down," I said.

There was a blast of fire and a deafening roar and I heard a crash and tinkle on the barn roof. Heavy drops sprinkled around me. It took me a second to understand that Hank had fired the shotgun straight up at the roof.

"Please, Lord, help us," I said. "Help Hank to calm down, and show us what to do."

It come to me what Ma Richards would say to Hank. I heard her say it in my mind. "You think you're so important the Lord would make a special flood just for you?" I said. "This flood is happening to everybody."

Hank didn't answer. I could smell the burned gunpowder.

"There ain't nothing special about your troubles," I said. It was hard words, but they was the truth. I was so scared there was nothing to say but the truth.

"Don't make no difference what I do," Hank said.

"You're just feeling sorry for yourself," I said.

"I should kill us both and have done with it," Hank said. The cow bawled and thunder slammed the roof of the barn again.

"You won't do it," I said. "You're just showing out." It was a chance I had to take, to shame him back to his senses. I had to do something to get him calmed down.

The gun fired again, and it sounded like sand was ricocheting around inside the hayloft. I hoped that was the last shell Hank had.

"Think of the baby," I said.

"I can't think of nothing," Hank said.

"Let's go back to the house," I said. "We're going to freeze to death out here."

"We'll get drowneded," Hank said.

"I think the water's going down," I said. It did seem the water in the hallway of the barn was not as deep as it had been.

"Might as well get washed away," Hank said.

"Do you want the baby to die?" I said. "Do you want the baby to freeze to death?"

"This ain't no world for a baby," Hank said.

Anger boiled up in me. All the confusion and scaredness in me started turning to anger now that Hank was a little calmer. "Get down from there and act like a man," I said, and pulled at his leg.

"Wait till the water goes down," Hank said. "Be foolish to go back now."

I seen he was right. I was so cold and angry I was jerking, and I couldn't stop. I had to get out of the freezing water. "Let's climb up in the hay and get warm," I said.

My feet trembled on the rungs as I pulled myself up the ladder in the dark. Even when there was a flicker of lightning you couldn't see much up there except the cracks between boards. I took Hank's hand and we felt our way to the pile of hay and crawled into it. I covered us up with straw and leaned against Hank and tried to stop shaking. The hay smelled like must and old apples. I hadn't been inside a hay pile since I was a girl.

The flood roared outside and the horse whinnied and banged the stall below us. But I didn't hear the cow anymore. She hadn't bawled since Hank fired the shotgun the last time.

"You don't need to blame yourself," I said, and pushed up against Hank and held his waist.

Hank didn't say nothing. I guess he was wore out by all that had happened. He put his arms around me and we laid there in the scratchy straw. I quit shaking finally, and I must have drifted off to sleep, for I thought somebody was calling to me. They was calling from a cellar, or down in a holler. And then I found it was the horse neighing.

I jerked up and listened. The floodwaters wasn't so loud around the barn as before. Hank had dozed off too and I shook him.

"Listen," I said.

"What?" he said and twisted hisself around.

"The water is quieter," I said.

"I can still hear it," Hank said.

"We've got to get back to the house and put on dry things," I said. "We're liable to catch pneumony."

"You don't want to go back out in that," Hank said.

"We've got to," I said.

We pushed the hay aside and felt our way to the ladder. I was stiff and sore, but no longer jerking as I found the rungs with the tips of my shoes and lowered myself into the water. The flood had gone down some, but was so cold it burned my ankles. I held on to Hank's leg and then his hand as he climbed down. When we got to the barn door everything was so dark we couldn't even see the house.

"We'll have to feel our way," I said, "the way we come out here."

"I ain't no good," Hank said.

"It don't matter if you're any good or not," I said, "we've got to get back to the house."

The flood tore at my legs as I stepped into it, but I pushed my feet hard against the ground and held on to Hank's arm, both steadying him and steadying myself.

"If I fall down just let me go," Hank said.

"If you fall down I'll fall down too," I said, "and we'll all be drowneded." But I knowed he wasn't going to fall down. Hank was strong as a big Percheron horse. He was shaky in his head, but he wasn't shaky in his big shoulders and powerful back. He was strong as a rock wall. Without a lantern we couldn't see the crazy water, but it splashed up on my chest and took my breath away. I held on to Hank's arm like it was an oak tree.

"Oh!" I said when an icy splash hit my neck. The shock of the cold water on my chest and belly made me forget myself and stop.

"Come on," Hank said and jerked my arm. I held on to him as the flood thrashed between my legs. Now that he was out in the wild stream Hank come back to hisself a little. Lightning flashed and I seen the porch was not where I'd thought it was. We had been pushed by the current below the corner of the house, past where the washpot and clothesline was. We swung to the left in the ghostly light, and then it was dark again.

By the time we got to the steps my feet was too numb to feel anything. Hank had to help me up and across the porch.

"Let's go upstairs where it's dry," I said.

"I'll have to find a lamp," Hank said.

• • •

WHEN WE GOT to the bedroom in the attic everything looked cold and damp. The day of rain had made everything clammy, and with the fire out the house was getting cold. I stood at the top of the stairs to let my muddy shoes and the bottom of my skirt drip as much as they would. In the bedroom I put the lamp on the table and went back to the stairs and wrung out the hem of my filthy skirt. It was a good thing we had not moved downstairs to Mr. Pendergast's room after Lou and Garland visited us. Thank goodness most of our clothes was upstairs.

"There's nothing to do but take off our wet things and get under the covers," I said. But Hank didn't answer. He had set down on the bed and put his face in his hands, and he was crying. A chill went through me, like an icicle had been drove down my spine. I went to Hank and took him by the shoulders. He sobbed into his hands like a baby. It didn't seem possible a man as big and strong as Hank could be so unstrung as he had been that night.

"Let's jump in bed and get warm," I said. I got down on my knees and untied his wet boots and pulled them off. I slipped off his soaking-wet socks. "Get out of them wet overalls," I said. He let me undress him like he didn't care, like he was a sleepy baby that didn't pay no attention. I was shivering with cold as I got his flannel night-shirt on him. I took off my own clothes and put on my flannel gown and got in bed beside him. Our feet was cold as snow. Hank had turned on his side away from me. He wasn't sobbing anymore; he was just sullen and quiet.

"We'll be warm and dry up here," I said. I listened to the rain and to things rubbing and knocking on the house. I reckon boards and trees in the flood was washing against the walls. Once I felt the walls jar, and wondered if the house had broke loose from its foundations. It was strange to think that I was stronger than Hank. He was wore out and I still felt like fighting. I felt of my belly where it had begun to swell a little. I cupped my hands around my belly like I was protecting it.

"I'm afraid," Hank said.

"I'm afraid too," I said. The fact that he was so scared made me feel less afraid. I couldn't explain it. Hank turned and put his face against my breast, and I pulled the gown to the side so the nipple was exposed. The nipple got hard and long and he put his lips to it. I run my fingers through his hair.

He leaned his head over and nibbled at my other breast, like he was hungry. He was so hungry he could never be filled.

"You don't never need to be so afraid," I said.

When I put out the lamp it was so dark in the bedroom you couldn't see the dark. Most times you can see the dark because there is just a little bit of light. But it was so dark I might as well have been blind. The sight had been took away, and there was no way of seeing. The house shuddered as big trees or logs washed up against it. The house creaked and groaned, as if something was pushing it. There was a kind of bark, of one board slapping another. And suddenly there come a flash. And I seen the one window in the bedroom lit up with blinding chalk dust. It was lightning again. The brightness burned my eyes.

Thunder hit the air like a timber slammed down on the roof. The house shook and seemed to rock on its foundation. Thunder followed thunder, as though a pile of big rocks was falling on the roof. Doors was slamming all over the sky. And as soon as it quieted down there was another flash of blue. And thunder followed like a train busting out of a tunnel. It sounded as if the sky was crumbling in big chunks and crashing down the mountainside. Thunder echoed off the ridges and repeated itself and echoed again.

And just when it felt like I couldn't stand to hear another thunder, I heard the wind. Suddenly wind brushed the house like it had been released by the thunder. Wind appeared as if it had been turned out of a cave and shoved up against the house. The eaves whined and windows shook. And trees across the valley and on the ridges above roared. I could hear another roar too, of a waterfall further up the valley, where floodwater was dropping hundreds of feet in the dark and breaking trees and churning up roots and boulders.

"Sounds like the end of the world," Hank said.

"Nothing is the end of the world," I said. I said it off the top of my head, but then I seen how true it was. If everything in the world come crashing down, the world would still go on. It would start all over again. The creek would go back to its banks and broke things would rot and turn into mulch and fertilizer. The sun would dry out the mud and silt, and weeds would start growing again.

Wind hit the side of the house again and flung drops pinged on the window. "It's Christmas," I said.

"Don't seem like Christmas," Hank said.

WHEN I WOKE up, Hank was gone from the bed. The place beside me was cold and everything about the bedroom seemed wrong. I looked around and tried to see what it was that was so bad about the room. Everything looked ordinary, except for our wet clothes on the floor. And then I thought that it was light, which meant it was much later than I was used to getting up. I had slept too long and I was uneasy in my stomach.

Another thing that was odd was the wind had stopped. The windowpanes was quiet and there was no rain on the roof. It had rained so long it sounded eerie not to hear drops on the tin roof. It was the quietness that was so strange. There was no dripping from the eaves. I listened to see if Hank was stirring around in the rooms below. The house was still.

. . .

WHEN I GOT dressed my shoes was still wet, but I put on dry stockings and climbed down the stairs. Opening the door into the living room I expected to see water standing on the floor, but there was none. Instead there was things laying on the floor, scattered here and yon, like an animal had been loose in the room. It was stuff that had been floating and was left when the water went down: soaked cardboard boxes, pieces of wood, bottles and jars, corncobs from the kindling box, clothespins, a broom. But the thing that struck me was not the look of the living room: it was the smell. There was the smell of a place wet and already sour. It was a stink of moldy rotting things. The water had only stood in the house a few hours, yet the house smelled like it had been rotting for months. It was a stink of soot and charred wood in the fireplace, and bitter soaked ashes. It was a stink of wet cloth and filth and festering mud. The floor was slick with a film of mud, and silt stuck to the bottoms of the curtains. The Christmas tree had mud on its lower limbs.

"Hank," I called. I looked in the kitchen and seen the floor was littered the same way the living room was. "Hank!" I hollered. But there was nobody in the house. The kitchen smelled worse than the living room. The wood was all soaked and sticks was beginning to mold and sour. The water had brought out all the stink of the charred wood and soot inside the stove. And there was the stench of rancid grease and bits of rotted fat and crumbs from the table that had been found and loosened by the water. The floor was slick with red silt.

I put a hand over my nose and hurried to the back door. I expected to see water standing in the yard, but there was only a few puddles. The yard had been tore and scrubbed by the flash flood, and most of the grass had been peeled away. Wood had floated out of the woodshed and was scattered over the yard and pasture. A chicken coop had been carried away and washed up against the pasture fence. The outhouse had been knocked over. Otherwise the buildings was all in place, and sun sparkled on the puddles. But I didn't see but six or eight chickens pecking in the mud.

"Hank," I called.

My voice echoed off the side of the barn. The air was so warm it felt like early fall, but the trees on the mountainside was bare. The ice was all gone and the trees flashed silver in the sun. It had indeed turned warm after the sleet. I called for Hank again, and then I seen him come out of the hallway of the barn. He was leading the horse, and he took the horse to the pasture and turned it loose. After he put up the bars of the milkgap, he started back toward the house carrying the milk bucket. I could tell something was wrong by the sag of his shoulders.

"The cow is dead," he said when he got closer.

"Drowneded?" I said.

"Hung herself," Hank said. "She climbed up to the top of her stall as the water rose and caught her collar on a nail. Then hung herself when the water went down."

"I don't believe it," I said.

"I didn't believe it either," Hank said. "But the cow is dead, strangled by her own collar."

"We got a baby coming and there won't be no milk," I said.

"I never heard of a cow hanging herself before," Hank said.

"Can we eat the meat?" I said.

"It has already started to rot in this warm weather," Hank said. "And beef won't keep the way pork does."

"You can't salt it down?" I said.

"It has already started to rot," Hank said, "because the blood is still in the carcass." I wondered if the meat could be boiled and canned, but I didn't say nothing. I didn't want to argue with Hank, now that he was calm, after the way he had acted the night before.

When I went back into the kitchen I had to adjust my eyes to the dark. But the stink hit my nose quick. It was a sweet, sickening smell, worse than mildew. It was the smell of rotten things.

"First thing is to mop the floor," I said.

Hank raked the wet ashes out of the stove and went to find some dry kindling in the barn. He didn't mention what he had done in the flood, and I didn't either. I got the bucket of fresh water from the back porch. It was clean and clear and had only been touched by rainwater. I took a drink, for I was parched from the long night of worry.

"The spring will have to be cleaned out before we get any more fresh water," Hank said when he come in.

"We'll have to keep fires going in the stove and in the fireplace to dry the house out," I said.

I DON'T THINK I'd ever faced such a job as cleaning up Mr. Pendergast's house after the flash flood. Looking at the red mud on the floor and on the chair legs and table legs, and smelling the stench of wet wood and ashes, you just wanted to walk out of the house into the morning air and never come back. The smell threatened to make me sick. I felt like grabbing a coat and a head scarf and staying outside.

The first thing that had to be cleaned was the floors, for we was tracking red silt all over the place and it caked on the bottom of our shoes. It was like walking in red grease. The mud smeared on everything and was too deep to mop directly. Hank got a fire started in the stove, and then he went into the living room to start one in the fireplace.

From the toolshed I got a hoe and an old bucket we had used in the hog killing. I lit a lamp in the kitchen so I could see better, and with the fire roaring in the cookstove, I begun to scrape the floor like I was peeling soft paint, and put the scrapings in the bucket. By the time I got to the living room Hank had a fire roaring and prancing there. I moved the Christmas tree so I could scour under it. With the fire cracking and snapping, the house already smelled better, as if the fire was eating up the smells.

When I toted the bucket of mud out to the backyard to dump it, I seen Hank was digging a hole beside the barn. It was a grave for the cow. It would take him most of the day to shovel out a hole deep enough. I wished I could do that job. It would be good to get out of the smelly house.

After the floors was scraped clean as I could make them, I heated water on the stove and shaved some soap into it. With the mop I scoured the kitchen and living room and front bedroom. I lifted all the curtains and bedclothes and hanging clothes in the closet away and tried to wash in the corners and melt the mud in cracks. Afterwards I washed my shoes on the back porch and put on some water to boil for grits and ground some beans for coffee.

Just about the time the coffee was ready and the grits was cooked, there was a knock at the front door. Who could be out visiting the morning after a flood? I was more startled and flustered than I had a right to be. I guess I was still shook up from the night before. I wished Hank was in the house and not way out behind the barn. I hoped it wasn't Timmy Gosnell drunk on Christmas morning. Drying my hands on my apron, I walked slowly to the front door.

It was Preacher Gibbs and his wife from Gap Creek Church. I hadn't seen them since Mr. Pendergast's funeral. "Merry Christmas," Mrs. Gibbs said.

"Merry Christmas to you," I said and wiped the sweat off my forehead. "Won't you come in."

"We come to see about you," the preacher said. I led them into the living room and Mrs. Gibbs handed me a little poke with a ribbon on it. Peppermint candy canes stuck out the top.

"Thank you so much," I said. "Won't you set down. I don't think any of the chair seats is wet."

"Did you get flooded too?" Preacher Gibbs said.

"We got at least a foot of water in the house," I said. "I've spent all morning cleaning up the mud."

"The Goins house washed away," the preacher said. "Two of their younguns was drowned."

"And the mill got washed away," Mrs. Gibbs said. "One of the Henderson boys was in the mill laying drunk on Christmas Eve and he got drowned."

"Now, Mother, we don't know he was drunk," Preacher Gibbs said.

"Everybody knows he was drunk," Mrs. Gibbs said.

"We shouldn't speak ill of the dead," Preacher Gibbs said.

"Can I take your coats?" I said.

"We can't stay but just a minute," the preacher said. "We wanted to see if you and Hank was all right."

"We was lucky," I said.

"You have been blessed by the Lord," Preacher Gibbs said.

"The cow got killed," I said. "She got killed in the stall. Hank is digging a hole to bury her out by the barn."

"The Lord reminds us he's in charge from time to time," Preacher Gibbs said.

"It was a terrible flood," I said.

"We come to wish you all a Merry Christmas and invite you to church," Mrs. Gibbs said.

"Could I offer you some coffee?" I said. "I just made a fresh pot."

"We can't stay," Preacher Gibbs said. "But we do want to invite you and Hank to service."

"We've been worried about what we was going to do," I said, "when Mr. Pendergast's heirs show up."

"Nobody has heard from them," the preacher said.

"They never was friendly to Mr. Pendergast," Mrs. Gibbs said, "not like real children would be."

"Young folks starting a family need a church connection," Mrs. Gibbs said. She looked at my belly like she could tell I was expecting. I don't know how she could tell, but she seemed to know.

"We don't know where we'll be living," I said.

"You should buy this place," Preacher Gibbs said.

"I wish we could afford to," I said.

"When the heirs are found, maybe you can make a down payment," Mrs. Gibbs said.

"We don't have much money," I said. I didn't tell them about Caroline Glascock and her husband. I didn't think it would do any good to tell them how we had been fooled. And I didn't tell about the lawyer that took the jar of money either.

"The Lord will protect his own," Preacher Gibbs said, "if you go to church and trust him."

It was good to hear somebody who was so confident about how the world worked. And it was a pleasure to see somebody from the community, after the awful night of flood.

A voice hollered outside and I thought at first it was Hank, sounding like he was hurt or in trouble. "What was that?" I said.

"Piieendergaass!" the voice yelled.

"It's Timmy Gosnell," Mrs. Gibbs said. A shadow passed through my chest. There was something shameful about having a drunk man raving in front of your house, especially on Christmas Day, when the preacher was visiting.

"He always gets drunk on Christmas," Mrs. Gibbs said.

"Piieendergass!" the voice hollered. His voice hurt like a saw raked across my skin.

"Maybe he'll go away," I said. A rock banged on the porch and rolled against the door.

"Poor Timmy," Mrs. Gibbs said. "When he gets like this nobody can help him."

"The Lord can help him," Preacher Gibbs said. "But I doubt if anybody else can."

Something hit the porch again, and then I heard another voice. It was Hank, who must have heard Timmy hollering and come running from the barn. I opened the front door and stepped out on the porch.

Timmy Gosnell stood in the yard by the boxwood, but except for his voice I would not have recognized him. He looked like he had been made out of mud, the way a snowman is made out of snow. He looked like he had been rolled in mud and soaked in mud. Every inch of his clothes was caked with clay and silt. There was dirt and silt on his neck and face. And there was filth and river mud in his ears and pasted in his hair. His hands was crusted with mud, and his shoes was caked in layers of sand and clay. He looked like something that had been buried for weeks and rose from the dead. Only his eyes wasn't covered with filth.

"What do you want?" Hank said. Hank was holding the shovel he had used to dig the grave for the cow.

"You owe me monneeeeyyy," Timmy groaned.

"I don't owe you nothing," Hank said. I seen how scared Hank was by his voice. Under the dirt Timmy could have been a rotten corpse rose from the grave.

"It's Timmy Gosnell," I said.

"You get out of here," Hank said and raised the shovel.

"You ooooowe me," the drunk man moaned.

The preacher and Mrs. Gibbs had come out on the porch, and the preacher stepped down into the flood-scoured yard. "What happened to you, Timmy?" the preacher said.

Timmy turned and studied the preacher like he wasn't sure he could see him. "Rained on me," he said.

"You need to go home and wash up and change your clothes," the preacher said. "It's Christmas."

Timmy pointed toward the house like he was having trouble saying what he wanted to. "Owe me money," he said.

"Julie and Hank don't owe you money," the preacher said. "And Vincent Pendergast is dead."

"They tooook his money," Timmy hollered.

Hank stepped closer to the drunk man. "We ain't took nothing," he said. I seen how scared and angry Hank was, and how embarrassed. I was so scared I couldn't hardly get my breath.

"Now you come with us," Preacher Gibbs said to Timmy. "We'll take you home."

The drunk man swung at the preacher like he was trying to drive away a yellowjacket. "I done been saved," he said. "Didn't do no good."

"You need to get cleaned up," the preacher said. "And have something hot to eat. It's Christmas."

"Won't hold water," Timmy growled at the preacher. "Your preaching won't."

"There's been a flood," the preacher said. "Half the valley is washed away. Looks like you got caught in it."

"All whooores," Timmy said and pointed first at me and then at Mrs. Gibbs.

"Now we don't need to talk that way," Preacher Gibbs said. Hank raised the shovel, but the preacher waved him back.

"Timmy, you just come along with us now," the preacher said. He tried to take Timmy by the elbow, but the drunk man flung his hand away.

"Owe me monneeeyyy," he groaned and turned away, staggering toward the road. His clothes was so heavy with mud they dragged to the ground.

"What a pitiful sight," Mrs. Gibbs said.

"All we can do for Timmy is pray," the preacher said.

"Somebody ought to teach him a lesson," Hank said. He drove the shovel into the mud of the yard.

"You can't teach a drunk man any lesson," Preacher Gibbs said.

When the preacher and Mrs. Gibbs was gone I thought how quick the world could be turned upside down. Awful things and crazy things was there waiting for a chance to happen. I had to go into the house and stand by the fire to warm myself and calm myself.

Ten

The Christmas flood not only killed the cow and washed away the chicken coop, the water in the cellar made the taters rot. I saved some spuds and sweet taters that hadn't got moldy by wiping them off and laying them in the sun on the back porch. But most of the taters got soft and turned to filth that had to be shoveled into a bucket and carried to the gully.

After the flood a lot of things got carried to the gully below the spring: rags I'd used to wipe off mud, cloth that had soured and mildewed, shoes that had got soaked and moldy. After Christmas it seemed half the things in the house had to be throwed away. There was dried apples and dried peppers that got wet and rotted in the kitchen. And where the flood rose to the lower shelves in the smokehouse some of the pork middles got the salt soaked out of them and started to rot.

By the time I'd finished cleaning the house, I felt the floodwater had been poison and killed almost everything it touched, except the tools. The foundation of the house itself had been soaked and the mortar crumbled off between rocks. It looked like the floodwaters had acid in them, and everything they touched was burned and eat away. The yard and road had been swept bare down to rock or hard red clay. The road up Gap Creek had always been rough, with long stretches of mud in wet weather and washboard ripples in dry weather. But there was now places washed out deep enough to bury a horse in. A big rock had been exposed in the roadbed high as a wagon axle. The branch run through the road in places and the creek cut across the routes and back above the Poole place. Some ruts was washed out so deep the dirt in the middle of the road come up to a wagon tongue.

If we had been broke at Christmas, we was worse off by New Year. All the meal we had was ruined, along with the taters and some of the meat. It was when Hank went out to the crib to shuck corn to take to mill that he discovered a lot of the ears had been ruint too. Mud and silt was stuck like paint to the ears in the bottom of the crib, and some of the kernels had begun to swell and sprout. Others had got moldy, or was just starting to rot. It was a mess, and it was beginning to smell.

"This is like the plagues of Egypt," Hank said when he showed me the rotting corn.

"We'll have to dry it out," I said.

"How can you dry out a crib full of corn that's soaked and molding?" Hank said, like he was accusing me of making light of our problems.

"We'll have to shuck it," I said, "and carry it into the house to dry by the fire."

"There ain't room by the fire, and there ain't time," Hank said. But I figured he was arguing more with hisself than with me. Since the night of the flood he hadn't said much. I tried to forget him standing on the ladder in the barn firing the shotgun.

"We'll save what we can," I said.

"That won't be enough to brag about," Hank said. I think he was mad at hisself for being mad, and for talking like Ma Richards. He meant to act different, but he couldn't help it. I guess nobody changes completely.

It was the day before New Year when we lit in to shuck the wet corn. We piled the dry corn to the side and pulled out the mud-stained, wet ears. The shucks was soggy and dripping muddy water as we stripped them off. My hands got cold quick and I found some old gloves in the barn and kept working with a shucking stick. Some of the kernels had been stained with mud, and they would have to be washed off after they dried out. We shucked several bushels of corn and toted them into the house and spread them on quilts on the living room floor. They nearly covered the whole room.

Hank built a big fire in the fireplace and made it hot with hickory wood. Soon the whole house smelled like moldy corn, a sweet almost fermenty kind of scent. The heaped corn looked like some kind of treasure in the firelight. You could imagine the kernels was bits of gold. I warmed my hands and then went back and shucked some more.

IT WAS AFTER we had got most of the wet corn shucked and piled by the fireplace, and I was ready to wash the mud stains off my hands for the hundredth time that week, that somebody knocked on the door. It was Preacher and Mrs. Gibbs again.

"Howdy," Hank said. "I'd invite you all in but the living room is full of corn. We're drying it out."

The preacher stepped inside and looked at the piles of wet, stained corn. "We was just stopping by to greet you," he said.

The preacher and his wife come and stood by the fire, and I didn't know what to say. My hands was dirty and cold and my dress covered with mud. The preacher held out his hands to the fire. "I've come by to wish you all a happy New Year and to invite you again to church," he said.

. . .

I HAD ALWAYS thought of myself as a churchgoing person and not somebody to be exhorted and converted. And I knowed Hank thought of hisself the same way. But in Gap Creek we was new to the community, and new to marriage and to each other, and we had not gone to church. It come to me that we must look like godless people to Preacher Gibbs and the folks of Gap Creek. They didn't really know us at all.

"We don't know many people on Gap Creek," I said.

"Then come to church and get to know your neighbors," the preacher said.

"If God is everywhere, you can worship wherever you are," Hank said. "I can pray in the corn crib same as in the church."

"But the church is where we strengthen each other and support each other. The church is the family of Christ," Preacher Gibbs said.

"I would be afraid to start the New Year without the Lord," Mrs. Gibbs said.

I was a little offended by the way they talked, but at the same time I was flattered that they had come back up the valley on New Year's Eve just to invite us again to church. It irritated me that they looked down on us as some kind of sinners. Preachers always look down on those they are trying to convert. But I appreciated the special attention they had showed us. It had been awful lonely on Gap Creek.

"We have been too busy to go anywhere," I said.

The preacher looked at the corn heaped on the floor. "It won't help to heap up your treasures in this world," he said. It was a little bit like he could read my thoughts.

"We're just trying to save a little corn to get us through the winter," I said.

"After New Year's it's only two and a half months till spring," Mrs. Gibbs said.

"It's the hardest two and a half months of the year," Hank said.

"We've got to get us a new cow somewhere," I said.

"The Lord will provide what we need when we need it," Preacher Gibbs said.

"The Lord helps them that helps theirselves," Mrs. Gibbs said.

"I reckon Christians have to work as hard as anybody else," Hank said.

"They have to work as hard," the preacher said, "but it means more." It struck me that he didn't say Christians enjoyed work more, or had it any easier. But saying that their work meant more sounded more than just talk. It sounded like the truth, or at least the truth as he seen it. I had never met a preacher like Preacher Gibbs. He had walked all the way up Gap Creek valley to visit us again and invite us to church on New Year's Day. And he appeared to really think about what he said. He was a man with silver in his hair and red in his cheeks. He was a farmer like everybody else on Gap Creek, and he looked like he had worked outside in a lot of wind and weather.

I felt what Preacher Gibbs had said went to the heart of things. "We'll try to come to church tomorrow," I said.

"You will be welcome," Mrs. Gibbs said.

"We'll try to come," Hank said. He give me a look like I had spoke too soon.

"That's all I can ask," Preacher Gibbs said.

When they was gone Hank said, "You may have to go to church by yourself."

"Don't you want to go?" I said.

"I don't know nobody here," Hank said. "And we may be leaving here anyway."

"That's the way to get to know people," I said. But it sounded strange to hear myself talk to Hank that way. Because he had always been the sociable one. He was twice as sociable as me. He loved to go to church, and he loved to sing in church. It was the fact that he had lost his job, and was worried about the baby coming and the loss of his money, and embarrassed by the way he had acted in the flood, that made him standoffish. I had to help him out. The night of the flood had took away his confidence.

"We can go one time," I said. "And if people ain't friendly we don't have to go back."

THE NEXT DAY was cold and clear. The ground was spewed up in places with ice and crumbs of dirt stood on hairs of ice on the banks of the road. There is a feeling about the morning of New Year's Day. It appears like the slate has been scrubbed clean. In cities they celebrate New Year's at twelve o'clock at night. But New Year's always seemed to me to start at sunrise, in the new light of morning. The early light on New Year's Day looks different and the air feels different. I always imagine I can smell fresh lumber and fresh pine needles. I fixed hot coffee and grits and eggs to go with the molasses. I knowed I had to go to church. It was the first day of the new week, and the first day of the new century.

"We'll take the buggy," Hank said. I'd been afraid I might have to walk by myself down the valley, but he must have been studying overnight about going and changed his mind. I heated some bricks in the fireplace to put on the floor of the buggy to keep our feet warm. And I wrapped myself in my overcoat and put a scarf around my head. It felt like a ceremony we was taking part in, getting ready to go to church, driving down the rough road to the forks where the church was. Hank had to drive real slow because of all the ruts and washouts. Our breaths smoked in the biting air.

I hadn't been to the little church-house on Gap Creek since Mr. Pendergast's funeral. It was really no bigger than a chapel, made of clapboards that had been whitewashed. There was big old boys standing outside smoking their pipes, like there always is before a church service. Everybody nodded or tipped their hat as we went in.

It felt like everybody in the church turned to look at us as we stepped through the door. I knowed Hank wouldn't want to set in the choir on the left with most of the older women. And I didn't figure we would set up front on the right in the Amen Corner. We walked up the aisle between the benches, and Hank stopped halfway up toward the pulpit and we set down on the right side. I don't guess there was more than twelve benches on either side anyway.

It had been so long since we had gone to a service I felt tense, like I didn't know what to expect. I thought, How silly to be worried, for it was just a worship service on New Year's Day. But it felt like something important was about to happen. I touched my stomach and hoped I didn't get sick.

A man with curly gray hair and red garters on his sleeves stood up. He held a song book and he turned to the woman that set at the organ. "Number two hundred and forty-three, 'Let the Lower Lights Be Burning,'" he called out. I opened the hymnal that laid on the bench and the organist begun to play. I was pretty sure her name was Linda Jarvis. I hadn't heard any music for months, except what I tried to sing with Hank on Christmas Eve. The organ notes filled the little church like they was coming from deep in the ground. The deep notes was like air blowing out of caves, and the higher notes was like birds singing in the sky.

What a wonderful thing music is, I thought. I had forgot how good music is in a public place. It was just a little organ, but it gathered and pushed the air in the sweetest breath. There was such color in the notes. I seen purples and blues and greens in the air. The organ music was living breath.

And when the song leader started to sing and we joined in, I seen I had forgot how voices joined together. One voice may be beautiful, and some voices not so beautiful by theirselves. But when they all joined in the church it was something different. All the voices blended and helped each other make a fuller kind of harmony. All together the voices seemed to raise the air. They made the church-house feel like it was lifting off the ground.

I seen how I had missed singing. I had missed singing with other people and I had missed the praise of singing. Hank sung beside me.

When the song was over the preacher prayed. "Lord, make us thankful for the privilege of being alive to see this new day and new year and this new century," he said. "Make us grateful for the honor of being alive, for the honor of your presence and blessing. Make us thankful for your love, which is showered without condition on our unworthiness. Help us to grow in wisdom in this new year and new hundred years. Help us to see your face and your love in the faces around us, and wherever we look in the world. For there is no place where your love has not already gone before us."

It was the best prayer I'd ever heard. It was the kind of prayer I would have liked to make myself, if I was able to. It was a prayer meant especially for me. If Preacher Gibbs had been able to read my mind and look into my heart he could not have spoke to me any better.

"We will sing another hymn," Preacher Gibbs said, and the song leader stood up again. "'We Are Going Down the Valley,'" he announced.

We are going down the valley one by one,
With our faces toward the setting of the sun.

Down the valley where the mournful cypress grows,
Where the stream of death in silence onward flows.

We are going down the valley, going down the valley,
Going toward the setting of the sun.

We are going down the valley, going down the valley,
Going down the valley one by one.

243

When the song was over Preacher Gibbs stood up behind the pulpit. It was made of ordinary planks with old varnish, small enough for him to lean over. "I will read two short texts today," he said. "One is from Matthew and one is from Revelation. 'Go therefore, and teach all nations, baptizing them in the name of the Father, and of the Son, and of the Holy Ghost. Teaching them to observe all things whatsoever I have commanded you and, lo, I am with you alway, even to the end of the world.'"

The preacher turned his Bible to the very last pages.

And the Spirit and the bride say, Come. And let him that heareth say, Come. And let him that is athirst come. And whosoever will, let him take the water of life freely.'"

The preacher read in a slow, deliberate voice. As he read he made every word sparkle, like it was a living thing he held up to the light. I had heard those words before, but I'd never heard such force in them.

"These are the words I want you to think about this New Year's Day," Preacher Gibbs said. "These are the words of the great promise of Immanuel, and the Great Commission. 'For, lo, I am with you alway, even to the end of the world.' And that is what I want to say to you today, that he is with us. He is with us right here on Gap Creek in the state of South Carolina. He is with us in the air of this church, and he is with us in the sunlight of New Year's Day.

"The Lord is with us as we go about our work. He is with us when we milk the cow or chop wood. He is with us while we sleep, and when we are sick. He is with us in the still small hours, and he is with us at the hour of our death. He will hold our hand in our moment of grief, and he is present in our greatest joy. He is with the moth͡ nurses her child, and he is with the mother who loses

͡ in eternity, but he is with us in time also. His is present in each hour and each minute and second. The blessing of his presence is in each moment and the thought of each moment. The Lord is in the fullness of memory, and the fullness of hope for the future. The Lord is in the promise of tomorrow. And in the last words of Revelation, in the last words of the Bible, in the last words the Savior spoke before the Second Coming, he tells us that salvation is for whoever will accept it. Salvation is not just for the chosen people, or the best people, or good people. Salvation is for the sinners, and for those afraid and those persecuted. Salvation is for those afflicted and those crippled and those troubled in their minds. Salvation is for the liar and the adulterer, for the blasphemer. Salvation is for whoever is athirst and will take the water of life freely."

What Preacher Gibbs said explained something I had always wondered about. Why would the Lord exclude so many people from heaven if he loved everybody, the way most preachers said. If only good people could get to heaven then there wouldn't hardly be anybody there.

"Salvation is not something you have to search mightily for," Preacher Gibbs said. "Salvation is here now for anybody who will accept it. Salvation is free as the air and the sunlight and the water in the spring. Salvation is close as the dust under our feet and fertile as a newground in April. Salvation is here, now. It is not in some vague future. All you have to do is accept it."

Preacher Gibbs was the best preacher I'd ever heard. He spoke calm like he was thinking about everything he said. He spoke almost quiet. There was no shouting and pounding the pulpit, no ranting about hellfire like a lot of preachers did. He spoke like he was talking to you from the heart, and like he respected you. He talked like he was talking to equals, and he talked like he was speaking directly to you. He spoke like he already understood your worries. And he talked like he believed in you, and wanted to cheer you up, not make you more afraid. The way he talked you could feel his respect for other people. He was trying his best to tell the truth and make people feel at home with theirselves.

"Now if anybody here would like to come forward and dedicate their life to Jesus on this New Year's Day, I will pray with them, and I will rejoice with them," Preacher Gibbs said. "The only thing we have to be ashamed of is not accepting his love. We are here in the fellowship of the Spirit, and in the spirit of welcome."

The song leader stood up and the organist started playing "Just As I Am." There was a hush in the church. The air was charged so tight it wanted to bust into flame. I seen it was time I rededicated myself. It was time I made a new profession of faith. Even though I had been baptized and was a member of the church on the mountain, I seen it was time I humbled myself like a little child and confessed my need for a new covenant with the Spirit.

"If the Spirit moves you, come forward," the preacher said. "Begin a new life with the New Year. We are entering a century of the telephone, of steam and speed. Are you ready to face it?" I stepped out toward the aisle. I felt like I was gliding and couldn't hardly feel my feet moving. I think Hank reached out to hold me back, but then let his hand slide off my elbow. As I stepped forward I could feel all eyes pressing on me. I was pushed by their attention. It had been a long time since I had been looked at by so many people. But I was doing what I had to do. I walked slow to the front of the church and knelt down at the altar in front of the pulpit.

"We will pray with this our sister," Preacher Gibbs said. I put my hands on the varnished wood of the altar, like I was holding on to a railing. The air was warmed by the woodstove on the left, in front of the choir. The air was warm and smelled of burning oak.

I have always wondered what people mean when they say they are converted or sanctified. The Pentecostals talk about the baptism of fire. Some people, like Paul in the Bible, talk of seeing a blinding light, and preachers talk about being washed in the blood. I have heard of women that fainted, and I've heard of women that danced and shouted and spoke in tongues like Ginny Powell on Green River. But I didn't know what to expect. Something was moving me, but I could do whatever I wanted to. I was free to do what I chose, and what I wanted was to rededicate my life.

"Lord, we are here to pledge our lives to you," Preacher Gibbs said. "We are imperfect and sometimes confused. But we know there is no safety and no comfort except in your will and in your love. Give us peace and give us the patience to know peace and to accept your love."

As the preacher spoke I seen how it was such a little thing to be humble and to accept the gift of life, to face the future, to look at the future calmly. It was different from speaking in tongues, and it was different from the kind of frenzy and rapture you hear about. It was the still, small voice I wanted to hear. I didn't want to be wrenched apart by feeling. I wanted to be calm and open and wise as the light on New Year's morning.

While they sung another verse of the hymn in quieter voices behind me, I prayed myself. Lord, I said, make me worthy to have a baby and raise it. Life with Hank is going to be hard, as everybody's life is hard. Give me the strength to face the pain, and to eat the pain like bread. And give me the sense to know joy and to accept joy. For I know I'm weak and can't sustain myself alone. Teach me to accept what is give to me.

When the singing stopped Preacher Gibbs reached down and took me by the hand and helped me stand. "Sister Julie," he said, "do you accept Jesus as your personal savior?"

"I do," I said. It sounded like a marriage ceremony.

"Do you dedicate your life to his will and glory and his work?" the preacher said.

"I do."

"Do you wish to join the fellowship of this congregation?"

"I do," I said. I hadn't thought about joining the church. I had only thought about rededicating my life to the Lord. But I seen it was the thing to do. Since I was living on Gap Creek I should belong to the Gap Creek church. Our fellowship could only be with those around us.

What I felt as I looked out into the faces of the congregation was not any sweeping whirlwind or flash of light. The joy I felt was steady as music you hear behind you, sustaining and clear. The faces looking at me was not of saints, but ordinary people. And that was the congregation I wanted to be a part of, just ordinary people like myself. I didn't need to be part of any special group. I was just a sinner that had accepted grace, and I needed the fellowship of other sinners.

"Shall we open the doors of the church?" the preacher called out. There was nods and several of the deacons said yes. "All opposed?" the preacher shouted. Nobody spoke up.

"Do you come to us on profession of faith?" Preacher Gibbs said.

"I do," I said.

"Let's all come forward and give Sister Julie the right hand of fellowship," Preacher Gibbs said.

I stood there beside the preacher while the organist played "By Jordan's Stormy Banks." And one by one the people in the room come forward. The women in the choir come first, and some shook hands with both hands and looked me in the eye. And some only shook with one hand and didn't look me in the eye. Some of the older women hugged me, and some of the younger women had tears in their eyes. I looked into their faces as each one come up. I didn't usually look people I didn't know right in the face. But I wanted to stand closer to them and be close to them. I wanted to be near people. There was young boys that come up, so young you wouldn't hardly think they was members of the church, and they wouldn't look at me. They shook hands with faces turned aside and hurried on. And some big old boys that had outgrowed their clothes so the pants come up to their ankles grinned and looked like they would like to kiss me if they dared. And older men wearing overalls and flannel shirts, and blushing because they was not used to shaking hands with a young woman, come forward and took my hand for a second. The only grown person left standing in the church that didn't come forward was Hank. He stood by hisself and looked down at the bench in front of him.

The last people to come forward was the elders, the deacons on the right side of the church. Some of them was very old, and stumbled up to the front of the church with their canes. Some had long white beards stained around the mouth with tobacco juice, and some had not shaved in a week and looked grizzled. Some was clean shaved and their faces was weathered like shoe leather. Some of the old men's eyes sparkled, like they was young boys looking out of their wrinkles at a pretty girl. And some had cloudy eyes, like they didn't see too well and wasn't even trying to see.

As I shook all the hands I had a sweet, calm feeling. In front of everybody, I didn't feel exposed. I felt the warmth of their attention and acceptance of me. The church was a warm and welcoming place. In the cold January day the warmest place was in the fellowship of the congregation. It was the place of music, the music of fellowship and communion.

After I went back to my place beside Hank, he didn't look at me. He looked straight ahead like he didn't even know I was there. But I wasn't sure why. After all, he was a member of the church at Painter Mountain, and he had been baptized and he liked to sing hymns and lead in prayer. He looked off into the dark corner of the church like he didn't hardly care, or was still thinking of the night of the flood.

. . .

AFTER I JOINED the church I felt better about living on Gap Creek. We didn't have no money, and we didn't have a cow, and Hank didn't have a job. But there was a fellowship at Preacher Gibbs's church that made you feel connected. In the worst times there is, you can get through with the support of other people. In fact, you can only get through with the help of other people. When I lived at home I had always been helped out by Mama and my sisters. I had never really been left to the mercy of myself before.

Every time I went to church after New Year's, to a prayer meeting or a preaching service, to a singing, I felt better. And when one of the women from the church, Mrs. Gibbs or Elizabeth Rankin or Joanne Johnson, come to visit and set with me in the kitchen or by the fireplace talking, I felt like a human being again. A woman has to have a woman friend to talk to.

"I didn't think you wanted to join the church down here," Hank said. "Does that mean you think we're going to stay here?"

"They are mighty friendly people here," I said.

"If they are so friendly why ain't they helped us find Mr. Pendergast's heirs?" he said.

Sometimes Hank acted like he didn't care what happened, but his worry always circled back to the house and finding out who owned it. We couldn't afford to move nowhere, unless he got a new job, and we could only stay in the house until the real owners showed up. The uncertainty of it wore Hank down, that and the worry about the baby coming. It was like a man to show his worry but never talk much about what was making him angry.

BUT FOUR WEEKS after I did, Hank joined the Gap Creek Baptist Church too. I knowed he would change his mind, because he loved going to church and singing just as much as I did. And I knowed he would change his mind without telling me, that he would not admit that he was wrong but would go ahead and join. I had learned Hank's ways and I thought that was what he was going to do, and it was.

It was late January and we was attending Sunday service though the road was froze and there was ice in puddles and along the edges of the creek. The air in the church was toasted by the little stove in front of the choir, and the church was filled with the smell of hot metal and burning oak and the lift of the preacher's voice. When Preacher Gibbs called out the invitational hymn and give the altar call, Hank stepped out in the aisle and went to the front of the church. He done it like he had planned for days to do it. He had made up his mind without telling me. That was his way.

Hank didn't kneel down at the altar like he was praying. He stopped in front of the preacher and said something to him. And I seen him reach out his hand like he was going to shake hands, like he had said he wanted to join the church by profession of faith. And then I seen him fall forward like he was going to lean on the preacher's shoulder, but he sunk out of sight.

I must have hollered, for I heard somebody cry out as I run down the aisle to see where Hank had fell to the floor. I'd heard a knock like a rock hitting a block of wood, which must have been Hank's head hitting the floor. He sprawled in front of the altar just like he had fainted. I bent over him and the preacher rolled him over. "Hank," the preacher said.

Hank's face was white as a pocket handkerchief, and his eyes was rolled back. I wondered if he had died or had some kind of fit. "You folks stand back," the preacher said. The singing had stopped and people was gathering around to look at Hank.

"Bring him some water," Preacher Gibbs said. Somebody brought a dipper of water from the bucket at the back of the church. The preacher lifted up Hank's head and I held the dipper to his lips.

"Wake up, Hank," I said. I tipped the dipper against his lips and water spilled down on his chin. Hank opened his eyes and some color come back into his cheeks. There was a startle in his eyes when he seen all the people gathered round and looking down at him.

"Stand back," the preacher said and waved his left arm.

"What . . . ," Hank said.

"You must have fainted," I said. "Have a drink of water."

"Don't want a drink," Hank said. He put his hands back against the floor to push hisself up. The preacher and me helped him to his feet. There was a red mark on his forehead that was beginning to swell to a pumpknot. Hank took a deep breath like he was trying to catch his wind after a struggle. He grinned and looked embarrassed. Everybody was gathered round and there was no way he could escape their attention.

"Brother Hank has asked to join our church by profession of faith," Preacher Gibbs called out. "How do you vote on his membership?"

"Yea!" several voices called.

"All opposed?" the preacher said.

Nobody said nay and the preacher declared the yeas carried the motion. "Let's all come up and give Brother Hank the right hand of fellowship," he said. He motioned to Linda Jarvis at the organ and she begun playing "Bringing in the Sheaves."

People formed theirselves into a line and come forward to shake hands with Hank. He grinned cause he didn't know what else to do, after fainting in front of the whole church. But I think he was relieved too. For he wanted to sing with the congregation and pray with the congregation as much as I did. For Hank liked to lead in prayer, and he knowed as well as I did it was better to sing with others than to stand off silent by yourself.

Eleven

It was a good thing Hank and me joined the church and had the support of the church, for things got harder that winter. Along in early February it come the hardest freeze I had ever seen or heard of. It reminded me of Cold Friday.

The sun come out on Gap Creek but it didn't do much good. The sun was little and cold in the sky as the tip of an icicle. The ground was set like steel. It got so cold frost started growing like white ferns and fancy lace on the windowpanes, and fire in the fireplace couldn't heat the house enough to make it melt. It got so cold the mud puddles and low spots in the road set hard.

"Can't stay this cold for long," Hank said when he come in with his face and hands red.

"What if it snows?" I said.

"Too cold to snow," Hank said.

"How can it get too cold to snow?" I said.

"It can't snow when it gets near zero," Hank said.

Almost all our taters had been ruint, and some of the canned stuff. The flood had rotted all the meat on the lower shelves of the smokehouse, and we had eat up most of the rest of the meat by the beginning of February. The cow was gone and there was no milk or butter. It was too cold for Hank to want to climb up on the ridge looking for turkeys.

"Everything is hiding away in thickets," Hank said.

We had some cornmeal and grits and a little bit of shoulder meat left. But we was fast running out of coffee and sugar and things that had to be bought. We didn't have but a few cents of money. By early February my belly was beginning to show. Everybody could see I was expecting.

"You should eat more than you do," Hank said.

"I eat plenty," I said.

"You ought to eat more to grow a strong baby," Hank said.

The thing I begun to crave in the cold weather was jelly, hot biscuits and cold jelly. I had eat all the jelly Mama had sent with Lou and Garland. There was still a few jars of blackberry jelly and grape jelly and apple jelly in the basement, but only a few. I brought them up one at a time and wiped off the dust and eat jelly three times a day. I had to stop myself from eating jelly between meals. I put jelly on cornbread, and I put it on oatmeal. I wanted jelly so bad I could have eat it with a spoon. I thought constantly about the cool quivering softness of jelly melting on my tongue. There is something about the firmness of jelly that makes it taste better. Jelly has body and has to be cut; it won't pour like honey or molasses. Jelly is soft rubies or amber. Jelly is almost alive. I craved jelly so bad I put it on grits and mush when I run out of biscuit flour. I wanted jelly so much I smeared it on whatever else I was eating.

I dreamed about jelly and imagined I was eating it with butter and toast, long after we didn't have any butter. I dreamed I was eating jelly and drinking milk, and that was the perfect thing for the baby. I dreamed about jelly and feared we would run out of jelly before the baby was born. I counted the jars; there was only four left.

. . .

ON THE FOURTH day of the cold spell, when the sky was clear as a big bubble the sun played its light on, there was a knock at the door. I wondered who could be out in such withering cold. I prayed it wasn't Timmy Gosnell. It was Elizabeth Rankin and Joanne Johnson. They had scarves wrapped around their heads and around their faces. Their noses was red as coals.

"Come on in before you freeze," I said. Even after I closed the door I could feel the cold air falling off their coats. I led them to the fireplace.

"We wanted to see how you was doing," Elizabeth said and looked at my belly.

"Takes all my strength just to stay warm," I said.

They unbuttoned their coats but didn't take them off. I asked them to please set down.

"We can't stay but a minute," Joanne said.

"I'm mighty glad you come," I said.

Elizabeth opened her coat and took out a bag she had been carrying beneath it. "Here is a few things I thought you could use for the baby," she said. She opened the bag and took out a little flannel jacket that looked small enough for a doll.

"Most of these is for a bigger baby," Elizabeth said. "But you'll need a few things for when it is first born."

"And because it's yellow you can use it for either a boy or a girl," Joanne said. I took the little jacket and it looked no bigger than a glove. The flannel was soft as velvet.

Elizabeth reached into the poke and pulled out a little gown and another jacket. She took out a coat and cap. "My Jessie wore these a few years ago, but they're practically new," she said.

"I certainly do thank you," I said. I felt my eyes get moist. I'd never had many women friends and I was touched that they had walked in the cold to give me the baby clothes. They made the cold February sweeter, and the heat from the fire sweeter.

Joanne reached into the pocket of her coat and pulled out something wrapped in tissue paper. "I have brung you this," she said. It was a pair of knitted booties and a cap to match. They was made of lavender and blue yarn, in a pattern that reminded me of a picture I'd seen of stained glass windows. The yarn was so bright it seemed to glow.

"I figure these colors will suit either a boy or a girl," Joanne said. Her fingers looked too rough and swelled at the joints to do any knitting. I leaned down and hugged her I was so touched.

"You have both saved me a lot of work," I said.

"When a baby comes, a woman don't have time to make clothes," Elizabeth said.

I set down and held the baby clothes on my lap and just looked at them, stroking the soft flannel and the warm knitted yarn of the cap and booties.

"Do you crave sour things or sweet things?" Joanne said.

I hesitated to say I craved either one, because it sounded so silly.

"Sometimes a woman craves salty things," Elizabeth said.

"I never heard of that," Joanne said.

"I guess I always had a sweet tooth," I said, and giggled.

"Well, I brung you this," Elizabeth said. She reached into her coat pocket and pulled out something dark. It was a jelly jar. "This is cherry preserves," she said.

"How did you know what I craved?" I exclaimed.

"I was just guessing," Elizabeth said. "I remember how I craved jams and preserves." Her face was wrinkled and she had a few gray hairs, but she looked utterly happy, happy the way people are when they give to somebody or please somebody.

Cherry preserves was one thing I hadn't had in years. It was something different from blackberry and grape and apple jelly. I felt like gobbling it up right there. There was nothing Elizabeth could have brought that would have been more welcome. "How can I thank you?" I said.

"And I brung you some of this," Joanne said. She reached into her other coat pocket and brought out a jar. The jar looked almost black, but when I held it up to the firelight I seen the contents was deep red.

"It's raspberry," Joanne said.

I put the two jars on the mantel and felt tears in my eyes when I turned back to Joanne and Elizabeth. "I don't know how to thank you," I said.

"Nothing but a little jelly and some castoff clothes," Elizabeth said.

"Best way to thank us is to have a healthy baby," Joanne said.

"The world wouldn't have lasted this long if women didn't help each other," Elizabeth said.

"The world would be a better place if people helped each other more," Joanne said.

I held up the baby things with their fine stitches and knitting done for little arms and legs and heads one by one. "You all are mighty good to me," I said.

"It's the least we can do," Elizabeth said.

THAT NIGHT AS I laid in bed, I kept thinking about how kind Joanne and Elizabeth had been to me. It made me feel growed up and kind myself to be treated that way. It made me feel like I was a bigger person. They made me want to be better.

There was a crack, like a shotgun blast, not too far from the house. Hank jumped up in bed like he hadn't been sleeping sound either.

"What was that?" I said.

"I heard it in my sleep," he said.

"You must not have been asleep," I said.

We listened in the cold dark. It was the coldest night I could remember. The air in the bedroom felt prickly and needled with cold. The house creaked in the roof, as a house will when the temperature drops to zero.

"I know what it was," Hank said.

"What was it?" I said.

"That was a tree exploding," Hank said.

"How can a tree explode?" I said.

"When it gets real cold and the sap freezes in a maple or poplar, some tree where the sap is starting to rise. And when the sap freezes it will bust a tree wide open."

I laid in the dark thinking of a big poplar that had busted to splinters. I had heard of such a thing a long time ago but had forgot about it. The tip of my nose was cold and firm.

"I guess a person would explode if they froze," I said. I thought of some poor soul like Timmy Gosnell that might have lost their way in the dark and fell in a sinkhole.

"People has too much salt in them to freeze," Hank said.

"People freeze to death," I said. "Drunks freeze to death."

"But they don't freeze solid and explode," Hank said.

There was another blast come out of the dark. It sounded like a hammer fell out of the sky onto a big rock. It sounded so loud it hurt the air. The sound echoed off the sides of the valley two or three times, off the cliff I called Old Fussy Face.

"Sounds like there's a war going on," Hank said.

"I'm glad I'm inside," I said.

"And I'm glad the baby is warm inside you," Hank said. We laid in the dark talking like that. I could remember hearing Mama and Papa talking in the dark when I was a little girl. It felt good to talk when you couldn't see anything. Under the warm quilts we laid like we was in a nest or a tent, or maybe a cave.

"What are we going to name the baby?" I said.

"If he's a boy we'll name him Lafayette after my daddy," Hank said.

"That's a long name for a youngun," I said.

"People will call him Fate," Hank said.

"We could name him after Papa," I said.

"But he will be a Richards," Hank said.

"What if the baby is a girl?" I said.

"Then we'll name her after your mama," Hank said.

I was glad he had said that, for I sure would hate to name my daughter after Ma Richards. "Delia is a beautiful name," I said.

There was another pop, but it was in the house, and it was not as loud as the others. We laid still and listened to the creaks and groans in the house. And then there was a crash in the attic, like a ham of meat had fell.

"This house is going to fall apart," Hank said.

"Its bark is worse than its bite," I said. We both giggled. And then there was another explosion out in the woods across the creek where a hemlock or poplar, or maybe a cucumber tree, had busted wide open in the cold.

I'D HEARD THE rumor that Timmy Gosnell had been arrested in Greenville for public drunkenness and was being held in the county jail. And it must have been true, for I hadn't seen him on the road in weeks, though sometimes his name come up when I was talking to Elizabeth or Joanne, or the preacher's wife.

"Poor Timmy," they would say. "Ain't he the saddest case."

"He never was no count," one would say.

"I reckon his daddy was worser than him."

Elizabeth asked me if it was true I had run Timmy out of the yard with Mr. Pendergast's walking stick.

"I was so mad I didn't hardly know what I was doing," I said. I was ashamed to think of that day.

"He scares me," Joanne said, "the way he stares at you sideways, and the way his voice rips out in such an ugly way."

"He could mark a pregnant woman's baby," Elizabeth said.

"How come?" I said.

"He's got a demon in him that makes him drink," Elizabeth said. "He's possessed by a devil that will mark a baby."

"Mark it how?" I said.

"Mark it so it'll stagger and roll its eyes and won't have good sense, just like him."

HANK AND ME was eating dinner on Saturday when we heard somebody holler from the road. All we had was cornbread and green beans, but they tasted mighty good. There come this holler from out front, and it sent a shiver through me, for I knowed on the spot who it was.

"Piieendergaasss!" the voice yelled.

"Is that Timmy Gosnell?" Hank said.

"I think it is," I said.

"That drunk," Hank said. "I thought he was in jail."

"I thought so too."

"Piieendergaasss!" the voice hollered, "come outch hhhrrrrr."

"He can't come here and bother us this way," Hank said. I seen Hank was scared, because this was something he wasn't used to facing. And because he was afraid I was afraid. But I wasn't as much afraid of Timmy Gosnell as of what Hank might do that he'd be sorry for later. When Hank was scared was when he lost his temper. And Preacher Gibbs wasn't here to help out this time.

Hank pushed back his chair and hurried to the front door, and I run after him. When he flung open the front door I seen Timmy

Gosnell standing halfway between the road and the steps. He had on his long black coat, but he had lost his hat and his head was mostly bald. There was a scab on top of his head like he had been hit or cut there.

"Where's Piendergaasss?" he said, and gulped, when he seen Hank and me on the porch.

"Mr. Pendergast is dead," Hank said.

Timmy Gosnell stood in the sun like he was trying to take in what Hank had said. He bowed his head and looked at us through his eyebrows. "Piendergaasss is hiding," he said, "cause he ooowes me money."

"We don't owe you money," Hank said again, and moved toward the steps.

"You're by G-g-god lying," Timmy Gosnell said.

"Don't call me a liar," Hank said, and his voice rose with the strain of anger.

Timmy Gosnell looked sideways and squinted in the sunlight. "Piendergaass is hiding," he said.

"Get out of the yard," Hank said. "You go on home."

"Ain't your house," Timmy said.

"Get away from here," Hank said.

"The hell you . . . ," the drunk man said and waved his arm at Hank.

Hank looked around and seen a rocking chair on the porch. It was a chair I sometimes set in on warm days to mend socks. Hank grabbed the rocker and held it in front of him as he descended the steps. "You get on away from here," he said.

"Don't do nothing," I said to Hank. I could tell how scared Hank was. I was afraid he would lose control of hisself, like the night of the flood.

"You stay out of this," Hank said to me.

Timmy Gosnell shaded his eyes and looked at me like he hadn't noticed me before. "That woman has got Piendergaass's money," he said.

"You shut your mouth!" Hank said. He shoved the chair into the drunk man's chest and he fell backwards.

"You can't cover up," Timmy said. "Piendergaass knows what he done."

"Don't hurt him," I said. "He's just a drunk man." I was afraid that if Hank hurt Timmy Gosnell, the sheriff would come and arrest Hank. After all, we was the newcomers on Gap Creek. I remembered what Elizabeth had said about Timmy being demon possessed and apt to mark the baby of any woman that looked into his red eyes. I tried not to look at him directly.

"Get on away from here," Hank said, and pushed the drunk man down on the ground again.

"You don't hold water," Timmy said, as his voice rose to a scream, "going to church and stealing Piendergaass's money."

"I ain't took nobody's money," Hank said.

"Let him go," I said. I reached out to take Hank's elbow but he jerked away. And then it was like everything happened at once. I seen Timmy Gosnell pull the knife out of his coat pocket. It was not a pocketknife and not a butcher knife, but maybe an old hunting knife. And at the same instant I felt Hank lose control of hisself. It was what I had been afraid of. He drove the chair into Timmy's chest and face, hitting him in the mouth with a rocker.

"Go on ahead, kill me," the drunk man laughed, "'stead of pay- ing me." He wiped blood from his mouth with the back of his hand and laughed again like he didn't feel no pain.

"Get on away from here," Hank said. He swung the chair and hit Timmy upside of his head. I seen blood on the bald head where the scab had been knocked loose. Timmy laughed again and held his ear.

"Hank!" I yelled, but Hank wasn't listening to me. He tossed the chair aside and grabbed Timmy by the collar of his coat. He drug him backwards across the yard to the road. There was blood on the drunk man's chin and on his forehead. He squealed like a hurt pig. Hank drug him across the road and pushed him over the bank into the creek.

"He'll drown," I hollered, and run to the creek bank. Timmy Gosnell was laying in the water like he was too weak to get up. He thrashed around and raised his head out of the water. In the black coat he looked like an animal that had crawled out of the mud.

"He'll freeze to death," I said.

"Let him freeze," Hank said, out of breath, and rubbed his hands on his pants like he was trying to get rid of filth.

"And you'll be arrested for murder," I said. "And then where will we be?" I worked my way down to the creek and tried to take hold of Timmy under his arm. He was heavy as a sack of rocks.

"Drown me, all I care," Timmy said and spit through the blood in his mouth.

I stepped into the water to get a hold on him and still couldn't move him. I pulled him a little way toward the bank before Hank come down and helped me. It took both of us to haul the drunk man out of the water and drag him through the weeds back up to the road.

We got Timmy on his feet and the water appeared to have sobered him a little. He was bleeding from his nose as well as from his mouth. "I'm gone tell Mama and Daddy what you done," he said. He started walking, taking short steps. His coat was wet and covered with mud and pieces of straw.

"You're so crazy you think your mama and daddy is still alive," Hank hollered after him.

"Gone tell them," Timmy cried and kept going.

"He's an idiot," Hank said.

"That was awful," I said. "He don't know what he's doing."

"Maybe that will teach him a lesson," Hank said. But I could tell

Hank was beginning to be embarrassed, the way anybody is after they lose their temper. I had a bad feeling as I watched Timmy Gosnell shuffle on down the road.

"Would you just let him insult you?" Hank said.

"He's a drunk man," I said.

IT'S SHAMEFUL TO admit that you have been hungry, that you have been hungry as a grown woman, as a married woman. It's even more embarrassing to admit you've been hungry while carrying a baby. We made do with what we had on the place and what church members give us. But there was a time in the late winter when things got lean and hard, and we just had to outlast them.

By the end of March all our meat was gone, down to a little fatback. The smokehouse smelled bare and stale. The taters was gone, and the canned stuff that had survived the flood was all eat up. There was nothing left in the house but a little cornmeal and grits from the corn we had saved from the flood.

Hank took Mr. Pendergast's shotgun and went into the mountains every day, but the turkeys had all been killed by the hard winter, or shot by other hunters. They had disappeared from the holler where they had been so plentiful. It was the wrong season for shooting squirrels and rabbits, but sometimes he killed a squirrel and I would make it into a stew. And then he run out of shotgun shells.

"A shell costs so much it's not worth wasting on a squirrel," Hank said.

"Couldn't you borrow more shells?" I said.

"I'd be ashamed to ask to borrow shotgun shells," Hank said, "unless there was something bigger to kill than squirrels."

"It'll be spring soon," I said.

"Not soon enough," Hank said.

I knowed that if I asked Elizabeth or Joanne or Preacher Gibbs or half a dozen other people they would help us out. But they had already helped us out, and besides, everybody had had a hard time that winter. It was up to us to look after ourselves. If we was going to be grown up married folks who was about to raise a family, we would have to learn to take care of ourselves. It would be a disgrace to depend on other people to bring us things to eat.

When all the dried beans and dried apples was gone, we had nothing but cornmeal and the eggs the chickens laid. There was half a dozen hens left after the flood, and they almost quit laying in late winter. But I was still getting ten eggs a week, and you can live a long time on grits and eggs if you have to. But there wasn't enough eggs for both Hank and me to have one every day. When there was only one egg I would scramble it and give Hank half.

"No, you have the egg," Hank would say.

"I don't want the whole egg," I'd say.

"You're eating for the baby," Hank would say.

"The baby don't want the egg," I said.

"It would turn my stomach to eat that egg," Hank would say. "It would taste like sand."

I discovered hunger don't make you resentful. Hunger makes you slow and brooding, like you are just waiting and waiting. You don't feel like going anywhere or doing anything. Hunger makes you set around, makes you want to go to bed early and sleep late. You don't want to think about nothing, for if you think you will think about good things to eat. When you're hungry you don't want to think at all. You want time to pass. You are waiting for something to happen. You don't want to waste effort. You are saving the fat on your bones and the strength in your blood. You are saving your breath. When you're hungry you don't even daydream a lot. You just drift through the hours and the first thing you know another day is over, another night has gone by. Mostly you want to forget.

. . .

ONE NIGHT I was waked up by wind shivering the bedroom window. Hank was waked up too. We laid there in the dark several minutes. I kept thinking about what we was going to do.

"Couldn't you find work as a carpenter, now that it's spring?" I said.

"I've tried," he said.

"And ain't you worked as a mason too?" I said.

"As a mason's helper," Hank said.

We just laid there in the dark. I reckon you don't go back to sleep so fast when you're still a little hungry.

"Why don't you go over to where they're building the store in Tigerville and get a job?" I said.

"Too long a walk," Hank said.

"No further than Lyman was," I said. But quick, I was sorry I'd said it. It was the wrong thing to say.

"That's my business," Hank said.

"I know it is," I said.

"Don't tell me where to look for a job," Hank said.

"I wasn't telling you," I said. We laid in the dark and listened to the wind roar on the ridge like a hundred freight trains. A gust hit the house again and made it shudder. It's hard to lay close to somebody in the dark when they're mad. I knowed it was better not to say nothing else. There was things about Hank I didn't understand, and it didn't do no good to try to make him talk.

I didn't know whether to put my hand on his chest and slide closer to show how much I loved him, or roll away and let him get over his anger on his own. I didn't feel like going back to sleep. The wind had woke me up, and Hank's resentment had took away all my sleepiness.

"I know you'll find another job," I said, and pushed up close so my cheek was on his shoulder. I tried to say it so it sounded like I was not just trying to cheer him up. I waited to see how his mood was going to go.

"I won't get another job," Hank said.

"Of course you will," I said.

"Word has got out," he said.

"Word of what?" A cold silver wire went down the middle of my back.

"Word that nobody wants to hire me," he said with a sigh.

"That don't make sense," I said. "You are such a good worker."

"They didn't fire me at Lyman just because all the bricks was made," Hank said.

I didn't say nothing. I had to wait for him to go on. It was better for me not to say a thing.

"I got in a fight is why," Hank said.

"With who?" I said.

"I hit the foreman upside of the head," Hank said.

The wind sounded like an ocean of doom coming down the valley.

"He cussed me and I hit him upside of the head," Hank said.

"He must have needed it," I said.

"He was a rawhider," Hank said. "I knowed if he kept mouthing off I was going to hit him. That's why nobody's going to hire me."

"Not everybody will blame you," I said.

"Word has got round," Hank said. I pushed up closer to him.

"I hit him before I even thought," Hank said. "He just kept cussing at me, and I knocked him on the head. It was not the Christian thing to do."

"You will find another job," I said.

"Nobody will ever hire me again," Hank said.

. . .

SINCE THERE WAS no cow to milk, Hank went out every morning to feed the horse and chickens and gather what eggs had been laid in the nests in the henhouse. Some mornings he would come back to the house with no eggs. Sometimes he would come back with an egg in each hand like he was a magician and had plucked them from the air. One morning while I was boiling water for grits he come back into the house but he didn't have any eggs. He looked like he had seen the devil hisself.

"You won't believe this," Hank said.

"Believe what?" I said.

"Come out and look at it," he said.

I left the pot boiling on the stove and followed him out the back door. He marched across the yard and I followed, wondering if the horse had died or he'd caught a thief in the feed room or seen a spook in the barn loft. But he strode right to the chicken house and flung the door open on its leather hinges. "Look at that," he said and stood aside so I could see into the henhouse.

At first I didn't see a thing in the dark except the roost poles and the boxes nailed to the walls with pine needles in them for nests. The chicken house smelled sweet and bitter as it always did. But I could smell blood too. And the place was quiet. There was not a cackle and there wasn't a cluck, as you would expect in the early morning. The chicken house was still as the smokehouse. "What is it?" I said.

"Look," Hank said.

And then I seen a hen laying on the ground in front of me. It was laying flat with its neck stretched out and there was a little blood on the neck. And then I seen another hen laying in the dust beyond that one. I strained my eyes in the shadows and seen all six hens laying on the ground. "What done it?" I said, and felt my face go pale.

"I'd say a mink," Hank said. "Only a mink'd kill them all for a sip of blood from each neck just for the fun of it." I thought of the mink I'd seen in the springhouse in the fall.

"Bad luck goes in a streak," I said. As I looked at the dead hens I thought that if we had plenty to eat and Hank had a job, and there wasn't a baby coming, that mink wouldn't have slipped into the henhouse to kill the chickens. It would have slipped into somebody else's henhouse. It would have found somebody else down on their luck and out of money to rob.

"The Lord taketh away," Hank said.

"And lately he ain't giveth too much," I said. But quick I was sorry I'd said it.

WHAT WE DID that morning was boil water in the washpot and scald all the dead hens. We plucked them and dressed them. There wasn't any way to keep them, so I fried two of them. And then I boiled the other four and made stew and chicken soup, which I put in jars. One of the fried chickens I had Hank carry down the road to Preacher and Mrs. Gibbs. We hadn't give anything to the preacher, and we didn't have no money to tithe into the church. And there was no way we could eat both chickens at once. The stew would keep a week maybe, and the soup even longer. But the fried chicken had to be eat in a day or two.

Just when we needed the eggs most, and just when there was grass for the hens to eat, as well as bugs and beetles, the fowl had been took. It was the kind of thing that made you just want to set down and cry. It made me want to give up.

We had fried chicken for dinner, and I made some cornbread and grits to go with the chicken, and I still had just a little bit of molasses to go with the cornbread.

Hank and me set down at the table with that hot chicken and cornbread and steaming grits, and Hank said the blessing. He returned thanks for the chicken we had to eat. We set at the table and eat real slow. We didn't have any butter for the cornbread and grits.

"This chicken's mighty good," I said.

"It is," Hank said. I knowed he was feeling low, and I didn't want him to get in one of his moods. His jaw was set in a hard line.

"Maybe the Lord seen fit to give us some meat when we need it most," I said.

"Maybe the Lord wants to feed us now so he can starve us later," Hank said.

"It's near about spring," I said.

"It better be," Hank said.

As soon as he finished eating Hank pushed back his chair. "I'm going out," he said, wiping his chin.

"Where you going?" I said.

"I've got to get out of this house," he said. And before I could say anything else he was gone.

Twelve

y living on stew and cornbread and then the chicken soup and cornbread, we got pretty far into spring without starving. I still craved jam, but after I eat what Elizabeth and Joanne had brought I didn't have no more. I craved something fresh, something green, too, but it was a late spring. Sarvis was blooming and buds on the maples was getting red as little match heads.

"Do you think the creesie greens is out?" I said to Hank.

"They're up, but too little to pick," he said. "It'd be easier to pick a mess of four-leaf clover."

But I thought there must be sheltered places along the creek or one of the branches running into the creek where the creesies was big enough to gather. One evening I took a bucket and walked down the valley to where the little branch called Briar Fork come into the creek. There was green grass along the creek bank, but the fields that had been plowed in the fall was still muddy. I walked along the edge of the plowed ground looking for new shoots and sprouts.

Briar Fork led back into a narrow cove. It was almost a toy valley, with corn patches along the branch no wider than a front yard. There was just enough room between the mountains on one side and the mountains on the other for the stream to cut through with a little bit of cleared ground on the sides. They was the kind of patches you could make with a hoe. A crow called somewhere on the ridge, and I could hear a waterfall further up the holler. Pines stood out black on the ridge almost straight above me, against a blue sky with a few white clouds. I was hid from the world, deep in the cove.

As I was looking up at the rim of the mountains my feet touched something soft. It was lush weeds at the edge of the plowed ground. I looked down and seen I had been stepping on creesie greens, growed up several inches, big enough to gather. I knelt down and took a handful of the leaves. They was so tender and soft some of the leaves crushed between my fingers, leaving a green stain. I picked them more gently. The leaves was so fresh they almost melted if you pressed them. Rain had splashed grit on some of the leaves and I tried to gather the cleanest ones.

As I squatted on the ground I seen the mud had caked on my shoes. It was like extra soles had thickened there. Layers of different colors of mud had built up. It was hard to stoop over with my feet raised so high on the mud. There was a pain in my belly from bending over. I stood up and stepped over to the grass to kick the mud off my shoes, swinging my feet hard across the grass to wipe off the thick layers, driving one foot and then another into the grass, knocking off tongues and wedges of mud. I kicked harder, trying to clean the soles. A pain shot through me from deep in my belly. It was like I had colic, a bad gas pain. I stood still to let my insides settle.

The roar of the waterfall upstream sounded closer, like the air had got damp and was passing the sound on. A crow called from almost straight above me. As I stood still, the hurt went away, but there was a hotness in my belly, like something had been stretched or strained. It was probably nothing. It was some kind of cramp from bending over. I wanted to pluck more creesie greens for a good mess. Because they boil down to almost nothing, you have to gather a lot just to cook up a good bowl. Nothing goes better with hot cornbread in the spring than creesie greens. I needed the bucket full just to have a decent meal. I wouldn't have any boiled eggs to put on them, but I still had some vinegar to tame the wild, bitter taste and make it perfect.

I stooped over slow and started picking more greens. They are really just wild mustard, somebody said. But we always called them creesie greens. A pain stung through me like you had plucked a tight wire. This time the pain went right down into my groin. I stood up, and the hurt went away a little. I stood and waited, looking at the clouds easing over the rim of the mountains. What was I to do? I wanted to get a bucket of creesies after coming all that way and finding the patch. Hank and me needed them for a spring tonic. We needed something to thin our blood and get us ready for hot weather. And I needed the minerals in the greens for the baby, to help it grow strong bones and strong nerves. I hadn't had any milk since New Year's. I had to get a good mess of greens to go with our cornbread.

But the pain in my belly didn't go away. The throb worked its way around to my side. It was not so much a tearing pain as a hot burning inside me. I tried to recall anything I had eat that would give me such a pain. Would bending over tear something loose inside me? I patted my belly with green-stained hands and waited for the pain to dim again. Surely my insides would cool off if I stood still long enough. I needed to outwait the pain and get my creesie greens.

But the throb didn't fade. I stood with my weight on one leg, and then I stood with my weight on the other. I listened to the creek and the waterfall above. The pain was not sharp enough to be birth pains. And it wasn't time for the baby to be born anyway. If the baby was born nine months from the time we got married, it would be early summer. If the baby went to full term it would be hot weather before it saw the light of day. That would be another six weeks, before the baby was due.

I leaned forward and my belly felt a little better. But I couldn't stoop over and pick any more greens. There was no way I could squat down and gather more. I had got all the sallet I was going to that day.

Taking short steps and not bouncing any and not twisting any, I carried the bucket back down the branch, walking stiff as a kid does that has a load in his pants. Taking care not to jolt myself, I climbed over fences and through fences. When I made it to the road along the creek, I walked careful as an old woman with arthritis all the way back to the house.

Once inside, all I felt like doing was laying down on the couch. I pulled off my muddy shoes and just flopped there. I could feel my face had went pale.

"You look poorly," Hank said when he seen me.

"It's nothing," I said. "I have just got a pain in my belly."

"Is it your time?" Hank said.

"Just a gas pain," I said. I leaned back on the sofa and held my belly like I could soothe it with my hands.

AFTER I LAID still for a while the pain seemed to go away a little. I thought I could wait it out. I stayed on the couch till suppertime, and then got up and fixed us a little pone of bread to go with the creesie greens. It wasn't the supper I'd planned, but it was enough. I didn't really feel like eating anyway. My belly was too uneasy.

"Are you sick at your stomach?" Hank said when he seen how I picked at my greens and cornbread.

"Just a little gas," I said.

"It's close to your time," Hank said.

"I'd say I had at least another month," I said.

"I'm going after Ma," Hank said. "I told Ma she could come down and help when it was your time."

"It'll be another six weeks," I said. I didn't want to say I'd rather do without any help than have Ma Richards there. I guess Hank was scared, and he didn't want to be alone with me when the baby come. That's why he had thought of going for Ma Richards. Ma could tell him what to do when it come time to go after a midwife.

"I'll be fine tomorrow," I said. I wished I hadn't bent over picking the creesie greens.

BECAUSE OF THE pain burning low in my belly, I didn't sleep too sound that night. I kept thinking about what was going to happen, and about Hank going after Ma Richards. All night I laid there thinking of nothing but bad things. It wore me out, trying to get to sleep. When Hank asked me in the morning how I felt, I said better, for I didn't want him to think no more about going after Ma Richards.

"Now that you're feeling better it's time to go," Hank said.

"What do you mean?" I said.

"I don't want to wait until the labor starts," he said. "Then it'll be too late."

"You could go get Mama," I said.

"Your mama's too busy," Hank said. "And it would hurt Ma's feelings if you had the baby and she wasn't here."

I felt too weak to quarrel about it. Even having Ma Richards to visit didn't seem as bad as quarreling with Hank again before the baby was borned.

Hank left that morning after breakfast. He marched out and

hitched up the horse to the buggy without saying another word. When he was scared he tended not to talk, for if he talked he might talk out his anger. He didn't want to lose the strength and firmness of his anger and be weakened by what scared him. I understood how he felt, but if I told him it would just make him madder. I watched him out the kitchen window as he put the collar on the horse and then the hames, then backed the horse between the shafts of the buggy. Hank could hitch up a horse faster than any-body I ever seen. He made harnessing a horse look easy as tying your shoes.

I watched him swing up into the buggy and flick the reins. And then I hurried to the living room to watch him drive up the road till he was out of sight at the bend where the road begins to climb. The pain in my belly got sharp and sideways, and I felt a little sick at my stomach. I put a hand on my throat and set still for a long time, until the feeling went away. Then I washed the breakfast dishes and tossed out the dishwater into the yard. And I got the broom and swept in the living room and kitchen. I thought the best way to cheer myself up was to keep working.

Along at midmorning there was a knock at the door. When I opened it I seen a slim man with silver hair and a fine gray suit. He looked like he might be a preacher or a lawyer. "How do," I said, not opening the door all the way.

"Ma'am, I'm Wilson Caldwell," he said and tipped his hat.

"Pleased to meet you," I said. I expected him to say something about representing the heirs of Mr. Pendergast's estate. "My hus-band's not here," I said.

"It's the lady of the house I came to see," he said.

I invited him into the living room and asked him to set down. Then I noticed the case he was carrying. It was like a lawyer's case, but thicker.

"I represent the Palmetto Apothecary Company," he said. He

opened the case on the couch, and you never seen such an assortment of little bottles and jars and pillboxes. "Since you are a ways from any drugstore, I bring the pharmacy to you," he said.

"We ain't got any money," I said. A pain kicked through my belly.

"Our prices are the most reasonable in the state," Mr. Caldwell said.

"I'm sure they are," I said. "But we're flat broke." I pressed a hand against the stab in my stomach. That seemed to help.

"Nothing is so precious as your health," the peddler said. It was clear he didn't believe me when I told him we didn't have no money. Maybe because I was living in a big old house he assumed I could not be broke.

"I can supply you with any ointment or salve, tonic or painkiller. I have bismuth of violet and magnesia, camphor and oil of cloves."

Because of the pain in my belly, I didn't feel like arguing with him. I set down on a chair and let him show me laxatives and worm medicines, Epsom salts and smelling salts, paregoric and soothing syrups, boneset tea and poppyseed tea, blood thinners and blood thickeners, peroxide and alcohol. "Now this is our most special product," he said and held up an amber bottle with a purple label.

"What is it?" I said.

"It's our Mineral Spring Tonic," he said. "It makes the old feel young, and the young feel stronger." He winked.

"I just need something for a bellyache," I said.

"This is the perfect medicine," he said. "Would you care for a sample?"

"I ain't got no money," I said.

"This is a free sample," he said. He took a spoon from his case and poured it full of the tonic. The stuff looked like molasses except it fizzed a little. When I took the tonic in my mouth and swallowed, it burned like corn liquor. I felt it sink all the way to my stomach.

"This tonic was invented by my papa," Mr. Caldwell said. "He spent his life studying herbs and remedies learned from the Cherokee Indians. He walked all over the mountains gathering herbs and roots."

"These mountains?" I said.

"All the mountains of South Carolina," Mr. Caldwell said. "He knew the foothills and the mountains of this state."

The tonic give me a warm feeling, but it didn't make the pain go away.

"The most remarkable thing was my papa was completely blind," Mr. Caldwell said. "Yet he drove his buggy over South Carolina and stopped at all the houses."

"That is amazing," I said. The pain in my belly throbbed harder.

"Not as amazing as the fact that he could find herbs in the woods," Mr. Caldwell said. "After all, he had the horse to guide him on the roads. But in the woods he had only a cane to find his way on trails. He dug ginseng and yellowroot and foxglove and konkajohn with nobody to help him. And he never fell off a cliff, though he climbed all over the ledges."

"How did he do it?" I said. The pain was so harsh it was making me sick.

"Nobody knows," Mr. Caldwell said. "It was a gift. He never got snake bit, though he killed a rattler one time. How would a blind man kill a rattlesnake?"

"And he was completely blind?" I said.

"He was born blind," Mr. Caldwell said. "He could just feel where trees and rocks and medicinal plants was. He was blessed and gifted that way. He could play the accordion too, and the guitar, and he could remember everything he ever heard. He could remember how many steps it was to somewhere. And he could tell by the sounds on the streets where he was in a city."

"He must have been a special person," I said. I wished the peddler would leave so I could go lay down.

"He invented this tonic," Mr. Caldwell said. "It was the work of his lifetime."

"Oh!" I said as the pain jolted through my belly. I couldn't help myself.

"Are you . . . ill?" Mr. Caldwell said.

"I feel a little sick," I said and put my hands on my belly.

"It must be close to your time," Mr. Caldwell said.

"I'm afraid it is," I said.

"I'll come through again," he said. "Perhaps you will need something for the baby in the future."

"Might be," I said.

Mr. Caldwell starting packing all the medicines back in his case. He handed me a little bottle of the tonic. "You keep this," he said.

"Thank you," I said, and pressed both hands to my stomach.

"I wish you luck with the baby," Mr. Caldwell said. He acted in a hurry.

"Thank you," I said, but another pain swelled through me and I turned my face away.

MY TROUBLES WASN'T over after the peddler finally left. Instead of getting better, the pain in my belly got worse. It was getting up toward dinnertime, but I didn't feel like fixing anything to eat, and I didn't feel like eating either. My belly was uneasy as quicksand. What if this is the baby coming? I thought. What if this is birth pains? But the baby couldn't be due for more than a month according to my figures. What I had must be appendicitis or locked bowels, or some kind of tumor inside me.

I looked up the road, but there was no sign of Hank or the buggy. The closest neighbor was George and Hester Poole a mile and a half down the road. Even if I got out on the porch and screamed nobody would hear. I was alone in the house, and I was alone in the deep valley.

The best way to fight pain is to ignore it. I would make some hot cornbread, to have for supper, and if I felt like eating a bite for dinner I could. But soon as I walked into the kitchen and bent over the meal bin, a new pain hit me, sharp as a piece of steel rammed through my bowels. It was a different kind of pain. It was bigger than any pain I had ever felt. The thought crossed my mind that it was the pain of a giant that had struck me by mistake.

The force of the pain was so hard I couldn't stand up straight until it passed. And when it weakened a little I stumbled to the table and braced myself by holding on to the back of a chair. I felt weak and trembly as a cobweb. What is this? I said to myself. I knowed this was a different kind of pain. It roared through my bones. But as the pain lessened I gathered my strength and limped back slow to the living room. Did I have a busted appendix? Should I get out on the road and try to walk for help? There wasn't a doctor on Gap Creek, so even if I walked to Elizabeth's or Joanne's or the preacher's house, there wasn't much they could do. Was there something in Mr. Pendergast's house for the pain? The laudanum had been used up when Mr. Pendergast died. All I had was Mr. Caldwell's little bottle of tonic. And then I remembered there had been a little corn liquor on the shelf where Mr. Pendergast kept his medicines. Maybe a drink of liquor would soothe whatever was wrong inside me.

I went back to the kitchen and was about to reach up on the shelf for the whiskey when the pain hit me again. The pain come from the side like a train slammed into me. The pain was so bad I lost my breath and gasped like somebody hit on the back. "Eiiiie!" I screamed without meaning to. It felt like this pain was worser than the last. I held to the edge of the shelf, like my legs couldn't bear my weight. "Oh God," I said without thinking about it.

The pain drove down into my belly like a steel spike hammered into my groin, a long steel spike drove on and on. I thought I was going to fall, but gripped the shelf board and rode the pain. I rode the pain like it was a bucking horse and I was about to be throwed over the wall of a gully. The pain blowed up inside me and rose and rose and I couldn't escape it, for the pain was right in the center of me.

As the pain begun to fade I thought my legs was going to crumble. I held on to the shelf and felt the sweat all over me. The pain was burning hot and sweat dampened my forehead and temples. Pain is like a terrible heat. I felt like somebody that had been scorched in a furnace. But as my strength returned I reached for the pint jar of liquor. It was about half full. I took the jar to the table and unscrewed the lid. The fumes flared up around my face. I took a quick drink, so it would go down without me tasting it. The whiskey burned my throat but felt calm and settling in my belly. I screwed the lid back on the jar.

As I walked back to the living room it was clear I was having birth pains. It was the easing away and the spell between the pains that showed me. How long had it been between seizures? I tried to recall what I had heard about labor pains. If you knowed the time between them you could figure when the baby was coming. I tried to think what else I remembered about delivering babies. For I was on my own, and there was no way I could stop the baby from coming. It might be dark before Hank and Ma Richards arrived, and that was hours away. I tried to think what I would need to do. I tried to think what things I would have to have. We had to boil water when Mama give birth to my younger sister and Masenier. And we used a lot of clean washcloths and towels.

They say Indian women used to go out in the woods and have a baby on their own. They would walk up and down a riverbank until the baby was ready to come. And then they would pull it out of their-selves and chew the birth cord in two. I didn't see how they had the strength with all the pain. I limped to the closet and got a bunch of clean towels and washcloths. And I put wood in the cookstove to build the fire up. I was about to take the towels to the bedroom but wondered if that was the best place to go. Would it be better to have the baby in the bedroom, or close to the fireplace in the living room? Or would the kitchen floor be the best place? I could put a blanket on the kitchen floor and then clean it all up later. The hot water would be close by in the kitchen. That seemed like the best plan.

Quick, before the next pain come, I put water on the stove to boil. And I swept the kitchen floor clean as I could. There was still red silt from the flood in the cracks of the boards, but I cleaned it all I could and spread a blanket and quilt on the floor in front of the stove and laid the towels and washcloths beside it. I even got a pillow from the bedroom and put it on the quilt.

Even though I knowed it was coming, I was not prepared for the force of the next pain. It come from behind, like a saw ripping through my backbone and innards. The teeth of the saw felt an inch long and so dull they tore flesh in gobs and strings. What am I going to do? I thought. I can't stand this much suffering. I can't do this all by myself. The pain was so hard my legs folded under me and I sunk down on the quilt. I laid down on my side trying to ease the hurt. I curled up trying to make it hurt less. Nothing helped. I pushed the palm of my hand against my back and that helped a little. The pain was a wall slamming into me. I seen the pain was going to get worse, not better. The pain was going to be worser than anything I had ever imagined.

I was so weak I couldn't do a thing but lay there. The ceiling of the kitchen wobbled and stretched and spun around above me. I held on to a table leg to make things get still. What hope is there? I thought. What hope is there for the baby? And I seen how I had to do everything for the baby. It didn't matter about me. If I was finished I was finished. But the baby had to be saved. The baby had to be protected. But I was near helpless on my own.

The only sweetness in the world I could think of was that Jesus might be looking down on me with love and concern. There was nobody else to see me in my misery. There was nobody else to help me through. "Please, Jesus," I said, "show me some mercy. Not for my sake, but for the little baby."

I was sick and weak and scared, and I was flat on my back. The pain between my legs come worser than before. But it felt like somebody took my hand. It felt like there was a firmness in the air around me. I clinched my fists and gritted my teeth as the pain got bigger. There was a scream in the house and I wondered who was hollering. And then I seen it had to be me that screamed. The water was boiling on the stove and light through the window showed it was getting on into the afternoon. I had lost track of how long it might be between the pains. It seemed I was in pain almost all the time. I thought of the passage in the Bible where it says, "I will multiply thy sorrow and thy conception; in sorrow thou shalt bring forth children." The word "sorrow" sounded more dignified than "pain" or "hurt." Sorrow was about understanding, about a long time passing.

The hurt was so bad I twisted on the floor and hit the quilt with my elbows. "Lord, help me through this sorrow," I said. My face was so wet the sweat was getting into my hair and making it all tangled. My back was so sweaty it stuck to the quilt. I would be wore out and ready for rest if it wasn't for the pain. Even though I didn't know how much further, it was certain I had a long way to go before I was done. It was a full day's work. And I remembered that's what they called giving birth: labor. I was in the *labor* of giving birth. It was hard labor. I would try to think of it as work and not as pain. I had a mountain of work ahead of me. I might as well pitch in. There was no way I could get out of it. There was no way I wanted to get out of it.

This is *my* work, I thought. This is the work only I can do. This is work meant for me from the beginning of time. And this is work leading through me in an endless chain of people all the way to the end of time. Other women have done their work down the course of the years, and now it's my turn. There's nothing to do but take hold of the pain and wrestle with it. It was not a choice to give in.

But as the stab of pain got bigger and wider in my belly, a raging red flood of pain pouring through me and out of me, I seen I had to grip on to something. I couldn't just lay with my back on the quilt and push hard as I needed to. I had to push against the pain. I turned around on the quilt so I could hold to the table legs. That give me something to brace against, and I needed to brace myself to push.

The work was to push the baby out from inside. It was hard as pushing the whole world a few inches. Pushing the baby out was hard as shifting the earth and the heavens. I gripped the cold legs of the table like I was going to heave the table at the ceiling. There was still a little dried silt on the legs from the flood. The silt crumbled in my grip like talcum, melting in sweat. We are just earth, I said. But what a miracle of earth flesh is, earth shaped and changed so it takes on feeling and can breathe and think and remember.

The pain that hit me then felt like it was crushing my bones. It was pain so hard my breathing froze. Tears squirted from my eyes and mixed with the sweat on my cheeks and temples. I flung my head from one side to the other, slapping my cheeks on the quilt. The quilt was soaked with sweat. This is what it means to be a human being, to labor and to hurt, I thought.

When the pain was at its most terrible, I felt myself opening up. I set up on the quilt, the pain was so awful. I opened my legs wide as

I could. I opened myself wider than I ever dreamed I could. Inside the pain was the pleasure of stretching. It was pleasure so intense I couldn't name it. It was pleasure so hard I felt blood tearing out of my veins and through my skin. The pleasure stabbed through me like it was going to bust my heart wide open. The light from the evening sun was coming through the kitchen window on my face, near blinding me. The window was so bright it seemed to shine all on its own. The window throwed light on me like it was watching over me, like it was picking me out with the shaft of white light.

I leaned forward far as I could and put my hands between my legs. Sweat and hair got in my eyes, and I couldn't brush them away. What I felt coming through me was bigger than an onion, a hairy onion, or apple. I pushed with all the strength in the last inch of my body and the little head come out more. "Please, Jesus," I screamed. I took hold of the little head which was all slick and hot and wet, like it had butter on it, butter and blood. I cradled the head as tender as I could and pulled.

The light from the window shot right at the place my hands took hold on the little ears and I thought of seed and word, and the way preachers talk about the word in the womb. "Please, Jesus," I said again, and took hold of the head like it was the most precious fruit. I can't describe how good it felt to pull so hard. My eyes stung and bulged I was straining so. I pulled on the head, and then I felt the shoulders. It was a precious little body, just a handful, all bloody and sticky. I lifted it on out as easy as slipping a bean from its pod. I was so weak and wore out I was shaking. This is what leads to everything else, I thought.

I held the baby up into the gold light from the window and its eyes was closed and its face and body was slick with blood and a kind of gray butter that stuck to it all over. The blue, bloody rope that twisted from its belly back inside me had to be cut. But I didn't have any knife or scissors handy. And I couldn't put the baby down to go fetch them. There was nothing to do but pull the baby close to my face and bite the twisty cord. It tasted of the salt in the blood and slick stuff. Everything was salty and rich. I could eat the cord if I had to.

And I seen it was a little girl. I had been guessing it would be a boy without knowing it. And now it was a little girl I was holding. I cupped my left hand around the baby's belly to hold her and slapped the little bottom with my right hand. There wasn't any response. Could the baby be dead? I looked at the face. The little eyes was still closed. I slapped the butt again, and there was a low tearing sound, more like a lamb or goat than anything human. But it become a cry. It was the cry of a baby. The baby was breathing.

Her skin looked gray under the juice and blood. But where I rubbed it clean, the skin was pink. She was almost too little to hold. I held her in both hands and looked at the closed eyes and the wrinkle in the nose. I held her up in the light from the window. I was so tired I couldn't hardly set up, yet I felt stronger than I ever had before.

"THERE'S SOMETHING WRONG with that baby," Hank said. It was the first thing I heard when I woke up from the ocean of sleep. I had sunk into sleep after the pains of the afterbirth. I had cleaned myself up as best I could, then wrapped the baby in a blanket and put it beside me on the pallet. I had gone to sleep without knowing it, dreaming of the baby being born and turning into a flower. But it was a flower that had to be fed milk.

"That baby is gray as pipe clay," Hank was saying. But he wasn't talking in my dream. I was waking up.

"It's a skinny baby," I said. Hank was bending down to look at the bundle in the cradle of my arm.

"It's an early baby," he said. "I don't think the Lord was ready for it."

"I delivered her," I said. I had slept so deep I was calm. I wasn't going to let anything rile me. I had done all the work myself and I wasn't afraid anymore. I was sore inside and outside and my legs was stiff. But I was happy to remember what all I had done.

"That baby needs a wash," Hank said.

"Washing is not as important as feeding," I said.

"This baby looks too weak to nurse," Hank said. He bent down like he was going to pick up the baby, and without thinking I tightened my arm around the bundle. It was *my* baby, and I could nurse it.

"The kitchen floor's no place for a baby," Hank said.

"Where is Ma Richards?" I said.

"I didn't bring her," he said. "I got halfway up the mountain and turned back, cause I thought something might have gone wrong."

"Bless you," I said.

"Now we could use her help," Hank said.

"Too late now," I said.

"Let me get you to the bedroom," Hank said.

"I can walk myself," I said. I couldn't just keep laying on the pallet on the kitchen floor in front of the stove. Hank picked up the baby and I started to raise myself, but pain shot through my belly and I was too weak to move my legs. I was so weak I fell back on the quilts, helpless to set myself up.

"Be all right in a minute," I said.

"You just lay there," Hank said. He carried the baby into the living room and then come back and picked me up. I was so sore it hurt wherever he touched me.

"Be careful with the baby," I said as he carried me into the bedroom. I was too weak to do anything but collapse into his arms.

After Hank put me down he leaned close and kissed me. As his lips brushed mine our foreheads touched. He smelled like tobacco juice and he felt cool.

"You're burning up," Hank said.

"I'm just tired," I said.

"You've got a fever," Hank said. He lit a lamp and brought it to the stand beside the bed.

"I ain't got childbed fever," I said. I knowed that women who took a fever after childbirth got infected inside them, and most of them died.

"You're hot as a coal," Hank said, and his voice seemed to stretch out a little in the air. I could remember having a fever when I was a girl and people's words sounded stretched and broke apart.

"I just need a drink of cold water," I said. I knowed it would make Hank mad again to think I was sick. I wanted him to see I was just tired.

Hank brought me a dipper of water and I sipped it. The cold water made me shiver, and the shudder made me feel the ache in my bones. Besides the soreness in my middle and groin, there was an ache in my joints and in my legs. I shivered again. I could remember feeling the ache in my bones from a fever. I felt like I had been bruised in every joint.

"I just need to rest," I said. But my arm shook as I handed the dipper back to Hank.

"I'll go after the doctor tomorrow," Hank said.

It was long after dark by then, and Hank left the lamp turned down low. I laid in the bed shivering and I could hear everything Hank said from out in the kitchen. His voice wobbled in curves.

IT SOUNDED LIKE I was in the room with Hank. And then it was like he was far away and I was listening through a tunnel or pipe under the house. I could hear Hank humming to the baby. He had got a jar of milk from somewhere, maybe from the Pooles, and he was dropping it in the baby's mouth with an eyedropper. It was late at night, but it wasn't the night after the baby was born. It was two nights later, maybe. I wasn't sure. It was later than I had thought, and I had been sick a long time. Hank was trying to feed the baby from a bottle in which he had put sugar water or something like barley water, but it didn't work. The baby was too weak to drink more than a few drops at a time.

And I knowed where the baby slept. It didn't sleep beside me in the crook of my arm in the bedroom. It slept in a shoebox in a chair by the fireplace. I had heard Hank describe the place he was fixing for the baby. She was too little for a cradle, even though Hank had made a cradle out of poplar wood the week before. The baby was too delicate to move. The diapers had to be laid under it and over it.

"I HAVE GOT the baby clean," Hank called. I knowed he was worried. He wasn't used to handling no baby. "I'm going to make it a sugar-tit."

"It needs milk too," I said.

"I don't think you can nurse it," Hank said.

"I can nurse it," I said.

"You're too weak to set up," Hank said. "And you've got a fever."

"Bring the baby here," I said.

"The baby is too weak to move," Hank said.

"It's my baby," I said, "and I have got a right to nurse her." It sounded like I was talking somewhere faraway. It sounded like I was in another room.

"You're too sick to know what you're saying," Hank said.

"Bring me the baby," I said.

"I've heard fever ruins a woman's milk," Hank said.

"All a baby needs is its mother's milk," I said.

Hank went out to the living room and come back carrying the baby in two hands like she was a coal of fire he didn't want nothing to touch. She was wrapped in a diaper that swallowed her up. I took the baby in my hands and wrists and held her to my chin. Her little bottom in my palm was small as a hen egg.

"This girl needs a drink of milk," I said and pushed my gown aside. Soon as I brought the tiny lips to the nipple they started in to suck. "We know what a baby needs," I said.

The little lips kept working and working and then turned loose, and the baby let out a sad little cry. "What's wrong?" I said.

"You don't have milk," Hank said.

"What do you mean?" I said. I pulled the gown open on the other side and the baby took that nipple. I held her there as she sucked and hoped everything was going to be all right. But I knowed something was wrong. The breast should feel different somehow. The baby sucked and sucked and then broke loose and cried again.

"The milk will come," I said.

"Sometimes women don't have any milk," Hank said.

"I never heard of such a thing," I said.

The baby kept crying, and I tried again with both breasts, but it didn't do no good.

"What's wrong?" I said.

"You ain't got no milk," Hank said. He took the crying baby out of my arms and carried her, holding her in both hands like she was liable to fall apart, back to the fireplace in the living room. It was awful to hear her cry out there by the fire. She was my baby and she was hungry, and there wasn't nothing I could do about it. I was the one that was supposed to feed her, and there wasn't nobody else to do it. I hated myself for not having milk.

I DON'T KNOW how much time passed. I know Hank brought in a doctor once and the doctor looked at me and said, "In a case of fever, the best thing you can do is keep her warm."

"But she's too hot already," Hank said.

"Your best hope is that she will start to sweat and the fever break," the doctor said. He was wearing a high collar and a dark red tie. I don't know where Hank had found him.

"Please look at the baby," I said.

"Don't you worry about the baby," the doctor said.

"She's a little out of her head," Hank said.

"I'm in my head," I said. "I can't go outside of my head." I kept thinking I was so hot I must be ripening like an apple or tomato wrapped in foil. I was getting hot and mellow. And I would have milk later. And I heard music. It was the tinkle of strings. It was music somewhere in the air. It was harp music in golden light from the lamp.

"It must be King David playing his harp," I said.

"You're dreaming," Hank said.

"Ask him to play again," I said. For the harp notes stung the air and sweetened the air at the same time. The notes carved the air in shapes of blue and purple and red, like pulsing stained glass windows all around me. The notes carved time and colorful shapes too. I thought of the coat of many colors and the seconds of many colors. Minutes was made of shining pieces that formed pictures. I seen a picture of Moses from the Bible made of glowing seconds of many-colored glass. And I seen a picture of a dove which meant love and sounded almost the same as the moan of love.

The colorful pieces of time stretched bigger and longer, and they begun to move like big dust in the air. The colors danced in a shaft of light in the late afternoon. Motes juggled each other, and I thought the motes was notes. All the colors was sounds spinning. The colorful notes juggled in the air.

"Tell David to keep playing his harp," I said.

"You're not at yourself," Hank said beside the door.

"I'm inside myself," I said.

My bones ached, but the ache was sweet too. It was a deep

brown sweetness like heat from a hot bath. It was a sweetness that itched and made me shudder, like stretching when you're stiff. It was the sweetness of an itch just before you scratch it.

That's when I seen the doorway on the other side of the room. It was not a big doorway, but it was open. There was light behind it, but the light wasn't blinding. It was the light of a spring evening. It was a door that appeared to open on to a grassy knoll with a trail over it. The door was open and waiting. All I had to do was rouse myself to get up and walk through. And on the other side would be the wonderful world I had always dreamed about. The mowed grass and the grassy trail led to the pine woods and to an opening in the pine woods like a room or an alcove, a little cove. It was the kind of place young people might dance on a spring afternoon, surrounded by pine trees and with white clouds overhead.

I looked through the doorway and seen that the sky was clear except for the white clouds. And there was another trail beyond the grassy alcove, a trail that led off into the pine trees and up a hill. It was a path inviting me to follow it. It was a path that was alive, a path I could feel along with my feet even if my eyes was closed. It was a path that led right up toward the lip of the hill to the edge of the sky. It was the trail into heaven. One step at a time I could walk there, through the doorway into the evening light, on the cool grass.

WHEN I WOKE up Hank was bending over me with a cup of warm tea. The steam off the cup made my cheeks sweat. "Have a taste of this," he said.

"Am I better?" I said. I remembered the shining doorway I'd seen the night before.

"Your fever has gone down," Hank said.

"Then I'm better," I said.

"Fevers always go down in the morning," Hank said. "And then they go up again in the evening."

"How is the baby?" I said.

"The baby is so weak I can't feed it nothing but a sugartit and milk in an eyedropper," Hank said.

"Then I ought to nurse it," I said.

"You can't," Hank said. I felt the emptiness in my breasts.

"I want to see the baby," I said.

"The baby is too delicate to move," Hank said. "I'm keeping her in a shoebox by the fire."

"I want to see her," I said.

"You just need to rest," Hank said.

When Hank was gone I looked for the lighted doorway in the bedroom wall, but seen only the wall where coats and overalls hung on pegs. Yet when I closed my eyes and looked through the squint of eyelashes I seen the bright threshold. It was there all the time if you just looked at it right, like stars in the sky at noon if you can see them.

I closed my eyes and listened to the things outside the house. There was a dove calling somewhere in the woods across the creek. It was like the note when you blow across the mouth of a bottle. It was like a note coming out of a cave in the mountain.

Hank was getting clothes together in the kitchen to take out to the washpot. He had made a fire under the washpot and carried water from the spring to fill the cauldron and the tubs. As far as I knowed Hank had never washed clothes before. "The water is coming to a boil," Hank called. "I hate to leave that baby for a minute."

"You can't take the baby outside," I said.

"I'm afraid if I turn my back it'll quit breathing," Hank said.

"It's in the hands of the Lord," I said. But I didn't know if I was talking in my head or really talking to Hank. I couldn't tell the difference no more.

I could hear him talking like I was in the room with him. I

heard Hank carry the clothes out to the washpot, and I heard him singing to hisself as he stirred the clothes in the boiling water with the troubling stick. Hank had never washed clothes before, but now he had no choice. He was singing "By Jordan's Stormy Banks." He sung several verses and choruses while he troubled the hot water and then lifted the clothes out with the stick, streaming and steaming, and slopped them down on the washboard.

Hank left the baby in the shoebox on the chair by the fireplace while he done the washing and split more wood at the woodpile. I heard the *chop* of the axe and then the *hack* of the echo coming back from the ridge across the creek. *Chop-hack* it went. *Chop-hack, chop-hack.* His axe was making music and the dove was making music. Everything was making its own music. The dust in the air was music and the clouds in the sky was music. And the baby's little cry was music that hurt.

WHEN NEXT I woke up I was shivering. It was cold like ice water was pouring through the hollows of my bones and there was ice in the sockets of my joints. My teeth chattered and my elbows jerked. Hank bent over me and said, "You've got the chills." He wrapped the quilts tighter around me. But the quilts felt thin as muslin that let a cold wind through. There was nothing between me and the ice at the North Pole.

"Drink this," Hank said. He held a cup of hot tea to my lips. There was fumes coming from the tea. It was part whiskey. My jaws shook so I couldn't hardly put my lips to the glass. I swallowed a trickle of tea and it went down my throat like a lizard of fire. It crawled in my belly and curled up in a nest of glowing coals. I took another sip and the nest of coals got bigger.

"Drink all of it," Hank said. I took another sip and swallowed. The hot herb tea made me shiver even worser. Shivering shows you're still alive, somebody had said. I shuddered and jerked from one end of the bed to the other. My breasts was empty, but I wanted to hold the baby. But I couldn't even keep my arms still. I tried to lay still and my back jerked and rippled. My bones felt like they was rattling against each other.

As the warm juice in my belly started spreading, carrying its lights through veins and bones to my toes and fingertips, I stopped jerking a little. I laid back on the pillows and seen the door in the wall of the bedroom. It was warm evening light coming through the door, on the grass and among the pine trees. Somebody was calling to me on the path, just beyond where I could see.

Now I could think two things at the same time. I could hear Hank in the living room talking as he awkwardly lifted the diaper and gown from the baby and sponged the little body off with a piece of flannel cloth. The baby was so little a regular diaper almost covered it up. The skin was too delicate to rub. Hank just touched it with the wet flannel the way he might wash a sore place or a wound. He touched the baby like he was almost afraid to touch her.

"Be a miracle if this baby lives," Hank said.

"It's a miracle any baby lives," I said. But I didn't know if I was just talking in my head. I couldn't nurse the baby. I had failed her.

It was night outside the window where Hank was. Night pressed against the house and made it feel little.

But through the door in the wall of the bedroom come the light of a summer evening. Birds was singing in the golden trees and the grass was warm from the sun. You could tell where the path in the grass was because it was sunk a little. The trail wound off into the pines and up the hill. "Julie," somebody called among the trees, beyond where I could see.

Who could be calling me out into the late evening sun, into the woods where the sun didn't reach? I wondered if I should get out of bed. I had laid still so long I was weak and my legs felt like they was froze. If I had such a fever as Hank had said, should I get out from under the covers and walk outside?

"Are you coming, Julie?" the voice called. And at the same time I heard Hank talking from the living room. "I've heard of giving a baby ginseng tea to stimulate its heart," he said.

"Ginseng tea is too strong for a baby," I called. "I wouldn't give it nothing stronger than pennyroyal tea."

"You could give it a smaller dose, or a weaker dose," Hank said. He sprinkled talcum on the little girl and slid a diaper under her. Hank worked careful, barely touching the delicate skin. The baby was so soft a touch could bruise it. The skin was softer than a rose petal and would break just as easy.

After he got the diaper under the baby Hank laid the ends across the belly and pinned them. He held one diaper pin in his mouth while he snapped the other into place. Hank's hands was too big for that kind of work, but he was doing his best. I seen there was things about Hank I couldn't have guessed. He was talking to the baby. "She's a pretty girl, now ain't she a pretty girl?" Hank was saying. "Prettiest girl in the world. Ain't got a name, pretty little thing."

But while I heard Hank talking, almost singing to the baby, I could hear the voice calling from the pine trees also. "Julie," it said, "I want to show you something."

Whose voice was it? It sounded so familiar. "Julie," it called, "I want you to come out where I can see you."

Suddenly I knowed it was Papa's voice. I hadn't noticed that before, for it wasn't Papa's voice when he was old, but when he was young. It was his voice as a young man, when he first met Mama. He was calling to me in the voice of his youth. He was calling to me across the summer grass from the pine woods.

"I'm not supposed to walk," I called back.

"You can walk," Papa said, almost like a kid calling me out to play. I lifted the covers aside and got out of bed. My legs was stronger than I had thought they was. I had to walk slow, but I was steady. I took short steps to the door and walked out into the grass.

It was a world for a picnic out there. I had never seen a place so perfect. The grass was warm and trimmed smooth. The world was a park, a garden. It was like the world must have been in the beginning. There was bushes that smelled like perfume and flame azaleas in bloom. There was little bluets along the edges of the grass. It was grass you wanted to set down on. It was grass you wanted to lay back on and watch the clouds pass over.

Papa called to me again, but he was further out in the woods than I had thought. "Are you coming, Julie?" he said. It was like he had gone for a walk on the path up the mountainside and was waiting for me. We was going for a stroll on the trail that wound off through the pine trees to the edge of the sky.

But in the living room Hank was still talking to the baby. He laid a white flannel blanket over her up to her chin. "This little girl will live till the end of the century," Hank said. "She will live to see the end of time. For preachers say the world will come to an end at the end of the millennium. This little girl will start out in a shoebox by the fireplace and live to see Jesus bust out of the eastern sky in all his glory."

"How can time come to an end?" I said in my head.

"It will come to an end when the Word is fulfilled," Hank said.

"Time can't end, for what would follow would be time too," I said.

"Don't you believe the Bible?" Hank said. "Don't you know it says plain in Revelation that time will stop?"

"But what comes after that will be more time," I said.

The baby cried a little cry. It was a cry small as a bird might make. It was small as the memory of a cry. She was crying and I couldn't feed her.

. . .

"YOU ARE WALKING on sacred ground," the voice in the pines called to me.

"I'm walking barefoot," I said.

"Only a few more steps," the voice called. But it was now further up the trail. The voice was in the shadows under the pine trees. The pines had purple and green shadows. The grassy path wound deeper into the trees.

Now it was like there was music coming out of everything I looked at. The glowing grass under my feet had its own music, and the shadows blowed out deep organ music. I knowed the music was in my head, but it was seeing the wonderful world of grass and pine grove that made me think the music. There was music coming from under the ground so deep it hurt my bones and stirred through my guts. Everything had a different voice, but the voices all harmonized like a congregation at church.

"Julie," the voice called as I stepped into the alcove among the pine trees. It was a little dancing yard, a little cove. I looked for Papa's figure, but there was nobody there. The woods was lit with the evening sun, but I didn't see nobody. It was the kind of place where you expected to see a burning bush. I walked over the soft grass as easy as gliding.

"Papa," I called to the path going up the hill. There was nobody in sight among the pines, and nobody answered. But I thought I heard somebody speak, or maybe it was a dove calling. I stepped up the path knowing there was somebody waiting, for I had heard the voice call my name. The music was in my head, but the voice come from the pine trees. "Papa," I called again. But when I come around a turn in the path there was nobody there. "Please, Jesus," I whispered, "let me talk to Papa."

"Julie," the voice said again, and it sounded close by but above me. I hurried up the grassy trail and seen the top of the hill was bare. It was covered with grass and a bright, white cloud hung so close it appeared to lean against the top of the hill. It looked like I could step from the path right onto the shining cloud.

"Papa," I called. But I didn't see anybody on top of the hill. There was just me and the sky and the white cloud.

"Julie," the voice said behind me. I turned, and where there hadn't been anybody before stood a young man that looked a little bit like Papa. He had a reddish blond beard and hair. He was wearing a white shirt and he had slender shoulders and the whitest skin you ever seen.

"Don't you know me?" he said.

"I think I know you," I said.

I was standing on the top of the world and there was nobody there but him and me and the shining cloud almost at my elbow.

"I have come to show you my love," he said.

"Why have you come to me?" I said. I felt how shameful I was. I hadn't even been able to nurse my baby.

"Because you have shown the truest love," Papa said.

"How?" I said. My knees was shaking.

"Because you have loved others more than yourself," he said.

"I done what I had to," I said.

"You are one of the blessed," he said.

"What kind of dream am I dreaming?" I said.

But Papa didn't answer. He turned and walked further up the grassy hill. I was afraid he might just melt away into the light. He looked so slim and starved. I was afraid he would vanish before I could find out why he had come to me.

There was things I wanted to ask Papa, things I would never get a chance to ask again. "Will I live?" I said.

"I have come to tell you, you will live," Papa said. "You will live and you will continue to work and to love."

"That sounds simple," I said. "Simple and hard." They was two words that fit my life, the life I had lived. Ever since I could remember the work had been hard, work I often hated. I looked for Papa, but he wasn't on top of the hill. I looked behind me, but there was nothing but pine trees and grass there. The cloud had floated away and hung far out over the valley.

"I wanted to ask if the baby will live," I called. But there was only the whisper of air around me.

I stood on the hill until the light begun to fade. Far to the edge of the world I thought I seen a star come out like a crystal. It was time for me to start back down the hill.

I HEARD THE baby crying in the living room.

"I'll put some extra wood on the fire," Hank said.

"It's near bedtime," I said.

"Never mind what time it is," Hank said. "I'm going to make some more tea for the baby."

"What kind of tea?" I said.

"I'm going to put a little camomile in it," Hank said, "to help the baby sleep. To hush it up from crying."

I felt how warm and damp the sheet was around me. The quilt pressed down its warmth close to my sweaty skin. I reached a hand from under the covers and touched my forehead. My skin was wet with sweat, and cool. But I could smell the sickness on my hand, the smell of old flesh that has been cooked by fever and needs scrubbing. I was dripping with sweat.

Thirteen

Hank did go after Ma Richards after my fever went down and Ma Richards helped me take care of the baby while I was getting my strength back.

Ma Richards complained, but she helped me with little Delia like she was her own baby. I'll have to give Ma that. But it didn't do no good. The child had been born too early. She was too little to be able to live on cow's milk and sugar water and the gruel Ma Richards made. It broke my heart to see how tiny Delia was and how she wouldn't gain any weight. Her fingers and toes was tinier than match heads. Her little arms was the size of my fingers. Taking care of Delia wasn't like taking care of another sick baby, where you hold it and rock it, and give it tonic and warm milk. Delia was so tiny you didn't dare hold her upright. She was so weak you didn't want to move her no more than you had to. And she was so delicate you was afraid you'd break her skin or arm just by taking her up.

"The Lord will let this baby live," I said, "if it's his will."

"The Lord has his own plans for people," Ma Richards said, in her way that always irritated me.

"But we can still ask for what we want," I said.

"We can ask," Ma said. "But that don't mean the Lord has to answer."

I had been feeling better about Ma Richards as I got stronger. But maybe because I had decided to like Ma more, my guard was down. Before, I had been extra careful whenever she was around and held myself back because I disliked her so much. Now anger rose right out of my guts and filled my mouth.

"I guess you know all the Lord's secrets," I said. I sounded like Mama when she was mad. It just come out and I didn't try to stop it.

Ma Richards was folding diapers on the kitchen table. She stopped and looked at me. She wasn't used to people talking back to her. She certainly wasn't used to me talking back to her.

"I try to tell the truth," Ma said.

"Why should the Lord show you the truth more than anybody else?" I said. I could feel a shadow in the air around me, like the daylight was haunted. I had never gone so far quarreling with anybody, except maybe Lou. But I didn't want to stop myself until I'd gone farther still. It felt good to talk angry.

"I've learned a few things in my years," Ma said. "And one of the things I've learned is how foolish the young can be when they won't take advice."

"The only advice you want to give is to run things," I said. I had gone that far; I might as well go on farther.

Ma Richards went back to folding diapers. She finished one and started folding another. There was a grin on her face, like she had been waiting a long time for a fuss and nobody had obliged her. "Throwing off on me won't make the baby no better," Ma said.

"You don't care what happens, as long as you can be the queen bee," I said. My voice was shriller than I wanted it to be.

"I care enough to come down here and work day and night to take care of you," Ma said.

I wanted to drive her out of the kitchen. I wanted to fold the diapers myself. I grabbed a diaper off the pile and started to fold it. Hank was out at the barn and I didn't want him to hear me quarreling with Ma Richards.

"You don't think nobody knows how to do anything but you," I said. Now that my tongue was loose it just seemed to go of its own accord.

"What is wrong with you, Julie?" Ma said. "You must be out of your head."

"I believe in respecting old people," I said. "But I never run into anybody like you before."

"Hank don't seem to mind the kind of person I am," Ma Richards said.

"You've been bossing him around all his life," I said. "He's a good man or he wouldn't have put up with it." I figured I might as well tell the truth while I was at it. "You are the cause of most of his troubles."

"What troubles?" Ma said.

"The way he gets discouraged, and can't find a job," I said.

"Now you want to blame me for the way the world is?" Ma said.

"I blame you for the way Hank's world is," I said.

"You have got on a high horse all of a sudden," Ma said.

She reached for another diaper to fold, but I picked it up before she could touch it. "You're not used to people telling you the truth," I said.

"I ain't done nothing to be ashamed of," Ma said, "at least nothing to you."

"I don't care what you do to me," I said. "It's the way you run over Hank that riles me."

"Hank has told you that?" Ma said.

"He didn't need to," I said. "I've got eyes in my head."

"Some women get afraid they can't hold a man, and that makes them mean," Ma said. "I reckon you're one of them."

Tears come to my eyes. I couldn't help it. Suddenly everything in the room blurred and melted. It seemed Ma was smirking at me. "I just wish you would mind your own devilment," I said.

"It's a common weakness to blame other people for our own shortcomings," Ma said and laughed a dry laugh.

"You're mighty used to having the last word," I said, my voice rising toward a scream.

"Maybe that bothers you because you're afraid of everything," Ma said.

"It's my house!" I screamed. But even as I screamed I wished I hadn't done it. I had gone too far. I felt like Ma had tricked me into getting mad and screaming at her. Even though she had helped with the baby while I was recovering, she had tricked me into losing my temper.

"Julie, I don't know what's got into you," Ma said. But she said it like it was for somebody else's benefit. I guessed that Hank must have come into the kitchen while I was screaming. I turned around and there he stood in the door with a look of surprise. Even with my tears stretching and swelling everything, I could see the fear on his face.

"What's wrong?" Hank said, like he was short of breath.

"Julie is upset," Ma said.

"I have a right to be upset," I said. But I wished I hadn't. For it wouldn't do no good to try to set Hank against Ma. He would never turn against her, and she would make it look like the quarrel was all my fault.

"Has the baby got worse?" Hank said.

"I've done everything I could to help," Ma Richards said.

I seen what a mistake it had been to let myself go. But there was one last breath of rage left in me. "You've done everything you could to make me look bad," I said to Ma.

"I've done everything I could to help you," Ma said. She has beat me by sounding meek, I thought.

Hank looked at Ma and he looked at me. He stepped forward and put a hand on my shoulder, and he put his other hand on Ma's shoulder. "Let's get right down on our knees and pray about this," he said. "We're a family and we've got to live like a family."

The fizz and bite of rage was going out of me. The boldness that had took over my tongue melted away. I sunk down on my knees to the kitchen floor, and Hank put his arm around me and his other arm around Ma Richards.

"Lord, help us to love each other," Hank said. "Teach us to put aside our spites and grudges, our slights and hurt feelings. Teach us to put away our vanity and our pride. Help us to be the decent people we are deep inside." He pulled me closer on the left side and Ma closer on the right. I couldn't look Ma in the face, and I don't reckon she could bear to look me in the face either. I stared down at the floor.

"I want you all to kiss each other," Hank said.

I didn't make a move and I didn't say nothing. I reckon my lip was trembling.

"We're going to have to get beyond this," Hank said. "There's no hope for a family that quarrels all the time." I had never heard Hank talk so dignified and wise. It was usually him losing his temper and me holding mine. But here he was sounding like a deacon that led in prayer and was the head of the family. His calm moved me more than anything else had. I felt proud that he was a man I could rely on and trust. He was not only the father of my baby, who had took care of the baby, but he could show me what to do when I got all worked up and beside myself with disappointment and resentment. It was like Hank had got a lot older.

I reached over and put my arms around Ma Richards's bony shoulders and kissed her on the cheek. Another sob rose and broke in my throat. "I'm sorry," I said.

"I love you, Julie," she said, and I seen the tears streaming down

Ma's wrinkled face. I felt she meant it, that she was telling the truth. There was no sass and no edge in her voice.

I sobbed again and snuffed up my nose and wiped my eyes. My cheeks was wet like I had been out in the rain. I felt wrung out inside, but scrubbed and sweetened too. The world was firm again. That's when I heard little Delia crying the faintest cry.

"I'll go see about her," Ma Richards said.

"I'll go too," I said.

THE BABY WAS getting weaker instead of growing. It appeared she was losing weight. Her skin was so white it looked clear. Blue veins showed through like ink marks under her skin.

"She's awful weak," I said.

"Bless her little heart," Ma said.

"Ain't there no medicine for an early baby?" I said.

"The doctor just said to give her milk and sugar and a little barley water," Hank said.

"Her belly's too young to take anything," Ma said.

"They give babies paregoric for colic," Hank said.

"I'd hate to give one so little paregoric," I said. Delia wasn't squealing like a baby usually does with colic. She just laid there fretting and whimpering, and she didn't have a temperature either. There was no sign of a fever. There's nothing that makes you feel as helpless as a baby that's sick. It's your job to do something about it, but you don't know what. I was just getting back on my feet and I couldn't think clear.

"Maybe a little liquor will stimulate her heart," Hank said. It still surprised me that he had learned to take care of the little baby. Most men are scared of new babies and don't want to hold them the way they do bigger children. But Hank had had to take care of little Delia when I was sick. And he was as worried as I was. He kept the fire going in the fireplace all day and all night, even though it was late spring. Since Delia couldn't eat much, it was like she was living on the warmth from the fire.

"I'd be afraid to give a baby that little any liquor," I said.

"I've heard of giving babies mint tea with a drop of brandy in it," Hank said.

"We don't have no brandy," I said.

"A drop of liquor will serve just as good," Hank said.

There was some peppermint out beyond the washpot on the way to the spring. I sent Hank out to pick a pan full and I put the green leaves in the oven to dry. The leaves filled the house with the smell of mint as they cured. It was a kind of medicine smell. I took them out before they could burn or bake. As soon as I boiled the tea I asked Ma Richards how much liquor I should mix in.

"Just a few drops," Ma said, "in a tablespoon of tea."

I fixed up the tea and put it in the eyedropper Ma had used to feed Delia milk. I held the tip of the eyedropper to the baby's lips and squeezed out a drop in her mouth, then another. She twitched a little but didn't open her eyes. Her lips was pursed for nursing. It made me ache that I couldn't nurse her.

"The mint will soothe her stomach," Ma Richards said.

I dripped several more drops into Delia's mouth, and a little color appeared in her tiny cheeks. Maybe the tea was working to make her stronger.

WHEN I GOT up in the middle of the night to look at the baby, I didn't think anything was wrong at first. The baby was usually quiet and still. I had thought of warming up more of the tea. I thought of mixing a little liquor with sugar water to give her. I brought the lamp to the mantel of the fireplace and set it down. The baby was quiet in the shoebox. I looked closer and seen her eyes was closed and there was no color in her cheeks. She needs some more tea, I thought. I put my hand on her forehead and it was cold. I need to build up the fire, I thought.

And then it come to me that Delia's little forehead was really *cold*. I pulled back the blanket and took her little hand, and it was cold as an icicle. And I knowed she was dead.

This is the worst thing that has ever happened to you, I said to myself. If you live to be ninety this is the saddest moment you will ever know. It was so sad I couldn't really feel it. I would feel it later, maybe. Now it was happening to somebody else. It was sadder than when Masenier died, and when Papa died, but I couldn't feel a thing.

I set down by the fire and looked at my baby. In a few seconds I would have to go tell Hank, and he would go tell Ma Richards. But I wanted to wait a moment. If I didn't tell nobody, it might not be true. Maybe Delia would start to breathe again. Maybe my life wouldn't come to a stop the way it seemed to have.

Jesus, don't let this be true, I prayed. I thought how helpless and innocent Delia was. I thought how cruel it was to bring a little person like her into the world to suffer and then die, never knowing anything else. What kind of world would let such a thing happen? But I put it out of my mind because I had to go tell Hank. I couldn't bear such grief on my own. There was a numbness in my belly that reached out toward my toes and to the tips of my fingers.

AFTER PREACHER GIBBS come to the house and preached a little funeral in the living room for Delia, and after we buried her in a corner of the orchard in a little oak box Hank had fixed from planks he found in the barn, I felt different from what I expected. I felt like nothing was real, and I was so light I couldn't hardly touch the ground. I scrubbed the floor of the house to make things seem real, and I carried water from the spring and washed all the bedclothes. I hoed out the tater patch, making myself sweat. The harder I worked the lighter I felt. When I talked it didn't sound like my voice talking. And when I thought, it seemed like somebody else thinking. Finally I just set down on the porch in a rocking chair and waited for my weight to return to myself.

"Do you want me to start supper?" Ma Richards said.

"You can if you want to," I said.

"What would you like me to fix?" Ma said.

"Whatever there is to fix," I said.

THE NEXT DAY Hank drove Ma Richards back up the mountain. I hugged her before she climbed in the buggy, and I told her I loved her. There wasn't nothing else to say, after the way she had helped out with little Delia, and after the way she had acted after our fuss. What she had done had showed her love for Hank, and me. But even so, it relieved me that she was going. I felt better because she was leaving and I would have the house to myself.

Soon as the buggy drove out of the yard I got a bucket of warm water and a rag and washed the steps. I scrubbed the front steps and the back steps until they sparkled. And I scrubbed the front porch and the back porch until the planks was raw. Then I swept the yard so clean the dirt glittered like sandpaper. I took a bucket to the creek and got some fresh white sand and sprinkled it over the front yard and the backyard. The ground looked frosted with sugar. I tightened the clothesline and washed the outhouse. Then I washed the outside walls of the house high up as I could reach.

That evening I started cleaning up the house inside. I washed the floors and the walls and the windows. I polished the windows so clean they looked like they wasn't there. It seemed I didn't have control over nothing in the world except the work I done. I couldn't make nothing right, but I could make the floor and the dishes shine. I washed off the cookstove when it cooled and polished it. I want to make one little place in the world as bright and tight as a crystal, I thought. I want to make one tiny place as fit as it can be. After I polished the stove I shined the silver. And then I polished Hank's Sunday shoes and my own with saddle soap.

By the time Hank come back that night I was wore out, but the house sparkled. I had even washed the ceilings and the backs of the doors.

LATER THAT MONTH, after I had recovered my strength a little, I planted every seed I could find on the place. And in the South Carolina heat, and in the moist soil along the creek, they sprouted and growed fast. I planted bunch beans and half-runners, greasy backs and Kentucky Wonders. I planted peas and lettuce and okra, bell pepper and red pepper. I planted squash and eggplant and turnips. The summer squash growed like little yellow geese and the winter squash swelled like pincushions. I planted watermelons and mush melons in the soft loam along the creek.

The more I worked the more I had to work. I would give the preacher potatoes and carrots instead of any tithe. And I would help anybody else I could. I would give people that passed on the road new taters and squash.

Every time I thought about Delia I worked that much harder. I mowed the grass on the bank by the road with the sling blade, and I trimmed back the briars and brush and big weeds. We didn't have enough money for shoelaces, but everything I done was free. The sweat was free as water from the spring, as air and sunlight. But the greatest free gift was time that kept coming day after day. It seemed that time couldn't go on after the death of little Delia. But it did.

Every day led to another night, and night to another day. Time kept spilling down on me, and the only way I could take hold of the minutes and make sense of them was to work.

"You'll kill your fool self," Hank said. But he didn't say it ugly. He hadn't been able to find a job. He had asked in Tigerville and he had asked in Pumpkintown. I guess word had got out that he hit the boss at the cotton mill in Lyman, as he had feared, because nobody would hire him. Hank worked on the place as hard as I did. He put in a big field of corn and a field of sweet taters. He set out a row of tobacco he got from George Poole on credit, and he plowed around the trees in the orchard and did some pruning. The watermelons we growed by the creek was better than any watermelons I had ever seen on the mountain. He carried rocks on the sled and lined the branch in the pasture so the banks wouldn't wash away. He patched up the fence with pliers and pieces of wire found in the barn. He cleared out the hayloft and the corncrib. The fact that he didn't have money to buy nails and paint made him work even harder.

In late summer I helped Hank cut tops in the August heat. We stacked the corn tops in shocks in the field to cure, and in the September heat we pulled the fodder and carried it in bundles to the barn. The fodder made the barn smell sweet as green tea. We gathered apples and made cider in an old mill found in the toolshed. I cut up apples and dried the slices on sheets in the sun, to make pies in the winter.

While we worked that summer we attended every prayer meeting and church service, every singing and dinner on the grounds. I carried taters and cider and canned preserves to shutins and old folks. I made jelly and canned beans and peaches and tomato juice. I canned blackberry juice and grape juice. The days was thick and cluttered with grief, and I fought my way through every minute with work. I wrestled with every job like it was a demon, or an angel, and I picked my way like climbing from rock to rock on a tricky path. It was my sweat and my effort that made time possible. When I seen another woman with a baby, I turned my face away, and then I took hold of myself and tried to be glad for her.

I WAS DOWN on my knees weeding the okra when I heard somebody holler from the road. It was a voice I recognized quick. My knees hurt from the sharp clods, but the pain the voice drove through my chest was worse.

"Piieendergaass!" the voice called.

I hoped Hank didn't hear him. Timmy Gosnell had left us alone since Hank throwed him in the creek. Timmy was only trouble when he got bad drunk. I had seen him walk by on the road from time to time, and I doubt he was ever cold sober. But he only got to thinking about Mr. Pendergast and the ginseng money when he was terrible drunk. I kept working, bent over where I was hid by the sweet corn and tomato plants. Maybe Timmy would go on down the road if nobody paid him any mind.

"Piieendergaass!" he hollered again, and I heard a rock bang the side of the house. I prayed he didn't break a window, because we didn't have money to buy a new one. Another rock rung on the porch, making me wince.

"You owe me moneeeeyyyy!" Timmy yelled.

I feared what might happen if Hank got riled again. Since the baby died Hank had been in a quiet mood. But I didn't know what he would do if Timmy made him mad. I knowed I had to get Timmy to leave before Hank heard him. Hank was down in the patch by the branch hoeing sorghum cane.

I stood up and seen Timmy Gosnell standing at the corner of the house. He leaned over with his hands on his knees to steady hisself.

And then he reached down for another rock. I was dizzy from being bent over so long and I took a deep breath.

"You owe me moneeyyy!" Timmy called out to the house.

"You know Mr. Pendergast is dead," I said as calm as I could.

Timmy whirled around and almost fell over. His shirt was unbuttoned and he looked sunburned, as if he had been laying asleep in the hot Gap Creek sun. He shaded his eyes to look at me. "Piieendergaass owes me money," he said.

"Can't you understand, Mr. Pendergast died last fall," I said, trying to sound quiet and reasonable.

"Then you all," he said and pointed at me, "you all owe me money."

"If I had any money I'd give it to you," I said.

"You *have* to," Timmy said and took a step toward me. I backed away. I didn't like his smell, and there was sores around his eyes. He looked both confused and angry.

I held out my hands covered with dirt and weed stains. "See, I ain't got any money," I said.

"You will *pay* meeeee," he said and stomped his foot on the baked ground.

"You go on home," I said. I knowed he lived in an old house by hisself way back in the holler of Hominy Branch. It seemed strange that all he thought about when he got drunk was that Mr. Pendergast owed him a dollar or two.

"Ain't treated me squarrre," Timmy said and shook his finger at me. He blinked like he was having trouble seeing in the bright sun, and when he lurched forward I took another step back. "Ain't treated me squarrrreee!" he hollered and shook his head.

Just then I seen Hank coming up the trail from the spring with the hoe on his shoulder. "You better go," I said to Timmy. "Hank will be mad."

"Ain't afeared of *himmm*," the drunk man said.

Hank walked right up to Timmy and stopped, resting the hoe like a staff on the ground. He was so sweaty from work his shirt stuck to his shoulders. "I told you not to come back here when you was drunk," he said.

"You owe me money, Riiichards," Timmy said.

"How you figure I owe you money?" Hank said. "Mr. Pendergast is dead."

"Cause you got all Piieendergaass's money," the drunk man said.

"I ain't got a cent," Hank said. He didn't seem scared like he had before when Timmy come. He wiped the sweat out of his eyes. "You go on home," Hank said.

"Ain't afeared of *you*," Timmy snarled and leaned toward Hank, squinting with one eye. His face was peeling from sunburn.

"Don't want you to be afraid of me," Hank said.

Timmy stepped back as if trying to understand what Hank had said. He was used to people hollering at him. He studied the ground for a few seconds, and then looked around. "You're a goddamned liiiiar," he said.

"We don't want to talk that way," Hank said. He lifted the hoe, but let the end drop to the ground again.

Timmy swung around and pointed at me. "Her too," he said, "you're both . . . liiiiars."

I seen how much the drunk man wanted a fight. He wanted to be beat and bloodied and throwed in the creek. It was what he had come for. He wanted to be hurt and humbled. Hank must have seen it too.

"We want to do the Christian thing," Hank said.

"Don't talk to me no Chriiiiistian," Timmy said, and swung his arm as though swatting a fly. "I ain't got no confidence."

"We could give you some coffee and cornbread," Hank said. "And if you stay awhile Julie can fix you a bean and a tater."

"You ain't no preacher," Timmy said and swung his hand again.

"You'd feel better if you eat something," Hank said.

"You're a thief," Timmy said. "Don't talk to me no Chriiiistian."

"Nobody took anything from you," Hank said.

"All my life people has took from me," Timmy said. "Why, I ain't got nothing."

"We could give you some new taters and a mess of beans," Hank said.

Timmy looked at the house, and he looked at the sky, like he was trying to think what he wanted to say next. Things had not gone as he had expected. Nobody had knocked him down or threatened him. "I know what you all are," he said, "coming here and taking Piendergaass's money. Everybody knows what you all arrrre."

"We ain't stole from nobody," Hank said, and looked Timmy hard in the face.

I was sweating so hard the drops run into my eyes, but my hands was too dirty to wipe my brow. I used the back of my wrist, but it had dirt on it too. I felt I was melting like a tallow candle.

"You all are going to hell," Timmy said, "you and your whore both."

"It sure feels like hell out here in the sun," Hank said.

But Timmy Gosnell would not be humored. He looked at the ground, and he looked at Hank. He swung his fist and Hank stepped back, catching Timmy's arm. Dropping the hoe Hank took the drunk man by the shoulders and turned him toward the road. "Time for you to go home," Hank said.

"Won't go," Timmy said and braced hisself with his feet.

"You go on home and we'll pray for you," Hank said.

"Don't pray for *meee*," Timmy hollered. He wrenched hisself away and turned toward Hank. "I won't let you pray for meee," he said.

"We'll pray for you to feel better," Hank said.

"Like goddamn to hell you will," Timmy said.

And then I seen Hank get an idea. I seen when it come to him. All at once he knowed what to do to make Timmy leave. Instead of beating Timmy until he was bloody, which is what the drunk man had expected, Hank said, "I'm going to pray for you right now." He dropped to his knees on the hard ground in front of Timmy.

"Don't you pray for meee," Timmy hollered.

"Lord, we ask your guidance," Hank said, shading his eyes from the bright sun. "Brother Gosnell is in pain and confused. Would you soothe his heart and strengthen his will, and show him the way."

Timmy stood froze, listening to Hank pray for him. He started to say something and stopped. He swung his arm as if brushing away a gnat.

"Show Brother Gosnell the way to truth. Heal his pain and confusion," Hank prayed, sounding like Preacher Gibbs. "For he is a sinner, as we're all sinners."

Timmy took a step back like he was afraid, and then he took another. He looked at me, and then at Hank praying on the baked ground. "Ahhh!" he said and swung his arm again. Then he turned toward the road and started walking. I watched him lurch toward the bend.

When Timmy was gone a ways Hank opened his eyes and stood up. "If you come back we'll pray for you again," he hollered. But Timmy didn't look back. He kept stumbling down the creek road until he went around the bend. Hank looked at me and grinned. He had changed since last winter. He had knowed what to do to get rid of Timmy without hurting him. I hugged him with my elbows and wrists, since my hands was so dirty they would smear on his wet shirt.

IT WAS ALONG in late fall after the corn was gathered and put in the crib, after the taters was dug and the apples was picked, after the beets was canned and the foxgrape jelly made, the winter squash put in the hay, and the cabbage buried in a hill behind the barn, that Hank took up hunting again. In the summer he had caught trout out of the creek, and we fried them for Sunday dinner. But we hadn't had any red meat since the winter before. After the first frost Hank killed some squirrels and I made a stew. And then he killed a wild turkey. In November he shot a deer and we had more venison than I knowed what to do with. He salted down some of the deer meat and put it in the smokehouse.

We didn't have any money, and our clothes was wearing thin, and I kept patching Hank's overalls and mending his socks. His shirts was wore out at the elbows. But you can come to take pride in clean, patched clothes. You take pride in how you can keep things together with no money and just hard work. I was beginning to think about Christmas again, and about going up to the mountains to see Mama and my sisters.

THERE WAS A knock at the door one morning. It was a frost-tight morning with mush ice in the water bucket on the back porch. I dried my hands on my apron and opened the door. It was Preacher Gibbs and another man dressed up in a high collar and a black overcoat.

"You all come on in," I said. The cold air swept in with them.

"Julie, this is Mr. Raeford from Greenville," the preacher said.

"Pleased to meet you, sir," I said. "Please take a seat."

"I represent the heirs of Mr. Pendergast's estate," Mr. Raeford said.

"I see," I said.

"Since his heirs did not know about his death for over a year, they are only now claiming their property," Mr. Raeford said.

"I have explained to Mr. Raeford that you and Hank have done a fine job of taking care of the place," Preacher Gibbs said.

"I can see that," the lawyer said.

"Won't you all set down," I said. I figured this lawyer really did represent the heirs since he was with Preacher Gibbs. The two men set down and held their hats on their knees. The lawyer opened a leather case and took out some papers. It was the kind of papers that give you a feeling of dread. It was the kind of papers hard for ordinary people to read.

"The heirs have authorized me to sell the house for them," Mr. Raeford said.

"I see," I said. I hated to tell him we didn't have a cent and was living on the game that Hank shot in the woods and the canned stuff I had put up in the summer.

"And they have asked me to collect rent for the months since Mr. Pendergast died," the lawyer said.

"Rent?" I said. The word stuck in my throat.

"You have had the use of the house and land, as well as the horse and other livestock," Mr. Raeford said.

"Mr. Pendergast didn't charge us no rent," I said. The lawyer had a little powder on his face, and he smelled of some kind of toilet water.

"You kept house for Mr. Pendergast, the Reverend Gibbs tells me," the lawyer said. "Since his death the heirs have been owners of this house."

"Surely you are grateful that Hank and Julie have took care of the place, and the things on the place," Preacher Gibbs said.

"I'm only an attorney representing the interests of my clients," Mr. Raeford said. "They have asked me to collect back rent and to arrange for the sale of the property."

"That does not seem very neighborly," Preacher Gibbs said. "This young couple has put a lot of work into the place."

"I'm only an attorney," Mr. Raeford said again. "My clients are willing to be reasonable. They will settle for a hundred dollars in back rent."

"We don't have any money," I said. "And we don't have no way of getting any."

"Then I must ask you to vacate the premises," the lawyer said. "And I will ask the sheriff to seize any goods you have in lieu of payment." He put the papers back in his case and stood up.

"I'm astonished," the preacher said to the lawyer. "I would be ashamed to treat these people this way after all they have done here. They didn't know how to get in touch with the heirs. Nobody on Gap Creek did."

"I'm only an attorney," Mr. Raeford said again.

The lawyer handed me a paper. It was a paper that said Hank and me was being sued for back rent, and under South Carolina law we was liable to lose all we owned unless we paid the rent.

"We don't have no money," I said. I felt short of breath.

"Let's pray about this," Preacher Gibbs said. We stood up in the living room and Preacher Gibbs turned his face toward the ceiling as he prayed. "Lord, show us what is right," he said. "Help us to do your will in this world, so that we may earn a place in the next. For we know you are watching our every deed. And every single one of us must face your judgment."

AFTER THE PREACHER and the lawyer had gone I stood by the fire and looked at the paper like I couldn't understand it, though I understood what it said all too well. I stood there watching the words swell and swim in front of my eyes until Hank come back from hunting with a rabbit in the pocket of his mackinaw coat.

Hank looked at the page and swung it down like it was on fire and he wanted to put out the flames. He shook the paper till it fluttered like a paper bird. I had not seen such a look on his face for a long time.

"Does it mean we will be arrested?" I said.

"We might," he said.

"What can we do?" I said.

"We'll have to leave," Hank said, "early in the morning."

"Will we take the horse?" I said.

"We'll take only what we can carry on our backs," Hank said. "We'll take only what we brought here when we come."

"And leave all the canned stuff?" I said.

"We'll leave here the way we come into South Carolina," Hank said.

THAT EVENING I cooked a big supper of rabbit and taters and beans and cornbread. I even made a sauce out of dried apples. Since we couldn't take anything with us we eat everything we could hold. And then we went to bed early, since we would have to get up and leave so early. Once we was in bed it was like a great weight had fell away. We had been worried so long about the heirs showing up, and about where we was going to live. And now we didn't have to worry no more. We would be leaving. We would be shedding all the worries of Gap Creek and starting out again back up on the mountain. When Hank touched me on the breast I trembled. I was so freed up and charged by knowing that we was leaving that I didn't feel like myself. And Hank was trembling too. It's a man's desire that stirs a woman's desire most.

Hank touched me on the breast, and he touched me on the belly. He touched me between my legs. I seen it was better we was leaving. We would start all over again. We had everything we needed to start again. When Hank climbed on top of me I cried out. It was like we was going for a long walk over the hills and under the pine trees. I rolled and said something, and he turned and said something. We said things we had never said before. And we walked further and rushed up on cliffs we had never seen before. When he cried out I was thinking of little Delia, and I had never felt such love before.

We had never had such love as we did that night. I felt I had been stretched and growed more than I ever had. I felt time was slowed down and richer. I felt myself soar out over a sparkling river, and I felt myself settle finally down into the warm nest of the bed and Hank's arms.

THAT MORNING WHEN we left was the coldest of the year. It must have been about ten above zero, maybe colder. It was dark when I got up and lit a fire in the cookstove. Water on the back porch was froze, and I had to crack the cap of ice in the bucket. We was out of coffee, but I heated up some cider to warm our bellies, along with grits and cornbread and jelly.

It was sad knowing I would have to leave most of the jelly and jam I had made, the stuff in the basement, the taters and cider and molasses and corn in the crib. All our work would go to the heirs, except what we could carry in our pockets and on our backs. I made up my mind I would take three or four jars of jelly.

Since we couldn't carry much it didn't take long to pack. About all we could take was our clothes, which was mostly wore out anyway. Back on the mountain we would start over again with even less than we had to start out on Gap Creek. With a lamp I looked over the house for the things I had to take. In the bedroom I got my comb and brush set, the one Rosie had give me when I was married. And I folded up the quilt Mama had give us. On the mantel I got the little flower vase that Lou had give me. In the kitchen there was one frying pan we had brought from Mount Olivet.

I tried to recall if I had brought any spice or seasonings when we moved to Gap Creek. I climbed up on a chair and looked on the shelf in the kitchen. It was the shelf where Mr. Pendergast had kept bottles of cinnamon and sage and pepper, and also his liquor and camphor and other medicines. There was the box of Epsom salts and the bottle of oil of cloves. I had picked over the bottles and jars and boxes many times before. There was a little tin that I had never opened because it looked rusty and was covered with dust. It was the kind of tin that might have held tea or snuff at one time.

I decided to open the can since I never had before. It was hard to twist the lid because of the rust. I had to set the lamp down and use both hands to wring the cap off. There wasn't nothing inside but some crackly wax paper, the kind tea is wrapped in. I opened the paper and seen something shiny. I held the box under the lamp and seen a gold coin. I fumbled in the paper and found a twenty-dollar gold piece. It was Mr. Pendergast's secret bank. The money had been there all the time while we was broke and near starving.

"Look at this," I called to Hank.

"Where did you get that?" he said. He had gathered his tools up in a sack, along with his extra underwear and overalls.

"Mr. Pendergast must have forgot this," I said.

"The Lord has blessed us," Hank said.

"What do you mean?" I said.

"I mean the Lord has give this to us, for all the work we have done here," Hank said.

"You're not going to give it to the heirs?" I said.

"And them willing to put the law on us?" Hank said.

I seen Hank was right. The Lord had kept the twenty dollars for us till the last minute, when we needed it most. It was a sign. We was free and we had something to start over with.

"It's a little pay for all the work on this place," I said. I wrapped the coin in the wax paper and put it in my pocket. The little packet felt sweet as if it was sugar, and it felt warm in the cold morning air. I put all my clothes and the clean frying pan and three jars of jelly in a pillowcase. I placed the flower vase in my other coat pocket. There wasn't room for anything else, and there wasn't nothing else we had to take. I didn't have but one pair of shoes, and they was near wore out. I tied a scarf around my head.

Hank fed the horse some corn and fodder and turned it out into the pasture. It was about five o'clock in the morning and completely dark. The stars was out so bright they seemed just over the treetops. It was so cold my teeth chattered and wouldn't stop. A shooting star spit across the sky throwing off sparks. In the starlight the creek glittered and I could see skirts of ice around the rocks in the stream. There wasn't a light in all the valley, and the mountains loomed like shadowy animals on both sides of the road.

"You'll warm up when we start climbing," Hank said. He had not brought a lantern, so we had to find our way along the road in the starlight. The ruts of the road was froze like wood, and puddles had set under panes of ice. When I stepped on a puddle it crackled like brittle candy.

I knowed I could warm up if I breathed deep and kept breathing deep. The cold bit my nose and stung my face. My breath smoked in the air. Grass and brush along the road was covered with hoarfrost. After about a mile we started climbing. The road wound along the creekbank and then turned and started up the mountain. I slung the pillowcase over my shoulder and leaned into the climb. When you have to climb there's nothing to do but pitch into it. The only way to climb is slow and steady, to not wear yourself out at the beginning.

We had to step over a branch that run across the road and we stumbled on rocks that stuck up in the ruts. It was still dark, but you could see a little where starlight come through the trees. Something squalled on the mountainside. "What was that?" I said.

"Just a wildcat," Hank said.

"Or maybe a painter?" I said.

"Just a little pussycat," Hank said. "You want me to call it up?"

"Don't you dare," I said and shivered. I remembered hearing the wildcat on the night Masenier died. The climb was warming me up a little, but I didn't feel right. Maybe I had eat my grits and biscuits too fast. Or maybe we had been walking too fast. I slowed down a little.

"Are you tired already?" Hank said.

"I just need to catch my breath," I said.

"We have a long way to go," Hank said.

As the road zigzagged up the mountain, we worked our way from one switchback to another. Every step was lifting us out of the valley. Every step was taking me away from the cove of Gap Creek where little Delia was buried. Every step I took in the dark was raising me back toward the mountain and the rest of my life. The road ahead appeared to go up and up forever into the sky.

"How much further is it?" I said.

"We're only getting started," Hank said.

There was a pain in my belly, like the pain I used to feel in my side when I walked to the store as a girl with Mama. It was an uneasy place that got shook as we walked on the rough road. I slowed down more to keep from jarring my belly. I switched the pillowcase from my right shoulder to my left shoulder. My face was stiff with cold and my hands was stiff with cold. My left hand was just about numb from gripping the pillowcase.

"Do you need to rest?" Hank said.

"I'm all right," I said. I felt for the coin in my pocket. Its weight give me more strength and more hope. But the pain in my belly got worse. I swallowed hard and walked on. I imagined I was drawing energy from the tips of my fingers to walk on the ruts, and that I was drawing strength from my ears and from my knees. I was going to burn up every ounce of fat in my body to climb the mountain. I still had strength I'd never used, and I was going to use it. I was going to leave Gap Creek without looking back.

It was still dark as I followed Hank past a waterfall, and past a place the branch gurgled along the road. Further on the woods was open and you could see down the valley where we had come from. There was a light in a house miles below. My belly felt like it was twisting sideways. But I swallowed deep and kept going.

We must have walked for another hour in the dark. I was getting warmer and the pain in my belly was hot. Suddenly sour water belched up into my throat and the back of my mouth. I turned my head and the sour taste flooded over my tongue. I didn't want to be sick when we had so far to go in the cold. I stood still and swallowed hard. It was what I had learned to do to keep from being sick. If I stood still enough my stomach would settle. I had to slow time down by slowing myself.

"Are you going to throw up?" Hank said.

"I don't think so," I said. "It'll pass." As I waited in the road and got hold of myself the sourness in my throat went away.

When the pain was gone and my belly was calm again I took a step and Hank was beside me. It was getting to be first light so I could see him. "You hadn't told me," he said.

"I meant to," I said. I was going to tell Hank the day before, when the preacher and the lawyer had suddenly come to the house. But in the excitement of having to leave I had forgot.

"You'll have to have a cold drink when we come to a spring," Hank said.

I stood very still as another cramp hit me in the belly. But this time it passed quicker. Hank took my hand. He was strong and steady as we started walking again.

"We'll take our time," Hank said. "It's mostly down from here."

I looked around and seen the sun was just coming up over the mountains. We had reached the gap at the state line and was already in North Carolina. The valley was dark below us, but the sky was lit up and the east looked like it was on fire.

"Can you walk?" Hank said.

"Of course I can walk," I said. I felt as weak as a newborn colt but my strength was coming back as my stomach settled. I steadied myself for a moment before picking up the pillowcase. The red sun slipping over the ridge made me squint a little. My belly felt firm and calm.

We started walking again.